THE SUMMER OF CHASING MERMAIDS

Also by Sarah Ockler

#scandal

The Book of Broken Hearts

Bittersweet

THE SUMMER OF CHASING MERMAIDS

SARAH OCKLER

SIMON PULSE

New York   London   Toronto   Sydney   New Delhi

SIMON PULSE

An imprint of Simon & Schuster Children's Publishing Division

1230 Avenue of the Americas, New York, New York 10020

First Simon Pulse hardcover edition June 2015

Text copyright © 2015 by Sarah Ockler

Jacket photograph copyright © 2015 by Michael Frost

SIMON PULSE and colophon are registered trademarks of Simon & Schuster, Inc.

For information about special discounts for bulk purchases, please contact Simon & Schuster Special Sales at 1-866-506-1949 or business@simonandschuster.com.

The Simon & Schuster Speakers Bureau can bring authors to your live event.

For more information or to book an event contact the Simon & Schuster Speakers Bureau at 1-866-248-3049 or visit our website at www.simonspeakers.com.

Jacket designed by Regina Flath

Interior designed by Tom Daly

The text of this book was set in Chaparral Pro.

Manufactured in the United States of America

2 4 6 8 10 9 7 5 3 1

Library of Congress Cataloging-in-Publication Data

Ockler, Sarah.

The summer of chasing mermaids / by Sarah Ockler.—p. cm

Summary: After a boating accident takes her beautiful singing and speaking voice from her, Elyse d'Abreau, the youngest of six sisters, leaves her home in Tobago to stay in an Oregon seaside town where Christian Kane, a notorious playboy, challenges her to to overcome her fear of the sea.

ISBN 978-1-4814-0127-2 (hc)

[1. Mute persons—Fiction. 2. Communication—Fiction. 3. Loss (Psychology)—Fiction. 4. Dating (Social customs)—Fiction. 5. Community life—Oregon—Fiction. 6. West Indians—United States—Fiction. 7. Oregon—Fiction. 8. West Indies—Fiction.] I. Title.

PZ7.O168Sum 2015

[Fic]—dc23

2014034875

ISBN 978-1-4814-0129-6 (eBook)

For Jessi Kirby,
the mermaid of Crystal Cove

The Beginning and the End

This is the part where I die.

Don't panic; it isn't unexpected. The sea is prideful, after all, and Death never goes back on a deal.

Granna always believed that the d'Abreau sisters were immortal, even after her daughter-in-law died delivering the last of us (me). But among our six bodies, she said, there were only five souls. Twins were special. A single soul dwelling in two bodies.

So Natalie and I—the twins, the babies—were blessed. Blessed by all who loved us. Blessed by the gods and goddesses, by the lore and the legends of Trinidad and Tobago, our islands in the sea.

Our connection was unbreakable, and from the first time we sang together in the bathtub, instinctively harmonizing at age three? Well. We were bright stars, Granna promised. Put on this earth to make music, to share it with the world. No matter that Natalie grew into a soft-spoken beauty with a voice as comforting as a warm breeze, and I became the raging storm, fearsome and bewitching. Our destiny tangled as our limbs in our mother's womb. We were the first to know each other, the first to feel our matching heartbeats. Together, we made magic.

Two bodies, four lungs, one soul.

The beginning and the end. Completion.

Natalie and I sang for Granna and our father. We sang for our older sisters. We sang at Scarborough in Tobago, for fund-raisers and festivals. We sang in Trinidad, our mother's homeland. We sang for the guests—always rich, often famous—at d'Abreau Cocoa Estates, Granna's farm and eco-resort, the place we'd called home after my mother's death. We sang for the men and women who harvested the cocoa pods, who came in for dinner covered in dirt and laughter, eager to listen. During Carnival we sang on top of the big music trucks that traveled through the streets of Port of Spain, as masqueraders jumped up around us dressed like angels and princesses and mermaids. We sang for home, Trinidad and Tobago, twin-island nation, the proud red, black, and white. For our mother's memory— though for Natalie and me, she never existed.

We sang for fun. For our lives.

That's what it felt like, the music. Like being alive.

So maybe I was a liar, and maybe I should've told her years ago, but I didn't. Granna, I mean. It's just that she was wrong about completion, so wrong about the connection and the stars.

The thing about souls was that Natalie really *did* have her own, like each of our four older sisters.

And mine belonged to the sea. Always.

I was born into the sea, born knowing this. Natalie had been born on the boat, but by the time my turn came, we'd been tipped. My first breath outside my mother's body was salt water; the Caribbean Sea lay claim to my soul the moment it took hers.

I've never considered this soul more than a loaner, a broken-winged bird I've only nursed and borrowed. Granna might not believe it, but eventually, I knew I'd be called upon to return it.

One night last spring, just after Carnival, the moonlight sparkled on the waves not far from where our mother had delivered me, her last, and I came so, so, so close.

Then I escaped.

For a time.

Even a fool knows you don't cheat Death more than once. And technically, after my watery birth, that night last spring already made it twice.

There's peace in acceptance. Death in it, always. Inevitable. With the acceptance of one thing comes the dying of another: a new belief, a relationship. An ideal, a plan, a what-if. Assumptions. A path. A song.

Consider: Pregnancy dies upon birth. Plans die upon action. Dreams die upon waking.

Not to ruin the story, but if you've come this far, you should know how it happens.

The end begins, as all things must, in the water. Now.

Ropes of black hair twist before my eyes, swaying like reeds. One by one, red clips loosen from the braids, tiny jeweled starfish that drip-drip-drop

into the deep.

My body is sinking, sinking, sinking. Cold . . . And a memory stirs. The warm sea pressing against me, leaking into my lungs. Stealing my voice.

No, wait. . . . That was then. The spring. That last time, when I came so, so close. *Then* was the Caribbean, my Caribbean. *Now* is the Pacific, and though it's late summer here, the Pacific isn't as patient, isn't as warm. My limbs will soon turn as blue-blue-blue as my silk dress.

It's midnight now, the in-between, and the only person who knows where I am is asleep above, in the berth of our boat, the *Queen of Cups*. He was dreaming when I left; I knew from his sleep sounds. Beautiful, he was, stretched out alone where moments earlier we'd been entwined.

When he realizes I'm gone, he'll search the water, dive beneath the boat. Frantic. Desperate. But he won't reach me.

There's blood in my mouth now, blood in the water, black-not-red at these dark depths. My lungs burn.

I'm ready.

But as my heartbeat stalls, as my limbs give their final tremble, as all around me turns to darkness, I can't help but wonder. . . .

If the sea had offered me one last chance—if I could've bargained with Death to make this broken wing mine, a soul with all its beautiful imperfections—would I have taken it?

Even after everything I'd lost?

Six Weeks Earlier

Chapter 1

After spending the day in Aunt Lemon's gift shop with a sticky note in the shape of a crab stuck to my boomsie (and no one even told me until *after* I'd escorted a pair of surfers to our collection of mermaid dashboard ornaments, and then my cousin Kirby sent me the picture, all, *u got crabs!*), I decided a little alone time was in order.

If not for the crab incident, I probably would've just gone to Lemon's Summer Solstice party tonight like I'd promised. Instead, I was slithering around the Chelsea Marina docks, hoping to reach my boat before Kirby ensnared me in her net.

"Elyse!" Kirby shouted. "The party's starting!" In a gauzy white dress and fitted denim jacket, she stood like a beacon in the sand, hands cupped around her mouth. Her voice skipped across the waves. "Where *are* you? Elyse!"

She wasn't my blood cousin—Her mother, Lemon, was Dad's best

friend, all the way back from their graduate-school days in Miami—
and before this summer I'd only seen Kirby twice: the first time five
years ago when they'd visited the islands, and then again a year
later when our two families met up at Disneyland, my first visit to
America.

But I'd been in Oregon a month already now, living in her house,
our toothbrushes cohabitating in the zebra cup in the bathroom, and
still she couldn't get my name right. *Uh-leese*, it was like.

Close enough, maybe. It just didn't sound-feel-comfort like home.

Sing for us, Ay-leese. . . .

Ay-leese, stop drowning yourself in hot sauce. Give it to me!

Granna, you hear? Our Ay-leese, she got a boyfriend.

Ay-leese, breathe! Fucking breathe, Ay-leese. . . .

"But it's the Solstice! And there's . . . cake?" Kirby's voice lacked
conviction. She'd been searching the edges of the marina for twenty
minutes, and I felt a little thrill that she hadn't found me.

Unseen in the shadows, I crept to the slip that held the old Albin
Vega—last place on earth she'd check, since from a strictly "owner-
ship" perspective the boat wasn't mine. I waited until Kirby finally
retreated, white dress vanishing like a sail in the mist, and then I
climbed onto the deck and ducked through the companionway into
the saloon.

Freedom.

For a holiday that was supposed to, according to Aunt Lemon,
"honor the full strength of the Sun God," the Oregon night was a

bruise. I took in the blackness that seeped into the boat, the salty air, the mustiness that clung to torn seat cushions.

But for the damp suck of the sea, all was soundless.

The Vega rocked gently in the tumult, steadying herself, and my view of the sky—pink-purple-black through the starboard window—straightened.

Tipped.

Straightened again.

The ship was a castaway among the polished vessels surrounding us, a forgotten relic here in Atargatis Cove. I didn't even know her proper name. *Queen of* was all it said on the hull, once-gold letters peeling from the aqua-blue fiberglass. Could've been the *Queen of Hearts* or the *Queen of the Damned* for all I knew. But there was something special about that emptiness,

the unknown,

the unsaid.

Potential undefined.

She was abandoned, a fate we shared, which made her the perfect hideaway.

The boat jostled as a wave hit, and I took a deep breath, fought a shiver. *The sea can't hurt me here. . . .* I repeated the mantra in my head until fear left my limbs. Until I could breathe again.

I lit the big candle I'd brought from Mermaid Tears—Lemon's shop—to chase away the mustiness. OCEAN BREEZE, it said. It smelled like chemically enhanced coconut.

Soft yellow light flickered into the saloon.

Everything was as I'd left it. Straightened up, wiped down, cans of expired soup discarded. A fuzzy new blanket spread out in the V-berth, and another on top, for curling up. Scattered on the cushions, a few books Kirby had brought me from her volunteer job at the library. Some extra clothes, flip-flops, sunglasses I never seemed to need here in Oregon. My iPod. A box of crackers with the peanut butter already spread between them. A bundle of Sharpies, rubber-banded together, different thicknesses.

My shoulders relaxed. The Vega was still unclaimed.

I freed a mass of black curls from beneath the hood of my sweatshirt, and from a pocket in my denim cutoffs, fished out a handful of sea glass. Lemon was looking out for me this summer, so in addition to helping at Mermaid Tears, I tagged along on her morning beach combs. She collected glass to forge into sculptures, some for sale in the gift shop and others on display in the gallery above it. She valued each piece of glass like a gemstone, but she always let me keep some of the haul. I'd been saving it in an empty Costco jar that formerly contained a decade's supply of pitted olives—my hourglass. Once the glass reached the top, things would be right again.

Repaired, renewed, recovered.

Rejuvenated.

Restored.

All the REs complete, and I'd be whole.

Fucking breathe, Ay-leese. . . .

My hand tipped into the jar, and I watched the colored bits clink and settle among the others, an inch of green-gray-blue rising like the tide.

Whole.

I didn't really believe it, but it sounded nice, like a poem. Even if it were possible, what then? Where would I go? Not back. Not forward. I was here, drifting on the current, eighteen years old and totally unmoored.

I pushed the jar back along a shelf in the triangular V-berth, way at the front of the boat, and settled into my favorite spot. My iPod still had a little charge, so I popped in an earbud and scrolled to a new playlist. Lemon had plenty of instrumental on her laptop—Native American wood flutes, classical, wind chimes, dolphin calls, ambient weirdness. On my first night in the States I'd desperately replaced my soca and calypso with it, erased even the reggae—anything that reminded me of home. Of who I should have been. Tonight I was onto Bach's unaccompanied cello suites, track one. Music hummed in my right ear as I cranked the volume, but I wasn't fool enough to sit alone on a boat with both ears covered.

A calm ocean could change in an instant.

Sing for us, Ay-leese. . . .

By the time my screen read "Suite No. 4 in E-flat Major," my heart rate finally mellowed, and I grabbed a Sharpie from the bundle. I found a clear spot among the tangle of words overhead—some nights my notebook wasn't big enough—and pressed the tip to the low ceiling.

Words spin and spill
ink from a ~~bottle~~ of ~~blood~~

Queen of lurched left, a game we nightly played, and I tightened my grip on the marker, waiting for her to settle. She perpetually lost. Her body was inked with the evidence.

A smudge, a smear, a shaky line of
~~black~~ letters stands erect, marches
around my fingers, encouraging,

Back on the island of Tobago, 7,040 kilometers—no, make that 4,375 miles—off the coast of my heartbeat, Dad and Granna had an old Albin Vega in the resort fleet, the *Atlantica*, a twenty-seven footer like this, one of three boats reserved for our guest charters. They'd taken the fourth out of commission in March, part of a long string of before-and-after afters that ended with me leaving for the States, but as far as I knew, the *Atlantica* was still going strong. It was the ship my twin sister Natalie had been born on. The one I'd been born next to.

The last thing my mother saw.

It was a dark and stormy night, our birth story. So they say.

inspiring,
yet ever

Now, out here on these chilly summer nights, the pale scar of the moon cutting the Oregon haze, I wondered if Dad was out on the Vega too. Lying in the V-berth, staring at the same moon, thinking of me as I thought of him. Of my sisters and Granna. The cocoa pods, red-orange-yellow, stacked in pyramids after first harvest, spicing the air with their intoxicating plums-and-tobacco scent.

Home.

Do you miss me?

soundless.

"Keep your skirt on! Let me check it out, make sure she won't sink." A male voice accompanied shadows through the companion-way and into the saloon. The boat bobbed under new weight, and I yanked out my earbud and bolted upright, narrowly avoiding a head injury.

His image flickered in the candlelight. When he spotted me, he put one hand on his head, as if he'd anticipated the crash that never came, and said in a tone much softer than what he'd used on his friend, "Well. Hello there."

Unlike me, he was unalarmed, the ghost of a smile hovering on his lips. Something softened him around the edges—alcohol, probably—but his gaze was sharp and clear.

Toes to curls, a shiver shook me. This boy wore the ocean in his eyes, green-gray-blue, ever shifting, and I recognized him immediately.

Knew before he said another word that he was as dangerous as he was beautiful.

Christian Kane. Official summer scoundrel of Atargatis Cove, fresh off his first year at Stanford. Aside from the upcoming Mermaid Festival and Pirate Regatta, the Kane family's annual return was the talk of the town. And this son, the eldest? Kirby had him to thank for the cake tonight.

Christian Kane had his own mythology, his own devoted following, much like Lemon's Sun God. Fitting that they shared a birthday.

I was frozen on the blanketed cushions as he scanned the scene: writing on the fiberglass walls and ceiling, damning black marker still clutched in my fingers. Somewhere beneath my elbow, two battered novels about the sea, ancient legends retold. A half-empty can of Coke on the shelf behind my head. A postcard from home, blank, tacked up on the wall. The yawning jar of sea glass, there next to the soda. Nautical charts and manuals once scattered throughout the saloon, now stacked neatly on the table beside the candle, held in place with a large rock carried in first by the tide, second by me.

This ship had belonged to no one. I'd been so certain. And rickety and neglected as she was, I'd called her my home away from my home away from home, my sacred space. Now Christian's gaze swept back to me and skimmed the unfamiliar legs stretched across the V-berth, brown skin made lavender by the moonlight.

When he finally looked at me full on, his stormy eyes changed course.

Confusion.

Surprise.

Intrigue.

The last was the most worrisome.

I tugged the hood up over my head, tied the strings across my seashell necklace and the scar gouged into the hollow of my throat.

Breathe. . . .

"Christian?" someone said, flirty and singsong. The breeze shifted, carrying a whiff of spicy vanilla perfume, and a girl crashed into him from behind. Her silver-tipped talons curled over his shoulders. "What's the deal? I'm freezin' my ass off."

Christian didn't take his eyes off me, just raised a curious eyebrow that lit a spark in my chest.

The girlfriend noticed me then, and around a faint smile, still watching me, Christian spoke plainly.

"There's a girl writing on my boat."

I basically ran.

Chapter 2

For centuries poets and fisherman alike have written about the loneliness of the sea. Yet on this particular Solstice, all the gods of witches, men, and merfolk conspired to thrust me into social interaction.

My right hand was smudged with the ink of my unfinished poem. I rubbed it against my thigh, but the blackness stuck.

I wondered if the boat was really Christian's, like he'd said, or if it belonged to his parents.

I rubbed harder—no luck. Behind me the Pacific stretched and yawned, deceptively placid.

My footsteps quickened.

I drank in the salty air and marched along the grassy dunes toward Starfish Point, the very end of Atargatis Cove, where Lemon's place stood sentry at the top of the hill with an equally impressive neighbor: the Kane house.

The Kanes lived at the Cove only in the summers, but they'd owned both properties for generations. Lemon had been leasing hers from the family for about twenty years—first from Christian's grandfather, and now from his father.

Ahead, a wooden staircase stretched up the dunes to the houses, and from the top you could look back along the shore, see the ocean and the whole town. I'd walked it every night after my writing sessions at the marina, but the sight still stole my breath.

Now I took the stairs slowly, my hand on the rough banister, and the twin homes rose before me like glimmering spires. Like most houses in the Cove, these had dark-gray shingle siding, shimmery windows trimmed in white, expansive second-floor decks with endless ocean views. This morning, just before sunrise, Kirby and I had stretched out in chairs on Lemon's deck, shivering under blankets as we listened for the mournful calls of the whales.

"Ahoy! Look what the tide dragged in." Kirby was already halfway down the deck stairs when she called out to me. "I've been looking *everywhere* for you," she said. In preparation for tonight's feast, she'd strung tiny white lights along the railings, and the house sparkled behind her. "You okay?"

I waved. It was both an acknowledgment and a nonanswer, one of my go-tos.

Her gazelle legs launched her off the stairs and into the grassy dune next to me. She was a little breathless, but not from exertion. Kirby was just perpetually excited.

"Status update," she said. "Vanessa went off with Christian the instant they all got into town. Okay, he's totally hotter, like that's even possible, but still. I've been telling her about you for weeks!"

A gust of wind tossed Kirby's red-brown curls into chaos, and as she plucked them from her mouth, I looked back toward the marina, a half mile down shore.

Christian.

Totally hotter.

Vanessa.

Even possible.

Oh!

I thought about telling Kirby I'd already met them, but "met" wasn't the right word. My insides churned again, thinking about the poems I'd scribbled all over the boat. The stuff I'd left on board, set up as if it were mine.

The story required more words than my lips had energy for, and from the bounce in Kirby's step, I knew she was eager to get inside.

As I followed her toward the house, she ran through the attendee list, prepping me on the lives of our party guests. The Kane family. Vanessa, Kirby's best friend, whose parents were big on the Texas political scene and summered at the Cove like the Kanes. Mayor Katzenberg, whose son, Noah, had the power to turn Kirby's bronze cheeks a deep plum. Noah couldn't make the party tonight, but he worked at the Black Pearl Café near the marina, and in my short time here, Kirby and I had made dozens of reconnais-sance-style coffee runs.

Lemon had also invited her coven friends, a mix of locals and out-of-towners from Coos Bay and Bandon-by-the-Sea, and Kirby said they'd come bearing Solstice goodies.

"Give those women a theme and take cover," Kirby said. "Kat and Ava—the ones who just opened that cookie bar on Main? You should've seen the cookies they made when I started my period. They threw me a moon party. It was basically horrifying. But don't worry, tonight they just made sun cookies. As far as I know. Witches are kind of unpredictable. Are you hungry?"

There's a parrot in Tobago, the orange-winged parrot it's called, and it chirps and chatters so often, for so long, you start to think it's conversing with you. Sometimes it sounds like it's laughing, sweet and high, and even though you don't understand a word, eventually you're just listening to it. Listening, and sometimes telling your secrets, and laughing right along.

Words, after all, aren't a requirement for friendship.

That's how it is with Kirby.

These birds, oh. They the death of me, my father often said, pitching mauled cocoa pods into the mulch pile. The flying menaces had caused so much damage to our crop that he finally brought in hawks to scare them off, but now I missed them. I missed the hawks and I missed the orange-winged parrots, who'd never survive the chilly Oregon summers, and as Kirby chattered on, filling me in on

the people I'd soon meet, I felt bad about trying to ditch; she and
Lemon had been talking up the party for weeks, and she was glowing
with anticipation.

Kirby stretched her hand backward, seeking mine with wiggling
fingers. Her palm was warm and kind, and for a moment it felt like
home when she squeezed me. Like if I closed my eyes, I could imagine
my sisters were inside, waiting with fresh sweet bread and stories
about the crazy tourists back home. Maybe Natalie was there. My twin
heart. Not crying and full of regret, as I'd last seen her. But smiling,
sweet and happy, like before.

*Ay-leese! I been working on this harmony; come see. You do the
alto, and I'll . . .*

Kirby led me around to the front of the house, through gardens lush with feathery herbs and the pinks and purples of Lemon's
flowerbeds: angel's fishing rod, African lily, Japanese anemone. From
here we entered through the gift shop and took the back-office stairs
to the second floor, which housed Lemon's sculpture gallery and the
expansive living space. This way we'd come up into the kitchen, sparing
me a big embarrassing entrance.

I pushed my hood back, shook out my curls.

Kirby glanced at me over her shoulder as she gripped the kitchen
doorknob. Laughter and music floated behind it, light and joyful, though
no one was singing or dancing, not like they did at parties back home.

"If you're not up for it," she said, "I can make an excuse. Sneak you
to your room."

It was sincere. Lemon loved hosting dinner parties, and her coven was famous for its late-night revelry; Kirby had bailed me out before. But the look on her face was so hopeful, so earnest. I knew it meant a lot to her that I was here, not just for the party but for the summer. Half-Trini herself, Kirby didn't have any other connections to that part of her life—she was a Carnival baby, and her father had lost touch with Lemon long before she even discovered she was pregnant. The first time I met her, on that visit five years ago, we'd all stayed up laughing, trading stories and jokes. Mine were absent a mother, Kirby's a father.

That connected us too.

Later she'd asked me and Natalie what a Carnival baby even was.

Here in Oregon, despite my nightly disappearing act and regularly scheduled mood swings, Kirby was trying.

Words weren't a requirement, no. But it wasn't exactly cake and ice cream, being friends with someone who didn't talk.

Being friends with *me*.

I rubbed my inked hand against the cutoffs again, silently mouthing my answer without meeting her eyes. *No worries. I'm okay.*

She bounced on her toes, curls springing against her shoulders.

"Time to meet the summer people," she said with a laugh. "At least you're not going in unprepared. I already told you everyone's story."

I pressed the shell necklace against my throat, grateful I wouldn't have to tell mine.

But that's the thing about permanent

the accident . . . the damage was too great

irreversible

you're lucky you can still swallow, still breathe

vocal loss.

we're so sorry, Elyse, so very sorry

When you don't feel like talking, no one can force you, no matter how many stories and secrets might be locked inside.

Chapter 3

"It's no secret." Mayor Wesley Katzenberg swirled the scotch in his highball, his proclamations drowning all other conversations. "Without Parrish and Dey's expansion plan, Cove's a sinking ship."

"We're fine, Wes," Lemon said. With her shoulder-length auburn waves and a dress dotted with red and yellow suns, my aunt looked like living fire. Trailed by the mayor, she blazed through the gallery to check on the food. She was a strict vegan, but she'd gone all out for the guests; the long table at the center was a riot of sea death, dark red lobster tails and crab legs and bright white shrimp swimming in cocktail sauce.

I thought the shrimp tasted like erasers.

"It's a good plan, Ursula," the man said. "More tourists mean more exposure for the gallery." His hand flopped onto her shoulder like a beached fish as he followed her around the room. He was a big man, well over six feet, with a barrel chest and broad shoulders that made me nervous as he marched past Lemon's delicate glass creations.

"Wesley." Lemon picked up a tray of sun cookies that matched her dress and shoved it into his hands. "Be a dear and see if anyone wants one of Kat and Ava's goodies."

It was hard to like him. I'd been in the house less than an hour, and twice he'd asked me if I was the caterer, handing me his empty glass even though it was obvious I was the family friend from T&T Lemon had been telling everyone about. Atargatis Cove was small-town, coastal Oregon, and far as I could tell, Kirby and I were the only different-looking people around. Who else *could* I be?

"Oh, it's not a race thing," Kirby assured me when I brought it up. We were standing in the white-and-turquoise kitchen, a breezy space that flowed into the gallery beyond, divided by an island lined with barstools. She hefted the blender from its base, poured strawberry-banana daiquiris into three glasses. "When it comes to Wes Katzenberg, it's a—"

"Vagina thing," Vanessa said. In her Texas country-music accent, it sounded like va-*john*-a. "Oh, don't give me that look, Kirby Jane. You know he's just like that. Women belong in the kitchen, rubbin' on his feet, breedin' his minions."

Kirby sighed. "It's not *what* you say. It's how you say it."

"Minions?" Vanessa laughed. "Or vagina?"

She'd arrived at the party alone soon after my exit from the marina, and if she'd been upset about finding a castaway on Christian's boat, she'd kept it secret. If not for the covert wink she'd given me when Kirby introduced us, I would've thought she hadn't recognized me.

The birthday boy had yet to arrive; likely he was waiting at home, trying to put some distance between Vanessa's entrance and his, lest anyone figure out about their high-seas adventure on the boat.

The boat.

My stomach rolled every time I thought about it. Christian and Vanessa, catching me in the V-berth. Writing on the walls. Hiding.

A vandal *and* a stowaway. Perfect.

"I just feel bad for him," Kirby said. She shook a can of whipped cream, topped each of our drinks. "He's only mayor because no one else ran, and now he's desperate to prove himself. On top of that, his wife bailed last year—Noah told me his dad gave Terra an ultimatum to quit her job or quit the marriage. Guess what she picked? Right after that she moved to Newport. And Terra's in Mom's coven, and the mayor doesn't even know she comes to town every month for the gatherings."

"Jesus, Mary, and Josephine," Vanessa said. "You tell your cousin everyone's business? What'd y'all say about me?"

"Nothing true," Kirby teased, pressing a fresh strawberry onto each glass.

We sucked down half of our daiquiris without taking a breath, the girls eager to hide the evidence before the adults caught us with booze. The way they treated each sip like a stolen victory made me smile. Back in Tobago there was no need to sneak.

At least not with alcohol.

"Good?" Kirby asked me, and I nodded. The rum was strong; it tasted like home.

I wiped my mouth on the back of my hand and gestured toward the hallway off the kitchen. *Can we go in my room?*

She leaned in for a closer look at my lips. "Sorry. Maroon?"

I shifted toward the bedrooms, but she and Vanessa were looking out across the gallery again. I dropped it.

"Where *is* that boy?" Vanessa said. "He should've been here by now."

"Probably off with some cheetah," Kirby said. I looked from her to Vanessa, then back to Kirby, confused. The couple had looked pretty cozy on the Vega, but Vanessa didn't flinch at Kirby's comment.

"Christian's not a poster boy for monogamy," Kirby explained. "Last year, there were these three sisters, the Lorettis? And they—"

"Good lord," Vanessa said. "You really need a silencer, Kirbs."

"What?" Kirby said. "Honestly, I don't know how you can be so cool about it."

"I don't care who he hooks up with. I'm liberated."

"Oh, that's one word for it." Kirby snorted. "Wait until the rest of the summer renters roll in next week. The line to 'liberate' with Christian will stretch from here to Astoria."

I thought of his smile when he'd caught me on the boat, the glint in his eyes as he scanned the words I'd left on his walls.

Around here, liberating with Christian was probably like high tide. Regularly scheduled. Alluring, yet slippery. Dangerous.

Vanessa only laughed. "I'm tellin' him you said that. Anyway, worry

More than a stolen smoke break, Mr. Kane was hiding something. An old wound, perhaps. Some thinly concealed resentment.

"Shall we?" His arm was extended in front of him, and it took me a beat to realize he wanted me to lead the way into the gallery, to find and meet his family.

His wife, however, was on her way to meet us.

With one hand glued to her phone, Meredith Kane power-walked across the gallery. When she reached us, she smiled at me without showing her teeth, then looked at her husband.

"I can't get ahold of him," she said. In a sleek brunette bun, crisp white blouse, and navy dress pants, she looked even more polished than her husband. Kirby had told me that both Kanes ran their own tech businesses from home—he had started some big-deal social networking platform, and she built websites for other tech companies. Wherever the Kanes went, it was clear that the work went with them. Even to their son's birthday party.

"Did you start with him again?" Mrs. Kane asked. "Because I thought we agreed this morning—"

"Meredith." His eyes flicked to me, then back to his wife, pleading. "Can we not—"

"So check *this* out," Vanessa said. She came around the front of the island and stepped between us. It was like she hadn't heard them bickering, just hopped up on a barstool, legs dangling. "At school this year, my friends and I caused some major capital-D drama. It was in the paper and all, and one of the reporters got snarky and called us—ready?—feminist killjoys. Direct quote."

Vanessa tossed her long, chestnut hair over her shoulders. She kept her eyes on me as she laughed at the story, but the look was as friendly and curious as ever, assessing but not judgmental.

"You're kidding," Mrs. Kane said, a smile finding its way through the cold.

"Swear to God, ma'am," Vanessa said.

Just like that the tension in the room evaporated.

It was easy to see why she and Kirby were friends. Kirby had a heart the size of Oregon, and Vanessa was a magnet, a sweet girl with a gorgeous smile and a fearless tongue, the girl everyone simultaneously loved and wanted to be.

Except for me.

I'd already been that girl, and it didn't work out.

"Anyway," she said, "that only served to galvanize us in our mission."

Soon she had the Kanes enraptured with a story about how she'd rallied the girls sports' teams at her school in Fort Worth, and, together with a few supportive parents, they'd gotten the school to start a new women's literature core. Her mother had even ordered T-shirts for all the girls' mothers that said PROUD MOM OF A FEMINIST KILLJOY.

The way Vanessa told it, I wanted to be a killjoy too.

Vanessa wasn't bragging, though. She'd done it as a diversion, I realized. The Kanes were newly focused on her, listening attentively. Mr. Kane was asking questions about how she'd organized so many girls, and Mrs. Kane was laughing about the T-shirts.

Vanessa knew how to work them. She'd likely been in the middle of it before. Maybe she'd tried to save Christian and his brother from the arguing.

Despite my ability to read people, I felt like an outsider, like someone watching a party from the other side of the glass. I could see these things unfold, but I couldn't quite understand the dynamics, the deep knowing that comes from growing up with people you care about.

I missed my sisters.

I'd met so many people tonight, Vanessa and the Kanes, the mayor, Lemon's friends. And though I was smiled at and asked to pass plates or glasses, no one really spoke to me. No one asked me about Tobago, or my family, or what I did before arriving in Oregon. No one asked how the party compared to celebrations back home, or why I called my aunt Lemon instead of Ursula, her real name. They hadn't heard me say it, after all. They didn't know that Natalie had invented it. We were four years old, failing miserably at sounding out Lemon's last name.

Langelinie.

I felt the loss of my voice like a fresh wound, a cold blade against my throat, and I closed my eyes to keep the sea from spilling down my cheeks. No one knew me like my family in Tobago, but they'd known me always as Elyse, beautiful songbird, weaver of music that could bring a man to his knees. Music was my life, a rare gift that Natalie and I had shared, had grown into, had grown *because* of.

And now, without the music, I was just . . . Elyse. Broken.

My family didn't know me anymore. Natalie didn't know me. *I* didn't know me.

Pictures of Granna and Dad flickered in my mind, my five sisters following with pleading eyes—Juliette, Martine, Gabrielle, Hazel, and Natalie, my twin, the one whose absence had carved the biggest trench in my heart.

I blinked them all away, my family and the cocoa pods and the chatty orange-winged parrots. Tobago. *This* was my home now— Atargatis Cove, Oregon. My own bedroom in a beautiful house by the sea with Aunt Lemon and Kirby, an informal job hunting sea glass and helping out at Lemon's gift shop. No pressure greater than this party, no expectations for a big bright future, no expiration on the offer to stay. As far as Lemon was concerned, as long as my visa was in order, I could linger here the rest of eternity.

If I were still the type of girl who made long-term plans, that would've been it.

Linger.

Eternally.

"So now I'm a feminist killjoy." Vanessa dusted her hands together. "Done and done."

In the crush of laughter that marked the end of her tale, I took the back stairs down the way we'd come up, and slipped away to the sea.

Through the blackness I retraced my path to the marina, keeping a respectful distance from the waves. Nighttime was the most dangerous, the time when she lay in wait, thick and hazy, lulling us with her otherworldly beauty.

Along the dunes I passed the larger homes first, grand palaces with names like The Captain's Shack and Heaven by the Sea, then the smaller cottages closer to town. Here, signs staked the lawns, urging the Cove's residents to vote on Prop 27, the mayor's measure that would allow commercial development of the beachfront. With his support the real estate firm Parrish and Dey was backing it, buying up and revitalizing property to boost the local economy. The town was divided, Lemon had told me—yes for those who'd make money from the influx of tourists. No for people like Lemon, people who wanted the Cove to retain its quaint seaside charms, its wildness.

It's not that the Cove didn't get visitors—the wave action was amazing for surfers. Whale watchers and beachcombers liked it too. But it was a mystical place—a tiny cove situated between swaths of ancient forest and the sea, a place found neither on maps nor GPS directions. Getting here by road required four-wheel drive and the navigational skill of a pirate. According to Kirby, most people at the Cove were either locals like them, or long-term summer residents who'd been vacationing here since they were in diapers, generally in homes their grandparents had built.

The town didn't have a single hotel or B&B, something the mayor wanted to change.

We'd gone through similar things back home, especially after much of the country's agriculture was destroyed by Hurricane Flora. But unlike here, in Tobago people welcomed the ecotourist boom, the new opportunities it brought.

One thing was certain: No matter where on the globe you went, something was always changing.

I approached the marina with the same stealth I'd used earlier and stopped short at the sight. I wasn't expecting to see the birthday boy, yet there he was, standing on the dock near his boat, hands in his pockets, looking at the water. I couldn't make out his features, but the stance was unmistakable. In the slump of his shoulders, the resignation in the bend of his neck, I read his thoughts.

They were mine.

The yearning, the unanswerable questions, all the what-ifs that the sea—in its endless tumult—would never clarify.

It was strange, what churned inside me. A connection of sorts, some shared pain I couldn't quite explain. When I tried to look at it, the feeling vanished.

Christian shook his head and turned, and for a moment I thought he'd spotted me; his eyes seemed to find mine in the shadows. But then the invisible connection broke, and he marched along the dock and onto the shore, seemingly unaware of my presence.

Happy birthday, I mouthed to his back.

He was gone.

I slipped onto the Vega. It felt less like a victory than my earlier escape from Kirby, and I left the candle unlit, in case Christian drifted back in this direction. By the pale light of the moon, I searched the onboard cabinets until I found paper towels and Windex. The cushions in the V-berth were surprisingly unruffled, and I climbed onto them and sprayed, sprayed, sprayed the ceiling. Scrubbed, scrubbed, scrubbed the walls.

Outside, clouds drifted over the moon, and in the new darkness the ocean hissed.

Black as ever, my words remained.

I got to Lemon's upper deck just in time to catch the end of Christian's birthday song in the gallery, the scene warm and yellow through the windows. My absence had been undetected.

Surrounded by his family and Vanessa, Christian hunched over his cake at the head of the table, face glowing in the candle flames. He was smiling, but there was something unhappy there; it clung to him like mist on the dawn waves, a glimpse of what I'd sensed earlier. Again I felt the familiar tug that had gripped me at the docks.

His six-year-old brother hung on his arm like a monkey.

"Make a wish," Sebastian Kane said, and Christian smiled.

At Sebastian's gentle touch, all the angles of Christian's face changed, smoothed. My eyes traced the lines of him, the messy hair, the stubble along his jaw, full lips. Soft. Kissable.

"Hurry," Sebastian said. "They're melting!"

Christian smiled again, and his eyes, green and gold in the

flickering candlelight, shifted. For the second time that night he seemed to be looking at me in the darkness, though I knew it was impossible for him to see my face. Still, I met his gaze, and neither of us looked away, even as he pursed his lips and extinguished the candles, until nothing remained beyond the glass between us but smoke and wishes.

Chapter 4

Leaving early was unusual for Lemon's coven, but the mayor's real estate rants had cast a shadow over their revelry. It wasn't long before they said their farewells, one by one, until only the Cove residents remained—us, the Kanes, Vanessa, and Mr. Katzenberg, telling us how amazing the beach would be next summer, thanks to Prop 27.

"I don't know, Katz," Mr. Kane said. His tone felt both jovial and condescending. Like he could be insulting you, but you wouldn't know it until later, when you were brushing your teeth and auto-replaying the night's events, and your brain would suddenly go, *Wait.* "You've only been in office half a term. Already need a corporate bailout?"

"Bailout?" The mayor laughed, a throaty thing layered with the stuff he wasn't saying either. "This is prime beachfront we're sitting on. Atrophying, if you ask me. That's why I think you should sell."

"I already know what you think," Mr. Kane said. "Everyone in this room knows what you think." He laughed, again with the condescending tone. It didn't seem to bother the mayor.

As the two went on about property values, I watched Christian and Vanessa across the table. He played with her hair absently, and she smiled, eyes at half-mast in lazy contentment. Christian's other hand was tight around a glass of soda, probably spiked with something stronger, and every time his father spoke, his jaw clenched and unclenched. It happened so fast, so automatically that I wondered whether Christian even realized he was doing it.

"ROI in a place like the Cove is hard to predict," Mr. Kane said. "Risky investment, if you ask me."

Christian sighed. "You can take the corporate stiff out of the office, but you can't take the office out of the stiff."

I felt my eyes go wide. I couldn't imagine me or my sisters talking like that to Dad or Granna, but Mr. Kane didn't seem to notice the insult.

"Can we change the subject?" Vanessa asked. "All this expansion talk is puttin' me to sleep." Her tone was playful, but her eyes told a different story. I followed her gaze to Mr. Kane, who belatedly shot Christian a venomous look. Christian stiffened, alternately chugging the drink and clenching his jaw.

Mrs. Kane said nothing.

With five sisters, a single dad, and a grandmother living under one roof, along with all the field workers constantly on the property and an endless, rotating crop of resort guests, my family had its sticky webs too. I'd learned to navigate them, to find joy in those flickering moments of closeness even when they felt suffocating.

But walking into someone else's family issues? One false step, and even without speaking, I could end up tangled.

When the mayor resumed the conversation with more praise for Parrish and Dey's plan, I left the table, undetected and unstopped, and made myself busy in the kitchen. I was filling the sink with soapy water when I felt a tug on the hem of my sweatshirt.

From the height of my hip, a pair of vibrant blue eyes fringed in white-blond curls peered up at me.

I turned off the tap and smiled at Sebastian.

"I like your hair," he said, twirling a lock of his own, which was almost as springy as mine.

I patted my head. Humidity was a commonality the Oregon coast and T&T shared; like Sebastian's, my curls were everywhere, though his stopped at his chin, and mine coiled all the way past my shoulders.

He looked around to ensure we were alone. Satisfied, he waved me closer, cupping his hands around my ear as I leaned in.

"Can you please give me another piece of cake?" he whispered.

It was the best idea I'd heard all night, so I cut one for each of us from the leftovers on the range top, and together we sat at the counter.

Through a mouthful of chocolate cake, he said, "Did you know that Atargatis Cove is named for the very first mermaid? I'm going to look for her this summer."

I'd read something briefly about the legend of Atargatis on one of my library visits with Kirby, but Sebastian clearly had the inside scoop. I reached across the counter for a Sharpie so I could ask him more about the town's namesake, but then the air behind us shifted, and someone leaned in between us, warm and close.

"What sort of debauchery is going on in here?" Christian said. Immediately I rose from the chair, crossed back over to the sink with my plate.

"Well?" Christian said.

Sebastian giggled. "The usual sort."

"Hand it over, Trouble." Christian held out his hand, and after shoveling in a final bite, Sebastian gave up the rest of his cake. Christian finished it in two bites. He joined me at the sink, slipped his plate into the soapy water.

Sebastian darted back into the gallery.

And Christian just stood there.

Watching.

He didn't cross his arms or put his hands in his pockets or inspect his fingernails like most people would. He was just . . . *there*. So relaxed and confident that I had to resist the urge to give him something—a sponge, a dish to dry, anything. He'd obviously connected the dots on my identity, which meant he knew I couldn't speak, so by not saying anything, he was baiting me.

It worked.

There was a time when guys couldn't get under my skin, when I'd come right back with a flirty innuendo, a joke, a rejection. A playful shove. A tease. One step closer and an almost-kiss.

All that confidence, all that moxie. All of it wrapped up in my voice, my music.

All of it lost.

I grabbed the Sharpie from the counter, scribbled on my palm. I held it up to his face.

Something I can do for you?

He laughed, raspy. "God, yes."

I held his gaze and thought again of a hundred witty comments, all the flirty things I would've said if I'd still been able to say them.

If I'd still been me.

But of course I just waited, silently aflame.

It was Mayor Katzenberg who saved me.

"Chris," he called from the gallery. "Come on out, son. Something I'd like to run by you."

Christian rolled his eyes. "This'll be entertaining," he mumbled, turning away. When I didn't move from the sink, he looked back over his shoulder and said, "You coming?"

I followed him out, reclaimed my chair next to Kirby.

Vanessa's eyebrows were drawn close, pinched with worry. When Christian sat next to her, she put her arm around the back of his chair. It looked like she was about to say something, but the mayor barged ahead.

"Hear me out, boys." Mr. Katzenberg regarded the men over the lip of his highball, amber liquid stilled like the crowd at the table, all of us waiting. He sipped loudly, then lowered his glass. "Up for a little wager on the Pirate Regatta?"

Kirby leaned close, whispering in my ear. "The regatta happens every August during the Mermaid Festival. Christian races with Noah on Noah's boat, the *Never Flounder*? They—"

I cut her off with a look. I already knew about the festival; I wanted to hear the mayor's terms.

So did Christian. He folded his arms over his chest and leaned back in the chair, tipping it up on two legs. "I'm listening."

"I know you and my boy are close," the mayor said. "But if you're willing to race against Noah this year, and you win, you'll get the *Never Flounder*."

"You love that boat, Christian!" Sebastian wriggled excitedly in his mother's lap. "We could take her on mermaid hunts!"

Christian's eyes glinted for a moment, then dimmed. "Noah would never part with his baby."

"Noah doesn't own it," the mayor said. "I do."

"And if I lose, Katz gets the old Vega?" Christian laughed. "Hardly a fair trade."

"Hardly indeed." The mayor wiped his mouth with a thumb and forefinger, eyes shining like a pirate who'd just unearthed the treasure. "No, Chris. If you lose . . ." He looked at Mr. Kane, greasy lips twitching into a smirk. "Your father sells his property to P and D."

Mr. Kane laughed, hollow. "Should've seen *that* coming."

"It's a good deal, Kane," the mayor said. "They're offering well above market value. And if people see the Cove's prominent families selling the houses at Starfish Point, they're more likely to jump on board with Prop Twenty-Seven. It's a real chance to put this town on the map."

"This town doesn't want to be on the map," Christian said.

"That's exactly the kind of outmoded thinking that holds us back." The mayor rattled off local businesses, people who'd benefit from the expansion. Tax incentives, growth, sustainable local economy, and everybody wins, restaurateurs and surf shop owners alike.

Lemon wasn't on the list.

"It's a win-win, guys," he finished up. "You're walking with the boat, or you're walking with a hell of a profit on these houses."

"Houses?" Christian said.

"P and D's after the complete package." The mayor tapped the table in front of him. "Your house and the neighboring property."

Kirby's leg twitched against mine, and Lemon's eyes snapped to us, probably feeling the same shiver that passed through me. Lemon's house, Lemon's gallery, this very room, the sanctuary I'd been offered this summer . . . *we* were the neighboring property.

"Pardon the interruption of this little testosterone-fest," Lemon said. "But do I get a vote?"

The mayor sipped his drink, hissing through his lips. He looked at Mr. Kane, who didn't offer any reassurances either.

Lemon loved her home—the Mermaid Tears gift shop and gallery,

the sprawling gardens, the view. The fact that the two most powerful men at the Cove were treating it like a business deal, a generic summer rental whose fate didn't matter? Something they could toss around in a wager, with no care that Lemon's life could get turned upside down?

That told me every last thing I needed to know about them.

Thankfully, Christian wasn't taking the bait.

"Sounds like real good times, guys. But . . . pass." Christian rose from the table, went to the kitchen for a drink refill. When he sat down again, he said, "Vega's barely floating, and there's no time to get her ready."

"Nonsense," his father said. "Take a vacation from breaking hearts this summer. You'll have plenty of time to get her seaworthy."

"She won't sail past the docks, Dad. I was down there earlier. She's a wreck." Christian glanced at me, then back to his father. "What are you even playing at? The *houses*?"

"Don't do it, Daddy," Sebastian said. "Mama, tell him not to. I like it here."

"Don't look at me," Mrs. Kane said. "This is your father's game, apparently."

"My great-grandfather built these properties, Meredith," Mr. Kane said, smug. "I grew up here. They belong to me."

"Yes, I'd almost forgotten," she said. "For a minute there, I thought our marriage was an equal partner—"

"Hey, kids," Christian said, "we all know you two are bonkers for each other. No need to blind us with the sunshine of your marital bliss."

Mr. Kane cleared his throat. His wife leveled him with an icy stare. One of them was sleeping on the couch tonight.

"Should I start packing?" Lemon asked. Beneath the steely sarcasm I detected fear. She had to be nervous—I'd felt the shift in her energy, seen it in her eyes the moment someone mentioned "neighboring property."

"P and D isn't interested in tossing you out," the mayor said. "They simply want to corporatize the properties up here under one umbrella. You'd still lease it, just from different landlords."

"Different rent, too," Lemon said.

He waved a hand, swatting at her persistence. "Better services, more security. Other than that, not much would change for you. And Kane's house? It's empty in the off season. He's paying a maintenance company for upkeep when he could just let P and D rent it out year round, bring in more families, more money for the Cove."

"More money for Parrish and Dey," Lemon said.

"I'm sure they'll keep the rent fair," he said. "Whatever the market value supports."

"Market value will skyrocket if those plans go through," Mrs. Kane said. "Let's not pretend, boys. P and D invests in beach communities to make a profit, bottom line. They start building condos, hotels, a Starbucks, more roads. Everything gets more crowded, more expensive. Half this town would be forced to move."

"That's an exaggeration," the mayor said. "Sure, there'd be changes. Some folks would relocate, move somewhere off the beaten path. But we're talking about a few sacrifices for the common good. A real chance to save this place. To make it better for those of us who stay."

He seemed pretty certain that the plan would work, but it didn't make sense to me. If everyone was forced out, what exactly was he trying to save?

"The Jameses are on board," Mr. Kane said. "Right, Vanessa?"

Vanessa offered her disarming smile. "Don't you get *me* into this mess, Mr. Kane. I leave politics to the politicians."

"Neil told me he'd be listing your place this summer," he said.

"Yeah, but it's not for Prop Twenty-Seven. With all their campaign stuff, my parents just don't have time for long vacations anymore. Mom's not even coming for *this* season until next week, and Daddy won't make it up here at all. But y'all?" She looked from the Kanes to Lemon and Kirby, skipping pointedly over the mayor. "You guys *are* the Cove."

"Exactly." Lemon nodded. "And what do you think the Cove becomes if we commercialize it, Wes? Take a drive up to Cannon Beach—*that's* our future under corporate landlords."

"Yes." Mrs. Kane pointed at Lemon with the phone that hadn't left her hand all night. "Cannon Beach is a perfect example."

Cannon Beach was a great place for a day trip—they'd taken me up there a few weeks ago to see Haystack Rock from *The Goonies*. It had its own charms, but the town was overrun with tourists, a place whose original heartbeat was so deeply buried under the money it was no more than a faint throb. I couldn't imagine the Cove turning into that, or Lemon and Kirby being okay there.

Mr. Kane narrowed his eyes at his wife and set his highball on the table, harder than he needed to. "If what Wes says is true, Meredith, we'd make a killing. We could buy a beach house any-where."

"But I like it *here*," Sebastian said. "All the best mermaid watching is here."

Mrs. Kane ruffled his hair.

"We come here every summer, Dad," Christian said. "But . . . you know what? Whatever."

For a moment no one spoke. It seemed like Mr. Kane might be backing down, looking out for his family.

Then the mayor's eyes darkened. "What's wrong, Kane? Afraid your boy can't out-pirate mine? Is he into mermaids too? I hear that's inherited from the father's side."

Mr. Kane's jaw ticked, the gesture almost identical to Christian's, but whatever response hovered on his tongue stayed put.

I looked at Sebastian, his sweet face unmarred by the mayor's jab. As ever, my heart thrummed with the unsaids trapped inside.

Christian sighed. "You really are a douche bag, Katz."

The mayor laughed, but Christian wasn't being funny.

After a tense beat the mayor drained his drink, then got up and headed for the kitchen. He returned with the half-empty bottle of scotch, poured himself a refill. He stretched across the table and filled Mr. Kane's glass too.

Mr. Kane grabbed the drink. "I think we both know my son could swab the deck with yours, Wes."

The mayor only smiled. "This mean you're putting your money where your mouth is, friend?"

"Noah and I have sailed that race together every year for the last three," Christian said. "Now you're pitting us against each other? Forget the Vega. Without Noah, I don't even have a teammate."

"A little competition would do you boys some good," the mayor said. "Plenty of willing sailors at the Cove this summer."

I felt Lemon's eyes on me, but I refused to meet them. I knew what she was thinking—I could feel the impressions forming, drifting across the space between us.

She looked away, probably talking herself out of it, pushing an unbidden thought aside.

But not before it reached me.

My hand was curled on my thigh, and I looked down and read the message on my palm, smudged now with clamminess.

Something I can do for you?

Inside I felt an idea take root, bloom.

I'd been sailing my entire life.

But not anymore.

I was probably better than a lot of the sailors here, maybe even better than Christian and Noah.

But I couldn't go out there again.

I crushed my fingers against my palm, made a fist.

"All right, Katz," Mr. Kane said. It was like Christian wasn't even there. "We're in." He rose, stretched across the table for the handshake. "Your boy's finally got some competition this year."

It was a strange mix, Mr. Kane's vibe. On one hand, he treated his eldest with little more than contempt. But the mayor got under his skin in a different way, a way that made him react fast. He bet on Christian, talked him up at the risk of losing his home. Lemon's home.

"We'll see who brings the competition." The mayor downed his drink, lifted the empty glass toward Christian. "Let the piracy begin, Chris."

"It's Christian." Christian's voice was sour as he rose from the table, but he didn't say no, didn't back down from his father's bet.

Outside, the clouds that had been threatening all night made good on their promise.

Lightning pierced the sky.

Rain lashed the windows.

From the first moment Mayor Katzenberg had said the word "wager," it couldn't have been more than ten minutes. A blip, really, but a blip that left a chill in the house untouched by the earlier celebratory warmth. Silently I helped Lemon and Kirby carry the remaining dishes to the sink, and then I slipped into the shade beneath the sea glass tree, my favorite sculpture in the gallery.

Built along the north-facing windows in a dark corner, the tree was made from driftwood, bone-white branches that jutted out from a tall trunk. Tiny pieces of sea glass in blue, green, brown, and white hung from invisible wires like leaves that never fell.

The jewel-colored bits clicked together softly as Christian exited through the deck door, leaving his birthday party guests behind.

I pressed my forehead to the window and tracked him down the staircases, down to the sand below. He walked along the shore, past his house, unconcerned about the rain and the blue-white electricity streaking across the horizon.

I imagined his footsteps in the wet sand.

Dark, fading. Dark, fading. Dark, fading.

He disappeared in the mist.

My throat tightened, a feeling like tears rising, but they didn't spill. They never spilled anymore; I always stopped them. Crying never brought anything back from the dead. It only felt like the ocean trying to drown you from the inside out.

The men were back to talking investments, oblivious, but as I watched the lightning gather and spill on the horizon, I knew their bet had set things in motion. Irreversible, impossible things. Dangerous things.

I also knew how to patch up an old boat. I knew how to sail.

But inside my head, the only place that could still hear my words, the echo said no. It said that I shouldn't be thinking about the Kane family, the sticky web of it. I needed to keep my head down, help Lemon at the gift shop.

Not try to save the house from these dangerous, destructive forces. From men more powerful than the ocean.

I needed to collect sea glass. Keep my room clean. Do the dishes without being asked. Write poems and lyrics that no one would ever read, pretend I'd one day be able to sing again.

But maybe . . .

You're too afraid, the echo taunted. *You're a fool to even think it.*

I closed my eyes.

There was a time, not so long ago, I'd take a stage before hundreds of people. Grab my sister's hand, move the crowd without a second thought. Now, everything in me felt frozen and stiff, the stage bravery no more than a memory.

Natalie would've known what to do. She would've told me the truth. Held my hand, caught my tears when I let them fall, even if she'd been the one to put them there.

But she was gone.

I was gone.

Behind me, someone flicked on an overhead light, and I opened my eyes, catching my reflection in the glass. For an instant, a heartbeat, a breath, I thought it was my twin sister.

I pressed my hand to the window, and her fingertips met mine exactly. We spoke in unison.

Oh, gyal. What am I supposed to do without you?

Chapter 5

"Some say it's the entrance to hell," Lemon said, "but you shouldn't worry too much. It's probably just a legend."

Water surged against the rocks near Thor's Well, white froth sizzling in the wave's retreat. It was the morning after, and I'd awoken with the realization that it hadn't been a dream. That my boat was no longer mine and the house that had stood so firmly before the sea could be reclaimed just as easily.

And now I found myself in Cape Perpetua at church. Lemon's version, anyway.

Hell? I mouthed. It was the first time I'd accepted Lemon's weekly invitation, but it was starting to make sense why Kirby always turned her down. The sun hadn't even risen yet; the sea was cold and gray, and the jagged black rocks around us looked blue in the soft light.

"Think of it as a sacred doorway. The entrance to the underneath, the realm below the sea." Lemon tucked her auburn mane into a headscarf and yanked on the knot. "Ready?"

I glanced at my naked feet. Not wearing hiking boots to traverse volcanic rock was a recipe for injury, but on the drive up Lemon had insisted that the best way to connect with the earth was to feel it beneath your bare skin, sharp edges and all. She held out a steadying hand.

I pictured Granna and Dad at Sunday services. Natalie probably still went with them too. The remembered scent of frankincense filled my nose.

I longed for a hymnal and a smooth, firm pew, but, as the saying goes: When in Rome . . .

I grabbed Lemon's hand, held on tight.

At least at Lemon's church I didn't have to wear a dress. Granna would probably give me the evil eye if she saw. The thought made me smile.

I took a tentative step. Then another.

This stretch of Pacific coast was edged with jagged rock, left-overs from an ancient eruption, and somewhere in the middle lay the hole called Thor's Well. It was a craggy, bottomless pit into which waves crashed and poured, presumably sucked back out to sea. There was a paved pathway from the Cape Perpetua visitor center and a platform that offered a decent view, but at low tide like this, you could walk out on the rocks and get close to the well itself, depending on your risk tolerance.

Even with my death grip on Lemon's hand, when it came to tempting the temper of the sea, my risk tolerance was at an all-time low. I swallowed the urge to vomit.

Lemon led us to a flat spot in the rocks, still a safe distance from the well, and together we knelt down. Cold water soaked my pants, chilled my legs. With her hands spread flat at her sides, Lemon pressed her forehead to the exposed rock and whispered devotionals to the sea. Even at low tide the surf was restless; I couldn't hear Lemon's words, but likely she was thanking the Pacific for its gifts, for its beauty.

Acknowledging its power in the face of our infinite human fumbling. Our smallness.

I wrapped myself in a tight hug, fought off a shiver.

The water calmed around us. We sat in companionable silence, watching the first orange rays of sunlight poke through the mist, and I stretched out my fingers to catch them.

It still had the power to shock me, the lack of warmth here. My skin prickled with goose bumps.

"So, last night," Lemon said, finished with her morning prayers. No matter how delicate the situation, she entered conversations like she entered a room, suddenly and intentionally, and I braced myself for whatever was coming. "It was probably a bit much for you, meeting so many people at once. Strong personalities."

I scooched closer and shook my head, salt water soaking my clothes anew. Sure, I'd shaken too many hands, forced too many smiles, witnessed more of the Kane family tension than I'd wanted to. But it was a party, stuffed with people, and no one had really tried to talk to me. They'd looked at, but not questioned, the scar. They'd taken in the kinky hair, the dark skin that seemed so rare in coastal Oregon, and possibly wondered about where I'd come from, but no one voiced it. Not even when they looked at me again and again like an exhibit, each time anew. Not cruel, perhaps, but invasive. Invasive enough that I always waited for the questions, and when they didn't come, I shrank a little more inside.

I didn't have the word for it, but when it came to meeting the good people of Atargatis Cove, last night was closer to the *opposite* of "a bit much."

In Tobago, everyone knew everything, and whatever they didn't know they made up. Neighbors thought nothing of telling Granna she was "gettin' on in size," or that it was long past time for Dad to "find himself a new woman." Carnival before last, Natalie and I had gotten pretty wild, relishing our first time in a masquerade band in Trinidad unsupervised—Natalie linked up with some guy from San Fernando, giving him a hard wine, boomsie in the air and her hands on the ground, losing her mind as Machel Montano sang his hit, "Advantage." Natalie was taking advantage all right. As for me, I was doing the same with my last boyfriend, Julien, who was loving his wild, free Elyse. News of our partying had reached Granna before the sun rose.

After this year's Carnival, before I'd even been released from the hospital in Port of Spain, neighbors had sent cards full of advice on how I couldn't let this setback bring me down, how I was still a beautiful girl with lots of prospects. How fate altered our course, and it wasn't for us to question things or to linger too long in anger.

Anger, they'd warned, was an invitation for the devil.

And what were my new plans, they wanted to know?

I used to hate it, all their macoin'—being nosey. But now I couldn't decide which was worse—having neighbors spy on me, counsel me like they knew the workings of my heart? Or having them look right through me?

~~There, I was a celebrity.~~

Here, I felt invisible. Intriguing, maybe. Different. But ultimately unknowable.

I thought that's what I'd wanted when I left Tobago. To be left alone, to hunt sea glass in the mornings and write my poems at night, dreaming of the past. To hide out on a rickety old boat that wasn't mine, unseen.

But after last night, after seeing all that shared history, closeness and rivalry and dysfunction alike, I wasn't so sure.

I was a ghost still tethered to her body, and I didn't know how to move on. I didn't know how to explain all that to Lemon, either, especially without a voice. I held her gaze and let my eyes speak for themselves, but when she didn't question me further, my attention drifted back out to sea.

A rogue wave lashed the rocks before us, spraying us with mist. I put on my bravest face, not wanting to worry her. When Lemon finally spoke again, she had to raise her voice to outshout Mother Nature.

"Your granna called last night," she said, licking sea mist from her lips. "You were asleep. I told her about the situation with the house. She thinks you should return home, that this whole regatta business might complicate things."

I shook my head. Lemon was the one who'd invited me to the States, who'd convinced Dad and Granna it would do me good to get off the island, away from the constant reminders of everything that could no longer be. It was like she'd sensed my ache across the oceans, and I knew she could still sense it now. That she understood I needed time. Space. Distance.

From the moment she'd sent the ticket, I promised myself that I'd earn my place here. Do what I could to help at the gallery, even when she'd tried to insist that I relax. As long as Lemon would have me—as long as she had a place for me and I could continue to help out—I had no plans to return to Tobago.

Besides, there was a chance Christian could pull this off. Kirby had told me that when Christian and Noah raced together, they'd won every time, three years running.

"That's what I told her," Lemon said. "Your dad, too. He knows as well as I do that you're not going anywhere until—and unless—you're good and ready. I don't care what those cocky old fools do with our house."

Lemon looked out across the Pacific, the horizon endless and gray despite the rising sun.

"I grew up with those boys," she said. "Wes and Andy. Ever since they were kids, they've been pissing in each other's shoes. Sometimes I think the only reason Andy left the Cove was to prove he was better than Wes. When Wes ran for mayor, Andy sent campaign contributions, even though there wasn't an opposing candidate. He just wanted Wes to know how much throwaway money he had." Lemon shook her head. "Either of them would save a baby from a burning building, but bet your ass they'd be sure the other one heard about it after."

I tugged on her jacket to get her attention. When she looked at me, I mouthed carefully, *Why bet houses? Why not just sell?*

"Andy didn't show up here wanting to sell," she said. "Unfortunately, bets are his weakness, and Wes knows how to use it against him. He set the hook; Andy bit. Walking away would've made him look weak, especially after that jab Wes took at the boys."

I thought again of Sebastian, the excitement in his eyes when he'd started telling me about Atargatis, and Christian, his body strung tight in his father's presence.

I thought of the Vega, all the work it needed. How I *knew* that it needed all that work, not just because it looked like a wreck on the outside, but because I knew boats.

I closed my eyes, drifted into a memory at the resort, Natalie and I taking Bella Garcia out on our own Vega. Bella was one of our regulars, sailed like a pro. She was also famous, one of the most popular soca artists in T&T. Earlier this year she'd taken the coveted Queen of the Bands title at Carnival.

Natalie and I had been there.

Caribbean Sea, from the edge of the Arctic. But for them, it would always be home, no matter how far they'd traveled, how many adventures they'd embarked upon.

Port of Spain, Trinidad, was only fifty miles from our resort—much closer than the other continents across which my sisters had traversed. But looking out at the islands from that hospital window in the city, when my twin sister and a doctor who looked not much older than me said I'd never sing again? That was the day I lost my home.

I didn't want that for Lemon and Kirby. Even if what Mayor Katzenberg had said was true—that Lemon could keep on renting, just from a new landlord—I knew it would change. That the rent would double, at least. That the house wouldn't be the same, wouldn't feel like hers. That the face of the entire town would change. Lemon was taking it all in stride, but she faced the possibility of losing the home she loved, shutting down the gallery she'd worked so hard to build, relocating to a strange new place.

And I had the skills and the time to do something to help her keep it.

Despite my fears, how could I *not* try?

As if to answer, the sea threw an icy wave our way, fully dousing us both. Lemon squealed, and inside, I shrank and shriveled.

"Time to make our exit," she said, "before the tide comes in and sweeps us down to the underneath."

She rose from the rocks and turned back toward the horizon,

offering a small bow of thanks to the sun just before it slipped fully behind the clouds.

I did the same, ignoring the tremble in my limbs, the warring thoughts that tugged me from one side—offering Christian my help with the Vega—to the other—steering clear of the treacherous sea, of Christian and his family. Beyond that, even if I could trust the ocean, even if Christian could take me seriously, how could I get involved in anything connected to Wes Katzenberg and Andy Kane? Men like that ruled the world, always getting their way, always knocking people down in the crossfire.

Against that, what power had a broken girl with no voice?

On our return march, I waved away Lemon's offered hand. Despite my careful steps, I sliced my foot on a jagged edge, and now I limped my way onto the path that led back to the parking area.

"Let me see." Lemon cradled my heel, the skin warming at her touch. "You're bleeding, but you'll live. We'll clean it up when we get home."

She smiled when she released my foot, but there was a look I'd come to know, one that meant she was about to unleash some mystical wisdom, feed me some foul herbal tonic, or cause a minor explosion in the kitchen.

Betting on the first, I lifted my eyebrows in question.

"Your blood has mingled with the ocean," she whispered ominously. It was a little melodramatic, even for her, but I smiled anyway. "Whatever you were thinking about on our walk across those rocks? You've just made an oath with the sea."

Chapter 6

Fog had crept up the coast during our drive back from the Well, and whorls of mist still clung to the sand when I set out for the marina. It wasn't yet seven in the morning, and the beach was cloudy and deserted, save for the oystercatchers scrabbling around the tide pools. I zipped the hoodie up to my neck and picked up the pace, jogging toward the docks at a clip only slightly hampered by my earlier injury.

Christian was there when I arrived, his back to me as he stood at the stern, one foot propped up on the coaming. His hands were shoved into his sweatshirt pockets—light gray, just like mine—and the fabric pulled tight across his shoulders as he stared out at the sea.

I'd thought this might be a problem, him being here. The boat needed a major overhaul; of course he'd want an early start. But I couldn't just leave my stuff. Without a few coats of paint, my written words would remain forever—I could at least apologize and collect my physical belongings.

Christian hadn't noticed my approach, and I took a second to gather my thoughts, to observe this boy whose grit and seaworthiness would determine Lemon and Kirby's future at the Cove.

He was taller than me by a head, with those strong-looking shoulders and narrow hips, dark jeans that hung loose on his legs. His hair was short and thick, soft and messy. It was darker than his father's, but sandy blond at the tips, like he'd spent much of his Stanford hours basking in California's famous sunshine.

I wondered if it was hard for him, being here. I wondered which place he thought of as home. Whether he'd ever felt untethered, like me.

The breeze kicked up, blowing the curls back from my face. I gathered them into a hair tie, took a deep breath, and marched down the dock. I stopped beside the *Queen of*.

Christian had left a tape gun and a couple of flattened cardboard boxes on the dock, awaiting assembly, and the boat's aqua-blue deck was already littered with stacks of stuff. Much of it had probably been in the saloon since they'd first docked the boat here, but some of those stacks were mine. It reminded me of packing for Oregon, boxing up my room in Tobago. Trying to decide what was worth bringing, what had to be left behind.

A fierce wave of protectiveness rose in me, but I let it pass. Christian wasn't dismantling my room. The Vega was his; he was simply removing a stranger's junk, getting her ready for the voyage ahead.

Uncertain of how to get his attention, I unfolded one of the flat boxes and attacked it with the tape gun. Christian turned around at the noise, the pensive angles of his face reshaping.

"Aha!" He pointed at me with mock accusation, a slow grin spreading. "My stowaway. I was hoping you'd turn up today."

The seashell around my neck felt heavy. My fingers found their way to it, fidgeting as I tried not to break his gaze.

"Sorry to be the bearer of shitty news," he said, "but you're being evicted."

I scanned the sight of my belongings, a half dozen piles on the deck.

In a softer tone he said, "I was just boxing it up to bring to your aunt's."

I gave him a quick nod of appreciation and got back to work assembling the box. When it was all put together, he held out his hands for me to toss it up. He caught it and set it down on the deck, then waved for me to climb aboard.

"Come on, now," he said when I didn't budge. "You came all this way. At least help me pack it up."

His smile hadn't faded, but it didn't reach his eyes. Not now, and not last night, either. It was the ghost smile, that look, there but not. His gaze was far away, adrift on another sea, and his real smile wasn't for me. Vanessa—she probably got to see it. But not the girl who'd stowed away on the boat that didn't belong to her. The girl who'd written volumes on the walls but never said a word.

Ignoring his outstretched hand, I stepped over the gap between the dock and the boat, heaving myself over the rails. When he tried to steady me with a gentle touch on my lower back, I shook loose. Even with a sore foot, I could make that climb in the dark—I'd done so on many nights before his arrival—but thought better of confessing.

"She's a beauty, yeah? In her own way." Christian palmed the side of the companionway, caressing it lightly.

I offered a wary smile.

"She smiles," he said, one hand on his heart, and I wondered if he knew that my smile wasn't the real one either. "I suppose there's no need for the grand tour. Just help me get the rest of this stuff out of the saloon."

He took off his sweatshirt and tossed it onto the coaming, and when he leaned forward through the companionway, a black line peeked out from beneath his T-shirt sleeve. I followed the markings to the larger shadow beneath the fabric. He was tattooed across most of his right shoulder and upper arm, but I couldn't make out the design.

"First, there's this." From inside the saloon he turned to face me, holding out a black Moleskine notebook, Sharpie clipped to the front. The notebook had a waterproof cover and sturdy paper, unlined, the kind that didn't bleed the ink. The pages themselves were rippled from some earlier spill, but intact. On the inside cover there was a silver music-note sticker.

Without Christian opening the notebook, I knew all of this.

It was mine.

Save for what I'd written on the boat and on my hands, all of my words were in that notebook. Songs I'd written with Natalie, poetry I thought one day we'd turn into music. Ideas for our future tours. All my hopes and dreams and, once I'd lost them, the fears that took their place. The secrets.

Now they were pinned in Christian's hand.

My heart sank.

"It was on the table," he said. "With the candle. Figured it belonged to you, since I'm the only other person who uses the boat, seeing as how it's mine and all, and I'm not much of a writer. But you? Regular wordsmith."

When I didn't respond, he leaned closer, waving the notebook between us. His voice was low and raspy, like a secret. "The thing I can't figure is, how did all the words escape this paper and end up on my walls?"

Inside, I felt like an eel, slithering and squirming under his glare. But outside, I was a rock.

And my God, that boy would *not* give me a break.

"Relax," he finally said. The mask of seriousness dropped suddenly from his face, and I let out a breath. "Just giving you a hard time. I didn't read it. Flipped through enough to figure it was yours, probably private."

I didn't have to scrutinize him long to know that Christian was telling the truth. I grabbed the offered notebook before he changed his mind.

He watched me a moment longer, then ducked back into the saloon, taking it all in. "She needs a lot of work. I don't even know where to start. Guess once I clear it out, I can assess—"

I held up a finger to interrupt. I knew he was mostly talking to himself, but I had a few suggestions. I plucked the Sharpie from the notebook cover and flipped to the first free page inside. I'd never started up the engine, but after my month-long visitations with the *Queen of*, I was intimately familiar with her other trouble spots— all the things both small and large that could sink this ship, sink his chances at winning the regatta.

He waited silently, patiently, as I let the words flow.

The Queen's Issues
Leaks around starboard window.
Condensation gathers on the sill beneath.
Mainsail & jib seem sketchy; unfold and hoist for full assessment.
Wiring issues are not my area of expertise, but a probable concern,
given her age and condition.
The nav instruments are cracked.
Condensation on their casing indicates damage.
Externally, gel coat needs another application.

*Interior woodwork is original, mostly solid,
despite a bit of interior mildew, likely
cleanable.*

*Underside? Now there's a question for the
experts.*

Final thoughts on the Queen of:
A seaworthy vessel in need of some love.

I tore out the page and handed it over, satisfied. After reading it, Christian got that ghost of a smile again. When I didn't flinch under his gaze, he raised an eyebrow, like, *Who are you?*

"Does everything you write come out like a poem?"

I hadn't done it on purpose, but he was right. Every list or letter came out that way, like a verse, a story I could set to music. Natalie was the same way—Dad often teased us about it. *I thought you were making a grocery list, little songbirds. Now you'll have me singing about coconut milk and Cheerios."*

"Speaking of poetry," Christian said. "When you say here 'interior mostly solid,' is that with or without your body of work?"

My cheeks flamed. On a fresh page I scribbled again. Christian stepped back through the companionway and onto the deck, closer, bringing with him the smell of the sea and whatever shampoo he used—something like mangoes, which reminded me of my sisters.

The boat bobbed beneath us.

He read my words upside down as I wrote.

Thought she was abandoned.
I'll scrub & paint everything.
I'm sorr

He grabbed my hand, cut off the rest. "Forget about it. Adds character. And, ah, thanks for the list." He released me and folded up my note about the boat's issues, stuck it in his back pocket. "God, I love a woman who knows the difference between a mainsail and a jib."

He held my gaze, eyes glittering.

Sometimes there's a fine line between sexy and crass, and Christian walked it with the best of them.

His looks helped, sure. The strong build, the confident stance, those mysterious green-gray-blue eyes. But more than that, it was his attentiveness. Just looking at him, a careful observer could see that he was there but not there, his thoughts in many places at once. Adrift, as I'd noticed earlier. But when he was with you, he was *with* you. In a shared moment, for however long it lasted—an instant, a minute, ten—he was the kind of guy who offered his undivided focus, no matter how many other girls might be in the room, no matter who he planned on taking home that night.

Clever? Yes. Cocky? Sure. But dismissive? Not part of his repertoire.

All of this I deduced standing too close to him on the deck of the *Queen of*, his sea-and-mangoes scent enveloping me.

"Gotta be honest," he said after a beat too long. "I'm not sure what to make of you."

My fingers reached instinctively for the shell necklace, gave it a twist.

Those eyes . . . He had me pinned. He knew it. I matched him, unflinching.

It was both thrilling and unnerving, the intensity that crested between us.

The boat bobbed. Tipped. Straightened.

And like a wave, the moment receded.

Kirby's words echoed, and I thought about the long line of "libera-tors" he'd soon face, once the rest of the summer renters arrived.

"Seriously," he said. "You know your boats." It wasn't a question, and I didn't deny it. "Good sailing in the Caribbean?"

I turned the page, wrote another message.

Yes. Family owns an eco-resort in Tobago
w/ small fleet nearby.
I lead guest charters. Used to lead.

When I looked up, he nodded toward the open maw of the sea, the waves that endlessly tumbled and turned as they made their way toward the *Queen of*.

"Used to? When's the last time you were out?"

That was a question whose answer I couldn't provide without trawling through the past, wading through pains too close and tender. The scar on my throat tingled.

I shrugged and mouthed a quick response. *Three, four months.*

"Formal?" he said.

I held up four fingers and tried again. *Months.*

"Four months," he said, nodding. "I couldn't go that long. I sail at school. Kayak, too, when I can. Sea's in my blood."

Mine too, I mouthed, but he was looking out across the Pacific again. He didn't know I'd said it, didn't know I'd felt my own blood stir at his words. My pulse quickened, warmth rising inside as old passions—for the first time in months—surged ahead of more recent fears. I didn't know the story with his old Vega, but Christian's love for the sea was plain, as deep as the Pacific herself, and the liveliness in his eyes tugged at something in my heart, too.

The doctors in Trinidad had warned me about possible nightmares. Post traumatic stress, they'd called it. Irrational fear, paranoia, depression, anger. All of those things they'd tried to prepare me for. But what they hadn't talked about was betrayal. How something you'd known and loved forever could turn on you, could break your heart even as it left you alive.

Now it felt as if the sea, that old treacherous lover, was giving me another chance.

Was I wrong to trust her? To *want* to trust her?

Did it matter?

Again I thought of Lemon, kneeling in her garden to trim the herbs she'd planted, blending them into tonics and lotions. Pacing the shore in contented silence, scanning for treasures. Reading tarot cards and books about witchcraft in her reading nook at the end of the hallway. Cooking meals for me and Kirby and her guests in the big white-and-turquoise kitchen. Assembling her sculptures, piece by piece, humming her otherworldly music as she did.

Home.

All of these things buzzed through my blood anew, making my skin warm and tingly.

I opened my mouth to make the offer at the same time Christian said, "What would it take to make you my first mate?"

My first thought was, *Boy, keep looking at me like that and I'll be whatever you want. . . .*

But that was just my skin speaking, all the soft parts that hadn't been touched by strong hands since Julien broke things off a month after the accident. I quickly dismissed the thought and looked up to the sky, as if to consider.

He didn't rush to fill in the silence, to sweeten the deal with some other promise, to convince me how much I'd like working with him. He just let it stand.

Christian Kane, I was quickly learning, knew how far he could push. Knew when to silence the jokes, the flirting, the sarcasm. When to give a conversation space to breathe, to expand.

The Vega took a hit from a large wave, rocked and rocked.

Water splashed up the sides, splattered us.

My heartbeat quickened, but my limbs remained steady.

Still Christian waited. Watched. Waited.

He didn't know that I'd already decided, some time between last night and this morning, catching the sunrays between my fingers, spilling my blood into the sea. Finding him here, adrift and back again.

I didn't know that I'd already decided either.

But somehow, I had.

I pressed the Sharpie to the page. He stepped closer, mangoes-in-the-sea.

I'm in.

Chapter 7

"Let's box everything up for now, get a look at her from the bones up," Christian said. We stood in the saloon together, wasting no time after my acceptance. "Sound like a good plan?"

A good plan.

No matter how far from home I'd gotten, the past had a way of tracking me, never giving up the chase. It snuck into my dreams, into those quiet moments when I'd been writing on the boat. It leaped out from the ocean, cresting on waves when I was certain I'd spotted a sea lion or an otter. Now, at Christian's words, the past found me again.

Last year, it was. Natalie and I sat in the shade of the cherry trees passing my notebook between us. We were supposed to be with Granna on a meet and greet for new resort guests, but we'd snuck out, ducked under the trees in a fit of giggles. We were working on our set list and choreography for Carnival. The festival was still months away, but the music had already taken us; we both knew it would hold us hostage until we finalized every word, every step.

The sun was low on the horizon when we finished that day, and Natalie closed the notebook, satisfied. When our eyes locked, she said, "Gyal, we got ourselves a good plan here. Real good plan."

I missed us all over again, each time as raw as the first.

"You okay?" Christian's hand on my elbow tugged me from the grip of the past. When I nodded, his concern changed to relief, then excitement. "Shall we get this good time rolling?"

Christian may have been pissed about the fact that his father made the bet without consulting him, but he wasn't talking about it, and the idea of fixing up the boat seemed to buoy him. I felt it too, the lightness in him emanating outward. For me, fixing up the old *Queen* wasn't like prepping for the stage at Carnival, or even for the show my sister and I put on for the resort guests. But it felt good having a purpose again, a project with a clear goal. A partner.

I swallowed the lump in my throat and nodded, and together Christian and I got a system going. Mostly it involved him tossing things from the saloon through the companionway, and me catching them, dropping them into boxes.

"You spent a lot of time here, I think." He flipped through a dark gray book I recognized as *Moby Dick*. "Yeah. This one was never my favorite. Look alive." With a flick of his wrist, he tossed it.

I caught it, dropped it in the box with my blankets. After the notebook incident, I'd decided to cast my lingering embarrassment out to sea. After all, Christian didn't seem bothered by the fact that I'd taken up residence in his boat, painted the walls with poems. Why should I be? Anyway, I meant my apology about the writing, and if he wouldn't let me paint over it, the least I could do was work my boomsie off getting the boat regatta ready. Christian depended on me now; I'd put myself in his trust, as far as the boat went.

But more than that, Lemon depended on me too. Even if she'd never say it.

Still digging out the V-berth, Christian said, "Since you obviously like stories, allow me to regale you with the tale of how I came to own this fine fixer-upper."

I sat down on the saloon bench, starboard side, and Christian said, "Oh, it won't take that long."

I rose.

"Dad won her in a poker game in Coos Bay," he said. "Two years ago. Later that summer, after Noah and I won the race on *Never Flounder*, Dad gave me the Vega. Said we'd build her up together, make her gleam until she outshone Katz's boat."

I looked on, waiting for him to explain how the project got derailed.

Christian's laugh was bitter. "Sweetheart, this boat is so damn metaphorical it could bring tears to the soul." He considered that a moment, then the fog lifted, his half smile back in place. He pointed at my chest. "That's some poetry, for you. Tears to the soul. Write it down."

Behind the sarcasm, the clenched muscle of his jaw told me that we'd reached the end of the story—as much as he was willing to share, anyway. I pulled out my notebook and scribbled a question.

What's Noah say about this bet?

"Haven't seen him yet—we just got into town yesterday. But I'm sure he'll be pissed. We've always raced together. But our dads? Everyone knows they won't back down from a bet."

"Never could," a voice said from the docks. I knew it immediately, thanks to all those café runs with Kirby and the times I'd spent alone at the Black Pearl, doodling in my notebook over a cup of coffee.

Noah gave us a smile, a broad and unabashed thing that lit up his face. Other than the lack of a suntan—common in this misty gray part of the world—he had the hot-surfer vibe going on, complete with blond dreads and an easygoing gait.

Christian hopped off the boat, grabbed Noah in a rough hug.

"Good to see you, man," Noah said. "You're tanner than I remember."

"Get out of Oregon once in a while, dude. Might see the sun," Christian said. I was still on the boat, and he started to introduce us, but Noah waved him off.

"Elyse and I go *way* back," Noah said.

Christian folded his arms over his chest. "That so?"

Noah only shrugged. "But seriously, dude. What the hell with our dads, right?"

Christian ran his hands through his hair, leaving it all sticking up.

"They were in their chest-thumping, dick-measuring glory last night."

"This sucks even harder than the lobster incident," Noah said. "Remember that shit?" He turned to me to explain. "This was, like, ten years ago, right? The Cove used to have this lobster race for kids, back before people got all animal rights and put an end to it."

"The lobsters were fine. They should've put an end to our dads." Christian shook his head, laughing at the memory. "Our fathers made one of their stupid bets. The loser's dad was supposed to buy fresh lobsters for the winner for the rest of the summer."

What happened? I mouthed.

"We both lost," Noah said. "Because Christian's jerk-off lobster attacked mine, and all the other lobsters piled up, and everyone freaked. A bunch of kids started crying, and parents were running around chasing the lobsters back into the ocean."

"My lobster was *not* a jerk-off," Christian said. "He just had some anger issues."

"Dude." Noah laughed. "My father never forgave me for losing that race. He still gets twitchy around lobsters."

"My dad's like that with swordfish. Remember *that* one?"

Noah sighed. "Remind me not to have kids. It's our sworn duty not to pass this shit on to them."

"Agreed," Christian said.

I pulled out my notebook, wrote another question for them:

What if you guys just said no? Didn't race?

They both bristled.

"The whole sea-in-the-blood thing," Christian said. "Can't *not* race." He scrubbed a hand through his hair again. "Anyway, you don't say no to sirs Wesley and Anderson. If Noah and I blew them off, we'd be out on our asses. We'd probably have to sleep at the Black Pearl. Or maybe move in with you guys."

Not Vanessa? As soon as my lips formed her name, I regretted it.

Christian only laughed. "For a quiet chick, you ask a lot of questions."

I left it at that, wondering if he'd backpedal, try to erase the "quiet" as if it were some kind of unintentional insult. Others had, especially in Oregon. The polite state, it was. The smile-bright-and-keep-your-thoughts-buried state.

But this boy let the joke stand.

Maybe Kirby, well-intentioned as she was, was wrong about Christian Kane.

At least a little bit.

After a final sweep of the saloon, Christian and I packed up the remaning items, and Noah helped us stack the boxes on the dock. After I handed over the last of them, I saw a tiny blond boy materialize from a spot in the distance, running fast and clattering with gear: flippers, scuba mask, a bucket full of shovels and sand molds.

"Sebastian! Over here, bud!" Christian called with a wave. I noticed Mrs. Kane then too—she waved when she saw us, then turned back toward the houses, probably returning to her work.

The kid lit up, zipping toward us with a turbo boost of energy.

When he reached us, Noah scooped him into his arms for a welcome hug, then transported the little guy onto the boat. I grabbed his hands, held on until he got his footing.

"All right, dudes," Noah said. "Gotta head to work. Shift starts in ten. Stop by later if you're hungry." He and Christian exchanged a fist bump.

"Guess this is it," Christian said. "From now on, we're mortal pirate enemies."

"Arrrrgh," Noah said with a fierceness that surprised me. "Oh, but we're still on for crabbing next week, right?"

"Wouldn't miss it," Christian said. "Just don't bring your dad."

As he backed up along the dock toward the marina, Noah pointed at Christian and smiled. "Same, dude."

"You guys cool to hang out a minute?" Christian asked once Noah had disappeared. He pointed in the distance toward a sleek yellow-and-blue boat at the other end of the marina. "That's the *Never Flounder*. I need to do a quick recon. Be right back."

"Hey." Sebastian set down all his stuff, then looked up at me with a wide grin. "You're the birthday cake girl."

I smiled and held up my hands, guilty as charged.

Sebastian sat down on the bench, gesturing for me to follow.

"Here's a game I just invented," he said as I sat beside him. "Let's pretend we're underwater. Only it's like a dream, because we can breathe underwater and we can talk."

I frowned and pointed to my throat. *Can't talk*, I mouthed. *No voice.*

"Are you a mermaid?" he asked.

I grinned. *Maybe.*

After regarding me with open curiosity for several long but not uncomfortable moments, Sebastian said, "I read a story about a mermaid who couldn't talk because the sea witch cut out her tongue."

I stuck out my tongue to alleviate his concern.

Relived, he said, "Did you know some mermaids are boys?"

He was right. I wondered if he'd read about the mermaids back home. Men, the old ones. Maybe Granna could send over some of the books, the island fairy tales she'd read to us growing up—I'd have to ask her next time we Skyped.

I pulled out my notebook and made a quick sketch for him, something I remembered from those stories. He stayed utterly silent, watching each stroke with awe. At the bottom, I wrote:

A mermaid from the Caribbean Sea, where I used to live.

When I tore out the page and handed it to him, he said, "I can *keep* this?"

I nodded. Sebastian considered me with those wide, genuine eyes, and when he reached up toward my throat, I didn't flinch. His pink fingers found the shell around my neck, touched it softly. He lifted it and saw the scar. His brow furrowed.

He whispered, "Is your voice inside the shell?"

I smiled a little sadly.

"That's okay," he said. "We don't have to talk to be friends."

"What are you two conspiring about over here?" Christian was back, standing on the dock with his arms folded. I wondered how long he'd been watching us, how much he'd heard.

"I'm goin' on a mermaid hunt," Sebastian said, as if this explained everything. He rose from the bench and gathered up his gear. A thin silver camera dangled from a strap around his wrist.

"Think this is the year you'll find her?" Christian asked.

Find who? I wanted to know.

"Remember when I was telling you about Atargatis?" Sebastian said. Even his curls bounced with excitement. "She used to be a star, and then this one time she fell in love with a shepherd. And he loved her too, so he was always watching her. But he should've been paying attention to where he was going, because one night he tripped and fell into the sea and then he died."

My eyes widened. Sebastian was not one for the cartoon versions of fairy tales.

"It's true," he said. "Right, Christian?"

Christian nodded. "According to the legend, she was so heart-broken and guilty over the death of her lover that she broke her oaths with the moon and the gods, and flung herself into the sea. She wanted to drown so she could find him again."

"Yeah," Sebastian said, "but the sea was like, 'No way. You're too beautiful and I can't kill you. But I can't send you back home, either.'"

Goose bumps rose along my arms.

"And then the sea turned her into the world's first mermaid," Sebastian said, "and she's cursed to live in the ocean forever, and I'm going to find her."

Christian ruffled Sebastian's curls. "You've been chasing mermaids a long time, kiddo. This *has* to be the year. You've earned it."

I raised my hand. *Can I come?*

Sebastian beamed. "Awesome! Christian, too?"

"I've got a few things to wrap up here," Christian said, "but you guys go." He nodded toward the boxes, my stuff. "I'll bring these by the gift shop later. Unless you're planning to contest the eviction and move back into the Vega tonight?"

I let his ghost smile linger between us.

We helped Sebastian off the boat, and after doing a quick check to ensure I hadn't left my notebook behind again, I climbed back onto the docks.

"I know the best spots." Sebastian grabbed my hand. His gear clattered with every step.

Before we reached the sand, Christian called out for me. "Elyse?"

It was the first time he'd said my name, I realized, and he'd gotten the pronunciation perfect. I turned to face him.

"Thanks for doing this." He tapped his foot against the side of the boat. "We've got a ton of work to do. But somehow I've got a not-so-terrible feeling about this race."

With my free hand I gave him a quick salute, sealing the deal.

He returned the gesture. "Later, Stowaway."

The cut on my foot throbbed anew.

Thunder roared in the distance.

Lemon would probably call it a bad omen.

I pretended I hadn't heard it, but a shiver rolled through me.

As if he'd read my mind, Sebastian tightened his grip on my hand and said, "Don't be afraid. That's probably just Atargatis. She knows we're coming."

Chapter 8

Sebastian and I gathered an impressive haul of sea glass, two intact sand dollars, and a bald, one-eyed doll head. But we didn't spot any mermaids, and soon the deluge came, chasing us into the Black Pearl for cover.

"See anything out there today?" Noah wanted to know once we'd settled into our booth. There were only two other occupied tables—a pair of men in suits who were clearly out-of-towners, and a group of girls about my age, whispering and giggling over milkshakes. Noah sat down with us.

"No mermaids," Sebastian said, shivering beneath his wet shirt. "But we did find this." He set the doll head on the table, making Noah jump clear out of his seat.

"That's creepy, little dude."

Sebastian smiled.

"So what am I making for you guys?" Noah asked. The Black Pearl didn't have a fixed menu—they brought in fresh meat, seafood, and produce each morning, and whatever concoction you could imagine from the available goods, they'd whip it up for you. "Bacon burgers are hot today. I'm also experimenting with chickpea salad. Nontraditional, but pretty good on a pita with some red onion and celery. Feeling adventurous?"

When I nodded, he said, "Did you bring your hot pepper sauce?"

I patted my pockets, realizing my error. I'd made a batch at Lemon's and carried a bottle with me whenever I planned to eat here.

"I'll bring out the store-bought stuff," Noah said. "Won't be the same, but it might spice things up a little."

I offered a grateful smile.

"I want chicken peas too," Sebastian said. "But I also want curly fries. And a root beer float."

I held up two fingers at that.

When Noah came back with the floats, he said, "No Kirby today?"

Library, I mouthed. It was inventory season, and there was a lot of work to do, culling the collection, cataloging new books for the summer. She told me she'd be spending practically every Sunday afternoon deep in the stacks.

"Right on," Noah said. His smile slipped, just a little, before he ducked back behind the counter.

I texted Kirby with this latest development.

Her response was immediate: *screw the stacks. lunch break—on my way!*

While we waited for Kirby, Sebastian dried his gear with napkins and continued to fill me in on the lore of his beloved mermaids, a subject on which he was a living encyclopedia. He knew everything about them—mythological origins, the difference between mermaids and sirens, all the ways in which the recent string of so-called mermaid documentaries were fraudulent and even detrimental to genuine ocean conservation efforts.

He was cleaning the lenses on a pair of binoculars that covered most of his face when he stopped suddenly, looked at me seriously across the table. "Atargatis is real, you know. I saw her once, but only for a second."

For weeks now I'd walked the shore day and night, and I'd yet to see her myself. But I believed him; the legend was tragic and beautiful enough to be real.

"We were on Noah's boat last year," he said, "and all of a sudden, she was just *there*. Sitting on these rocks, like nothing." His voice had dropped to a whisper, and his eyes were twin moons, round and glittering with awe. "Noah said it was probably a sea lion. But Christian believed me. I knew it was her because of the starfish tattoo." He touched his throat, and my scar tingled beneath the shell necklace.

I scribbled on a napkin and slid it across the table.

Is she evil?

Sebastian shrugged. "No one knows." He dunked the ice cream in his root beer, pondering as it bobbed up to the surface. "Probably she's so sad, she doesn't even remember how she got there."

When Kirby arrived, she was surprised to see my lunch companion.

"Last I saw you," she said to me, squeezing water out of her hair, "you were heading out for a beach walk after church. How'd you snag such a cute date?"

Sebastian rolled his eyes. "It's not a date. We were looking for mermaids." He crawled under the table, popped up on my side of the booth, then announced randomly, "Elyse is gonna help Christian win the regatta."

Kirby's eyebrows shot straight up into her hair as she sat down across from us. "You're gonna who with the what now?"

"Two chickpea surprises, two orders of fries-es." Noah arrived with our lunch, set the plates before us. Kirby immediately quieted, but her smile was impossible to hide. Noah mirrored her joy and, without words, returned minutes later with a vanilla latte, her favorite.

When he left us again, I drew a heart on a napkin, encircling their initials: *NK + KL*.

Kirby snatched it off the table and shoved it into her bag, lasering me with a pointed glare. "Anyway, about this regatta business . . . you can't just sign up for that, Elyse! What were you thinking?"

On another napkin, I wrote:

He asked. And I want to help save the houses.

Kirby sighed, but if she was worried about losing her home, she didn't let on. "Why would Christian ask you for help? He's obviously just trying to get in your . . . your you-know-whats." Her gaze drifted to Sebastian, then back to me. "You need to be c-a-r-e-f-u-l, that's all I'm saying."

"Christian's a good sailor," Sebastian said. "He's always careful."

Kirby smiled, brow furrowed as she tried to find a more cryptic way to warn me about the elder Kane. But before she figured it out, the door swung open, bringing with it a stiff breeze and a pair of beautiful fish caught in a net.

Vanessa and Christian.

They tumbled in through the doorway, rain soaked. Christian had his arm over Vanessa's shoulder, hers was looped around his waist, and he whispered something in her ear that made her laugh.

They looked for all the world like a couple who'd sooner drown than be separated, the kind that could finish each other's sentences and share inside jokes with just a look. More than lovers, they were friends. The closest kind.

I wondered how they survived the off-seasons.

Across the café, one of the milkshake girls waved. "Hey, Christian!" Her friends elbowed one another, all smiling.

"Hey there . . . um . . . you!" Christian said. "Good to see you again."

Kirby raised an eyebrow. "Case in point," she whispered. "Calla

Loretti, the one who just said hi? They hooked up last summer. He doesn't even remember her name."

"Whose name?" Christian said, suddenly in my space. Without asking me to move over, he slid into the booth. I was a Kane sandwich, and he smiled at his brother on my other side and leaned in close, breath hot in my ear. "Looks like you've got a new fan," he whispered, nodding toward Sebastian.

Across from us, Vanessa sat next to Kirby and laughed. "Eww. Get a room, y'all."

Her words held not a hint of jealousy.

I couldn't figure that girl out.

"Don't encourage her," Kirby said, talking about me, and if I wasn't so perfectly sandwiched between the Kane brothers, I would've kicked her under the table. Vanessa might've claimed an open mind about Christian's female companions, but that didn't mean I wanted her thinking I was one of them.

No matter what Vanessa said, the green-eyed devil could rise any time. I had five beautiful sisters. Jealousy trailed us so often she may as well have been the sixth.

"What the hell is that?" Christian poked the doll head on the table.

"Elyse found it," Sebastian said.

Before I could defend myself, Christian was leaning in again. "Elyse, if you need something to cuddle up with at night, there are much better options around here."

"Hello!" Vanessa said. "Room! Get one!"

Christian gave me a wink, then waved to Noah at the counter.

"Bring us two of whatever's good today, Katz. Preferably heavy on the dead animal and vitamin G."

"Greasy specials on the double," Noah called out from the grill. "Ten minutes."

"So, ya scalawags, how's tricks on the ol' *Queen of*?" Vanessa wanted to know. To me, she said, "Don't know what kinda trouble y'all got into with your aunt, but if someone made *me* work on that floating piece a' sh—"

"Watch it," Christian said. "You're talking about my girl right there."

Vanessa laughed. "SS *POS* ain't nobody's girl."

"What's POS?" Sebastian asked.

"Piece of . . . stupid," Christian said.

"Mom isn't making her do anything," Kirby said. "My cousin drives her *own* crazy train. But she's probably more qualified than most of the sailors at the Cove." As if I weren't there, Kirby launched into an overview of my boating skills, told them all about the resort, about how I'd been born in the sea. Short version, anyway. "Elyse pretty much belongs to the water."

She'd probably meant *in* the water, but I didn't correct her. No one knew the whole story—not even Lemon. Not even Natalie, and she was there the last time the sea tried to take me.

She was the one who'd fished me out.

Dead, mostly.

I closed my eyes, tried to hold back the shiver I knew would come anyway. It started in my feet, rolled up through my insides until even my scalp was covered in gooseflesh.

Next to me, Christian stirred, whispered in my ear. "Sorry. Didn't mean to drip on you." He shifted over, putting some space between us. His eyes were full of concern, a softness that clashed with his usual cockiness. "Better?"

It wasn't. I nodded anyway.

"So how bad is it?" Kirby asked Christian. "Like, *Extreme Makeover: Boat Edition* bad?"

"Piece of stupid bad?" Sebastian giggled.

Christian took out his phone, set it on the table where everyone could see. He scrolled through some pictures he must've taken today, soon after I'd left the ship. My boxes were still on the deck, but Christian had covered them to keep out the rain; the tattered blue tarps enhanced the fixer-upper vibe considerably.

"Gross," Vanessa said. "Looks like patchin' up that ol' girl is gonna take a lot more than an eighties music montage."

"Do I even know you?" Christian said. "It's like you're speaking another language."

"Back me up, girls," she said to me and Kirby. "The rah-rah, we-can-fix-it-up montage is essential to any romantic comedy."

"You see me laughing?" Christian's face was all angles, stone cold. The phone buzzed on the table, and he picked it up to check the incoming text. He looked up immediately, waved again at the girl across the way. "Calla," he whispered to us. "*That's* her name."

"You might need to change your phone number," Vanessa said.

He stowed the phone in his sweatshirt pocket. "Again?"

"Your ninety-nine girl problems are fascinating," Kirby said, keeping her eyes on me, "but back on point. Is the boat that dicey?"

"Piece of stupid dicey?" Sebastian laughed again.

"In a word, yes." Christian gave her an overview of the damage, glossing over the part about my redecorating. Just like at the docks, despite the grim report, he seemed excited about the project, getting more animated as he talked. Without breaking stride on the conversation, he leaned in front of me and grabbed the Sharpie I'd left on the table. He made a sketch on a napkin, an illustration to aid the description.

"She needs a major overhaul," he said, capping the marker and tossing it onto the table. "But she's longer, lighter, and faster than *Never Flounder*. Plus, I've got a better first mate. We're taking this race."

When I met his eyes, Christian winked at me, and in an instant I felt the force of his confidence, of his faith, a sudden weight around my neck.

Intentional or not, gratitude could so often turn into expectations, into hope. It was one thing to have your own kind of hope, an ember you could nurture inside, something to inspire you when things got dark. If it died, it was on you; no one else even had to know about it, and you were free to reignite it, or to give up and walk away. But when you were carrying it with another person, *for* another person, it was a dangerous dream. Treacherous as the sea, yet fragile as a bubble.

Faith was a funny thing.

He was seriously counting on me, I realized then. It was more than his desperate need for a partner, for someone to help fix up the boat. He really believed in me.

I gave in to another shiver.

Christian nudged me with his elbow, then raised his voice, called out across the restaurant again. "Hear that, Katz? *Never Flounder's* going down this year, dude."

I guess the piracy had started.

"Keep talking, sailor boy." Noah laughed as he flipped two burgers off the grill and assembled them on plates, topped with cheese and bacon and mountains of fries. "Anyone ever tell you not to threaten the dude cooking your food?"

"Poisoning the competition?" Christian said. "Kind of an obvious move. I'm unimpressed."

"Poison? Yeah, not what I was thinking." Noah came out from behind the counter, set the plates in front of Christian and Vanessa. Fries toppled from each, and for a moment, Christian stared, probably considering how far Noah would really go.

The door swung open again, ushering in the cold and another guy in a suit. He clomped over to the table where his two clones were waiting. "Surveying's done in sector four," he said. "That's probably our best bet for the new boardwalk."

"We've just secured Starbucks," one of the others told him. "McDonald's is interested, but they're hedging. Peterson's trying to get a location scout out here next week."

Our table went silent as we eavesdropped. I wondered if sector four was Starfish Point, but then I realized it wouldn't make sense to put a boardwalk that far up the Cove.

Of course, if they turned the houses into high-end vacation rentals, maybe it would.

"P and D vultures," Christian said, his voice low.

"Starbucks?" Vanessa whispered. "I mean, I love a good half caf, triple shot, no foam, cinnamon latte as much as the next girl. But not at the Cove. That's just not right."

Kirby nodded. "Mom will freak if they put a McDonald's here."

Seconds passed in silence, everyone—including Sebastian—apparently lost in private worries about the Cove. About how things inevitably changed, no matter how much you wanted them to stay the same.

"That does it," Vanessa finally said. "I'm game."

Christian raised a flirtatious eyebrow, and she laughed.

"To help you guys fix up the boat, perv," she said. "Vanessa James, at your service."

Christian laughed. "Considering you hate cleaning, you've never touched a power tool, and you don't know jack about sailing, what exactly *are* your services?"

Something burned inside me, a flash and a spark, and then it was gone. Vanessa shooed him from across the table, then turned to Kirby.

"You're in, right?" Vanessa asked her. "I mean, with four of us? We got this."

"Five," Sebastian said. "I'm a good helper."

"Thank you, sugar bean," Vanessa said. "Five."

"Four." Kirby's eyes darted from Noah at the grill to Vanessa, back to Noah, back to Vanessa, and finally settled on Christian's fries. "Sorry. I . . . there's a lot going on at the library, and I just . . . I can't."

"It's because she wants to marry Noah," Sebastian said, and everyone roared.

But not Kirby, who was trying to shrink herself to fit inside her coffee mug.

And not me, whose roar died months ago.

"That's not it," Kirby whispered. Even her hair looked embarrassed. "I'm just too busy. The inventory, and . . . and with Elyse working on the boat, I'll have to pick up the slack at Mom's store. And helping out with the art stuff. You know?" She looked up at me, eyes brightening. "But Elyse is definitely perfect for the job and I know she can do it and you won't regret it because she's amazing, and you'd better look out for her and not do anything stupid or I might have to kill you in your sleep."

Kirby grabbed my root beer float, sucked down the rest through the straw.

"Damn." Vanessa laughed. "So much for sisters before misters, Kirbs."

"Christian's a mister," she said.

"Hardly," Vanessa said.

"It's cool." Christian nodded toward Kirby. "Sleeping with the

Enemy here can side with Noah all she wants. Me and Stowaway?
We've got it covered. Right?"

I felt his eyes on me, but didn't look up.

"Hey. We good?" Christian asked.

They were all watching me, even the creepy doll head.

So I closed my eyes and said what I said best.

Nothing.

Chapter 9

No good would ever come from a sticky note in the shape of a crab.

Elyse,

Good morning, beautiful! No worries about treasure hunting or the shop. Kirby & I have it covered. Left coffee on for you—one of my magic brews, perfect for a day of new experiences. Mixed up some new lotion, too—it'll put some pep in your step! Have fun on the boat & be safe!

Blessed Be,
Lemon

As soon as the storm broke last night, Christian had shown up with my boxes, slightly damp but no worse for it. Between that and Kirby's not-so-subtle comments on the matter, I'd had no choice but to tell Lemon about our regatta plans.

I hadn't meant that I'd abandon everything else in my now-quiet life, but Lemon seemed to think that was the best approach. She'd left me high and dry this morning, long gone on her sea glass hunt before I'd even finished my shower.

My own sea glass jar, relocated to the windowsill in my bedroom, was about to be seriously neglected.

It was only my second day as first mate, and already I ached for the quiet beach walks I'd be missing, the meditative steps along the shoreline as Lemon shuffled ahead of me, lost in her own silent reverie. As I drank the last of the "magic" brew and turned off the coffeepot, I realized I'd even miss my shifts at Mermaid Tears.

Not my idea of heaven, maybe, but a new routine I'd begun. A new life.

Now it was changing again.

For the second time in as many months, it felt like my future was about to walk the plank, all of yesterday's bravery a show whose curtain was thin and tattered.

I shook off the feeling as I made my way to the docks. I'd made a promise that I'd do whatever I could to help save the house, and I meant it. The regatta was still almost six weeks away—long before I'd have to face the open water.

Christian was on the boat when I arrived, crouched down with a box of tools and oily rags. A pair of college-aged girls chatted him up from the dock. They looked as if they'd just breezed in from Aruba or Maui or some equally sunny place where the summers were warmer, the beaches less rocky.

Monday after Solstice. Let the official summer season at the Cove begin.

"Are you planning on sailing this thing?" one of them asked. Shimmery black hair cascaded down her back, curled but not frizzed, and her shorts would better serve as a swimsuit. Her legs were covered in goose bumps.

I was cold just watching her, but Christian had no trouble basking in her warmth.

"Rebuilding her first," he said, his voice slightly huskier than usual. "Pirate Regatta this August."

"Seriously?" Short-Shorts said. "Sounds dangerous."

Christian shrugged. "They don't call it the Pirate Regatta for nothing."

Her friend, a cute redhead in ripped jeans and a thin NYU hoodie, also trying not to shiver, rolled her eyes. "I told you about the regatta, Gracie. They do it every year."

"Maybe I can help." Short-Shorts casually tossed out the offer, as if she interrupted her summer vacation all the time to help wayward sailors, but I saw the smolder in her eyes. The way she held her shoulders taught, exposed her collarbone, and arched her back.

"Smooth, Gracie. God." NYU laughed playfully at her friend.

"Shut up, Brenda." Shorts flipped her luscious locks and looked back to Christian. "I've been on a boat before. Lots of times."

"That so?" Christian rose to his full height, a wrench gripped in his hand. It was like the opening of a really bad movie. Not a family-friendly one.

He saw me then, standing at the end of the dock. His smile changed as I approached, flirt to friend in five seconds flat.

"Oh, hey," NYU said, elbowing her friend when she noticed me. I nodded a hello at both of them, though Short-Shorts—Gracie—wasn't particularly welcoming.

"Do you need help or what?" Gracie asked Christian.

With his eyes on me, he shook his head. "Thanks for the offer, ladies. But we're all set."

Their sigh was weighty and collective.

Then Brenda narrowed her eyes at me, scrutinizing. "Wait. You're Kirby Langelinie's cousin, right? From Trinidad?"

I nodded. *Tobago, actually. Twin islands.* I'd tried to mouth the words clearly, but both girls stilled.

"Lose your voice or something?" Gracie said, and Brenda elbowed her again, the gesture an obvious reminder that *I* was the girl they'd talked about. Not *to*, but about. "I mean—oh, right. I'm—sorry? Sorry." Gracie lowered her eyes, nudging Brenda as if they'd both made this huge blunder, calling attention to my inability to speak. Her once pink cheeks were red, and Brenda clearly didn't know what to say either.

So often it fell to me to smooth things over, to make people comfortable even when I was anything but.

I shook my head like it was no big deal, forced a smile that I wanted so badly to be real.

But it wasn't.

The girls looked relieved anyway.

"Elyse is my first mate," Christian said, and Brenda and Gracie brightened, though I couldn't tell if it was because they were impressed with me then, or just grateful for the subject change.

"Oh, cool," Brenda said. "We'll be rooting for you guys."

With her eyes and smile aimed at Christian, Gracie said, "Do you want to maybe hang out for lunch or something?"

Christian shook his head. "We've got a lot of work to do. But," he said, and Gracie's renewed hope was enough to float all the boats in the docks. "I'll probably be at Shipwreck later. Stop by if you're around. It's reggae night."

"I remember," Brenda said.

"See you there, sailor," Gracie said, and Christian winked.

Back home, in the vacation bungalows that bordered the resort property, we had our legendary boys too. Three, most infamously. The Maharaj brothers. My sister Juliette lost her virginity to Deo, which just about crushed Martine, who claims to this day that she kissed him first. Over the years those boys drifted like flotsam and jetsam between the d'Abreau sisters and the tourists that flocked to the island each year.

Every coastal destination had its legends, all the drama that

comes from the seasonal clash of locals and tourists, romantic sunsets over the sea, sizzling nights, the hormonal forces at work. I
hadn't expected anything less at the Cove, especially after hearing
Kirby's warnings.

But this boy was ridiculous.

"No need for the green-eyed monster," he said. The girls had finally
said their good-byes, and Christian held out a hand for the bucket of
cleaning supplies I'd brought—Lemon's organic, nontoxic stuff, just to
be sure we didn't damage any of the *Queen's* old rubber seals. "I'm
spending almost every waking moment with you, after all."

I gave him the evil eye, but the truth was, I wasn't jealous—not of
Christian's momentary attention to Brenda and Gracie. It was something I could never explain to him.

I saw myself in those girls, the way Natalie and I used to wait for
Julien and the boys at the steel-drum competitions, twist and wine
against them during Carnival like it was all this party game, this tease
that drove the boys wild and never meant anything more than that.

Until now.

Until I couldn't have it back.

I wasn't jealous. I just missed it, our carefree fun. The music and
the laughter. Julien. Natalie.

Christian watched me, waiting for a smile. When I didn't offer it,
he said, "Sit tight. I know what you need."

He ducked through the companionway, returned with a cardboard holder of to-go cups and pastry bags from the Black Pearl.

"I lost you for a minute there." He let out an awkward laugh. "Let's go. You're freezing."

When I didn't move, he squeezed my shoulder, gave me a gentle nudge. "Here, walk on the inside."

I followed him, letting him take seaside as we made slow and careful steps up to Starfish Point.

"Want to talk about it?" he asked.

I saw his eyes on my scar, knew what he was asking.

He was the first.

It was nothing like I'd imagined, that question. And now that it was there, an opportunity to tell my story, I couldn't find the words. Just like I couldn't find the words to explain why, even from safe distances, the ocean could still sneak up on me, bring my darkest nightmares to life.

Christian didn't force it. "The first time I was on a boat," he said, "I was five or six. Dad chartered a sailboat, nothing fancy, but he wanted to take me and Mom out on the water. Mom made us all wear life jackets, even though he'd insisted there was nothing to worry about, since we weren't going out far. But Mom didn't back down."

Smart thinking, I mouthed. The ocean was unpredictable. Our resort guests were required to wear life jackets at all times, even when we were just parked at the dock.

"Hour into the trip," he said, "the sky turned black, black, black. Storm rolled in faster than anything I'd ever seen—we're talking minutes. Waves hit us from all sides. Raining so hard we couldn't tell whether the water was coming from above or below."

I shivered just imagining it. It sounded a lot like the night I was born. The kind of stormy sea that had taken my mother.

"I remember thinking I was going to drown," he said. "Like, I *knew* it. But I didn't scream. I just held on to the rails until my hands turned white, puked all over my life jacket. I couldn't move."

Another wave crept up, tickled our feet. Christian guided us closer to the dunes, still walking seaside.

"Gotta hand it to the old man," he said. "Mom was freaking out, but from what I remember, Dad kept it together. Got the sails under control, navigated us back to the marina. Your aunt was there at the docks—said she was about one minute away from calling the coast guard. We all went to the Black Pearl for hot soup. Mom was still crying. I didn't talk for three days."

I smiled up at him. *You? Silent?*

He nudged me with his elbow. "Yeah. The only time in recorded history." He took a deep breath of salty air, looked out again at the restless ocean. "It was almost three years before I got in another boat. I couldn't explain it then, but when I think about it now, it's like . . . like I'd gotten away with something that day. Escaped death, or whatever." He laughed nervously again, ran a hand through his hair as though he was embarrassed. As though I'd think it was silly.

But I shocked him instead, stopped in the sand and pulled him into a hug. It was quick, but tight, real. It seemed like we both needed it.

We climbed the dune stairs that led to the houses, and just before

I turned for Lemon's place, he tugged on my hand. "Feel like meeting up at Shipwreck later? Reggae night, like I was saying. Pretty decent music. Dancing, if you're into it."

Still warm from the hug, I flashed him a smile. *A date?*

He smirked. "What if it is?"

Despite the flutter in my chest, I folded my arms and gave him a look that I hoped conveyed an approximation of . . . *hell no.*

"Why not?" he said, laughing.

I reached for the notebook in my pocket, but I'd left it at home this morning. I came up with a Sharpie, no paper.

Christian held out his palm. "Go ahead. Tell me."

I yanked the cap off the Sharpie, grabbed his hand and held it flat. It was warm, steady as I wrote.

Gracie, Brenda, Calla? Hands full.

Just before he pulled away, I added another word along the edge of his palm.

LoverBoy.

"You don't hold back, do you?" he said.

I matched his teasing smile, but inside, my heart dropped.

Words were one thing, letters on the page. On the walls. On the skin.

But he was so, so wrong. Without a pen, without a surface on which to let the letters run, I held back everything.

"I've known Brenda forever," he said. "Her parents have a cottage down shore. She's always bringing friends to the beach. Last summer, she brought her two cousins, and . . ." Christian smiled, lost in a memory, then shook his head. "Anyway, a bunch of us go—Cove summer tradition. Noah and Vanessa. Sometimes Kirby, especially if she knows Noah will be there. I won't say it's awesome, but it doesn't suck."

Whatever his motives, Christian's invitation was sincere.

Just as Kirby's had been when she'd mentioned it last night.

But after all the excitement these last two days, I needed to be alone. Me and my words and all the things trapped in my heart.

Held back.

Sorry, I mouthed. *I don't dance.*

Chapter 10

March.

Our first day together on the boat, Christian asked how long it'd been since I'd been sailing, and that was it. My last time on the open sea. But it was also the last time I'd let the music infiltrate my limbs, the last I'd felt my dance steps sync with the soulful, upbeat rhythms of Bella Garcia. She'd always been our favorite, mine and Natalie's. That last time, that last dance, my twin and I had stood side by side on one of the resort boats, singing and laughing, timing our moves with the currents of the Caribbean Sea. The stars glittered overhead, as if they'd shown up and turned on their eternal spotlights just for a better glimpse of the soon-to-be-famous d'Abreau sisters.

The day before, after accepting her Queen of the Bands crown, Bella had introduced us to her manager exactly that way: *These are the soon-to-be-famous d'Abreau sisters.*

Now, standing alone on the cold shores of the Pacific, I was in the dark; no stars shone through the Oregon haze. Lemon was deep in creative thought in her studio. Kirby, Christian, Vanessa, and Noah were at the club with all the other kids summering at the Cove. I'd no one to coordinate with but the waves, no audience but the last gull of the night, bobbing on the surface.

I looked for Atargatis but saw no one. Heard nothing but the sea.

I slipped the earbuds in—both of them this time—and sucked in the salty air.

One song. Only one.

I'd erased all the others long ago, but this one I couldn't bring myself to forget. I'd hidden it, voted it down to the bottom so it would never turn up in a shuffle. But I couldn't delete it. It was like my own personal lighthouse; just knowing it was there was enough to give me a tiny sliver of light.

Dancing, if you're into it . . .

Like the gull diving beneath the waves, I waded through Lemon's new-age playlists, all the wood flutes and whale calls and songs about fairies, and finally found it.

"Work Ya Way Back" by Bella Garcia. Just seeing her name on my iPod again was almost enough to fillet my heart. But it felt good, too, that old pull. Although I was tired from cleaning the boat, my legs tingled with anticipation, muscles warming like they'd been waiting for this night all along.

Like all our favorite soca stuff, "Work Ya Way Back" never failed to lift us from a foul mood, never failed to inspire a head swerve or a good old wine—a twist-and-roll from the waist, the hips, the very soul. The song was about the obvious—shaking your boomsie, working the crowd—but it had another meaning too. It was about dancing through the darkest and most lonely nights we faced. It was about getting up again, fighting your way back from even the scariest, lowest places the human soul could go.

In all my years of listening to this song, it had never once failed to lift my spirits, to chase away the darkness.

I'd been afraid to listen to it for so long. Afraid it wouldn't work.

Now, with my thumb hovering over the screen, I hoped it would still have the same effect on me.

Flame. Ashes. Phoenix. Flame.

I tapped play, cranked the volume.

Closed my eyes.

Dug my bare toes into the cold, damp sand.

And finally I let the familiar beat seep through my ears, calling to a deep place inside.

A smile twitched at the corners of my mouth. My hips swayed. The music took hold. And for the first time in too many months, I danced.

You can't have me, Atargatis.

Chapter 11

"How much is this?" A woman in a giant straw hat picked up one of Lemon's best-selling sun catchers, a delicate wire-wrought snowflake tipped with pieces of blue and white sea glass.

Nine, I mouthed. My brain automatically converted it to Trinidadian dollars. Fifty-four. I shook my head to stop the endless calculating, smiled again at the customer.

Kirby was cutting back on her library hours to fill in at Mermaid Tears, but this morning she'd been called back to the stacks over a Harry Potter emergency, by which I assume she meant there was dark magic at work, and Lemon was on a rare-book hunt in Florence, Oregon, a mission also dark and magical.

So I found myself on newly familiar ground, miming my way through customer interactions at the shop, wishing someone would bring me a scone and a latte from the Black Pearl.

"Nineteen dollars?" The woman held the ornament to the light. "Is this even *real* sea glass?"

Yes, I mouthed. I'd harvested it myself. *And it's fifty-four. Sorry. Nine.*

The tide was rolling in outside, waves shifting from a distant *hiss* to a closer *hush*. The air felt heavy, damper than it had last night. Storm warning. The woman seemed immobilized with indecision.

"Sorry." She squinted at my lips. "I can't seem to . . . What?"

I grabbed my Sharpie and the crab sticky-note pad.

$9 or IX or NINE. + tax.

She probably thought I was crazy. I dropped the Sharpie, reapplied my neutral, nonthreatening smile.

"Okay. I'll take it," the woman said.

I wrapped it in tissue, bagged it. She set an American twenty on the counter and took off without collecting her change. I stuffed it into the jar I'd started on my first day behind the counter, when I realized just how many people would rather leave without their due than try to make conversation with a mute.

That's sixty dollars back home, my brain rattled off.

I slipped out from behind the register to straighten the shelves. I'd just finished rearranging everything the woman had unsettled when the bells over the door chimed, followed by a cold blast.

Mayor Katzenberg took up all the space in the doorway. "Waves are really whipping up out there."

I was pretty certain he wasn't here for the sun catchers. I ducked behind the counter, hoping he'd state his business quickly and be gone.

His presence put me on edge.

"Good afternoon, Miss d'Abreau," he said, finally acknowledging my name. A step up from the Solstice-party caterer, at least. "Don't suppose your aunt is around?"

When I shook my head, he approached the counter, leaned in close. I could smell the cheap gel in his slicked-back hair, like Windex and rubbing alcohol.

"That's all right," he said. "This concerns you, actually. Got a minute?"

I looked around. There were no other customers on the premises. No one watching but the mermaid dash ornaments, a shelf of fish-tailed girls in seashell-and-coconut bras who tittered with every footstep.

Minutes, unfortunately, I had.

"Noah tells me you've volunteered as first mate in the regatta with Chris," he said.

Christian, I mouthed.

"Sorry, didn't catch that." He lowered his eyes to my lips.

I waved him off. He wouldn't listen, anyway.

"Miss d'Abreau—Elyse—I'm not sure how they do things down under, or . . . Africa? You know, I don't think I've ever really thought about Trinidad and Tobago." He laughed as if it was funny, this knowledge gap. "Where exactly are you on the map?"

I grabbed the Sharpie.

West Indies.

I started to write about our proximity to Venezuela, since that narrowed it down for people unfamiliar with the islands, but he was already moving on.

"India, right. Like I said, I'm not sure how things go on over there, but here at the Cove? We've never had a . . . a girl . . . woman . . ." He assessed me, searching for the right word. "We've never had a female in the race before. It's unprecedented."

I waited, not sure what I was supposed to say.

"I'm not trying to be discouraging," he said. "I just think you might be more suited for—rather, more comfortable—with something like the mermaid parade. Or you could help your aunt sell her arts and crafts at the street festival." He looked around the shop, came back to me with a condescending frown that matched his tone. "Leave this regatta business to the boys."

Va-john-*a thing*, I thought. I suddenly wished for Vanessa, that she'd roll in with her "feminist killjoy" T-shirts and a bullhorn and say all the things I couldn't. When the chimes on the door announced a new customer, I thought maybe I'd conjured her, that she'd somehow heard my plea.

But it was Christian.

"Well, if it isn't the king of the Cove," Christian said. "Slow day at the office, Mayor?"

The man laughed. "Plenty enough to keep me busy these days. You'd be surprised how much paperwork rezoning entails."

Christian cocked his head, narrowed his eyes. It was unnerving, the kind of look that could make criminals confess to crimes they'd only *thought* about committing. "Is that why you're down at Mermaid Tears, harassing my first mate?"

The mayor's smile slipped. "You know, Chris—"

"Christian."

"Yes. I was just telling Elyse here . . . frankly, kids, I'm not sure it's even legal to have a female first mate. We'd have to consult the rule book, but as far as I know, regatta's a man's race."

Christian's jaw ticked, just like it had with his father the night of the party. "Damn. Must've hit my head on the way out of that time machine. 1850, are we? I might need some new clothes. Elyse, you sew, right? Don't all girls sew?"

"Very funny, son." The mayor's laugh was choppy, a machine gun in the glass store. I felt useless in its path. "I think we both know I'm the most progressive mayor this town has ever had." Mayor Katzenberg gave me a once-over as he cleared his throat. "But the regatta is a physically demanding event, requiring hours of hard labor, strategic thinking, and a strong stomach. You know that, Chris. Christian."

"You think my first mate can't handle herself out there?" Christian said. The mayor didn't respond.

"You're underestimating her," Christian said.

"Be that as it may, the Pirate Regatta is a long-held tradition at the Cove. I don't think its advisable to, ah, rock the boat. Forgive the pun." *Rat-a-tat-tat,* went his laugh. I wrapped my arms around my chest to keep from jumping out of my skin. Lemon had said Wes Katzenberg would save a baby from a burning building, but as I watched him now, the way he looked at me and Christian with smarmy contempt, I figured he probably *ate* babies.

"Careful, Mayor," Christian said. "One might think you're trying to enforce sexist policies. For a man in public office . . . well there's something that could get into ugly legal territory."

"Trust me, I'm all for equal rights." The mayor winked at me like we were in on some secret. "Just trying to spare you some grief."

Christian waited, giving me a chance to respond. To defend myself. To put this man in his place. The words hovered on my tongue. I wanted to send the mayor away. To tell him that people who found it necessary to say things like "trust me, I'm all for equal rights" generally weren't.

But of course I couldn't. Wouldn't. I hated myself in that moment, hated how I'd let myself shrink before this man, the bloated self-proclaimed king whose presence made my skin crawl.

My sisters would be ashamed. None of them would ever let someone treat them like they were less than. Like they didn't matter, didn't belong, didn't have or deserve a voice. Granna and Dad instilled that lesson from a young age, reinforcing it often.

Everything was different for me now, and I wondered again if this would be my life, me letting everyone else talk for me, talk over me, talk around me.

Not so long ago I'd been convinced that losing my voice was the worst thing that could ever happen to me, the worst tragedy. But since then I'd been losing my whole self, everything I stood for, believed in, felt. Everything I ever wanted to be. Everything I ever was.

"I'm not sure the people will accept a woman sailor," the mayor said. Christian didn't wait another beat.

Inside, I shriveled and burned.

"Eh, you're probably right." Christian slapped a hand on the mayor's back, hard. "Guess it's a good thing the people aren't sailing in my boat. Hey, I think Noah's looking for you."

The mayor narrowed his eyes.

"Try the docks," Christian said. "*Never Flounder* was giving him trouble, and his first mate was MIA."

"First mate?" The mayor's brow furrowed, his over-gelled hair firmly in place above it. "I wasn't aware he'd found someone."

Christian smiled, devilish. "That would explain the whole MIA thing."

Like the blustery wind he blew in on, the mayor disappeared in a huff. The temperature inside Mermaid Tears rose a few degrees in his absence, and I let out a frustrated breath.

Crumbling under the mayor's chest-beating was one thing. The fact that Christian was star witness made it utterly mortifying, especially after he'd stood up for me.

"He's gonna be a pain in our ass from now until race day," Christian said, pointing at the space the mayor had formerly occupied. "Now that he knows we're partners, he's got you in his sights." He scrubbed a hand over his mouth, shaking his head. "It's only gonna get worse, Elyse. He wants my parents to sell the houses more than anything."

I nodded.

"You hear what I'm saying?"

I raised an eyebrow.

"My own father can't even say no to this guy, and look where that got us," Christian said. When he looked at me again, his eyes were fiery, intense.

I grabbed my sticky notes, scratched out my response. Ink and paper were the only place where my voice didn't falter, didn't betray the real me.

Stop trying to get rid of me, Kane. I said I'm in, I'm in.

I handed over the note, watched the tension in his jaw loosen as he read it.

He was relieved.

I was buoyed.

His eyes met mine again. "Do you think we could—"

"I'm back, I'm back!" Lemon crashed through the doorway with an armload of books, all of them wrapped in her rainbow-colored shawl.

Christian rushed to the door, scooped the heavy tomes from her arms.

He set them on the counter, and Lemon spread them out to dry. They looked old, yellowed, and musty.

"Herbology," she said, tapping the first, a cracked black-leather volume etched with a silver tree. "The others are mostly folklore, but still instructional. Took months for the bookstore to track them down, but boy, was it worth it. This one," she said, pointing at a book with a golden fish on the cover, "contains some of the world's oldest poetry and symbolism about the sea."

Lemon could hardly contain her excitement as she told us about the poems she'd already looked at, how she was newly inspired for her next sculpture series and needed only to find more sea glass.

I gave her a wary smile, my insides tightening again when I thought about how much the Cove meant to her, how hard it would be for her to make a life somewhere else.

"Thanks again for filling in today, hon." Lemon winked at me and turned to Christian. "And thank *you* for lending me your first mate. She's all yours."

Christian only smiled, his eyes lingering on me a moment before shifting back to Lemon. "I'm actually here on an important mission. Mermaid stamps? Sebastian said you'd know what that meant."

"Oh, of course!" Lemon scooted around the counter, pulled out a small paper bag from a shelf beneath the register. "I threw in an extra glitter-ink pad for him too. I know how he loves glitter."

"Who doesn't?" Christian said.

Lemon rang him up, dropped a few pieces of candy from her pocket into the bag. When Christian reached across the counter to take it, their eyes locked. Something passed between them.

Christian sighed as he tucked Sebastian's bag into his sweatshirt pocket. "I don't want Dad to sell, either, Ursula."

It was soft and sad, the way his brow curved over his left eye, and I imagined running my thumb over it. It straightened when his eyes met mine again. "I'll do my best."

I wrote on my palm, held it up so they could read it.

We'll do OUR best.

And there it was, so fleeting I almost missed it.

Christian Kane's real, unguarded smile.

Chapter 12

"Normally when I see a woman on all fours, I don't interrupt." Christian tossed his keys in the air, caught them right as I looked up from my crawl across the *Queen's* aqua-blue deck. I fixed him with a mean glare. "But, summer of firsts," he said. "Up for a hardware store run? Maybe get lunch from someplace other than Vanessa's picnic basket? That's not a euphemism. Seriously. There's only so much flavored water and finger sandwiches a guy can take."

I stripped off my yellow gloves and protective mask, offering a relieved smile. We'd been scrubbing grime and barnacles for a week straight; close quarters with Christian on this dirty little vessel had given new meaning to the phrase "cabin fever."

There was a decent hardware store on Main Street, but Christian said that the owner of Nutz-n-Boltz, a small shop tucked among the pines in the northeast part of town, was an old friend.

Right. Jessica Boltz was older than Christian by a decade, but that didn't stop her from eyeing him with the same look I'd seen on the younger tourists at the Cove—battle weary, but always up for another fight.

"Captain Kane." She didn't set down her magazine as we approached the counter, but the glint in her eyes told me she was watching our every move. "Been a while, sailor."

"Miss me, Jess?" Christian winked at her.

"Eh," she said with a shrug. "I could take you or leave you." She finally dropped the magazine, and her grin widened. "Enough with the mushy reunion, Kane. What can I do you for?"

Christian opened his mouth to say something crass, but Jess cut him off.

"No, that wasn't an offer." Her words were for him, but her eyes were on me, assessing. "Hear you two are the team to beat this summer."

"Heard right. This is Elyse, first mate."

"Did you say first date?" she teased. "Because I'm pretty sure the Cove's never seen a lady pirate at the helm."

"Don't start, Jess," Christian said. "We're taking enough shit from Katzenberg."

"Lighten up, sailor." She gave me a polite smile, her eyes flicking briefly over the scar behind my seashell necklace before turning back to Christian. "You're not actually putting the Vega in the water this year?"

Christian nodded.

"Don't get me wrong, Kane. You know that ol' girl holds a special place in my heart." She waited a beat too long before continuing. "But maybe you should put her out of her misery. Let Noah do his thing."

Christian leaned across the counter, tapped it twice. "If I let Noah do his thing, you may as well put up the For Sale sign here. Katzenberg has his way, you won't even recognize the Cove next summer."

"You're right," she said. "I might actually get more than two customers a week. Imagine?"

Christian's jaw ticked again, but whatever was bothering him, he stowed it. It wasn't the first time we'd encountered a proponent of the mayor's initiative. Whether it was snippets of conversation drifting from the other boats at the marina or full-blown arguments at the Black Pearl, we'd heard it all. Yea or nay, no one was on the fence. The town really was, as Kirby and Lemon had told me, divided. It seemed Jessica thought the changes—however they'd resurface the face of the Cove—would be good for business.

"Anyway." Christian reached into his back pocket and pulled out a list, slid it across the counter. "Here's what you can do me for."

She scanned the list, brow furrowing. "Afraid I'm out."

"You're kidding," Christian said. "Everything?"

For the first time since we walked in, Jessica's gaze dropped to the counter and stayed there. Absently she flipped a page in the magazine. "Had a run on sealants and gel coat last week. Lots of people patching up boats for the summer, I guess."

Christian turned to check out the shelves for himself.

"Save yourself the trouble," she said. "I know we're out."

"How about I just take a peek?"

"No!" she said, her confidence gone. "I mean . . . I've got it all on order. Might take a while, though."

Christian tugged the wallet from his back pocket, pulled out a shiny gold credit card and dropped it on the counter. "How long?"

Jessica hesitated, which is what Christian wanted, but the trick didn't work. "Three weeks, maybe?" she said. "A month? Try me again in August."

Christian grabbed the card and his list from the counter, stuffed them both into his wallet.

When Jessica finally met his eyes again, her mouth was turned down, shoulders drooping. It was a slight change, but like the look that passed between them on arrival, it told me everything.

She felt bad about something. And not just because she'd supposedly run out of sealant.

In an apologetic tone she said, "Christian, I'm just . . . Did you try Big Mike's?"

"Should we?" he asked. "Or will Mike be out of everything I need too? Mind giving him a call and asking? You guys do stuff like that, right? Look out for all the good people of the Cove?"

Jessica's freckles paled behind the rosy heat rising in her cheeks.

Christian smacked the counter with his palm and flashed a corporate kind of smile that would make his father proud. "Good seeing you again, Jess. Give the mayor my regards."

I didn't hear whatever apologies she fumbled next. With his hand on my lower back, Christian ushered me out the door.

At the far end of the parking lot two men were setting up surveying equipment. One of them adjusted a tripod while the other scanned the area, making notes on a clipboard.

Christian leaned back against his pickup, arms crossed as he blew out an angry breath. "Katzenberg already got to her. Guess I should've seen it coming."

Why?

"It's in the rules," Christian said. "The Pirate Regatta means legit pirate games. Cheating is encouraged, as long as it doesn't cause a safety issue or do any permanent damage to the boats. No one ever screwed with me and Noah, but now that I'm on the wrong side of Team Katz, it's a whole different shit storm. The mayor wants his kid to win, so he'll bribe people like Jess and Big Mike to dock-block us—refuse to sell to us."

I looked again at the surveyors across the lot. The clipboard guy was pointing at something in the distance, the other one smiling and nodding.

Kirby had said that Christian and Noah always won, but now they were competing against each other. The mayor was bribing local shops to fight us. P&D men were scurrying across the entire town like sand crabs. What chance did we have to win? To save the houses?

Christian must've sensed my fear, my disappointment. He grabbed my shoulders, looked into my eyes without flinching. "Elyse, I promise you we'll beat Noah. This is just a snag. Do you believe me?"

When I didn't respond, he ran his hands down my arms, grabbed my hands. "I need you to believe me," he whispered. "We're not going to lose."

He wouldn't look away.

Finally, I nodded.

When he released my hands, I pulled out my notebook and scratched out a message.

Jessica was lying when she said she didn't have our stuff.

"Bingo," he said.

I wrote again:

So why didn't we just buy it anyway? Could she refuse to sell? Is that legal?

"We could've done that," Christian explained. "But games like this are just understood. It's pirate season, and Jess made it clear that she's taken sides—Noah's. I have to accept it, otherwise I'm the dick. A bad loser, you know?"

But aren't you & Jess friends? I mouthed.

He smirked.

I wrote another note, delivered it with a smirk of my own.

You gave her the "grand tour" on the
Vega, then you didn't call again. Right?

Christian's eyebrows rose, playfulness returning to his smile. He
reached out and closed the notebook in my hands. "Enough questions,
Stowaway. Coos Bay should have what we need. Plus, there's this place
I want to show you." With no further clues but a mischievous glint in
his eyes, Christian thumped the roof of the truck. "Hop in."

Chapter 13

"He took you for Indian food? Did he pay?" Kirby leaned against my bedroom doorframe later that night, hyped up after finding my lunch leftovers in the fridge. Spazzy as she was, her eyes were at half-mast, and her auburn locks were rimmed with frizz. She'd been pulling double duty ever since I signed on to the regatta, keeping up with emergencies at the library and at Mermaid Tears.

I nodded from my computer desk, waved her in.

"Seriously, what are you doing?" She kicked off her shoes and flopped onto the end of my bed. "A lunch date? With Christian?"

Not a date.

"Maybe not for you. But Elyse, Christian never pays. It's his policy or whatever so he doesn't set up any expectations." Kirby barely took a breath. "So if he paid, that's a really big deal. What do you think it means? Are you guys, like, hooking up?"

She'd made air quotes around "hooking up," whispering the words as though they were foul.

I couldn't hold back my smile. Kirby was so worried, it was bordering on ridiculous. She reminded me of my sister Hazel, who was only a year older than Natalie and me and took her responsibility as our elder very seriously.

You're so macocious, I mouthed, but Kirby wasn't familiar with the word. *A busybody*, I tried again.

"How do you say 'concerned friend' in Trini? Because that's what I am. Vanessa got me worried," she explained. "She said you guys weren't at the boat when she went over there with the picnic basket, and you weren't answering my texts. Which reminds me . . ." Kirby grabbed the cell from my desk. "I'm putting Vanessa's number in here for you. Hey, this isn't even turned on!" She shook her head, waited for the phone to blink to life. "Honestly, Elyse."

I'd been on the laptop when Kirby found me, so I pulled up the notepad app and typed out a quick summary of our day.

The Coos Bay hardware store had what we needed, and after that, Christian had taken me to India's Palace for lunch.

"It's not strictly Trinbagonian," he'd said, "but I think you'll like this place."

He was right on both counts—I *did* like it. And it *wasn't* Trinbagonian. Not even close to the roti shops back home, to the fragrant feasts my friends' parents had cooked. But he'd been so excited to take me there; he'd done research online, read about the Indian influence on our food back home. He'd hoped India's Palace would bring me back to some of the best parts of the islands.

He was so sweet, almost shy about it. I didn't have the heart to tell him how different it was.

Christian had insisted I order, thinking I had this insider's knowledge. I was so touched by the gesture that I let him believe it, pointing out dishes on the menu like I knew what I was doing. I ordered enough food for a week—hence the leftovers in Lemon's fridge.

We had an amazing day.

But the best part wasn't the food, the spiciness, the cool mango lassi to wash it all down. It was the fact that Christian had been researching stuff about T&T, thinking of my home. The fact that he'd done something special, just for me.

"But what did you guys *talk* about?" Kirby wanted to know. "I mean, you were gone a long time." She tucked her legs up underneath her body, settling in for the gossip. For a minute it seemed like she'd forgotten her campaign against Christian—like he was just a regular cute boy, like she and I were just another pair of girlfriends talking about our crushes.

It was . . . nice.

Still typing, I told her a little bit about our conversation—how Christian had wanted to know all about the country, the history, what the food was like, how so many different kinds of people could come together on twin islands. I'd tried to keep up, responding in my notebook as quickly as I could, but each answer brought more questions.

It was as if the cleaning masks we'd been wearing on the boat had stifled all the words, and once we'd gone out without them, the torrent unleashed.

He was on his second helping of chicken vindaloo, still asking questions, before I'd even finished my samosa. When I jokingly pointed out the unfair advantage, he reached across the table, fingers brushing mine as he slid the Sharpie and notebook out of my grasp. He turned to a fresh page and scratched out a note, then passed it back silently.

We'd gone on like that for another hour, asking questions and talking through written words alone. By the time our waiter had asked us to wrap it up, my stomach, my notebook, and the restaurant were near capacity. Hours had passed. Neither of us had realized how long we'd been sitting, talking, writing. We'd been lost in our own world, lost in hundreds of words. Both of our writing hands were inked and smudged, evidence of our questions and answers—his about Trinidad and Tobago. Mine about California and Oregon. Favorite foods. Movies. Funny stories from school.

But none too deep about our families, about the scars they'd left.

It was like we'd both sensed it, the boundaries of conversation. The too-real words that would pierce our hearts, pop this fragile bubble of new friendship with shards from the past that neither of us was ready to face.

We'd gathered up our leftovers and driven back to the Cove in silence, as if neither of us wanted to break the spell we'd weaved on our long lunch break. Even after we'd parked the truck in the Kanes' garage and walked back to Lemon's house together, we'd exchanged only glances, shared only smiles.

Outside the gift shop door downstairs, Christian had grabbed my free hand, turned it over.

His skin was warm, rough from all the work we'd been doing on the Vega.

With his teeth he'd uncapped the Sharpie I hadn't seen him take from my pocket, and he wrote a final message on my palm.

Sweet dreams.

I peeked at it now, careful to keep it hidden from Kirby.

That part of the story was all mine.

"Sounds like you had a great day," Kirby said, her smile warm and genuine. "I'm glad, Elyse. It shows. You look . . . I don't know. Less depressed? Is that wrong to say?"

I barked out a breathy laugh. She was right. Today had felt more like a vacation than any of my days in Oregon. I could still taste the tangy mango lassi, and my stomach was more than excited for a midnight raid on the fridge later—a thought which only reminded me of Christian, his surprising attentiveness today. I wasn't ready to admit this to Kirby, but thinking of him fanned the spark inside me into an ember, red and glowing.

Still . . . with the house on the line I couldn't get sidetracked by fantasies about a boy whose main mission in life was making girls swoon. Kirby didn't know Christian fully, and maybe she was unfair in her harsh judgments. But that didn't mean she was *entirely* wrong. I'd seen the way girls looked at him, how he flirted. How it was obvious that some of them had gotten entangled with him in summers past. I had no interest in being one of those girls this time next summer, watching with envy whenever he brought someone home for the "grand tour."

I had to focus on the *Queen*, not her captain. That's what I'd been doing on the computer when Kirby had started her playful interrogation.

I updated her on the dock-block situation. After Christian dropped me off tonight, I'd spent the last two hours online, scouting out hardware and boating stores within a half-hour drive. Things worked out today, but the Vega would need a lot more work before she was seaworthy, and Coos Bay was too far to drive every time we needed a handful of bolts.

We need a closer hardware store, I typed for Kirby. *Not in the Cove, but not as far as CB. Any ideas?*

"You *do* realize the coast has about five billion state parks and campgrounds, and that most of them have their own marinas, right?" Kirby looked at me like it was the most obvious thing in the world. When I didn't make the connection, she said, "The bigger marinas have their own supply stores with camping and sailing gear. Some of them even sell boats and parts on-site."

She nudged me over, smooshing onto the chair next to me. Her

fingers flew over the keyboard, pulling up a map with all the parks and marinas in the area. From there we found the ones with supply stores or boat sale operations.

In a rare moment of unrestrained joy, I flung my arms around her.

"Wow," she said. "If I'd known my Google fu was the way to your heart, I would've shown off my librarian-in-training skills long ago."

I sent the page to print on Lemon's networked printer in the gallery, and off we went. Kirby beat me to it, swiped the paper from the output tray.

"One condition," she said, waving the page between us. I braced myself for another lecture about Christian, but Kirby only smiled. "In thanks for my services, you have to share those leftovers. I haven't had Indian in forever!"

I nodded toward the kitchen so we could start the late-night feast. But as Kirby set out clean plates and silverware, her smile slipped, and I froze. I recognized the look that had taken hold, rearranging her features.

Fear.

I tapped the countertop to get her attention. *What's up, gyal?*

"Noah doesn't like this any more than Christian," she said. Her gaze dropped to a water spot on the counter, and she dragged her finger through it as she talked. "I feel so bad for him. For both of them. And I'm trying to be super supportive for Noah, because I know how hard it'll be for him if he loses and has to deal with his dad's disappointment. Same as Christian, I guess. It's just . . . it's weird,

you know? And Noah's in the middle and I'm in the middle and I just . . ." She stopped playing with the water and met my eyes again, lowering her voice. "I like him, Elyse. I really, really, really like him."

I gave her an encouraging smile. Christian had teased her and called her Sleeping with the Enemy, and we all laughed, but I knew it wasn't easy for her. Everyone knew it, just like we all knew how much she liked Noah.

"This whole week, the library's been crawling with those P and D guys, looking at old blueprints and town infrastructure stuff." Tears gathered in her eyes. "I like Noah, more than anyone. But I don't want to lose the house. I don't want to lose the Cove."

It was the first time she'd admitted her fears to me, the first time she'd given any indication that losing the house was even a possibility for her. I reached across the counter and grabbed her hands, and as clear as I could form the words, I made her the same promise Christian had made me.

We're not going to lose.

Chapter 14

Nothing shone through the blue-gray morning mist but a crooked silver crown.

Standing on the shore where the ocean lathered the sand, Christian waved his trident, a cardboard wrapping-paper tube spiked at the end with three toilet-paper tubes. He was bare chested and barefoot, wearing only a pair of dark gray sweatpants and that crown.

"Fear me, sea-ling!" he roared, pointing the trident at Sebastian.

Dressed in Bermuda shorts and a plastic-coconut bra, the younger Kane squealed and dove behind the nearest dune.

Neither had seen me, and I sat atop the dune at the edge of Lemon's property to spy. Christian was relaxed and happy. Every time Sebastian laughed, Christian lit up too.

It was the first I'd seen him shirtless, confirming my suspicions that his shoulder and upper arm were fully tattooed. It was some sort of nautical design: a ship and compass, maybe a map. It was all blacks and grays, no garish colors or cartoonish lines. It seemed like such a part of him, almost like he'd come out that way, marked by his love for the sea.

Before I could finish cataloging it for private, late-night recollection, he was gone, zipping around the dunes in search of his brother.

"Looks like you've got a rescuer, little mermaid," he called to Sebastian, pointing his trident my way.

Heat rushed to my face, but I held my head high, rose from the dune, and approached them as though I'd been on my way all along. In truth I'd been en route to the Kane house, excited to catch Christian early. I'd wanted to tell him about Kirby's state park marina idea.

"Elyse!" Sebastian stretched out his bare arms, two pale fins. The plastic coconuts of his costume squished together. "Get to the sea stack! If Neptune touches you with his trident, you'll turn into sea-foam!"

He took off running toward the rock formations, waving for me to follow. It was low tide, and the beach was littered with sand toys and smooth rocks, orange and lavender starfish lounging in the Oregon haze.

Christian waved the trident threateningly as I passed. "I am Neptune, king of the sea! All shall bow to me!"

Sebastian and I huddled behind the largest sea stack, an ancient black column that rose above its neighbors like a giant crooked fang. Sebastian held my hand tightly, beaming. I'd seen him a few times since our failed mermaid hunt, but always it was on the boat, where I'd been too busy for mermaid sketches and talks of old legends.

He cupped his free hand around his mouth and shouted over the sound of the waves. "There's only one thing that can stop the evil king of the sea. True love's first kiss."

My throat went dry, but Sebastian was all giggles and innocence, thrilled with the new twist in the game, and before I could get myself out of that particular mess, Neptune—our tyrannical tattooed king—ducked out from behind an adjacent sea stack.

Sebastian sucked in a breath. "Oh no. He found us."

Christian's eyes sparkled with mischief. "Did I hear something about a kiss?"

Sebastian sighed. "You can't kiss her until you're married."

"In that case," Christian said, laying down his trident and kneeling in the wet sand before me, "I do."

"Hold on." Sebastian darted out from the rocks, leaving me alone with my soon-to-be-husband. Overhead, the sun was enjoying a momentary cloudless stretch, bathing us in a swath of golden light.

"If I'd known today would be my wedding day," Christian said, looking down at his bare chest, "I would've worn something a little more . . . well, more. Alas, if only you'd called first." His eyes drifted to my hands, lingered on the faintly visible writing he'd left on my palm last night.

Sweet dreams

I folded my fingers into a fist, but before I could think of a response, Sebastian was back with a red bucket full of water.

"Sorry," he said, breathless. "I had to get some holy water."

He told me to kneel in the sand next to Christian, and then he dipped his fingers into the water and drew wet, drippy hearts on our foreheads. Then he placed his hands on top of our heads and said, "By the power invested in me, with all the starfish before us, I now announce you god and goddess, king and queen of the sea. Christian—I mean Neptune—you may kiss the mer-bride."

Christian raised an eyebrow, sea-eyes glittering in the light. "How does the mer-bride feel about this?"

My lips curved into a smile, an old familiar smirk that matched my groom's, and we both knew what it was. A dare. Despite the rapid pounding of my heart, the chill in my legs from the encroaching tide, outside I was still and serene, and I let that smile float between us.

A baited hook, a blessing.

An offering.

A request.

Kiss me, Christian Kane.

The clouds above shifted, dimming the light as Christian leaned forward, bringing with him that freshly showered, mangoes-and-sea scent. His lips brushed so close-but-not-quite-touching, soft and tender as an island breeze. The moment was over quickly; chaste play to Sebastian, but a dangerous tease between me and Christian.

But as he pulled away, looking dazed, I realized I'd been waiting for Sebastian's telltale giggles.

They'd never come.

He was gone.

Caught by a wave, the red bucket tumbled endlessly in the surf.

I shot to my feet, dragging Christian up with me. Without waiting, I took off toward the great cold maw of the sea, eyes scanning frantically. I cupped my hands around my mouth, screamed his name instinctively, but of course no sound came. Only pain, only the reminder.

My heart slammed against my bones, everything in me alight with fear. The bucket lolled in the water, and I told my legs to move. To carry me there. To launch me into the surf so I could swim, dive under, look for him.

But I was frozen on the shore, the water no higher than my knees. Like my voice, my body had abandoned me.

The water had reached the base of the sea stacks, swirling and churning, and from the top of the tallest stack, our crooked fang, the mermaid Atargatis looked on, indifferent. Blue hair swirled around her in the breeze, hiding her face. Her fish tail, silver and aquamarine in the mist, curled out before her.

Help us! I cried. Behind me the twisted white ribbon of sea-foam hissed, creeping ever colder up the shore. *Why won't you help us?*

Atargatis only laughed. Cruel, icy. She shook her head, wild hair parting to reveal bloodred lips.

Hush, hush, little one, she warned.

Everything you wish for

I will take.

Everything you've ever dared to love
is already mine.

My legs gave out, and I dropped to the water, waiting for the chill that never came.

"Easy, Elyse. Breathe. Just breathe." Christian's voice was gentle in my ear, his bare chest warm behind me as his strong arms encircled me. He held me like that, whispering against the back of my neck until I calmed down, then he led me out of the shallow water, back to the shore where the tide hadn't yet reached.

When I looked up at the sea stack, Atargatis was gone.

"Okay?" Christian said, scanning my face. Tentatively he reached up, stroked my cheek with his thumb.

I nodded.

"It's just a bucket," Sebastian said, reaching for my hand. "I've got lots of them. Well, that was my only red one. But I have a blue one and a green one, too."

Sebastian was here, right here. He'd been here all along. I closed my eyes, inhaled the dense morning air. My body was functioning again, shivering from head to toe. Christian put his arm around me, rubbed my shoulder.

I felt like a freak.

As ever, the ocean laughed behind me. My first great love. My endless torment. How could something I knew so well, something that had been such a part of me, betray me like that? How could such golden, shimmering things so quickly turn black?

But no one could hear the questions in my heart, so I swallowed them down. Tried to smile. To reassure Christian and Sebastian I was fine—just a momentary lapse.

"Boys?" Mr. Kane's deep voice broke through the haze as he crested the nearest dune. I wondered how long he'd been watching us. "Breakfast is almost on the table. Christian, shirt. Let's go."

"Daddy," Sebastian said, releasing my hand and running toward his father. "They're married. They kissed and everything."

With his eyes fixed on Sebastian, Mr. Kane interrupted the story. "Okay, kiddo. Time to put away the toys and wash up for breakfast." When he looked at me, his smile changed, stretched unnaturally at the corners. "Elyse. Nice to see you again. I assume you'll be joining us?"

Christian looked at me, leaned in close again. His breath fluttered against my ear. "Stay with me."

The Kane house was laid out like Lemon's, only their main living area was on the ground floor with more rooms upstairs, while Lemon's had the shop and office downstairs. The whole house smelled like maple syrup and coffee. My stomach rumbled as they passed the dishes around the dining table.

"I'm glad you're here, Elyse," Mr. Kane said. He sat at the head, across from his wife, and each of them had a pile of mobile devices at their fingertips. "I've been thinking about this whole regatta business, and—"

"Here we go," Christian said. His father flashed him a warning look, but Christian was undeterred. "Dad, unless you're calling off the bet, Elyse and I don't care."

"Well, that depends on you, Christian," he said.

Mrs. Kane set her fork down. "Andy, honestly. This is not the time to discuss it." She tossed a smile in my direction, a reminder of my outsider status. It was the first I'd seen her up close since the Solstice party, and she hadn't warmed a single degree.

I wasn't sure how she and Lemon could be friends, but all Lemon ever said about it was that Meredith's soul had gone faint—that she'd spent so much time cultivating an image, the real her was pushed down, locked away deep inside. Still there, though, Lemon believed, aching to rise.

Next to her, one of the devices buzzed. She reached over and silenced it.

"Thith ith not the time to dithcuth it," Sebastian lisped. He'd capped his front teeth with a giant strawberry, and I winked at him across the table. Christian laughed.

"Cut it out, guys," Mr. Kane said. "Anyway, hon, I've been thinking about what Wes told us. About P and D's offers? Neil got twenty percent above his appraisal. Maybe we should just sell, skip the whole race."

"I told you, I don't want to sell." Mrs. Kane silenced another buzz rattling through her phone. "We've always summered here. The kids—"

"One of the kids is an adult now," he said. "We have other things to focus on. Christian has a future to think about. I've got a new software release to contend with this fall." He pointed his fork at his wife. "You're taking on more clients than you can handle as it is. That doesn't leave much time for lazy summer fun."

Christian shoved in a bite of waffle. With a full mouth he said, "We're doing the regatta, Dad. So this conversation is irrelevant."

After a beat Mr. Kane nodded. "Assuming you can win. Pass the maple syrup there?"

I reached next to Christian and grabbed it, handed it over.

"I'd stand a better chance if Team Katz hadn't dock-blocked us." Christian told his parents about yesterday's hardware store adventures.

"Slick bastard," Mr. Kane said. "Funding his kid's win." His tone held a note of approval, one that wasn't lost on Christian.

"You put him up to it?" Christian asked his father.

"Simmer down, boys," Mrs. Kane said. "Elyse, how's Ursula? Will you let her know I'll be there for dinner on the fifth? I haven't had a chance to call her back yet."

I reached for my notebook so I could jot down a response for her, but remembered that I'd left it at Lemon's. I nodded mutely, took another sip of coffee.

There were so many things I wanted to say. To the parents. The boys. All of them.

"Sounds like you need to step up your game, son," Mr. Kane said. Next to him, a tablet beeped. He tapped something into the screen, then turned his attention back to Christian. "Right?"

"Team Katz isn't playing fair," Christian said. "About what I'd expect from the old man."

"A lot riding on this race," Mr. Kane said, going back to his tablet. Mrs. Kane followed suit, checking her phone.

As the parents focused on their digital communications, there was a break in the conversation, an undercurrent of electricity as forks and knives clanked against plates and lips slurped hot coffee. Outside the big floor-to-ceiling windows, the sea was quiet again.

"Enough with the devices," Christian said. "I see the wheels turning, Dad, so just say it."

Mr. Kane removed the cloth napkin from his lap and blotted his mouth. To Christian, he said, "I'm thinking about what you just said—that Team Katz isn't playing fair. But you've got a gold card funded by your parents. How is that any different?"

Christian's hand tightened around his mug.

"I don't like to win with unfair advantages," Mr. Kane said. "If Wes Katzenberg wants to grant his son that level of entitlement, fine. We'll show him we're better than that."

Christian shook his head. "At the risk of sounding like an entitled bastard—"

"Why risk it?" Mr. Kane said with a wink.

Mrs. Kane stood from the table, gathered her devices. "Sebastian, all finished? Be a good helper and clear the table for Mommy? I've got some calls to return."

Sebastian eagerly followed, scooping up his dishes and an empty strawberry bowl.

"Dad," Christian said, "you forbade me to get a job all year."

"You needed to focus on your studies."

"Studies at the college you chose for me," Christian said. "Had your friends write letters of recommendation, pulled all the right strings. Paid the tuition in full."

Mr. Kane sipped his coffee. Glared. Sipped again.

"I did as you asked. And now I'm broke, but for that one credit card," Christian said. "So you're cutting me off, no warning? The first time I'm using the funds for anything other than food and textbooks?"

The Kane family puzzle was clicking into place, a few more jagged pieces every time I saw them. The father, decision maker. Homeowner. Controller. Christian, stifled by his father's contempt and expectations. Sebastian, soon to follow. But I still couldn't peg the mother. She was smart, managed her own career, carried herself with a sense of power and determination. Yet whenever things heated up with Christian and his father, she backed off. Completely.

Leaving her boys to the sharks.

"It's summer," Mr. Kane said plainly. "No classes until September. You're free to find work now."

"Where, at the Black Pearl?" Christian shook his head. "How would I find time to work and fix up the Vega?"

"This is your responsibility, son. If you can't find a way—"

"You made the bet."

"And you assured me you could handle it."

"That was before you yanked the rug out."

"Christian," his father said, patience finally cracking, "a boy your age is capable of supporting himself. Look at Miss d'Abreau, here. I doubt Ursula's given her an unlimited credit account. Right?"

I shook my head, but if he'd waited for me to explain, I would've told him that what she'd given me was far more valuable than a credit card. Money, my family had. But Lemon had given me a home when mine felt like anything but. She'd given me shelter, a room of my own, the space to breathe. She'd given me respite, encouraged me to explore and grow at my own pace. No pressure.

She'd given me love, with neither strings attached nor expectations for anything in return.

Her gifts to me were priceless.

But Mr. Kane wasn't interested in any of that. He continued to ride Christian. "Hard work builds character."

"I'd gladly work," Christian said. "You wouldn't hear of it, and I got tapped out. Now you're changing the rules."

"You're a privileged kid, Christian. Educated. Good-looking. Strong and healthy. No reason you can't figure this out." A self-satisfied smile tugged at the corners of his mouth. "Think of it like a business problem. You can impress your Stanford profs with the whole story when you get back."

Christian dropped his fork. It hit the plate with a clang that rang out through the dining room.

I don't know how, I typed.

"Call your sister. Text her. Skype her. Send her a note."

I shook my head rapidly. Reflex, self-defense, denial . . . Call it what you will, but Natalie was the very last thing I wanted to discuss with Granna.

She banged her fist on the counter. "You know what the gyal say to me, Elyse? Just yesterday. She say, 'Oh, Granna, it's like half my soul missing.'"

She couldn't have made me feel worse if she'd tried. I knew Granna wasn't guilting me on purpose—it broke her to see our family in tatters, to explain the family rift to neighbors and resort staff, to make excuses with my older sisters about why I ignored their calls and e-mails, to know that the once-unbreakable connection between her twin granddaughters had shattered—but it still felt like a knife twisting in my side.

I knew I was a bad sister, a bad friend.

Jealous, spiteful. Selfish, awful.

Wouldn't forgive, couldn't forget.

Broken heart, everything black and sticky inside.

But how could I pretend to be anything else, anything other than utterly wrecked and ruined?

Sorry, I typed. I left it there; there were just too many things that word could cover.

Granna frowned. "She got some good news, wanted to tell you about it. The lady, Bella Garcia?"

My heart jumped; blood rushed to my head. After the accident Bella had tried to get in touch, had sent cards and flowers. But we all knew there was nothing she could do—it's not like we had a close personal relationship, and no amount of sympathy would bring my voice back. I hadn't heard from her since I came to the States.

"She call Natalie, say she has another chance to go on singing. She wants your sister to take lessons in Trinidad, an exclusive place Bella knows there. They only take referrals, so Bella offered one."

Another chance to go on singing.

Another chance, as if she'd lost her voice that night too. Her future. Her dreams. But for Natalie it was only a temporary setback, something that could be fixed with lessons at an exclusive place.

Granna's eyes softened, along with her voice. "She miss you, Elyse. She just miss you real bad."

My fingers hovered over the keys, the letters that spelled out the response in my heart:

Right.

She miss me so much, I hear her news only from you.

She miss me so much, she never asked for my new phone number.

She miss me so much, she forgot.

Forgot that just because I have no voice, doesn't mean I don't want to hear hers.

Forgot us, all the ways we used to be, all the things we shared.

Forgot a thousand summer days,

a hundred promises sealed with

a million tears and

*two fragile dream bubbles, so afraid anything louder than
a single whisper would break them.*

Forgot all of our hopes and plans.

*Forgot how they'd been altered in one moment, one wrong
move, a bad choice.*

*Forgot that sometimes a tarnished life was worse than a swift
death.*

*And that after, all the dreams once singular and shared had to
be divided.*

One side for her.

One side for Death.

Nothing left for her twin heart.

Yeah, Granna. She miss me that much.

My fingers stilled, scared and stiff over the keys. Across the
invisible distance, Granna frowned again, though I couldn't bring
myself to actually type any of those words.

How's Dad? I typed instead. He didn't trust the Internet, was certain it was a tool for spies and thieves, and since I couldn't talk on the
phone, our communications had been relegated to postcards. He'd
sent two each week, without fail, but after the first few I couldn't
bring myself to read them. He never played the guilt-trip game—
went instead to the other extreme, pretending all was well, as if I was
on some vacation with his dear friend Lemon. He never mentioned
my voice, my sister, everything that had happened. Never asked me
when I'd be coming back.

He just assumed I would be.

Eventually.

My older sisters were too busy with their own lives to focus on my shortcomings, but Granna and my father—well-meaning as they may have been—made my heart ache.

"He miss you too," Granna said. "Everyone miss you. What else can I say?"

I grabbed the seashell at my throat, twisted and turned.

"Oh, I see what's going on, gyal. The devil keeping you company now," she said, which is what she always said when one of us girls was being stubborn and mean-faced, but this time I wanted to tell her no, it wasn't the devil. It was Death himself, shadowing me, lying in my bed, whispering against my skin. Death himself, come to remind me of his deal with the sea, and if I turned my back even for an instant, he'd drag me back to the depths to fulfill his end of the bargain.

In so many ways he already had.

"The devil with you," she said again, certain. "You call back when allya done visitin'. But best you send him away quick, Elyse, or he move in with you."

I nodded solemnly, eager now to wrap things up. I typed my final words, asked if she'd send over those books for Sebastian and a few pieces of clothing I'd left behind.

She said she would, but she wasn't saying good-bye. Instead, she rose from the counter, stirred the soup, and disappeared.

There was muffled conversation, a spoon clanging to the floor.

Granna cursed under her breath. Despite the downshift in my mood, I smiled.

The screen flickered, darkened, brightened again.

Suddenly a familiar face smiled back at me.

A mirror.

A memory.

My twin.

Her eyes glazed with tears, and for an eternity we stared at each other, locked in silence as warring emotions drowned my heart.

"Elyse?" she whispered, stretching her fingers toward me.

I slammed the laptop shut, crushed her fingers and erased her face. Her tears. Everything about her that looked exactly like everything about me, save for the silver star in the hollow of my throat.

The scar that had changed my life.

The scar that had shattered my dreams.

The scar that my sister had put there.

Chapter 16

"In total defiance of American tradition, they don't do Fourth of July fireworks here," Kirby said. "The Cove saves them for the Mermaid Festival. But if we were anywhere else in the States? Fireworks."

Why are we going? I asked. After weeks of turning down invitations to hang out with Kirby, Vanessa, and the gang, I'd finally agreed to this one, mostly because Lemon had threatened to make me an herbal-lotion lab rat if I didn't leave the house tonight.

Kirby shrugged. "We always go. And I've been working my butt off lately, so I need a fun night out. And anyway"—she grabbed my sleeve; she could sense I was about to turn back, and she held firm, kicking up her campaign—"there's a bonfire, with hot dogs and s'mores and sparklers. Sometimes people bring beer. I mean, usually they do." At my ongoing reluctance she tossed out a final bone, though with markedly less enthusiasm. "Christian and those guys will be there."

Noah? I wanted to know. Even in the twilight haze, her face brightened. I smirked and marched ahead, but she ran to catch up, linking our arms.

"One more thing. Um, Vanessa? I already told her you wouldn't go for it, but she has this kind of fun but also crazy idea that the three of us should sign up for the—"

"My girls!" Vanessa bolted for us as soon as she saw us cresting the last dune. Behind her they'd already gotten the bonfire going, a roaring orange blaze that the folks over at Coos Bay could probably see. "Let's get this party started, y'all."

She handed each of us a plastic cup filled with something that smelled like peaches and burning.

I downed a few gulps, let the alcohol soak in and loosen the tension that had been building steadily since my call with Granna earlier. With Natalie.

But I knew that no matter how much I drank tonight, no matter how many hours or days passed, I wouldn't be able to erase her image from my mind. Her voice from my ears. *Elyse?*

"Elyse? Did Kirbs tell you about my master plan?" Vanessa asked.

"She'll say no," Kirby said.

"She did?"

Kirby sighed. "No. But she will. That's not Elyse's thing."

I looked at Kirby. *What's not?*

Kirby held up her drink. "This? Peach schnapps and fruit punch. Vanessa calls it Texas tea."

"We're talking about the mermaid parade, Kirby," Vanessa said. "God, you two are, like, I don't even know." She grabbed my hand, flashed her impossible-to-ignore smile. "Before you say no, we'd all be doin' it together, and we'd look smokin' hot and it would basically be the most fun."

It was hard not to get caught up in Vanessa's current. I offered a guarded smile.

"Mermaid parade," she said. "Tell her, Kirbs."

"Fine." Kirby was ready with the full-on talking brochure. "It's all part of the festival," she said. "Friday night is the fellowship walk 'n' feast, where everyone sets up food and drink stations outside their doors, and people just walk around stuffing themselves silly."

"And fellowshippin'," Vanessa said. "Being neighborly and whatnot."

"Exactly," Kirby said. "And drinking, too. Hence the walking thing."

"Stumblin', more like," Vanessa said.

"Saturday is the big day. Arts-and-crafts festival, sea glass competition, parade, and then the regatta." Kirby paused for a sip of Texas tea, then went on. "After all that, there's a closing party at the Black Pearl for anyone left standing. That's when they do the fireworks, right off the back docks. The parade is awesome—totally campy, but super fun. We all compete for the mermaid queen crown, but unlike the regatta, our stuff is really good-natured."

Vanessa laughed. "Damn, girl. You should work for the chamber a' commerce."

"I would if we had one. Anyway," Kirby said, "the parade is usually over by ten, ten-thirty, rain or shine. And the boats sail at noon. You could get there on time. I mean, if you were thinking about it. Which I totally understand if you're not. But if you *were*, and you don't mind sailing in your mermaid gear, you could swing it."

Gear? I mouthed.

"Costumes and accessories," Vanessa said. "I don't think there's a girl in town who doesn't march. Local or not. It's, like, the *thing* to do. People start planning months in advance, but I don't need that kind of lead time—give me sequins and a glue gun, and I'll *Project Runway* us a whole school a' mermaids." She looked at Kirby, her eyes fuzzy. "Are they called schools? Or gaggles?"

This sent the two of them into a giggling fit. If I wanted to last the night, I needed to catch up. I finished my drink and grabbed Kirby's, downed the rest.

The mermaid parade sounded a little like Carnival back home. Playing mas, we called it—masquerading. Soon as one Carnival season passed, we were already thinking about the next, planning our costumes, mapping out the best parties and fêtes, scheming ways to stay out all night and hit them all.

"Anyway," Kirby said, finally taking a breath. She looked around for her drink, not even realizing I'd finished it. "We could get ready together. Ooh, we could do a theme!"

"Far as I'm concerned," Vanessa said, "any day we get to wear glitter eye shadow and seashell bras is a good day. Am I right?"

"It's a good day for *me*," Christian said. He'd come from behind the dune, carrying a plate of bun-wrapped hot dogs that smelled fresh off the fire. "Wiener delivery. I've come to tempt you gorgeous ladies back to the fire with my extra-long—"

"Check yourself before you wreck yourself, hot stuff." Vanessa grabbed three dogs, passing one to each of us. Mid-chew, we followed Christian back to the bonfire, where Noah and a few other people had gathered. I didn't know the newcomers, but I'd seen most of them around, passing through the marina or getting shakes or coffee at the Black Pearl. As usual, they looked at me with a mix of curiosity and over-politeness, a strange blend I'd come to expect in Atargatis Cove.

Christian's friends from the docks last week were there too—Gracie and Brenda—and I was relieved when they offered a matched set of genuine smiles.

There were blankets spread out around the fire, and I settled down next to Vanessa, kicking off my shoes and stretching my toes toward the fire.

All around me the group chattered and gossiped, roasting hot dogs and marshmallows, their laughter set to the soundtrack of the sea. After a while Gracie and Brenda stood, sauntered closer to the shore to where a few kids were writing their names in the air with sparklers.

The beach party reminded me of our reggae fests on the island, outdoor gatherings full of laughs and food and strong drinks. But ours would last all day and night, pulsing with music, and this one was way too mellow for a true fest. Roasting hot dogs and marshmallows on a stick was fun, but they were no substitutes for the grilled kingfish and mangoes from home.

After the hot dog I'd been working on a marshmallow, but handed it to Kirby, needing suddenly to stretch my legs. I walked to the shore, away from the sparkler girls, and let the icy Pacific nibble my toes. The sun had set, but the sky was still fingered with purple and pink, the first of the night's stars glittering in the Oregon mist.

I kept a safe distance from the crashing surf. I had no intention of tempting Atargatis again.

My toes went numb in the sand, and again I wondered if I'd ever get used to things here, if I could ever learn to call it home. In this little cove, the music was soft, the food mild, so many of the people cool and stiff. I didn't mean it as an insult, only a comparison, a simple observation that left me wondering again and again where, exactly, I belonged.

Heaviness tugged at my heart as I thought of Granna and Natalie. Would they even *want* me back? Did *I* want me back?

"Don't take this the wrong way." Christian's voice should've startled me, but the ocean was so loud, so constant, I'd barely heard him.

I looked at him, raised my eyebrows in question.

"You're a tough one to crack," he said, stepping closer. The breeze whipped against us, and we instinctively huddled for warmth, backing away from the tide.

Even through his Stanford hoodie his body emanated heat, a slow and tender warmth that caressed my exposed neck. My throat.

I tugged my thin sweater sleeves over my hands to keep them from reaching for him.

"All this time we've been spending together, and this is the first you've hung out with us," he said. "Not working, I mean. And Indian-food day doesn't count."

No?

"Work related," he said. "You were practically obligated."

I shook my head, coughed out what passed for my laugh these days.

Christian ran a hand over his face, then leaned in even closer. With one arm around my shoulders, he bent his head toward my ear, and my heart raged at his familiar scent, at his closer-than-closeness. It was getting to be a regular thing with us, this casual intimacy. But each time it electrified my nerves anew.

In a raspy voice that sent a wave of desire through me, he said, "I think you have more than a few secrets, Elyse d'Abreau."

He pulled away, cocky smile back in place.

A joke. A flirty taunt. But still I sensed that he'd tried to go there again, to dip a toe into the waters of my real story, and scared as I was, the comment had done nothing to douse that spark inside. The ember. The flame. All I could do was close my eyes, shake my head.

Nearly two months ago I'd washed up on the shores of this little Pacific hamlet from the twin-island nation of Trinidad and Tobago, with little more than a pair of sunglasses I didn't actually need and a suitcase full of memories I didn't actually want. I had five sisters, a nosey but devoted grandmother, and a loving father, all of whom

orry," she said, handing me what looked like a tarred sock on
k.

I pitched the mess into the flames and grabbed a fresh stick,
eared two new marshmallows. When they reached golden perfec-
ion, I pulled two graham crackers from the stash and mushed it all
together.

"Whoa, whoa, whoa." Christian stole my s'more before I coud
take a bite. "Emergency intervention for the tourist. You can't make
a s'more without chocolate." With his free hand he dug through the
bag between us for a Hershey bar, but I recoiled as if he'd offered me a
snake.

That's not chocolate.

He examined the wrapper. "Well it's not vodka or whale blubber
or a shoe."

"Forget it, Christian," Kirby said from my other side. "Elyse's
family owns a cocoa farm. They're totally organic. We're talking legit
old-school cocoa roasting. All the pods are harvested by hand and
turned into chocolate the old-fashioned way."

Christian looked impressed. "Seriously?"

"Seriously," Kirby went on, "Elyse's dad was featured on the Travel
Channel and everything. You'll never get her to eat commercial chocolate. Even what we consider the very best stuff here? Like, expensive
stuff? She'll totally turn her nose up."

"Dudes." Noah opened the cooler he'd been sitting on. "All this
talk of chocolate is making me thirsty. Who needs a brew?" He passed

I'd walled out of my heart. Though they w

to my face, this entire town likely whispered

my story. I couldn't utter a word, I had a scar

necklace that hinted at some past tragedy, and de

Vanessa's and even Christian's efforts to include me,

time on the Vega and rare outings like tonight, I was se

self-imposed cocoon.

Of *course* I had more than a few secrets, Christian Kane.

I opened my eyes, flashed him a smile that I hoped couched .

fear.

Christian's cocky grin didn't slip, his mischievous gaze unwavering as he said, "Speaking of secrets. I could've sworn you told me you don't dance."

My body buzzed, skin almost as hot on the outside as the things Christian had stirred up on the inside. I opened my mouth to deny it, but he cut me off with a laugh.

"Don't even try it. I saw you out here the other night, gettin' your groove on."

I turned away, considered asking the sea to make good on its promise. But Christian was at my side, elbowing me with a playful nudge. "You're really good, Elyse. Amazing, actually."

We stood in silence for a moment, the heat between us fading as the breeze picked up again. Without words we marched back to the bonfire, where Kirby had done a first-rate job torching my marshmallow on account of her drooling over Noah.

beers to a few takers, Christian among them. When the two clinked bottles, Noah said, "I know we're supposed to be all *Fight Club* about this, but I'm buzzed and it needs to be said: This regatta blows."

Christian took a swig of beer, wiped his mouth with the back of his hand. "Preach."

"I don't want to lose *Never Flounder*. You don't want to lose the houses. What the serious hell, right?"

"Serious hell," Christian agreed, but he'd turned away from Noah, meeting my eyes instead. In the orange light of the flame his face was soft and warm, but those eyes held a dangerous fire all their own.

Gracie and Brenda had just returned for more sparklers, but on hearing the conversation, they sat down again.

Brenda said, "I don't know about you guys, but my parents are totally fighting this Prop Twenty-Seven thing. There's a reason they bought property at the Cove instead of some big tourist place. I mean, where else can you find whole sand dollars?" She procured a few from her pocket, stacked them in a pile at her feet.

"Right?" Vanessa said. "I mean, sure, I have to drive an hour for a decent pedicure, but so what? That's not what the Cove is all about."

"Guys, my dad cares about this place," Noah said. "Maybe it doesn't look like it, but he has a good heart. He's just also got a big, hard, stupid head. Which is presently shoved up his ass."

Everyone laughed, but the lightheartedness died out fast.

"Besides," Noah said, "it's not his decision. Everyone gets a vote. They don't have to follow his lead."

"If they do," Vanessa said, "this place will look a whole lot different come next Fourth of July." She pronounced it like *Joo-lie,* and it made me smile. I wondered what they'd say about my accent if they could've heard it. I pictured them laughing, telling me to slow down, to say it again. They'd try to sound out the words, imitate the Trini rhythm, and I'd be laughing too. Loud and bold.

A chill crept in among us, and for a moment no one spoke. In the distance someone lit a few firecrackers, whistling into the night.

"I still can't believe our dads made that bet," Noah said to Christian. "Dude, we always race together." Noah stood, chucked a bottle cap into the fire. "It's bullshit, man. Bullshit."

I'd never seen him get worked up before, not so much as lose his cool over a burnt sandwich or cranky customer at the Black Pearl.

I rose from my spot, put a hand on Noah's shoulder. I didn't know him well, but behind the counter at the Black Pearl, he'd become a constant for me, someone who knew how I liked my latte and had it ready the moment I set foot inside. In that way he'd given me a small sense of permanence, of belonging, and I'd always be grateful.

Noah pulled me into a friendly hug. "Just so you know, when Dad told me to try to scare you into quitting, I drew the line. I'm a lover, not a fighter."

I smiled, squeezing tighter to tell him it was okay.

As I reclaimed my seat in the sand, Christian shot Noah a mock-threatening glare. "I think you're getting a little too friendly with the competition, lover."

"Don't tell my old man," Noah said. "I'll have to deny it, say I'm interrogating her."

"You won't get anything out of her," Christian said, nodding in my direction. "My girl here's a *vault*."

"Your girl?" Noah raised his eyebrows. "When did that—"

"She's a girl." Christian swigged his beer, sighed. "She's my first mate. Simple."

"But you said—"

"Stow it, Katz."

Noah held up his hands in surrender. "Sorry, dude. Just wish I knew where to find a first mate like that."

"Okay, seriously?" Christian said. "We're sitting right here."

Noah only laughed. "Just rilin' you up, bud. Wearing you down. My strategy's already working."

"Think you can win with psychological warfare alone?" Christian asked.

"In the absence of a hot first mate, it's all I've got."

Christian tipped his beer toward Kirby. "Why don't you ask Sleeping with the Enemy?"

Kirby gasped. "Christian!"

"Already did. She doesn't sail." Noah leveled Kirby with an adoring gaze, and without being asked, he rose from the cooler, unzipped and shook off his hoodie, and draped it over Kirby's shoulders.

She smiled at him, shy and sweet. The two of them had stars in their eyes. It was practically a marriage proposal.

Vanessa pressed her hand to her heart. "What is it about young love and a bonfire on the beach?"

"Hey!" Brenda waved from across the fire. "We're cold over here, too, if anyone cares."

Gracie gave an exaggerated shiver. "Is there anyone in, say, a Stanford sweatshirt? Anyone who might offer to keep a girl warm for the night?"

With his eyes still on mine, Christian said, "Yeah. I've got you covered, ladies."

Everyone whooped and whistled. Christian handed me his beer and rose, dug out a blanket that was folded beneath the s'mores stuff.

"Heads up." He tossed the blanket over the fire, straight into Brenda's lap.

The girls grumbled as they unfolded it and draped it over their legs.

"Dude," Noah whispered as Christian reached over to reclaim his beer. "That's some cold shit, right there."

Christian only shrugged.

Noah laughed, his eyes shifting from Christian to me, then back to Christian. "What I wanna know is, when are you two crazy kids getting matching sailor hats? Monogrammed, perhaps?"

Christian punched him in the arm, but they were both laughing.

"Shoot, I'm dry again," Vanessa said. "Who needs a refill?" From the large jug she'd brought, she poured fresh Texas teas, passing cups to Brenda and Gracie, then to me and Kirby. "First, we get those matching mermaid costumes. Then hats." She held up her cup in a cheer, clicking it to mine and Kirby's, then to Brenda's and Gracie's. "Sisters before misters, right, girls? Don't make me say it again."

"You guys are marching in the parade?" Brenda asked. "I was just trying to talk Gracie into it."

Vanessa smiled at Gracie. "Oh, you have to, girl. Cove tradition."

Christian narrowed his eyes at me as we drank, a smile tugging his lips. "You're marching in the parade?"

I couldn't tell whether he thought this was a good thing or utterly frivolous. His eyes settled on my mouth, waiting for an answer, but I said nothing.

Beyond the fire, the Pacific raged on.

"Are you?" Christian was still watching me, still waiting. But soon Noah was talking about the regatta again, apologizing in advance for any future piracy he might have to engage in to save his boat, and the moment passed. The girls had lit new sparklers in the fire, attracting a few stragglers from a smaller bonfire nearby. One of the newcomers immediately set to hitting on Vanessa. He was on a mission, and she was loving every minute of it.

Christian switched seats and put his arm around her protectively, and in the jokes and jibes that followed, I slipped away.

Chapter 17

"Figured I'd find you here, Stowaway."

I sat up as Christian stepped into the saloon, windblown and a little buzzed. I'd been camped out in my formerly favorite spot in the V-berth, and I wasn't expecting him; it had only been half an hour since I'd left the bonfire.

"Vanessa took off with that mouth-breather, and Noah's out there trolling for a first mate. Even Brenda and Gracie turned him down. Kirby's trying to help, but the whole thing was pretty pathetic." He slumped onto the saloon bench, turned his gaze on me. His voice was soft. "I couldn't watch."

I nodded. Christian rarely showed it, but I knew it hurt him, having to race against one of his best friends. Having to follow his father's orders just because his father—Noah's too—was the kind of man whose orders were simply followed, no room for discussion.

"That yours?" Christian's attention was captured by something on the table across from him. It was a white envelope, a typewritten label stuck on the front with a single directive: FOR REGATTA EXPENSES ONLY.

I shook my head as he tore it open. Until now I hadn't even noticed it.

"Holy shit," he said. After a pause so heavy it threatened to sink the boat, he said, "Elyse. There's fifteen hundred bucks in here."

My mouth dropped open. *Nine thousand Trinidadian dollars*, my brain calculated.

"No note," he said, double-checking the envelope. "Someone wants us to win. Bad. Ursula?"

Again I shook my head. Lemon hadn't had any big sculpture sales lately, and the store was more of a hobby than a real source of income. She seemed to do all right with the art and herbal cosmetics, and she'd been a saver all her life—something she tried to instill in me and Kirby any chance she got. But I was pretty sure she didn't have that kind of cash just lying around.

Besides, Lemon wasn't one for keeping secrets. She would've told me if she'd planned to give money for the cause.

"One of the girls, maybe? Brenda? Gracie?"

I shrugged. I hadn't seen them leave the fire tonight, so if it was one of them, they would've had to sneak onto the boat this afternoon, before the bonfire started. It was possible, but neither seemed like the kind of person who'd leave a gift like that without taking credit.

"This is ... I mean, we could really use this. The boat needs electrical and cosmetic work, and we haven't even looked at the sails yet." His words quickened with excitement, imagination already spending the cash. "It's not yours? For sure?"

I almost laughed.

"Jesus. This regatta gets shadier every year. Not that I'm about to look *that* gift horse in the mouth." He counted the money once more, slipped it back into the envelope. After a beat he set it back on the table. "What are you up to in here, anyway? More poetry?"

I shifted over in the V-berth as he approached, making space to fit him.

He slid in next to me, and we both leaned back, looking at the walls and ceiling that held so many of my secrets. The heat I'd felt with him on the shore seeped again into the small nook, and outside, the Pacific churned and hissed, rocking us gently. There were no stars now, but the moon had found its way through the clouds, and pale silver light shone in the small window behind us.

Cozy. That's the word that came to me. Cozy and ... safe.

Christian reached up and touched the first words I'd written on his boat, a poem called "Plan B." It wasn't my best, but it was honest, exactly what I'd been feeling that night.

"This one," he said, keeping his voice low, "says a lot."

Plan B
Plan Battered and Broken
Plan Boxed in

plan Bailed on and Back from the dead

plan Better luck next time

plan Balled up

plan Backtracked

plan Backhanded

plan Backward steps

plan Blackballed, Black-marked, and Blacklisted

plan B-side, Bye-Bye Baby

plan Belly up and Beat down

plan Bad days ahead and the Best are far Behind

"I take it crashing at the Cove wasn't part of your master plan?" He looked at me so he could capture my answer, something I suddenly realized he'd always done.

So many people glanced but never saw, their eyes skimming the surface, then settling on some other distraction, something easier to understand. I didn't blame them, really—often it was automatic, our brains wired to seek the path of least resistance. But with Christian, whenever we were together, whether it was working on the boat, breaking for lunch, inside Lemon's store, or anywhere else our paths crossed, he looked at me. He focused on my lips as I tried to form words, he repeated them to ensure he'd understood. He read the words I'd written for him in my notebook, on his hands, on mine. He noticed me.

He *saw* me.

This time, when I didn't answer, he reached across the sliver of space between us and grabbed my hand, squeezed. He traced my wrist with his thumb, a gesture that somehow managed to both frighten and soothe, barely navigating the line between friends and . . . something else.

I waited until his eyes met mine again, then I nodded toward him. *You?*

"Plan B?" he said. "I never even had a plan A."

Not college?

"That's not the issue." His sigh was heavy with regret. He released my hand, rolled over on his side to face me fully. We were so close I could feel his breath on my skin, warm as the Caribbean air. He lowered his voice even more. "I'm about to sound like an ungrateful shit here, and I'm not. I love school—totally thankful I have the opportunity to go."

So?

"I thought I was cool with the business track, like my dad, you know? He has all the connections, helped me get in, his buddies already promising to hook up a job after grad. But the more time I spend away from him, the more it seems like I'm just . . . going through the motions." He sliced the air with his hand. "Following the path, like he always wanted."

The tide was coming in; a wave caught us on the side, rocking the boat beneath us. When she settled again, I reached for the Sharpie in my pocket. I uncapped it, pressed the tip to the ceiling. The words were a revision, a new last line on my old poem that only now needed to be said.

Christian watched as the letters appeared.

Plan But what do YOU want, Christian Kane?

Christian stared at the words a long time, and when he finally looked at me again, his eyes were blank. Unreadable.

"No idea," he whispered. "No one ever asked."

I thumbed my chest. *I'm asking.* Gently, I tapped the words out against his heart. *What . . . do . . . you . . . want?*

His eyes changed then, from blank and unreadable to a red-hot smolder, simultaneously vulnerable and certain. Behind the seashell necklace, my pulse pounded, blood rushing to my head. I was dizzy in the best kind of way, floating on the sea and the moonlight and all the unsaid things, the fragile silver hopes yet unspoken, yet unbroken.

Christian slipped his hand behind my neck, leaned in close, looked again in my eyes for an answer.

Yes.

Our lips brushed, gently as they had at our mermaid wedding, and the length of our bodies aligned, warmth seeking warmth.

I closed my eyes, welcomed the heat of his mouth as our kiss deepened, the heartbeat in my ears drowned by the Pacific's endless howl and a single word, whispering inside me again and again.

Safe.

Chapter 18

"How do you feel about trees?" Christian asked the next morning. I'd just arrived at the docks, and he hopped off the boat wearing a grin that held both mischief and hope. *Please say yes*, it seemed to say. "We're taking the day off—"

"We're going explorin'." Sebastian popped out of the saloon like a curly-haired gopher. He was laden with his explorer's gear. "I hope you brought your land legs, lady."

Christian laughed. "What this presumptuous little beast means is, we're planning a hike near Devils Elbow. You up for an adventure?"

"What's a prumptious little beast?" Sebastian stretched out his arms for a lift off the boat.

Effortlessly Christian scooped him up, set him on the dock. "*You* are. That's what the dictionary said. Your picture was in there and everything."

Sebastian giggled. To me, he said, "So, are you coming?"

Next to us, the boat bobbed in the water, creaking and clanking as always. It didn't seem like a day off was the most prudent course of action.

At my hesitation Christian said, "Relax, Stowaway. We're off boat duty today anyway. I've got an electrician coming in, courtesy of our mystery benefactor. Hired him from Coos Bay. Figured we could use someone who actually knows what he's doing. Cuts down on . . . electrocutions!"

He grabbed Sebastian, tickling him until the kid squealed with glee.

"Don't electrocute me!" Sebastian cried.

I'm in. I gave them the trademark salute, and off we went, piling into Christian's truck and setting out for uncharted lands.

Just over an hour and twenty-five consecutive games of I Spy later, we reached Devils Elbow State Park, hidden from the shore in the Siuslaw National Forest. Sebastian was the first out of the truck, tumbling into the lot with boundless excitement, then bolting back to us with sudden urgency.

"I forgot something important!" Sebastian opened the passenger door, fished an envelope out of the glove compartment. He handed it to me, beaming. "I made this for you."

It was a card, stamped with a mermaid in the center, colored and adorned with glittery starfish stickers and hand-drawn reeds in green and yellow. Inside, edged along the bottom with blue-green waves and encircled with a heart, he'd written a note:

Dear Elyse,

Thank you for being my new friend.

And liking mermaids.

And marrying my brother.

Your new friend,

Sebastian Kane

P.S. Are you a mermaid? Yes or No.

He scrutinized my face for the answer, but I only shrugged, offering a devious smile.

"I already know you are," he said, and then he zoomed away, heading down the hiking trail for the dark, dank forest beyond.

Christian and I followed. It was a holiday weekend, and the parking lot was crowded, but most of the visitors headed down toward the beach trail and the Heceta Head Lighthouse. Christian and Sebastian preferred to go off the beaten path, and once we entered the forest, it wasn't long before we'd lost the masses.

With every step the trees grew more immense, the forest more dense. Enshrouded in mist, spruces stretched into the sky, impossibly tall and lush. Swaths of hanging moss draped the boughs, and tiny green clover crept up every trunk from the forest floor. The air was cool, scented with the endless cycle of decay and green growing things. Much like the rain forest reserve on Tobago, it felt ancient and sacred, an impossible otherworld where precious secrets drifted on every breeze and the most wondrous magic was real.

Ahead on the trail Sebastian turned around a bend. When the last of his golden curls vanished behind a cluster of trees, Christian stopped.

His arms slid around me as he backed me up against a tree, his eyes full of fire, bright in the hazy mist that surrounded us.

Everything in me turned hot and gooey. After last night I wanted to kiss him again. To keep kissing him. But he'd made no promises.

Neither had I.

"It's taken a lot of restraint on my part," he said in a low growl, hot and close to my ear, "to wait this long."

He kissed me, slow and soft, his lips tender and full, fingers twisting in my hair.

I let my knees go slack as Christian pressed against me, pinning me to the tree, holding me up.

It felt like a dream.

Farther down the path Sebastian's voice floated on the breeze, broke our kiss. "Come on, slowpokes!"

Christian sighed, still so close and warm. "Until the next bend in the road, then," he said, holding out his hand.

I took it gladly, my body buzzing.

Once we had Sebastian in our sights again, a few dozen paces ahead, Christian said, "Thanks for coming with us today. Doesn't seem like it now, but this morning? Kid was a mess."

I looked at him with concern. *What happened?*

"Ah, usual bullshit." He shook his head, tipped his face toward

the treetops. "You know how he's obsessed with mermaids, right? This morning he comes down with a bow in his hair and lipstick and one of Mom's old swimsuits, stuffed with ... stuff." Christian held his free hand in front of his chest. "Mom and I crack up, because it's adorable and hilarious. Dad just grunts, goes back to his iPad. But then Sebastian announces he's working on his costume for the mermaid parade."

I nodded. Kirby and Vanessa were still pressing me to sign up.

"I figure, okay. Mermaids are his thing," Christian said. "I tell him I'll take him down to Main Street as soon as registration's open." Christian shook his head again, every gesture weighted with sadness and frustration. "Dad goes, 'I don't think so. Boys *never* march in the mermaid parade,' yada yada. I fist-bump Sebastian anyway, tell him he'll be setting a new trend. Dad blows a gasket. The kid leaves the table with his dreams crushed, and the whole time, Mom doesn't say shit. He only stopped crying because I suggested the hike."

His hand tightened around mine, tension radiating in waves. I squeezed him back, held on tighter, fury rising as I thought of Sebastian at breakfast the other day. I'd hated the way his father had dismissed him so coldly, so flippantly. I never knew my mother, but Dad always reminded us how much she loved us, how much she wanted her six baby girls. He and Granna had gotten into some pretty knockdown battles over the years—how much freedom we should have, how much responsibility, how to teach us to be independent but not stubborn—but they never treated us like an afterthought.

Like a burden. Like an interruption of their otherwise perfectly busy lives.

"My parents acted like nothing happened," Christian said. "On our way out, Dad was all, 'Have fun today, boys. Enjoy the great outdoors for us.'"

Sebastian wasn't my child; he wasn't my brother. But I felt protective of him, of his innocence, his sweet intensity. I wanted to look out for him. To speak up for him when his own parents wouldn't.

I released Christian's hand, slipped the notebook and pen from my pocket. I wrote:

Not my business. But I'm saying it anyway.

"Wouldn't expect anything less," he said.

Why do people have kids if that's how they're going to treat them?

Christian sighed. "Yeah. That's a sob story for another day." With a soft smile Christian leaned close again, brushed my lips with a gentle kiss. "I'm—"

"Bombs away!" Sebastian stood on the path before us, hands covered in goop. Before either of us could react, he lobbed a giant mud ball, hitting Christian squarely on the side of his head. "Ten points!"

Sebastian vanished around the bend in a fit of devious giggles.

Next to me, Christian wiped mud from the corner of his mouth, his expression unreadable. It was the first time I'd seen him bested. I could barely hold back my laughter.

"Don't even laugh, Elyse, or I swear to God . . ." He turned on me, wrapping me in his arms. "You two conspiring against me?"

Before I could mouth a denial, his lips covered mine, smearing mud on my cheek, rubbing it in with extra enthusiasm. I finally squirmed out of his grasp, and together we took off in search of our little mud warmonger.

We found him hiding behind a tree, both hands locked and loaded. Christian and I dropped to the ground, narrowly escaping Sebastian's assault. Our victory was short-lived; we'd unknowingly crouched into a muddy trough, painting our pants with muck.

Christian gave me the side-eye. "You thinking what I'm thinking?"

Without hesitating, we scooped up as much mud as we could, then launched ourselves at Sebastian, tackling him to the ground. Soon the three of us were covered in mud and leaves and sticks and probably bugs. The Kane brothers rolled around next to me, both still trying to win, and I thought of my sisters, the trouble we'd get into on the farm when we were little, ducking through the trees as the workers shooed us away, making mud pies inside the discarded pods and pretending they were the latest and greatest chocolate creations from Tobago's world-renowned d'Abreau Cocoa Estates.

After the boys and I had soaked up all the mud in Oregon, we rinsed off as best we could at a water pump near the trail marker, and climbed up onto a large, flat boulder for a lunch of string cheese, apples, baby carrots, and trail mix. Sebastian ate all of the M&M's.

"I was thinking," Christian said. We were lying alone on the boulder with our eyes closed, drying out beneath a rare stretch of sunlight while Sebastian explored a grove up ahead. "That whole mud-wrestling thing? Maybe we could try it again later. Alone. Without clothes."

I rolled over to face him, smacked his shoulder playfully. *Keep dreaming, dirty boy.*

"Don't worry. I will." He tugged my arm lightly, pulling me against his chest. We stayed like that for a year, or maybe just a few minutes, and he played with the tangled curls in my hair, stroked my cheek while I pressed my ear to his damp shirt and listened to the steady, even beat of his heart.

"Christian! Elyse!" Sebastian called from the grove, excited. "Hurry!"

"Bad timing, squirt," Christian grumbled. But his smile was care-free and relaxed, and his body showed none of the tension I'd so often noticed when his parents were around.

We slid off the boulder and followed the sound of Sebastian's laughter, found him standing in the center of the grove. A single beam of sunlight penetrated the thick canopy above, and Sebastian was bathed in it, his arms stretched out in front of him.

On the chubby part of his forearm, two monarch butterflies perched, a pause on their journey through time.

Sebastian was trying to hold as still as possible, his face alight with wonder and pure, untarnished joy.

Time came to a standstill as Christian and I watched the monarchs in their tiny dance, lost in the music of Sebastian's laughter.

I tried desperately to grab on to the moment, to the feeling, to hold it in my heart. But beauty is by its very nature elusive, slippery.

A fragment, a flash.

Here and gone again.

The trees shuddered with my heart, and the clouds shifted, returning the forest to its misty gray.

The butterflies took flight.

One.

Then the other.

Sebastian remained still, his only word a whisper on the breeze. "Wow."

When I looked over at Christian, his mouth was open. By this rare moment, he'd been so captured, he'd forgotten to cover with a joke, a smirk.

There were tears in his eyes. The ocean rose inside him, and I looked away, before it got me, too.

Chapter 19

"Tears mean the tarot cards are doing their job," Lemon said gently. The group of women gathered in the gallery were enraptured. "There's no weakness in crying, Meredith. Only illumination."

As quietly as possible, I crept into the kitchen. It was dark by the time Christian and Sebastian had dropped me off, and now the gallery was lit with candles, golden light mingling with the full moon outside, dancing through the leaves of the sea glass tree.

Witchcraft afoot.

Lemon's coven met here monthly—the ladies liked working with the power of the sea, and Lemon had the closest access—but this time Mrs. Kane had joined them, along with another woman I recognized immediately as Mrs. James. She looked exactly like Vanessa, only blond instead of brunette, and older. The same warmth and confidence emanated from her smile.

"I should've been honest with him," Mrs. Kane said, drawing my attention back to the card reading.

"Maybe," Lemon said. "But there are a lot of layers there, a lot to sift through with your marriage. Right now it's more important to be honest with yourself. Honest about what you want, what you need, and where there's room for compromise."

"Can we ask the cards for specific instructions on that? A manual, maybe?" Mrs. Kane ran her fingers under her eyes, laughing through her tears. It reminded me of what Lemon had said about her soul, hiding there beneath the surface.

"There you are," Kirby called out from the hallway, scattering my thoughts. She and Vanessa crossed into the kitchen. "We've been texting you forever. It's ladies' night. Where were you?"

"And we know y'all weren't working today," Vanessa said, "since I ended up having a picnic lunch with an electrician. A cute one, but still. Spill it."

"What happened to your pants?" Kirby's eyes widened when she finally noticed the mud caked to my cargos. I'd rinsed what I could at the water pump and park restroom, but my clothes needed serious laundering, and the mud was hardening into the ends of my loopy hair like putty.

I took out my notebook.

Hike at Devils Elbow. Sebastian started a mud fight.

Kirby squinted at me, one hand on her hip. "What's with all the extracurriculars?"

Vanessa laughed. "Give the girl a break, Nosey Nelly."

"Me? You just told her to spill it."

"Because I relish the details, whereas you get all judgy."

"I'm just looking out for her. You know that boy is bad news. And now they're hiking? Mud fights? That's, like, the gateway drug to making out."

Hello! I waved my hands in front of her. *I'm right here.*

"Kirby, seriously. Loosen up!" Vanessa winked at me and said, "Anyway, you're here, mud queen, so come meet my mom—she's been bugging me all night. Gotta warn you, she's a little over the top. But she means well."

Ambushed by Vanessa and Kirby, official social committee of Atargatis Cove, I was powerless to resist. I let them lead me into the gallery, where Lemon's friends were consoling Mrs. Kane, offering further analysis on the tarot reading Lemon had just completed.

I wondered what the cards had told her. Hopefully something about sticking up for Sebastian. Or sticking up for herself, putting her husband in his place.

"Mom," Vanessa said. "Come meet Elyse."

Mrs. James turned away from the cards, her smile widening when she saw us. She approached with quick, intentional steps, and I could tell immediately that this was a woman who

spoke!

In!

Exclamation points!

"Elyse!" she said. "I've heard so much about you!" In one warm hand she crushed my fingers, gripping my arm with the other. "I'm so sorry we didn't get a chance to connect before now! Gosh, I hope you don't mind me sayin', but you're a real inspiration to us here at the Cove!"

I held my smile in place, but my shoulders sank. Once upon a time my voice had the power to bring people to tears. Now I was "a real inspiration" just . . . what? Standing here in muddy cargo pants? Breathing?

Much like my tight-lipped smile, Mrs. James's grip hadn't loosened, and she continued to ogle me with a mix of sympathy and awe. "You've just overcome so much! And—"

"Mom." Vanessa finally stepped in, disconnecting her mother's grasp from my arm and replacing it with her own. "Let's not make her a cause, okay?"

"Oh, don't exaggerate." Mrs. James's smile didn't dim a bit. "I'm just so pleased to meet you, Elyse. Vanessa speaks very highly of you, and I know Kirby thinks the world of you!"

Next to me, Kirby fidgeted. I felt a surge of affection for her, of appreciation. Yes, she had her judgments, made her assumptions, spoke for me more often than she let me try. But she was never disingenuous, never hid ill intent behind a fake smile or too-polished words. Despite my hot-and-cold routine, she never gave up on me. She looked out for me. Texted me. Included me. Tried.

In my time at the Cove, I'd spent many nights scribbling in my journal, attempting to write my way into a solution, into some kind of clarity and acceptance about what I'd lost and where I'd go from here. But maybe clarity was like love, shooting through you when you least expected it, when you'd finally stopped seeking it. Standing there in my mud-caked pants between Kirby and Vanessa, bathed in the glow of Mrs. James's overadoring but sincere smile, I suddenly remembered what it was like to *not* be shy and fragile and closed off. I remembered, because I *wasn't* those things, even now. But I'd been acting like it, like I needed Kirby to speak for me. Like I needed her protecting me.

I hadn't given her a reason to treat me otherwise.

All our time together, our close quarters and cohabitating toothbrushes, and I still hadn't let Kirby know the real me. Only the damaged one, the one who hid behind a scar and a whisper, the one who acted like there were no other options. Maybe that's what Mrs. James saw too.

I looked at my cousin, gave her my real smile. And when Lemon called out across the gallery, asking for the next woman who needed a little guidance from the universe, something sparked inside.

Kirby gave me an encouraging nod, and before anyone else could volunteer, I sat down across from Lemon, inhaled the spicy incense that floated in the air around her.

Lemon's baker friends, Kat and Ava, shifted over to make room, everyone's eyes on me and the cards that were soon to come.

Granna occasionally hired tarot readers from Trinidad, a bit of overplayed folklore to entertain the resort guests when Natalie and I needed a break from our song-and-dance routine. But late at night, long after the paying customers had turned in, the good rum came out, tongues and hearts loosened, and the women read—honestly, no gimmicks—for my sisters and the people who'd worked the harvest.

I'd never let them read my cards, though.

I'd smile, tell them I didn't want to know too much about my future. But I knew the cards weren't fortune-tellers. They were clarifiers, magnifiers. Illuminators. They dove into your heart, into your soul, and brought forth the things you were often so afraid to face. The things you most needed to face.

I'd gotten away with it so many times, my dismissive excuses. But the truth was as clear on those Tobago nights as it was now: I was afraid. Afraid they'd dig too deep.

Here at the edge of the Pacific, after hiding away for too long, maybe digging too deep was just what I needed.

Lemon smiled warmly, raised an eyebrow. "Remember, the cards never lie. Even when you want them to."

Heat shot through all the places that were suddenly—thanks in part to Christian—coming alive again. My lips especially burned, twin beacons that I was certain told the story.

I nodded anyway.

Lemon shuffled the deck. The cards were black, longer and narrower than regular playing cards, etched with gold crescent moons.

"This deck takes energy and inspiration from the moon. The images are a bit on the dark side, but sometimes we have to face our own darkness before we can find the light."

I gestured for her to continue.

"You may want some paper, so we can communicate about the card meanings," she said.

"On it." Kirby rose from her chair, retrieved my notebook and pen from the kitchen.

Around me the women in the gallery went silent.

"This card represents your recent past." Lemon drew the first card, laid it on the black cloth spread between us. "The Moon."

A huge silver moon dominated the face of the card, and from it an elderly couple dangled by puppet strings, marionettes dancing.

"The moon relates to our intuition, our deep feminine knowl edge," Lemon said. "It's turned up a few times tonight, unsurprisingly, given the full moon. But here it may be warning of self-deception. Of a time when you ignored your intuition."

I met her eyes, uncertain.

"Things are not always what they seem by the light of the moon. You have to be careful, and most importantly, honest with yourself. Trust your intuition, and don't lie to yourself." Lemon smiled gently. "This card is in your past, Elyse. It represents forces that are moving out of influence. It's important to consider, though, because it points to how the present situation came to be."

"The moon is speaking to all of us tonight," Mrs. Kane said. She smiled gently at me, the first genuine warmth I'd ever seen from her. If she brought her devices tonight, they were stowed in her purse. "Turned up in my present position."

"It was my future card," Mrs. James said. "I keep thinking it has to do with the house. There's something sleazy about these developers."

"I was hoping Terra would be here tonight to shed some light on Wes's plans," Mrs. Kane said. "Has anyone heard from her?"

"Not about this." Lemon shook her head. "If Wes is keeping secrets, she's as in the dark as we are."

Lemon and Kirby exchanged a glance weighted with sorrow, and Mrs. Kane sighed.

"It doesn't matter," Vanessa said in her easy-breezy way. "Elyse and Christian will win the regatta. The boat is lookin' good, too. Christian had an electrician fix up all the wiring."

"Really?" Mrs. Kane brightened. "I hadn't realized he'd hired someone. That's great news."

"I think it's wonderful that you're sailing, Elyse!" Mrs. James turned her big smile my way. "This town could use some shaking up."

The women laughed, and I wondered what they'd think about Sebastian marching in the mermaid parade. Seemed like all of us were on a mission to disturb the peace this summer.

"The moon is certainly powerful tonight," Lemon said, bringing everyone back on topic. "None of us is immune to its energy, especially so close to the sea." Lemon tapped the card. "Elyse, the moon can be illuminating, but only if you're willing to look beneath the surface. To look deep within, and be honest with yourself about your limitations as well as your abilities."

She flipped the next card, placing it to the right of the Moon. "This card represents you. The present. Where you are right now."

The card had no printed name, but I knew instinctively it was Death. On its face a pitch-black woman with a horse skull for a head stepped on a small child who looked as if he'd planned to climb between her legs, to crawl back into the womb. Dead things surrounded her, in the burned grass beneath her feet, the factory-polluted ocean behind. In the distance a tattered ship sank into the muck.

But in her rounded belly, new life grew. Was imminent.

"You're resisting," Lemon said. "A change has come upon you, yet, like the child at Death's feet, you're clinging to old ways, trying to go back." She met my eyes, silently asking permission to continue. She knew we were getting into personal territory here, and I appreciated her thoughtfulness. But I was in it, enraptured by the cards and whatever message they might unearth, and from the collection of witches and neighbors that surrounded me, I felt only support. Imperfect maybe, but real.

I nodded for her to go on.

"You cannot go back to the past, or resist this change. It's already come. But you can't move forward unless you acknowledge and accept it. Again, the Moon reminds you of the importance of self-reflection and self-honesty." Across from me, Lemon touched her throat, lingering on the place where, on my own skin, the silver scar burned. "The changes you endured back home were in many ways a death for you. Death of your old life, your old self. But death isn't an ending, Elyse. Just part of a longer journey. Death begets life, remember. One does not exist without the other."

I took a shuddering breath. The cards were so obvious, so right. I'd been holding on to the past, clinging to something that had long ago died. I'd been lying to myself about it. Trying to fill up my sea glass jar as if that accomplishment could reverse the clock, could make everything okay again. I wasn't simply trying to fool myself about the past—I was trying to go back there.

Lemon laid the next card sideways on top of the Death card, forming a small cross.

"This is the energy crossing you. It's the nature of what's preventing you from moving forward from Death, an obstacle in which both challenges and opportunities lie." She looked at the card. "The Two of Cups."

Even more so than Death, this card was captivating and bone-chilling. A naked woman, half-black and half-blue, leaned against the wall. She wore long black braids tipped in starlight, her breasts adorned with golden crescent moons. One hand held a glass of red wine, and the other spanned protectively across her abdomen. A skeleton, pale and gruesome and wrapped in bandages, leaned into her, one arm blocking her exit as he touched his wine glass to hers. Unlike the woman, whose nakedness left her vulnerable, the skeleton wore a fine red coat with gold

buttons. At their feet, his bandages twined around her ankle.

Blood had been spilled on the floor between them.

"What do you see?" Lemon asked, watching me write.

They made some kind of deal. But it didn't come easy. He has power over her.

I touched the skeleton on the card.

"I agree," Lemon said. "The skeleton is another representation of Death. In this case, he's struck a deal with Midnight. There's some kind of bargain here, but it's not clear who's got the upper hand. Death looks more physically powerful, but Midnight is more in touch with her intuition. It seems she has more knowledge, more wisdom. In your case, I feel like the cards are telling us that you're holding on to some obligation, some deal that you think you've made."

In the silence that followed, the candles flickered.

Death. A deal.

This card was about the sea. All the promises and warnings it had been whispering to me since the moment I was born. Since it stole my mother. Tried to steal me.

"Again," Lemon said, "I'm sensing a message about trusting your intuition. You're stronger than you think, and you've got to start believing that."

Next, I told Lemon, eager to move on.

"This represents your future," she said, "given the energy of the

other cards and what you decide to do with these messages. Essentially, what you're moving toward." She flipped the card and set it upright, just to the right of the cross.

The Queen of Cups featured an ebony-black queen enshrouded in robes of aqua, midnight blue, and deep purple, all trimmed in gold. Her outstretched hands held a golden chalice, as if in offering to a friend. She reminded me a bit of Granna, the wise matriarch.

I wrote in my notebook, letting the words come to me.

A helping hand from someone in a position of strength. Wisdom. Compassion. Friendship.

Lemon laughed. "You're pretty good at this, Elyse."

I smiled at the compliment.

"Cups correspond with the element of water, which symbolizes our relationships, our hearts, our inner beings. The Queen of Cups speaks to me of compassion, like you wrote," Lemon said. "See, she's offering the hand of friendship, of love. She's on stable ground, holding a cup of water to someone in need. But notice her bare feet? She can't cross the terrain to you. You need to meet her halfway. Basically, she's saying, 'Hey, girl! I'm here to help you through this journey, but only if you open yourself up to me.' Do you understand?"

I nodded. Friendship. Love. I was surrounded by both. Logically, I knew it. I saw it every day in the way Kirby looked out for me, and the way Vanessa made efforts to include me, and brought lunch

to the boat for me and Christian. I saw it in Christian, past the smirks and jokes, right there in the way he talked to me and let me respond in my own way, no matter how long it took. I saw it in Sebastian, his pure adoration and excitement. I saw it in Lemon, in the way she'd opened her home to me, given me the space and freedom to explore and breathe. But I was so scared to trust it. So afraid that opening myself up to all the Queen offered also left me vulnerable and exposed, naked on the shore. It was a loop I couldn't seem to break.

I knew I had to let go, to make way for new growth, as the Death card said.

I just didn't know how.

And as I'd learned from the readings back home, from my sisters asking the readers for more answers, more clarity, the cards wouldn't reveal it after all. The universe was great for dropping hints, but when it came time to do the heavy lifting, the hard work, that was all on us.

Meet her halfway, I thought, picking up the Queen for another look.

Two of my cards had ships in the background: the Queen of Cups and Death. Death's was sinking. The Queen's was sailing steadily in a beam of light from a nearby lighthouse.

Lemon winked at me across the cards, then rose from the table with the others, the party shifting into the kitchen to dig into the potluck dishes the women had brought.

Absently I scooped up the deck of unturned cards, shuffled them gently as I considered the reading. A card jumped loose, landing face up on my lap.

The World.

I studied it a long time, heart pounding in my chest. I'd never seen this card before, never even seen this deck before tonight. Yet I felt like I knew her, the woman at the center. She'd been haunting me. I'd seen her in my dreams, caught glimpses of her out on the horizon.

I knew, sure as she looked at me through a single, bright eye, it was her.

Atargatis.

Half-woman, half-fish, she perched atop the world with flaming candles in each hand, her body draped in blue silk. She was the queen who'd fallen to the sea from the sky in search of her lost love.

Once, she was made of starlight.

Now, she was water.

Surrounding her, a serpent devoured its tail.

Though she hadn't appeared in my official reading, she was speaking to me. Somehow I knew, before my time at the Cove came to an end, I'd have to face her.

Queen of the realm, above and below, within and without.

The in-between place where nothing and everything existed at once.

Chapter 20

"**Me time,** or just starin'-at-the-wall-'cause-there's-nothin'-else-to-do time?" Vanessa asked.

She and Kirby stood in my doorway after dinner a few nights later, Kirby freshly showered and robed, Vanessa wearing black skinny jeans and a silver off the-shoulder top, her long hair woven into a loose side braid.

Monday. Reggae night at the club.

I waved them in and plucked out the earbuds, offering what I hoped was a warm smile.

Vanessa flopped onto my bed, picked up the iPod. "Oboe concertos? Oh, honey bun. Looks like we got here just in time. Don't worry. We have a plan."

"*She* has a plan," Kirby said. "For the record, I told her you wouldn't be into it."

"Let the woman speak for herself," Vanessa said.

"But she—" Can't speak. That's what Kirby almost said. She let out a breath, met my eyes. "Sorry. I didn't mean it like that."

"She knows that, Kirby." Vanessa plowed on. "We haven't even given her a chance to make up her own mind." She grabbed my foot, gave it a shake. "Here's the deal. We're going to Shipwreck and you're coming with. Get dressed."

Kirby laughed. "That's letting her make up her own mind?"

"It's motivational," Vanessa said. "Positive thinking."

"It's a wonder you don't have a book deal."

"I'm sayin'. Anyway, come on. Decisions to be made." Vanessa rose from the bed and attacked the closet, whipping through the hangers like a woman on a mission. She found a cute red mini with a fringed hem, one I'd worn on nights out back home. I wasn't even sure why I'd brought it, but I hadn't been thinking clearly at the time. That night in Tobago, plane ticket in hand, packing was the very last thing that stood between me and my escape.

"I need a certain kind of top for this," Vanessa said. "But I'm onto something here." She disappeared into Kirby's room, and while she was gone, Kirby filled in the silence.

"Shipwreck," she said. "The club? There's a deejay from Portland spinning tonight. Everyone's going. And it's under-over, so you don't need ID. After the club we can stop at the Black Pearl for pancakes or eggs. Late night breakfast is an after-dancing tradition. So. Um. I know you don't like going out and everything, but . . . please come?"

"No one's gonna force you to do anything," Vanessa said, returning from Kirby's room with a handful of wardrobe options. "I mean, other than forcing you to come with us. Once we're there, you can mope on a velvet couch all night for all I care. But I'm gettin' you out of this house and off this rocky-ass beach if it's the last thing I do. You feelin' me?"

Kirby giggled. "Elyse doesn't swing that way. But Christian'll probably take you up on that offer."

Vanessa closed her eyes, sighed through her nose. "For a girl who's never been naked with a boy, you sure have a lot to say on the matter. Here, put this on." From the pile in her arms she tossed Kirby a slinky, forest-green number.

"That's a slip!" Kirby said.

Vanessa added a wide black belt. "Now it's a dress, and the color is perfect with your skin tone. And don't say you'll be cold, 'cause it's a hundred degrees in that club. Put it on, my little sex kitten."

Kirby sighed, but she'd warmed up to the slip-dress idea, and changed quickly out of her robe. When it was all put together, she spun before us. "Yea or nay?"

Vanessa was right; Kirby looked sexy. Still sweet, though, in her usual Kirby way. I gave her the thumbs-up and pointed at the wooden jewelry box on my dresser, full of necklaces and earrings I never wore anymore.

"Does this mean you're in?" Kirby asked, clasping a rhinestone choker around her neck. It looked perfect with the dress, picking up the deep green silk, sparkling against her light brown skin.

Alas, I shook my head. I flipped to a new page in my notebook, scribbled out my excuse for Kirby. At least today's was a new one, utterly original and true.

No. Christian's mad at me. I broke starboard window, total mess. Not enough $ to fix.

My insides burned with embarrassment as I tried to pantomime what happened. After we'd caught Noah snooping around the boat twice this weekend and again this morning, Christian had set up camp above deck, inspecting the *Queen's* ratty sails and keeping an eye out for the would-be pirate. He'd left me in charge below, a position I'd assured him I could handle.

But I'd had my earbuds in, Bella Garcia inspiring me to move-it-groove-it, don't-have-to-prove-it, and in all my eagerness to be the dancing, cleaning queen, I'd smashed right through the window with a wooden mop handle.

It was a brilliant mess, glass raining down over the saloon, Christian rushing in, panicked. Then confused. Then annoyed.

"Jesus," he'd said. "At this rate, we won't need Noah to sabotage us. We're doing fine on our own."

I tried to apologize, and he tried to accept it, but the tension in his shoulders gave him away. I couldn't blame him. It was one more thing that would have to be repaired, one more cost added to the seemingly endless list. And finding the right-size glass, along with replacement aluminum and rubber for the frame and seal—all of which I'd damaged? The Vega was almost fifty years old. It would take a lot of phone calls and drive time to find a marina shop that had what we needed. The electrical work had eaten through a good bit of our mystery fund, and from the looks of it, we'd be spending more cash on new ropes and patch-ups for the chafed sails.

We'd finished out the day in awkward silence. Christian had been distracted from the moment he'd arrived, and that made me distracted. Did he regret the kisses? The time we'd spent together on and off the boat? Or was he thinking about his family, his father? Was he worried about the regatta? Upset about Noah? Did something else happen with Sebastian?

As easily as I could read his body language, his thoughts were always veiled, and once again I'd been left wondering who he really was, this boy who loved his brother fiercely, this boy who Kirby had so warned me against, this boy who alternately made me laugh and made me doubt, this boy who wore the sea in his eyes.

When he'd finally called it quits for the day, I skipped the salute that had become our good-bye. I just made myself scarce.

Part of me had hoped he'd follow. Or call after me. Or grab my hand, give me a reassuring squeeze and that heart-melting smile.

But he didn't, and when I glanced back over my shoulder one last time, he was standing on the deck, his foot up on the coaming as he stared out across the sea.

"I'm sure he knows it was an accident," Kirby said now.

"What was an accident?" Vanessa asked. After Kirby explained, Vanessa said, "Oh, I doubt he's mad. But even if he is, he'll take one look at you in this outfit, and all will be forgiven. Trust me." She pressed the red skirt to her hips, holding up a sleeveless white fitted blouse with black buttons down the front. She was right; the outfit looked cute. Hot, even. Especially if I borrowed Kirby's strappy silver sandals . . .

"You're in," Vanessa said. "I can see it all over your face. Yay!"

I wasn't sure what I was doing, only that the girls were right—maybe I needed to get off this rocky beach, get a change of scenery. I dressed quickly, let Vanessa do my eye makeup. On her advice I left my hair wild, my crazy curls stretching up toward the night sky.

"Wow," she said when all was said and done. The three of us stood in front of the bathroom mirror, arms linked, lips glossed and glowing, a trio of beautiful mermaids. "Eat your hearts out, summer boys."

It had been a long time since I'd set foot in a club—never in the States—and though they'd talked it up the entire thirty-minute drive here, I wasn't expecting it to be so legit. The space was dark but inviting, deep blue walls lit with turquoise sconces, strobe lights over the dance floor. It felt like an underwater lair, cool and otherworldly as bass pumped into the night.

We found a couch and table in the back and ordered a few sodas while we waited for Christian and Noah. When the boys finally arrived twenty minutes later, it was as if the entire club had been awaiting their grand entrance, everyone parting to let them pass, girls smiling, the energy in the room rising.

Noah nodded when he saw us, making his way through the crowd, but Christian hung back, looking everywhere but at us. I watched him scan the room, but he was only pretending—his eyes landed on no one, nothing. When a girl snuck up behind him and put her hands over his eyes, he looked startled and distracted. He grabbed her arms playfully, pulled her in front to identify her.

Calla, the girl who'd texted him at the Black Pearl that day with the milkshakes, dragged him into a dance. I couldn't tell if he was into it or just playing along.

My stomach knotted again as I recalled our day of disaster on the boat. I couldn't watch him any longer, couldn't deal with the summer girls and his mysteriously raging sea-eyes and his there-and-gone smile. I set my drink on the table, headed for the ladies' room.

I spent a good ten minutes at the sink, washing my hands, redoing my lip gloss, watching the exchange of sparkly girls pass through the door. Finally, I caught Vanessa's reflection in the mirror. She sauntered over, put her arm around me.

"You're hidin' out," she said to the glass. "And I couldn't help but notice that your whole duck-and-cover act started the moment Christian walked in. What's up?"

I shrugged, stared at the sink.

"Elyse, if you don't want to share, that's one thing. Tell me to mind my business. But don't be in here actin' like it's fine. I got a sense for this stuff."

Christian, I finally mouthed at the mirror.

"Christian what?" she said. When I didn't respond, she grabbed my shoulders gently, turned me toward her. "Listen, hon. I know Christian really well. And the boy's got issues, yeah. But he likes you. Okay? You've got nothin' to worry about. Just be you."

I shrugged again. I knew he had issues. But I wasn't so sure about the liking me part. Which would've been fine if I hadn't already liked him.

A lot.

"Are you worried about Calla?" Her eyes were full of concern. "Because I promise you he's not into her. She's already dancin' with someone else, anyway."

My heart sped up. I had to tell someone my secret, and as much as I wished it could be Kirby, I couldn't handle her freaking out on me tonight. I took a deep breath, steadied myself for the confession.

Christian and I . . . we . . .

I let the words fade away, unformed.

No. I couldn't tell Vanessa, either. No matter what she said about Christian liking me, I couldn't admit to kissing him, to liking him as much as I did. I still didn't even know how she felt about him.

Or how he felt about her.

Maybe I didn't even want to know.

I met her eyes again, surprised to see her devilish grin.

"I know you guys have been kissin' and whatnot, honey bun."

A spark shot through my insides, chasing away the denial my lips wanted to form. Christian told her? Was he happy about it? Or annoyed? Did he want to kiss me again?

Was Vanessa jealous? Upset?

I waited for her to say more, but I knew she wouldn't betray his confidence. Or her own.

"All the more reason you should be out there instead of in here." Vanessa smirked. "By the way, our little Kirby's finally gettin' her groove on with Noah. I knew that outfit would unleash her inner goddess."

I let out a raspy laugh, nodded to let her know I was okay.

Maybe she was okay too.

She looped her arm through mine and led me back out, the music and lights assaulting us anew as we stepped into the fray.

Vanessa was so comfortable in her own skin. Large and in charge, Granna would've called her.

Hands in the air and a sultry smile on her lips, Vanessa glided through the crowd. Past the couches, past the bar, she reached back for my hand, pulled me onto the dance floor where the sounds of the Caribbean called.

They were playing Bunji Garlin. A song from home.

The crowd roared.

The deejay tossed glow-in-the-dark necklaces into the mob, outstretched hands catching and twirling them in the air.

There were so many things about the past I'd been trying to out-run, an anchor I'd carried for months without ever really escaping.

There were things about the future that scared the hell out of me too—big impossible things I wasn't ready to think about.

But the energy around me surged and sizzled in a way it never could when I was dancing alone on the beach, and I felt it, way down to the bones. Right here, right now, for the first time since I'd lost my voice, I let it all go.

There was no lost singing career. No family drama. No Prop 27. No regatta. No heartache. No guilt about my sister. No fear.

There was this: my hands in the air next to Vanessa and Kirby, our bodies shimmering and shaking, curls wild and electric, our mermaid hearts on fire in the deep blue sea of the club.

I closed my eyes, let the music pulse through my blood, fill my soul.

The deejay played on and on, an entire Caribbean mix, Bunji Garlin and Alison Hinds and the wining queen, Denise Belfon. When Bella Garcia belted out the opening words of "Work Ya Way Back," I was in a full-on wine myself, rolling my hips, twisting and turning, all the old moves coming back even stronger than they had on the beach, infused again by the energy of the eager crowd. Like me, they'd been charged up by the music, the kind that made it impossible not to dance, not to feel it, not to move and be moved.

This is mine, I thought. Music. Rhythm. The intense rush that came from connecting with something so deeply, so right. No matter that I couldn't sing. I could breathe. I could dance. I could move. The music was still in me. It always would be.

When I finally opened my eyes, heart pounding madly with the beat, Christian stood before me. Wordlessly we held each other's gaze as the air between us evaporated. Christian's hands landed warm on my hips, thumbs grazing the skin that peeked out beneath the hem of the blouse. I wrapped one arm loosely around his neck, the other waving at my side, keeping my balance as my sway deepened.

Again I heard that word in my head . . . *safe* . . . and I closed my eyes, letting the beat run deeper into my muscles and blood and heart and bones, a familiar twining of soul and music, guiding me across the dance floor. Christian kept pace, moving toward me and away, his body swiveling but his hands never leaving my hips. Warmth gathered between us like a living thing, something that pulsed and glowed and tethered us together. I moved in closer, and his hands slipped to my back, pressed out the last sliver of light between us.

For a time we were no longer in Oregon, dancing in a club in the damp northernmost curve of Atargatis Cove. We were underwater, the very bottom of the sea where impossible things bloomed, and with all the naked boldness of the Pacific, I stood on my toes and pressed my lips to Christian's neck, savoring the hot, saltwater taste.

His arms around me tightened, and deep inside, everything stirred anew.

The dance mix finally ended, and our arms dropped. I pulled away, opened my eyes. Christian was watching me with new intensity, eyes wild with barely checked desire, but still he didn't speak, and as we quietly made our way to the bar for waters, I knew he wouldn't. Neither of us would speak of it, this momentary thing between us, this passion that had risen up like a wave, crashing against the sand, only to be sucked back out to sea.

Alone in my room later, wrapped in nothing but a T-shirt and cool white sheets, I closed my eyes and let the sounds of the ocean overtake me. For miles north and south, waves lashed the shore, ravishing the coastline, and something deep within—something long buried, forbidden—crept out from the darkest places in me. I thought of Christian, and with one hand between my thighs, sighed his name hot and damp into the night.

I still felt his warm hands on my hips. I imagined them roaming my body, slipping beneath my shirt, and my own hands made it so. I caressed my breasts slowly, one then the other, felt my nipples rise beneath the touch of cool fingers. With eyes closed tight, I let my hands drift down my belly. And maybe it was a dream, and maybe it was a fantasy I invited as I lost myself in the nearly forgotten ecstasy of music and dance, but one thing was certain: The scorch of Christian's desirous gaze set my skin aflame; the ghost of his touch would not soon leave me.

For that secret night and many more after, as my fingers slipped inside me and found their own pulsating rhythm, I was grateful no one could hear the sound that otherwise would've passed my lips, a moan as deep as creation, a howl as loud as the sea.

Twenty minutes later Vanessa showed up, Sebastian in tow, dressed to scrub. And despite the fact that she'd spent the previous night dancing and flirting with Noah, even Kirby answered our SOS, strolling down the docks in a headscarf, overalls, and rubber gloves up to her elbows.

It took us all day to clean up the mess. I suggested taking the remaining fish parts back to their owner, dumping them into the *Never Flounder*, but Christian was cooking up a different plan.

Christian said it was best to wait a few days to wage a retaliation, let the other guy think he was in the clear.

This morning, five days after the fish attack, we made our move.

"Piracy rule number one," Christian said on the drive to the pet store. "Pirates don't acknowledge the piracy to the pirate. When we see Katzenberg, it's like this never happened."

I nodded.

"Rule number two," Sebastian said. He was sandwiched between Kirby and Vanessa in the backseat, his white blond hair blowing all around. "Pirates don't need baths. Pirates are stinky on purpose."

Christian met his eyes in the rearview. "Overruled. If you want to camp out tonight, you're getting hosed down first. I'm not sharing a tent with a skunk."

Sebastian giggled. "You're the skunk!"

Christian navigated us into the pet store lot. He winked at me and got out of the truck, leaving it running with the rest of us inside. Ten minutes later he was back with the crickets. Boxes and boxes of them.

Chapter 21

"Who would've thought one little bug could make so much noise?" Vanessa peeked through the cage of her fingers at the cricket she'd just captured. "We're gonna be findin' them everywhere for weeks."

The morning after our club outing, Christian and I had arrived at the *Queen of* to find her filled with buckets of raw, chopped fish—an impressively disgusting feat that Noah must've stayed up all night to accomplish. The stench alone would've been enough to warrant pirate retaliation, but thanks to my shattered window, a dozen gulls had snuck in, lining up to feast.

"Gives new meaning to the phrase 'poop deck,' anyway," Christian had said. The sight was so incredibly awful, all we could do was laugh. With one hand on my shoulder, through tears of hilarity that teetered on insanity, Christian shouted at the sea. "Katzenberg! You pirate!"

The two of us had sat on the docks then, texting for reinforcements.

"I grabbed whatever they had," he said, securing them in the trunk. "Told them it was for Sebastian's pet python."

"I don't have a python." Sebastian's eyes lit up. "*Can* I get a python?"

Christian laughed. "Dude. We're *definitely* not sharing a tent with a snake."

Back at the marina we all gave the boat another scrubdown—the fish smell had yet to vacate, despite copious amounts of bleach—and then Vanessa went to pick up lunch for us at the Black Pearl, just to confirm Noah would be tied up at work for the next few hours. Coast clear, Christian and I snuck onto the *Never Flounder*, crickets in hand.

We opened the boxes, shook out the bugs.

With a wicked gleam in his eyes, Christian said, "Welcome to the apocalypse, Katz."

Now, hours after our cricket adventures, the girls and I were hanging out in my room, listening to a country mix Vanessa insisted was all the rage in her Lone Star State. I'd intended to curl up alone, finish *Moby Dick*, but they'd followed me in as though we'd always been friends, as though my bedroom had always been our hangout.

"Crickets won't *totally* mess up Noah's boat, right?" Kirby asked. "I know he deserves it after the fish thing, but he's under a lot of pressure with his dad, and he's trying to—"

"Kirby." Vanessa released the cricket out my window and reclaimed her spot on the fluffy carpet. "Don't fall apart on us now. We did the right thing."

"But . . . you guys. It's *Noah*." Her shoulders slumped.

"Yeah, and it's the Pirate Regatta," Vanessa said. "Your house is on the line, Kirbs. Get in the game!"

Kirby nodded reluctantly. "I know. It's just . . . What can we really do? Even if Elyse and Christian win—"

"*When* they win," Vanessa said.

"If, when. The mayor will just come up with some other stupid bet. If Mr. Kane really wanted to keep the house, he would've said no from the start. All this boat stuff, the pirate games? We're just prolonging the inevitable. Face it." Kirby brushed tears from her eyes. "The tides, as they say, are a-changin'."

"Times," Vanessa said. "The song is *times*, not tides."

Kirby rolled her eyes. "*Everything* is a-changin'."

The girls fell silent. Kirby was right. Everything was a-changin', and not just this business with the Cove. Regardless of what happened with the house, after this summer Kirby would finish out her senior year, then head off to college. Vanessa was spending next year in South America, eager for a few backpacking adventures before making any decisions on college and career tracks. Noah had dreams of buying the Black Pearl, but who knew if that place would even exist after P&D got done. And in a couple of months Christian would be back at Stanford, then on to some big, bright future, the map of his life created, curated, and perpetually sponsored by his father.

Me? Maybe I'd linger here with Lemon. Maybe my visa would expire, and I'd be forced to return to Tobago, forced to serve drinks to the resort tourists who didn't require friendly local conversation. But no matter what I did, where the tides swept me next, all of it would change again. Even if I stayed exactly right here, right on this bed in this room in this big house by the sea, the tide would carry in the sands, one grain at a time, until the house and I were swallowed up, sucked back out to sea.

"Well, this is pathetic." Vanessa blew a breath into her bangs. She switched up the mix on the iPod, picked out some old-school British rock to amp up the mood. "New topic? Anyone got any juicy gossip, particularly about cute boys named Noah?"

Kirby shot her a scolding glare. "Speaking of cute boys, whatever happened to that guy you were kissing at the bonfire? You two totally took off. And then you never said another word."

Vanessa laughed. "I'm shocked it took you this long to bring it up. Over a week? New record for you, Kirbs."

"So what's the deal? Fourth of July weekender, trolling the beach for kisses from beautiful girls?"

"Oh, there was more than kissin', sugar." Vanessa wiggled her eyebrows.

Kirby looked scandalized. "You didn't even know the guy!"

"His name was Vince. Or . . ." She wrinkled her nose, concentrating. "Vance? Vaughn? Definitely something with a *V*."

"Like you know *anything* about a *V*." Kirby shook her head. "Vanessa, God knows I love you, but you can't just have sex with every guy you meet. What about, like, consequences?"

"Kirby. Not everyone ends up pregnant or with some disease. You just . . . you take precautions. You know?"

Kirby frowned. "You can't put a condom on your heart."

Vanessa exploded into laughter. "Okay, that needs to be on a T-shirt."

Kirby was laughing too, but she was still doing her mom thing. "You guys know that saying, though, right? Why buy the cow when you can get the milk for free?"

"Who says the cow is even for sale?" Vanessa looked at her breasts and smiled. "Why sell the cow when you can go get milked for free?"

"Oh. My. God." Kirby was genuinely concerned about this milk situation. When she saw me grinning, her eyes got even wider. "You too?"

I shrugged. *Ex-boyfriend.*

"She tell you about the candy box?" Vanessa asked me.

"Vanessa!" Kirby turned purple.

I nudged her foot with mine. *I know,* I mouthed. Lemon had shown it to me my first night here, a box tucked into the linen closet of the bathroom Kirby and I shared, once made for a sampler of cheap American chocolates, now holding only condoms. "I never count them," Lemon had said. "They're just in there, whenever anyone needs them. If I notice it's getting low, I'll refill it. No questions."

"Candy boxes, ex-boyfriends, friends with benefits." Kirby sighed. "Am I the only one around here who's still—"

"Yes," Vanessa said playfully. To me, she said, "Now I wanna know the story about the ex-boyfriend. Cute? Or jerk-off?"

"Jerk-off," Kirby said. "Otherwise he wouldn't be an ex. Right?"

For once, Kirby's answer on my behalf was correct. I flung a pillow at her anyway.

"Girls!" Lemon appeared in the doorway, saving me from miming my way through that particular tale. She was lugging a large box, which she set on the floor with a grunt. "Each of you is free to make your own decisions with boys, as long as the cow and the farmer and everyone involved is consenting. But please try to keep the squealing to a minimum. I'm sketching a new sculpture for commission and I need to concentrate." She toed the box, smiling at me. "Elyse, package from Granna. Careful opening it, though—I think there may be a few stowaways. Suddenly I'm finding crickets everywhere."

In the wake of another wave of giggles from Kirby and Vanessa, Lemon padded back to her reading nook, the spot where she liked to do her sketching. Kirby helped me drag the box closer to the bed, where we sat down together and yanked off the packing tape, express from Trinidad and Tobago.

Vanessa peered inside.

Granna had sent a case of d'Abreau Estates fine chocolate in every variety—dark, milk, cinnamon, and a new blend they'd just released with orange peel and hibiscus. There was another postcard from Dad and the few sweaters I'd owned on the island, most of which were thin or crocheted, ill suited for chilly Pacific Northwest nights.

"Is that from your farm?" Vanessa eyed the chocolate stash.

Dig in, I mouthed. She tore into the case, fanned out the

rainbow-wrapped bars on the bed. She decided on the cinnamon flavor, and I watched with breathless anticipation as she took her first bite.

Her nose crinkled, then smoothed, eyes wide as the chocolate melted on her tongue.

"Oh, holy orgasmic hell!" She took another bite. "I get it. I totally get it. Consider me a convert."

Kirby picked out an milk chocolate bar, and I took a dark one, settling back on the floor with Vanessa. There were still a few more items in the box—the fairy-tale books I'd asked Granna to send for Sebastian, more clothes—but good chocolate took priority.

"What's it like there?" Vanessa wanted to know, her mouth full of chocolate bliss.

I opened one of the books, showed her some of the illustrations. An island of lush, green trees. Dark, green-blue seas. Generations of families fishing in the villages, grilling the day's catch as the sun dipped below the horizon. It was the idealized tourist version, but the truth nevertheless, and my heart ached with homesickness.

"I want to go back," Kirby said. "I've only been once, and I was mostly too cool for school to hang out with Mom back then. I didn't really appreciate it."

I smiled, imagining what it would be like to show her around now that we were old enough to do it on our own. The Heritage Festival was coming up soon in Tobago, with all kinds of celebrating and dancing and food. I'd take her to the Ole Time Wedding in Moriah, or treasure hunting in Pirate's Bay. Definitely the Sea Festival in Black Rock—we'd fill up on bake and shark, saltfish buljol, kingfish in coconut sauce, peas and rice, all the chocolate tea we could drink.

We'll go, I told her, the words out before I could stop them. *Someday.*

I closed the book, tossed it back on the bed with the chocolate wrappers. For a moment no one spoke, and I thought maybe she'd ask me more about the islands. About what it was like growing up there. About how my parents met in Trinidad, like hers had, and how Dad had moved us to Tobago after my mother died. I thought she'd ask about my sisters. About all the rehearsals, the competitions Natalie and I sang in. The music we'd made.

But Kirby, ever worried that too much talk of home would churn up bad memories for me, didn't ask. Maybe talk of the islands churned up bad things for her, too. Like the father she never knew. Kirby hadn't mentioned him again, not since her last visit, and I hadn't asked.

I smiled at her now. We were still getting to know each other. New friends. Closer than friends. Maybe that wasn't such a bad thing.

"Speaking of holy orgasmic hell," Kirby said to Vanessa, smoothly changing the subject. "What does Christian say about Bonfire Guy?"

"Christian?" Vanessa said. "He knows better than to get in my business. He's got his own business to mind."

My insides twisted. I still didn't know the exact nature of Christian and Vanessa's relationship, but they were definitely tight, definitely had a history. Whenever we were hanging out in a group where other guys were around, like at the bonfire that night, Christian was protective of her. They shared inside jokes, casual hugs, glances loaded with meaning that only the two of them could decipher. She hadn't seemed bothered by the fact that Christian and I were getting physically close—in fact, she acted like she was all for it—but she hadn't offered up any details on their past, either.

Not that I'd asked her.

I still had a lot to learn about this new friends thing.

Vanessa swallowed the last of her chocolate, licked her fingers clean. "You guys, Christian and I . . . we made out a few times. But it's not like we ever *did* it. Not even close."

Kirby rolled her eyes.

"I'm serious," Vanessa said. "We're just friends. Capital-*F* friends."

Kirby shook her head. "But you two are *supergood* friends. Like, communicating-with-just-a-look good friends. *And* you have a physical thing going on."

"Had. We had a physical thing. But no. It wasn't even a thing. It was just kissing. Just . . . something to do sometimes? It never meant anything more than fun."

"Then why aren't you together?" Kirby asked. "You have fun fooling around. You're great friends. What's missing? Why is he such a player?"

I bit into my chocolate, tried not to squirm, tried not to think of all the kisses he'd left on my lips, burning a trail to my heart. As passionate as they were, as blazing hot, they still hadn't been enough to make me presume anything between us. To make me think he wanted anything more than fun. We hadn't even been alone since discovering Noah's fish prank—Vanessa and Sebastian had shown up every day after that to help, and we worked so hard on those days that the nights left little energy for socializing. Even his texts were mysterious; morning messages were usually just boat details, but nightly for weeks he'd messaged me those two simple words: "sweet dreams."

For all I knew, Christian was just biding his time until I was ready for the "grand tour." Or maybe he'd been spending his nights grand-touring with other girls. Calla. Gracie. Jessica Boltz. The endless tide of summer girls who'd watched him at the marina, at the café, on the beach, dancing at the club.

I closed my eyes, tried to picture something else. Starfish. Seagulls. Mermaids. Boats. Tattoos. Christian.

All roads lead back to Christian Kane.

I opened my eyes, inhaled some more chocolate.

"We talked about it," Vanessa said. "But we both agree we're strictly friend zone. I mean, we're so different, we want different things out of life, all that. Like, I've always been more . . . some might call it opinionated."

Kirby cracked up, pointing at Vanessa with half a chocolate bar. "Understatement."

"I blaze my own trail, Mom says. And Christian's just . . . well, all that stuff with his daddy." She waved her words away, clearly not wanting to air the Kane family secrets. "We're just different that way."

I thought about what Christian had said that night of our first kiss, about not having a plan A. He'd told me he'd always followed the path his father had set out for him, and maybe Vanessa was right—he hadn't blazed his own trail. But like so many other things, that, too, was changing. I sensed it that night after the bonfire, the way he'd looked at me after reading my "Plan B" poem. The way his eyes smoldered when I'd asked him what he wanted.

Maybe there was something about Christian that Vanessa didn't know. Something new and young, just breaking out from the darkness into the light. And I'd been there to see it. The first one. The only one.

I pulled my knees to my chest, wrapped myself in a hug.

I thought of Christian's strong arms around me in Devils Elbow. His lips skimming my jaw, my neck. . . .

"We're close, definitely," Vanessa said. "But we don't have that spark, you know?"

"What spark?" Kirby asked.

Vanessa pressed her hand to Kirby's abdomen. "You know that gooey, falling-down feeling you get, right about here, when you're dancin' with Noah?"

Kirby pushed Vanessa's hand away, but she couldn't hide her smile.

"*That* spark," Vanessa said.

"So you don't get jealous about the other girls?" Kirby asked. "I get crazy jealous when Noah even *smiles* at a customer. And he's just doing his job!"

"Told you." Vanessa shrugged. "Nothin' to be jealous of."

Kirby considered this, then looked at me. "What if he hooked up with Elyse?"

Vanessa caught my eyes. I recognized the look instantly; it would pass between my sisters whenever they were talking about something Dad or Granna wasn't supposed to know.

Slowly I shook my head. No, I hadn't told Kirby anything about what was going on between me and Christian. I didn't even know if there *was* anything, really, and I didn't want to get her worked up over something that might not even exist.

With her eyes still locked on mine, Vanessa said, "Maybe a little." It surprised me—both the admission itself, and the matter-of-factness of her tone. "She's the only one who makes him smile that for-real smile of his. I haven't seen it so much since we were kids. And now, every time he says her name, it's like the damn sun is risin'."

This time it was my smile that wouldn't hide.

"Just remember, Elyse." Vanessa grabbed my hands, her face etched with concern. She took a deep breath, let it out slowly. "You can't put a condom on your heart."

This set everyone to laughing again, and inside, I felt something loosen. Warm. It was another ember, small but sparking to life again, and I held on to it, made it glow.

"What else did you get?" Vanessa crawled back over to Granna's box, took out the rest of the fairy-tale books. There was a letter from Granna too; Vanessa handed me a thick, white envelope. I tossed it on the bed to read later, in private.

"Oh. My. Silky. Stars." Vanessa's mouth hung open as she pulled a length of fabric from the box and stripped off its plastic dry-cleaning bag.

She rose to her feet, let the silk flow down the length of her, swirled with gossamer silver thread and delicate beading. It shimmered like moonlight on the water.

The dress.

It was the deep, midnight blue of the far-off ocean, the blue that lured explorers to seek out the world's oldest secrets, the blue that turned black in the shadows and bright as the Caribbean Sea in the sun.

There was only one other like it in the world. It belonged to my sister Natalie.

Granna had ordered them, custom-made for Carnival last March. She'd been waiting for us in the dressing room that day, smile as proud and excited as I'd ever seen it.

"This is it," she'd told us. "A shot at your dreams." Behind her a sheet like a white sail billowed over a clothing rack. She untied the ropes; the sail slipped to the floor. And the dresses, twin mermaids, shone before us.

With our hair in luscious waves, swirls of the sea painted on our glowing brown skin, Natalie and I dressed in silence.

"My beautiful singing mermaids," Granna said. "Today you take the world by storm."

Natalie twined her fingers with mine, the tremble of excitement faint beneath her skin.

"Are you ready?" she whispered, and I squeezed her hand once, so proud of her, so grateful that of all my sisters, she was my twin, my shared heart, my shared dream.

"Yes, love," I said. "I am ready...."

"This is almost as gorgeous as you are," Vanessa said now. It came out in a whisper, the kind reserved for great works of art or monuments or memorials.

The dress was a bit of each.

The last time I'd felt its cool silk against my thighs, I had an entire brilliant life ahead of me.

Yes, love. I am ready....

I froze as the memories washed over me, slow at first, then all at once, and my throat tightened. The dress was a time capsule, everything my old life was supposed to be.

All the potential.

All the promises.

All the failures, fate's cruelest twist.

Afresh, the sharp swords of the past pierced my heart.

Chapter 22

"Elyse!" Lemon flung open my bedroom door, tears in her eyes, and I rushed back to the present. Three in the morning, Atargatis Cove. Disjointed, disintegrated. "Were you . . . I thought I heard . . . singing?"

The sound of my voice—my old voice, the old me, rich and buttery and beautiful enough to give anyone chills—floated in the air, but my lips were closed. The laptop sat on my bed next to the mermaid dress, the video of my final performance looping.

Whoever shot this version had put it on YouTube. It had more than a million views, hundreds of thousands of likes.

"Okay, baby. Okay." Lemon sat on the bed next to me, gathering me in her arms. "Don't try to avoid this pain. You've gotta feel it."

I thought about the sharp rocks at Thor's Well, spilling my blood into the mouth of the sea.

I wondered if Lemon really believed that pain was necessary.

Everything in me hurt so much, I didn't even know what was real. Did it hurt now? Or was it just a memory of hurt?

Soon after I'd first been told I'd never speak again, never sing, likely never utter a sound greater than a hoarse whisper, I decided I didn't believe them. I was so certain I'd beat the odds, find a way to heal through sheer will alone. I spent my mornings with private tutors, finishing school from home. In the afternoons, I listened to my favorite music for hours, drank hot tea and honey, rested, followed the doctors' orders precisely.

One month. That's how long it took before I *really* freaked out. I was so angry, so filled with rage. But when my body tried to scream, I felt only pain. Emptiness. A raw, tearing ache, again and again and again.

I was still angry when I'd come to the Cove, still filled with confusion and resentment and fear and grief. I'd feel the frustration surge up in all the little things, like finding a funny video online and wanting to call Kirby over to check it out, only I'd have to get up and go look for her, physically touch her to get her attention. Things like knocking on the table to ask someone to pass the salt. Repeating my words, again and again, while people stared at my lips, trying to make sense of them, more often than not ending the conversation because it was easier than deciphering.

But those were the easy targets, the healthy ones. I could channel the frustration and anger there, let it simmer, watch it bubble over in my bed at night as I clutched my pillows and begged the tears to come.

They never did. But it was better than thinking about the *real*

damage. The fact that losing my voice meant losing my future. My dreams. My plan A, plan B, all the way to plan Z. For me there was never anything but singing, never anything but traveling the stages of the world, my beautiful sister at my side.

It'd been more than four months since I lost my voice. All things considered, I thought I was doing okay. Maybe Granna didn't think so. Or Dad, or my older sisters, or Granna's nosey neighbors, or the island therapists everyone had wanted me to see.

But these last few weeks at the Cove? The time I've spent with Christian on the Vega, fixing up that old boat? Getting to know him and Sebastian, Kirby, Vanessa, Lemon?

I'd almost thought it was possible to be happy again. Not now, but in the someday-maybe haze of tomorrow.

Even without a voice.

Granna's package undid all of that.

After Vanessa found the dress, I'd made up some excuse, some sudden headache and exhaustion, ushering them out with extra chocolate. Desperate for an explanation, I'd opened the letter.

There was a video message from my sister, a clip she'd recorded onto a thumb drive, slipped inside the envelope. I could only watch a few seconds of it before turning it off, my sister teary-eyed and concerned, wanting to tell me some big important news that I just didn't want to hear.

Granna knew I wouldn't watch it through. That's why she'd sent the letter too. It was their plan B.

Elyse, that Bella Garcia? She thinks Natalie has real poten-tial. Maybe she can make it big.

Natalie.

With a solo career. That's what the lady say.

My sister, twin dream maker, best friend, the harmony to my melody.

This is some good news for her, first in a long while.

A solo career. Solo. Career.

Natalie is going on tour with Bella Garcia, just like she always talked about.

Just like *we* always talked about. Until we didn't, because one of us couldn't. Now Natalie was going to see the world without me. Our package deal, repackaged for her alone. Solo.

It was as if I'd slipped underwater all over again, some great weight dragging me under like an anchor. Granna's words echoed in my head, over and over and over and over.

There were no words to make this okay, no declarations or appease-ments to make this right.

I was a bad person. Horrible, not to be happy for my sister. Not to be supportive.

Singing lessons on Bella's recommendation were one thing, but hearing that Natalie was going on tour without me, after every-thing . . .

Deeper the swords pierced.

Ripped out.

Stabbed again.

Sliced and carved and bled.

I thought maybe, you seeing your dress again, you could remember.

The last time I wore it, I was singing with my sister, singing for our future.

How much it means to her, this opportunity. How special this is.

Singing for our lives. Our hearts. That single soul Granna so believed we'd shared.

I know this is hard, baby. But it's hard for Natalie, too. She wants to share this joy with you.

As we once shared everything else.

I know you love her, Elyse . . . you miss her like she miss you.

As easy as the words had come to Granna—support your sister, be happy for her—I knew it was hard for her too. I knew it hurt Granna and Dad and my older sisters that I hadn't spoken to Natalie, that I couldn't share in my sister's joy. That our family was down by a sister, that I'd taken refuge in another country. Save for a few Skype sessions, I'd effectively cut myself off.

All of this I could see. I could write it down, underline all the mistakes I'd made, highlight my faults.

Maybe it was selfish.

Maybe it was normal.

I didn't think to ask permission.

I just wished that one time, someone on the island of Tobago, someone rocking on the front porch of the main house of d'Abreau Cocoa Estates, someone lying on the *Atlantica* under the blue moon, someone practicing all of our old songs in front of the bedroom mirror, someone someone *someone* knew how hard it was for me. That they'd give me one word of acknowledgment, one moment of space, one bit of understanding as to why this whole thing might hurt. Why I might need time, an undetermined amount.

On a shelf above my bed sat my sea glass jar. The one I'd kept in the Vega. The one I'd stopped filling. Not because I'd stopped treasure hunting with Lemon, but because I'd forgotten about it.

I'd stopped counting down the days.

This is important, baby. Please try to be happy for her.

Important? If anyone knew how important this was, it was me. I wanted to be happy for my sister, I did. I wanted to send her a note on the days of her big shows, flowers and champagne to her dressing room for each and every performance. I wanted to call her, to hear her ideas, to hash out lyrics, to harmonize the chorus, to whisper encouragements, to calm her nerves.

But I couldn't call, couldn't harmonize, couldn't even whisper.

And whenever I thought about sending her a text or a letter, the only words I could find were the wrong ones. Not *Good luck. I'm sending good thoughts. You'll knock 'em dead. I love you.*

No. It was one thing, over and over and over again.

Baby, it should've been me.

Now I looked up at Lemon, eyes hot with the tears I couldn't seem to shed.

"My brave girl," she said, taking my face in her hands. "It takes a strong woman to lose everything, then stand naked in front of the mirror and face herself again. You need time, honey. And I don't mean time for it to go away. I mean time to learn how to live with it. This is a pain you'll always carry."

I took a deep breath. Though it wasn't what I'd wanted to hear, it did feel like truth. Like something she'd experienced herself.

"That doesn't mean you won't find joy again," Lemon said. "A woman's heart is infinite. There's room for both."

Kirby was standing in the doorway, and when Lemon put her arms around me, my cousin slipped in silently, her eyes glazed with tears.

I reached forward, closed the laptop.

Cut off my voice. My past.

Kirby sat on my bed with her mother, and wordlessly they held me, the sound of their breath calming me as the sting of Granna's letter faded.

"See those stars? That's what we need." Lemon pointed to a bright constellation overhead, still glittering in the violet sky.

Since the three of us were already awake, we'd headed out together for church, arriving at Thor's Well earlier than usual. The sky was still quite dark. It was clear, though, littered with stars that were only just starting to blink out for the approaching morn. There wasn't enough light to risk climbing down near the Well, so we settled onto the wooden viewing platform above, spreading out a blanket. From a thermos, Lemon poured hot tea into three mugs.

Following her lead, I lifted my steaming mug toward the sky. Starlight tea, she'd called it. Not ready for drinking until it had been fully infused with the light of our celestial guides.

"That's Lyra," she said of the constellation. "It was said that Orpheus could charm stones with the music of his lyre. He played to drown the calls of the Sirens, allowing Jason and the Argonauts to pass through the seas without crashing to their deaths."

"That's pleasant, Mom," Kirby said. "Let's hope Lyra's a good-luck charm on race day."

I gave in to a shiver, careful not to spill my tea.

"That bright star, there at the top?" Lemon said. "Vega. She's practically our neighbor. Celestially speaking, that is."

My eyes widened. *Vega?* I mouthed.

"Christian's boat is an Albin Vega," Kirby said.

Lemon raised an amused eyebrow.

Coincidence? I wanted to know.

She laughed. "You girls know how I feel about that word. Tea's ready."

I leaned back against the platform rail and closed my eyes. My hands enveloped the hot mug and brought it close. My sister Martine was a master tea blender; she'd always said that proper tea drinking was a full-body experience—hands, head, heart, and soul.

"Elyse," Lemon said gently. I opened my eyes, and she set down her mug, her gaze weighted with determination. "Voice and speech aren't the same thing. You've lost your ability to speak, to sing. But the only thing that can take your voice away—your true *voice*—is you."

"Talk about T-shirt slogans," Kirby said. Lemon hushed her, but Kirby only laughed. Through the starlit steam that curled between us, Kirby said smartly, "'No one can make you feel inferior without your consent.' Eleanor Roosevelt."

Lemon tugged on one of Kirby's curls. "That's my bookworm."

"Some guy from Portland drove in a truckload of donations the other day," Kirby said. "All these old tomes of quotations and classics and rare books. There was even a first edition *Moby Dick*. The guy had no clue what some of his stuff was worth."

Kirby went on about the donation, how excited all the librarians were, how she'd suggested putting together a whole display of books about the sea and getting the local kids to paint paper murals, and maybe even seeing if Lemon could include some of her artwork. The staff was all for it.

As she and Lemon chattered about the library, and the sea whispered secrets at our feet, I reached up to my throat, wrapped my fingers around the seashell necklace. The one that I'd told Sebastian held my voice. Behind my fingers the scar tingled.

New possibilities, perhaps.

Guidance.

Friendship.

Starlight tea.

And behind all of that, next to the pulse of blood in my veins, the faintest flicker of something I'd long ago lost.

Hope.

I want to be here, I thought. *Whatever the past held, whatever the future is to bring, right now, I'm exactly where I belong.*

I released the shell. Released my breath. Welcomed the approaching new day.

Inside, my heart warmed again, the embers glowing. I thought of Natalie, her voice, her tears. I missed her. She'd be leaving the Caribbean for a new life on the road. The oceans of the world would become her seas, just as the Pacific was slowly becoming mine.

Maybe there was room in my heart for forgiveness. For happiness.

I didn't have to decide right now.

The Pacific was a calm altar this morning, only a gentle stirring beneath the breeze. It looked so peaceful from here—this moment, the jeweled sky, the black water, the savory tea spicing the air and warming me from the inside. A cool, salty breeze kissed my cheeks, and for the first time since I arrived, Atargatis Cove started to feel like something other than a temporary stopover, an escape hatch I'd been trying to convince myself was the real thing.

It felt like *home*.

And suddenly I really believed it could be—a place that made me feel I was running ahead toward something good rather than running away from something bad.

I'd left my phone in the car, but I knew it was almost time for Christian's text, sending me the day's plan for the Vega. I'd need a nap first, but I couldn't wait to get back there, to sand the barnacles and test the navigation instruments, to redo the gel coat.

To make Christian smile.

Home.

"Ah, there she is. Good morning, beautiful." Lemon spread her arms out as the sun opened its great sleepy eye across the sea.

Next to her, Kirby and I grinned, stretching our fingers to catch the light.

Chapter 23

By the time I'd awoken from my nap and made it to the marina, it was late afternoon, and the ocean was chilly and anxious.

Lemon was taking care of things at Mermaid Tears, and Kirby had gone to the library with Vanessa, so I was alone on the far edge of the docks when I heard a sound that made my heart soar.

The *Queen of* was running.

Not coughing and sputtering, but clean and clear and ready to work. I shot down to the last slip, eager to see Christian, the look of triumph on his face. But as I approached the Vega, another sound cut the air.

Mr. Kane's voice, severe and edged with frustration.

I froze.

"The only reason I'm letting this nonsense go on," he said, "is that I can't stomach the idea of handing that smug son of a bitch what he wants. Not without a fight."

"You should really get some therapy," Christian said. I pictured the tightness in his jaw, the spark of rage likely glinting in his eyes.

"Whoever left you that money had no right to get involved. This is between the Kanes and the Katzenbergs."

"You left this Kane high and dry," Christian said. "And now you're telling me—what exactly? That I can't race, because Kanes don't take bailouts?" Christian's laugh was hollow. "Or is it that I must race, but only because Kanes don't go down without a fight? Forgive me if I'm a little confused."

"You do what you have to do, son. But I do not want you encouraging Sebastian's little mermaid fantasies. I think we've let that go on long enough."

"Jesus, Dad," Christian said. "He's just a kid."

I didn't hear Mr. Kane's response, but the boat bobbed in the water, and he climbed through the companionway, out onto the deck. Christian followed, arms laden with coiled ropes.

I knew they'd spot me any minute. I shrunk, closing up like a sea anemone.

"Afternoon, Elyse." As he hopped off the boat, Mr. Kane smiled his usual greeting, carefully neutral. A cold flash in his eyes was the only indication that he'd realized I'd heard the argument. "Looks like a storm's heading in. Be careful today."

He nodded once and walked on.

On the deck, Christian's face crumpled, but the vulnerability was immediately replaced with anger.

I knew that face, that transition. Anger was easier to hold, to focus on, than grief. Anger was sharp edged and clear. Grief was messy, blurry.

But in the end both left you hollowed out inside.

Christian dropped the ropes. "I keep taking it, keep taking it. For what?" He looked at me for an answer, but all I could offer was an ear. He shook his head and said, "I can't figure out what he wants. To sell the house? To stick it to Wes? To keep the house, win the *Never Flounder*? Set me up to fail? Set me up to prove him wrong, some sick game to make him remember that he has a son he can be proud of? And Sebastian—God, it's like he hates the kid as much as he hates me."

I wanted to tell him how wrong he was, that his father loved them. That maybe he just didn't know how to show it, or maybe he was trying to protect them from life's disappointments the way my father always had; overprotectiveness often stemmed from good intentions. But even as all those words floated through my mind, I knew they weren't true. Christian's father had a deep, mysterious resentment for his boys.

I'm sorry, I mouthed. And I was. Not just for Christian and the way his father treated him. But for me, too. For all of us. Sorry for all the little ways that the people who were supposed to love us most could hurt us so deeply, despite their shared heritage and blood, as though their knowledge of our pasts gave them unlimited access to all the most tender places, the old wounds that could be so easily reopened with no more than a glance, a comment, a passing reminder of all the ways in which we'd failed to live up to their expectations.

Sometimes love was a tonic. Sometimes it was a weapon. And so often it was nearly impossible to tell the difference.

All of this I thought, believed, but there was no way to put it into words. This pain, this understanding. How in Mr. Kane's eyes I saw my grandmother's disappointment, how Christian's rage reflected the tumult endlessly churning inside me.

Christian shook his head. "I wanted to help you guys. Ursula and Kirby. Sebastian and me, too. Hell, I don't want to lose the houses. It's a crap sandwich anywhere you bite. But I just can't. I can't do this anymore, Elyse."

He seemed to be waiting for something, maybe for me to tell him it was okay. It wasn't okay, not by a long shot. But it also wasn't his fault.

Mayor Katzenberg wanted the houses to sell to P&D because he believed the new business plans would help the town. That much, behind all his rivalry with Mr. Kane and his sexist attitudes, was true— I'd seen it in his eyes that night, flickering behind the desperation. There was greed, yes; he was eager to impress the corporate developers, to take credit for whatever good fortune befell the Cove as a result. But somewhere in there was a man who'd wanted things to be better here. As wrongheaded as the approach was, I understood the root of it.

Mr. Kane's motives, on the other hand, mystified me. In sifting through all that Christian had told me, all I'd heard from Vanessa and Kirby and Lemon, all I'd witnessed and overheard, I couldn't find an explanation. Like Christian, I wondered whether his father wanted him to win the bet or lose. Was he looking for more reasons to dismiss his son? More disappointments to hold over his head? Maybe he'd wanted to sell the house all along but didn't want the argument with his family, and this way, if Christian lost, the blame would rest on his shoulders instead of Mr. Kane's.

I didn't want Christian to give up—not just for Lemon and the house, but for him. I knew he could win, and I knew how much he loved the water, loved sailing. He belonged out there on the sea, lines in hand, steering his own course. But when I thought of his father, of all their arguments, of all the ghosts in their family, the hurt in Christian's eyes that no amount of sarcasm could cover, I couldn't blame him for wanting to walk away.

"Screw it. We're done here," he finally said, as though he'd been arguing with himself and had finally reached the inevitable conclusion. He pointed at me. "You hungry?"

Even though I didn't have the right words to make it better for him, I wanted Christian to keep talking, to set loose the anger that was coiling inside him like a serpent. But whenever he got close to revealing anything, he shut down again.

The clouds shifted, fully dampening the sun, and all the joy I'd felt with Lemon and Kirby at Cape Perpetua this morning dimmed.

Still, I wasn't ready to call it a day. Being with Christian was its own elixir.

I nodded.

"Lucky day, Stowaway. I'm about to bust your fish-'n'-chips vir-ginity." And there it was, the smile that I'd come to know so well. Not the real one, not the rare one. But the version that broke through the clouds whenever they threatened to get too thick, too heavy.

Whenever he didn't want anyone to know he'd been hurt.

We drove south to the Chowder House in Bandon-by-the-Sea, a little blue restaurant adorned with painted wooden fish that Christian had assured me was the best place for the occasion. I saved us a picnic table outside while Christian ordered Pacific cod and loads of fries, and by the time he'd come out with our food, he was relaxed and happy again. I liked it down here; it felt small and quaint like the Cove, but without the developers and all the Prop 27 propaganda.

As we ate, I scribbled notes to him about our bake and shark back home, about how all the fishing villages had their own rules, their own secret codes, but still shared their catch with anyone who wasn't so lucky that day. Christian told me about the crab pots in the Cove, how he and Noah used to go crabbing for the Black Pearl, but the regatta had changed things between them this summer. Neither had had much time for anything other than race preparations.

"Guess I just freed up the rest of our summer," Christian said. "Try not to miss our deep conversations about sea cocks and aft holes." He winked at me over the fish. "Maybe I'll take you crabbing this week instead. Sound good?"

I swallowed my last French fry, chased it with a sip of Coke. I

thought about Mr. Kane, about all the things he'd said to Christian on the boat earlier, about the things I hadn't even heard but could only imagine. I thought about what Lemon had said about voice and speech, and Kirby's quote, too.

Don't quit.

"Sorry," Christian said, leaning closer. "Did you just say 'don't quit'?"

I nodded.

"I'm not quitting. Crabbing is fun. You'll see." He looked away, out to the sea beyond the restaurant. I knew he'd understood me. He was playing games.

I pounded the table between us, captured his attention.

Don't quit.

He held my eyes for an eternity, and in them I saw again the raging sea. He shook his head, but still didn't answer.

Christian—

"We should head out," he said, glancing at his phone. "I promised Sebastian I'd take him to register today."

I narrowed my eyes, confused. *Your dad?*

"The kid wants to be a mermaid, the kid gets to be a mermaid. That's one thing my father does *not* get the last word on." Christian swept up our trash, dropped it in the nearby bin. When he came back to the table, he sat on the bench next to me, straddling it, his knees brushing my thigh. I shivered at the closeness, and without a word he tugged off his hoodie, handed it over. "You never told me if you're doing the parade."

I wrapped myself in his sweatshirt, all Christian, all warmth, all mangoes-in-the-sea.

"Are you?" he said again.

I stuck my hand out from his too-big sleeve, scribbled the answer on my palm. He was eager to see it, but I folded my fingers around it, held my hand behind my back like some secret thing.

"You're in for it, Stowaway." He grabbed me, pulled me toward him. I crashed against his chest, and our lips brushed, warm in the chilly air. I melted into his kiss, but then he was unfurling my fingers, peeking, sighing at my words.

We've got a boat to race that day, Captain.

Chapter 24

Atargatis Cove was a small town, nestled between the sea and Oregon's rugged, forested coastline. I was shocked at the number of girls who'd turned up to register for the parade—it seemed every resident and summer renter brought a friend, a cousin, a mother. The line wrapped around the block, and that wasn't even counting the developers taking pictures, punching numbers into their devices as if every person on Main Street was stamped with a dollar sign.

"I think this is bigger than last year," Kirby said. "I don't remember registration being this crowded."

"It wasn't," Vanessa said. "This is out of control."

"And it's only getting bigger," a booming voice said, and with a sinking feeling I recognized the self-important tone of Mayor Katzenberg. "This time next year, the parade'll be big enough to get national attention." He noticed me then, offered his shark's grin.

"Miss d'Abreau! I see you've come to your senses. I think you'll be much more comfortable as a mermaid than you would've been as a pirate. Plus, you won't have to deal with all that nasty raw-fish business."

I raised my eyebrows.

"Impressed?" He winked. "One of my better ideas, not ashamed to say. Noah's an excellent sailor, but the boy just doesn't have the stomach for real piracy."

Christian stepped between us, but I grabbed his hand, willing him to ignore the taunts. The mayor was already moving past us, and I was just grateful he hadn't noticed Sebastian. Sebastian was so excited; I couldn't handle it if the mayor made fun of him again.

"Guess we should've dumped the crickets at city hall," Christian said. "Not the *Never Flounder*. Shit." His voice was heavy with guilt. I offered a small smile. It was pirate season, after all. Part of the risk.

We finally reached the registration area, several long tables staffed by women and littered with pink forms. Kirby and Vanessa fanned out to the next available stations, and Christian and I accompanied Sebastian to his.

"Sebastian Kane. Age six," he proudly told the woman. "Last year I was only five, so I couldn't sign up. I had to be in the kiddie parade, and I dressed up like a lobster. I did that for two years, actually. But now my lobster costume doesn't even fit and I'm old enough to be a mermaid. Did you write down my name?"

The woman gave him a placating smile. "Honey, the mermaid parade is for girls. You can be a pirate, though, and cheer everyone at the boat races." At the sight of his big eyes, she added, "Let's hear your pirate growl. *Arrrrrgh!*"

Sebastian shrugged. "Um. Argh?"

"You can do better than that! What kind of a pirate are you?"

"A mermaid," he said plainly.

"Aww, no crocodile tears," she said, and I wanted to scream. He wasn't crying. He wasn't whining or throwing a tantrum. He was just pointing out the obvious, and no one was listening.

Christian took a pink form from her, one hand on Sebastian's shoulder. "I'm his guardian. He has my permission."

The woman frowned. "Sorry, guys. I don't make the rules."

Christian leaned in close, squinted at the name tag pinned to her shirt. "Maureen, right? I'm Christian. I don't think we've met before. I would've remembered a smile like that."

She beamed.

"Listen, Maureen," Christian said, his voice low. "He's been looking forward to this all year. It would really mean a lot to me, personally, if you could find a way to make it happen."

Charm radiated from his smile, his eyes, his voice, the seductive tilt of his head.

Who could possibly say no?

Maureen blushed under his gaze, but still wouldn't budge. Her eyes dropped to the stack of forms before her, fingers folding the corners back and forth. "I'm sorry. It's just not possible. He's a *boy*."

I wanted to scribble all over the stupid form, tell her in a hundred Sharpie words how wrong she was, but she was already looking behind us, waving to the next girl in line, and Sebastian was walking away.

The thing was, she wasn't even saying it with conviction. It was just something she'd been told, that Sebastian's request didn't fit into the check-box-here rules. In so many ways, that was worse.

While she was distracted with the next person, I grabbed one of her pink forms and quickly filled it out with Sebastian's information. It would likely be rejected—it required a parental signature, and they'd already told him no—but it felt important to sign it and drop it in the box, anyway.

She saw me do it, took it out of the box immediately.

"Rules are rules," she said again, handing me back the form.

"Is there a problem here, Maureen?" Mayor Katzenberg was back, his smile plastered on as he looked us over. She explained the situation, and predictably, he laughed.

"Guys," he said, "we've been over this." He ruffled Sebastian's hair. "Forget the mermaids, little man. You'll thank me one day."

I was boiling, but the mayor was already gone, and Maureen was not going to help us.

Vanessa and Kirby were waiting for us inside Sweet Pacific, the cookie bar that Lemon's friends Kat and Ava owned. Every cookie was decorated like something from the sea: glittery starfish, seahorses, coral cookie sticks, and of course, mermaids. Christian and I were trying desperately to cheer Sebastian up with sugar, but it wasn't working.

"What they're doing to him is so wrong, there's not even a word for it," Kirby said after we'd explained what happened. "But Wes Katzenberg makes the rules around here. We can't just go against them."

Why not? I asked.

"Because...I don't know. That's how it is. He's in charge. Unless you want to run for mayor, you just have to deal with him."

"Such bullshit," Christian said.

"What's bullshit?" Brenda pulled up a chair and sat down, her friend Gracie in tow. I hadn't seen them come in, but each had a plate full of cookies and a cup of coffee. "What's going on?"

"Sebastian wants to march in the mermaid parade," Kirby explained. "But they won't let him."

"What? Why the hell not?" Brenda said. "I mean, heck. Sorry."

Kirby shrugged. "He's a boy. They said no boys."

"I'm sorry," Gracie said. "But that's just bullshit."

"I'm saying," Christian said.

Gracie sighed. "Have these people ever been to a parade in New York City? The Coney Island Mermaid Parade is . . ." She shook her head, laughed. "Diverse."

"Totally," Brenda said. "Anyone should be able to march. As long as you have a mermaid costume."

"I do," Sebastian said meekly. His face fell. "Well, I'm working on one. I mean, I was."

"Don't worry, sugar bean," Vanessa said. "We'll figure something out."

I couldn't take it anymore, the broken look on Sebastian's little face, the disappointment in his eyes. Christian and Gracie were right: "Bullshit" was the only word for it.

I still had the rejected form; I grabbed it and marched back out to the table, cut the line.

Christian was at my side in an instant, squeezing my arm.

"What are you doing?" he whispered.

Maureen looked up, her smile turning to a frown. "I really am sorry, guys," she said. "But it's against the rules to let a boy register for the mermaid parade. There's nothing I can do about—"

I cut her off with a hand. I flipped over Sebastian's form, and with my marker, I wrote furiously, Christian looking on over my shoulder.

Rules

If everyone followed rules
As they were written, as they were said
You wouldn't be allowed to vote.
The rule of thumb, as the saying goes,
comes from the old rules
In which a man was allowed to beat his wife
So long as the implement was no wider than his thumb.
If everyone followed rules
My family would not own a cocoa farm

And I wouldn't be looking you in the eye,
woman to woman.
    Lucky for you, someone defied rules.
    Lucky for me, someone spoke out against
them.
    Lucky for my friend, the little blond
mermaid
    Wait, he wasn't lucky.
    No one defied the rules for him.
    No one stood up and said that boys
marching in the mermaid parade
    are perfectly acceptable
    That HE is perfectly acceptable
    And acceptably perfect.
    Rules are rules, yet still
    trumped always by kindness and human
decency.
    Let. Him. March.

I returned the form, word side up. Automatically she set it aside, but then she noticed the words, and her eyes couldn't resist. I watched them as she read, widening, then narrowing.

A sigh.

I smacked the table before her. *Let him march.*

Regret.

Let him march.

A final apology.

Let him march.

She folded the poem, slipped it into the purse at her feet, just as the mayor stomped toward us again, brow furrowed.

Let him march.

A storm of words, all the sound and fury of my heart, raging on as the sea.

But alas, never strong enough to break the solid shore.

Chapter 25

"**You know what** bothers me?" Sebastian said. He was dressed in thin white pajamas with frogs all over them, hair wild and untamed, snuggled up on Christian's lap in the Kanes' upstairs family room. It was the only place the three of us wanted to be after the day's disappointments and another typically tense dinner with the Kane parents.

Christian closed the book he'd been reading aloud, one of the Caribbean legends Granna had sent.

Sebastian said, "Everyone around here dresses up for the parade, and they make all these rules about who can be a mermaid, and they buy all the mermaid postcards and mermaid stuff for their car."

"Why does that bother you?" Christian asked.

"Because they do all that stuff," Sebastian said, "but no one even *believes* in mermaids. They never saw one and they don't know anything about them. I know *everything* about them."

He'd been chasing mermaids all summer, scanning the shores through his too-big binoculars while we worked on the boat. His enthusiasm would never dampen, though, whether he found one or not.

I loved that about him.

Point made, he nestled back into the crook of Christian's shoulder, nudged him to continue the story.

"I think that's enough for tonight." Mr. Kane stood at the top of the stairs, watching us across the open family room. I didn't know how long he'd been there, how much of the Tobago legends he'd heard, how much of Sebastian's frustrations. It didn't matter, though—he wasn't here to talk about mermaids. "Let's get to bed, kiddo."

The room was dim, save for the reading light bent over Christian's chair, and across the blue-gray room Christian and I locked eyes. Sebastian wanted to hear the end of the story, and Christian was so at peace reading it. So content. I shook my head and willed Christian to take a stand, to say no to this one small thing that could open the door for all the bigger things to come. To say no when it counted, right to his father's face.

Christian held my gaze, intense as ever. I couldn't look away, though I burned inside, remembering our kiss from this afternoon. I was still wearing his sweatshirt, still wrapped up in the scent of him. We'd suffered so many disappointments today, so many letdowns. *Just this one thing,* I thought. *Just this one.*

"Mom's working late tonight," Mr. Kane said, "so I need you to be a big boy and get yourself washed up and into that bed, pronto."

"I already brushed my teeth and washed my face and had a drink of water and peed and put on my pajamas and peed again," Sebastian said.

"Great," his father said. "Let's get a move on."

"I'll take care of him, Dad," Christian said. Mr. Kane started to protest, but Christian shot him a firm look. "We'd like to finish the story."

It was such a small challenge, a small request, but everyone in the room knew they weren't butting heads about Sebastian's bedtime. Still, Mr. Kane backed down, mumbling a halfhearted good night as he retreated downstairs.

Christian went back to the story, and reluctantly I tore my gaze away, drifting instead to the sea. Waves rolled against the shore, neither calm nor fierce, and I lost myself in the lull of the water, in Christian's steady voice as he read aloud the tales of home.

Outside moments later, a spark caught my eye, the glow of a cigarette in the darkness. Mr. Kane was out there, pacing the dunes, his form a black shadow against the sea's green-gray backdrop. I spied on his stolen moment, watched the pinprick blaze of his cigarette trail through the night, imagined the smoke he blew out across the sea. Inhale, exhale. Again. Again.

Across the room, Christian shifted, closed the book. Sebastian was finally asleep, his mouth open, his breathing slow and even.

Carefully Christian rose, hefting Sebastian to his chest. He dropped his voice to a whisper. "Be right back. Don't go, okay?"

Christian turned down the hallway toward the bedrooms, Sebastian's limbs slack as noodles in his big brother's arms. His blond head lolled gently, one pink cheek pressed to Christian's shoulder.

"Elyse," Sebastian murmured. He didn't open his eyes, just stretched out his hands toward me. "Elyse too."

Without turning around, Christian paused in the hallway, waiting for me to catch up.

Together we got the kid tucked in, Christian and I kneeling on opposite sides of the bed. As Christian smoothed the white-blond curls from his brother's forehead, I leaned in and kissed his pink cheek. In so many ways Sebastian felt like my little brother now too. The youngest sibling I never had.

It was in my heart to take care of him.

I wondered, suddenly and warmly, if it was like this for Natalie, too. She was only a few minutes my senior, but older nevertheless, bound by destiny to look out for me. I smiled at the thought.

Christian was still stroking Sebastian's hair, and for a long moment neither of us moved to stand, just watched the little one drift off to dreamland. When I finally looked up, Christian was watching me, his sea-eyes full of the same intrigue I'd seen that first night on the boat, a smile to match.

Only this one was different. Deeper. More intense.

More real.

"What you did for him today . . . ," he whispered.

I nodded before he finished, but a frown tugged my lips. In the end none of it had worked. They still wouldn't let him register for the parade. No matter what we'd said or done, no matter what I'd written,

I heard the gulls crying, searching for fish, and I thought about that word. Limitless. Without limit. All potential, destiny unmapped.

"You probably thought I was crazy," Christian said, "agreeing to race when my father made the bet."

I didn't disagree.

"It *was* crazy. Winning . . . at first, it was all about sticking it to my father. Watching him eat his words. He doesn't think I can do it without Noah. But there was this other part of me that thought maybe, if I could actually win, he might . . . he'd look at me with something other than . . ." He waved the words away, and I watched his whispers turn to dust.

Why does he? I asked.

Christian's gaze slipped away, settled on a point beyond the starboard window, and I let my hand curl on his knee in a gesture that I hoped said it was okay, that he didn't have to explain.

He spoke anyway. "I almost wasn't his."

The regret in Christian's voice was nearly too much too bear, too raw and revealing in the tiny space of the V-berth. Beneath my hand the muscles in his leg tightened, and I knew he was wrestling with what to say, how much to reveal of his own personal tragedy to the girl who couldn't talk about her own, even if she wanted to.

When our eyes met again, his glazed with emotion. Quickly he scrubbed his hands over his face, erasing it all.

"I meant what I said to your aunt. I don't want them to sell the houses. Dad might not get it, but it's the one place that's been constant

in my life. No matter how much money he makes or where they relocate, the Cove has always been ours. Some of my best memories were
here." He held my gaze. "Are here."

Me too, I told him. And his smile turned, for just a moment, shy.

"It's your fault, you know. That word, limitless." He shook his head,
still smiling. It was hard for him to admit, whatever was coming next,
but I knew he'd do it. He leaned in, kissed me softly. Still close, he whispered against my lips. "You make me think things are possible. You
make me want things."

I waited for the joke, the playful tease about these "things" I made
him want. But when it didn't come, when his gaze remained on my
eyes, intense and serious, I knew he wasn't talking about the kisses,
our half-naked bodies tangling on his bed last night.

He was making me want things too. The kinds of things I didn't
think I could have anymore. Ideas. Plans. Opportunities.

Dreams.

Love.

My heart hammered inside, thrumming with energy.

"Last night," he said, still holding my gaze, "I didn't . . . I don't want
you to think it's . . . I didn't mean to—"

I pressed my fingers against his lips, gently silencing him. I already
knew what he meant; his eyes said all the things his words were
fumbling.

He nodded silently then, kissed my fingers and held them warm
in his hand again.

For all of Kirby's warnings, for all of Vanessa's defending, for all of the women who looked at Christian with longing and history in their eyes, none of them seemed to really know him, to see beyond the obvious.

I felt like he'd given me a rare gift, this precious glimpse.

Being with Christian was like nothing I'd ever experienced. Back home, there had always been boys after the shows, older boys who drove fast and kissed even faster, who talked smoothly with just the right words to leave us bewildered.

I'd met Julien at a lime at Crown Point, caught up in the way he played the steel pan. It was an informal thing, one of the all-night summer parties the island was famous for, and Natalie and I had wandered over to the music tent to sing along. We hadn't meant to attract attention, but the band heard us, invited us to perform with them. Soon we had the whole crowd dancing to our Caribbean grooves, everyone laughing and having a great time. I thought they'd riot when the band took a break, but then the limbo dancers started to perform, and there was enough homemade crafts, food, and rum to keep everyone satisfied. Julien, cocky and confident as all the rest, handed me a drink and said, in a deep voice that rattled every inch of me, "Me gyal, you have a sweet voice there."

I dragged Natalie back to the beach every weekend that summer, and the night he pressed his lips to mine in a kiss that made my toes curl, we were official.

Almost two years we were together. And even though I thought

I loved him, now I wondered if I just loved the fact that he loved *me*. That he'd always talked about our future, about how he couldn't breathe without me, about how my voice drove him crazy. I loved that he couldn't keep his hands off me, that he'd look at me with such hunger in his eyes. When I stood naked before him, I felt powerful, alive. Adored.

It was intoxicating.

Until I went dark after I lost my voice, and the magic between us fizzled out in a month. He said he just couldn't handle the anger in me, the raw pain so close to the surface. Granna had warned me about him months earlier. "You think it's love, but it's desire. Fair-weather boy, that one. First sign of the storm, you watch him run for cover."

Back then I shrugged her off. So many nights I'd stared up at the Tobago moon and wondered if she even knew what she was saying. Love and desire? Was there a difference?

Now, here, Christian and I were on equal footing, each of us scared and vulnerable in turn, each of us strong and triumphant in our own ways. He looked at me with want, so intense it sent shockwaves through my belly, but it wasn't desperation. Making him smile, kissing him, it didn't feel like manipulation, like some favor I'd be cashing in on later.

It simply felt right.

I grabbed the Sharpie and notebook from my pocket.

I wanted him to know me. All of me, all the things I hadn't been able to tell him before.

But the instant I set the tip against the paper, the mood sobered. Putting a thing to words gave it power; it pulled the maybe from the mist and gave it form, solid and black.

I took a breath. Wrote.

You asked about my Plan B
And how I ended up at the Cove.
Well, once upon a time, on an island far away,
I used to sing with my sister.
And we had a chance to go on tour
To record an album
Connections already made
But then I lost everything

He read it, his eyes drifting from the final word to my scar. I confirmed with a nod. *Doctors say permanent. Irreversible.*

Ever since I'd heard those damning words, I'd been fighting it. But deep down, I'd always known the truth. The doctors in Port of Spain were top-notch. Dad even consulted vocal injury specialists from around the world, but the prognosis was always the same. They may, in six months or a year, be able to do another surgery, possibly restore minimum vocal function. But given the nature of the injuries, surgery could make things worse. I could end up with a marginally stronger voice, but unable to breathe. Unable to swallow food.

And still I would be songless.

It was, by some cruel twist, my fate.

With the marker still pressed to the page, I went on.

Ashes to ashes, and all the old ghosts
Gathering on the seashore
They waited for me with eyes on fire
Accusing, burning, haunting.
I thought that if I pretended I couldn't
see them,
Maybe they'd blow away
Remnants, lost forever to time
But they didn't, and I couldn't pretend.
I couldn't stay in Tobago another minute.
So Lemon brought me here on a visa.
A place to linger, to catch my breath
However long I needed
It felt like an escape, a perfect
hideaway
To flee, to forget
It wasn't supposed to start feeling like
home.

Lemon had said I'd always have a home with her and Kirby, no matter what happened with the houses in Atargatis Cove. I knew she'd meant it, even if we lost the regatta and they had to move. But it wasn't realistic, me following them to some new place, setting up a new life again. Trying to fit in. Trying to help her come to terms with a loss I might've been able to prevent. I knew, and I sensed that she did too, that if Lemon lost the house, I'd be heading back to Tobago by the end of the summer.

But it does feel like home. It IS home.

I capped the marker and tossed it on the bed.

And my sister, I mouthed, unable to write her name. *Natalie?*

Christian watched me in silence, the boat swaying beneath us.

I closed my eyes, lips forming words too fast to follow.

She saved my life.

She made me breathe again.

Fucking breathe.

I never forgave her.

Never thanked her.

Never got over her.

Never stopped missing her, even now, when she's going without me.

Behind my eyelids the image of my sister faded. I felt the familiar slice of pain at my throat, but I knew it wasn't real. Like so many memories, it was just a ghost from that day in March, a spirit with unresolved business who refused to move on because I wouldn't let it.

"Elyse," Christian whispered, his fingers gently touching the scar on my throat. I opened my eyes, lost myself in the sea of his gaze. "What happened to you in—"

"Hope y'all are decent in there." Vanessa's voice cut through the somber air. She and Kirby climbed down through the companionway just as Christian and I hopped out of the berth, looking rumpled and supremely guilty.

"This boat needs a security system," Christian grumbled, running a hand over his hair.

Kirby was glaring at us, eyes wide with accusation.

Vanessa dropped onto the saloon bench, head in her hands. "Sorry, guys," she said, "but we just got some seriously shitty news."

Chapter 27

"You're positive?" Christian asked. We were all out on the dock now, pacing.

"Mom read the fine print," Vanessa said. "She wouldn't make a mistake on this."

According to Vanessa, Mrs. James had gone into town this morning to finalize details about the sale of their home—they'd been planning to list it all along, just as Mr. Kane had mentioned at the Solstice party. As she waited for all of the signatures, a Parrish and Dey developer had come in to pick up some paperwork, and she casually asked her lawyer about the firm's plans. The guys had a copy of the preliminaries, some permits the firm had applied for, and easily handed them over.

Parrish and Dey wasn't going to raise Lemon's rent.

They were going to bulldoze the whole site.

On the land occupied by the two Kane houses, they could build enough condos to house the entire summer population of Oregon. And that's exactly what they were planning.

"Makes sense," Christian said after Vanessa confirmed the details. "Even if they doubled what Ursula pays now—tripled it—it's still a drop in the bucket compared to the money they'd bring in with a new complex. They could make that monthly rent in a week, for one unit. Figure they turn this site into condos, and the sky's the limit. Ten floors, twenty? That's where the real money is."

"But what if Prop Twenty-Seven fails?" Kirby asked. "If the people vote no on the business redistricting, they won't be able to build condos and hotels here, right? At least, not as far up the coast as Starfish Point. I read all the zoning details at the library."

"That's true," Vanessa said, "but then you'd better hope enough of the Cove's residents turn out to vote this fall, and that they vote it down. Mom says a lot of people support it, guys. Plenty of folks feel the pinch, and Wes comes in with his song and dance about bringin' wealth and prosperity to the people. . . . It sounds like a good idea."

"Does Wes know about P and D's real plans?" Kirby asked.

"Doubt it," Vanessa said. "That man was never one for the details. Mom's got a call in to his office, but his people keep putting her off."

"Wes Katzenberg has people?" Christian asked.

Vanessa shrugged. "An intern, I think." Suddenly her eyes narrowed, lasering in on a target approaching from the marina. "Unless you count the traitor *Noah Katzenberg*."

Noah strolled toward the dock, hands in his pockets.

"Don't let him know we know anything," Christian mumbled. "Play it cool."

"What's up, lovely ladies?" Noah's eyes skimmed over me and Vanessa when he reached us, lighting up when he saw Kirby. "Damn. Team Kane's got all the babes this year."

"Pirate alert," Christian said. He tried to look casual, but his arms were crossed over his chest, shoulders tight.

"Not here to pirate, dude." Noah raised his hands in mock surrender. "Not my gig. Just here to see if any of you sea rats feel like hitting up Shipwreck tonight."

Christian nodded toward Kirby. "Sleeping with the Enemy's probably game."

Kirby smiled, ignoring Christian's dig. She still seemed totally in denial about what was at stake here, especially with this latest development. Her house was going to be bulldozed, yet even that couldn't dim the stars in her eyes for Noah.

She turned toward him, practically beaming. "Sure, I'll go."

Vanessa grabbed her arm. "Kirby. You don't fraternize with the enemy. At least not while the other enemies are watching."

"But, how am I supposed to—"

"You text him later, make arrangements to meet in secret. God, have you never hooked up with a pirate?"

"Have *you*?" Kirby asked, laughing.

Vanessa grinned. "A lady never kisses and tells."

"You kiss and tell *everyone*."

"I think you mean, *I* kiss, and *you* tell everyone."

The girls left with Noah, leaving me and Christian alone with the Vega. He pinched the bridge of his nose and let out a half sigh, half moan. "I think you know what we have to do." He stepped close, grabbed my hands, his thumb tracing the faded message I'd written on my palm yesterday about racing the boat.

I raised an eyebrow, hoped for the best.

"We have to save the houses," he said. "The Cove. We have to win this thing. There's no other way."

There was fire in his eyes again, so beautiful that there was nothing I wouldn't have agreed to in that moment, just to keep it going. I held his gaze and hoped my eyes said everything I was feeling, everything I'd lost the words for.

Yes, we were still in the race. Yes, we had to win. Yes, yes, yes to all of it, to anything.

He leaned into me and kissed my neck, hot words caressing my ear.

"All in, pirate?" he whispered, his voice ragged. He pulled back to watch my mouth, and with no more than a breath between us, I smiled, my answer crashing against his lips.

All in.

During the final days leading up to the big race, Christian called in reinforcements in the form of Brenda and Gracie, finally taking them up on their offer to help. Alternating with the girls and Vanessa, Christian and I stood guard on the boat, sometimes checking in at random intervals in the middle of the night. We plasticked the window, fixed it up with duct tape to keep out curious birds. Lemon had even cast a spell of protection on the boat, fitting the helm with a small stone gargoyle, all to discourage further acts of piracy.

None came.

Lemon believed it was her magic, which I wasn't discounting. But ultimately, this rivalry was between the Kanes and the Katzenbergs. None of the other sailors was interested in screwing with another man's boat. All along, Noah—and his father—had been our main concern on the pirate front. And rumor had it *Never Flounder* was still belching up crickets.

Rumor also had it that Noah had yet to find a first mate. The mayor had volunteered the city hall intern for the position, a college kid named Wayne from Colorado who'd probably never sailed a boat in his life.

The night before the regatta, as Kirby, Vanessa, Lemon, Noah, and most of the population of Atargatis Cove roamed the streets for the Mermaid Festival's fellowship walk 'n' feast, Christian and I slipped onto the Vega to christen the boat.

To celebrate the accomplishment of getting her seaworthy.

To offer some good-luck wishes for the big win on our horizon.

Chapter 28

Mrs. James's discovery lent speed and urgency to our final renovations, and though she'd ultimately confirmed that the mayor hadn't realized the extent of P&D's plans, he wasn't interested in challenging them once he knew. After all, he wanted the same golden-paved streets as they did, regardless of how they made it happen.

It was down to us, down to winning the bet.

For two and a half weeks we scrambled.

By day we worked beyond bone weariness and aching muscles and lack of sleep. We dry-docked the boat to inspect the hull, which—luck on our side—was intact, requiring only a good scrub and polish. We cleaned. Fastened and tightened. Primed and painted. Oiled and adjusted winches and tracks. Tuned. Checked and double-checked and triple-checked, prioritizing for speed and lightness, and finally getting her back in the water, where we repeated the process all over again.

By night we kept watch.

And tonight, with the fate of the Cove resting squarely on our shoulders, Christian looked happy. Confident. Why shouldn't he be? He was certain the Vega was faster than Noah's boat, and together we'd reviewed the charts, mapped out the course, talked through all the potential trouble spots. Prepared was an understatement.

In the warm glow of Christian's smile, I tried to relax. I thought of my family on the islands, my neighbors, all of them in Port of Spain this weekend for the Emancipation Day celebrations. We'd always gone together to watch the Kambule, a procession through the streets to mark the day the African slaves in the British Islands were granted freedom. Even from the sidelines, Natalie and I always danced along to the drums, cheering and chanting as they passed, admiring the dance troupe in their vibrant African clothing.

Last year Natalie bought me a handmade bracelet from one of the vendors, a delicate wooden hoop carved intricately with elephants and giraffes. For the first time since I left home, I wore it tonight.

From the warm memories it stirred I drew strength. The smooth weight around my wrist quieted, for a moment, the war with the sea that still waged inside.

I've been waiting for you. . . .

"Took her out this morning," Christian said excitedly, handing me a plastic cup from the spread on the saloon table. Grapes, crackers, cheese, champagne—he'd thought of everything. "Handled herself just fine with the mainsail and standard jib. One spot on the route looks a little rougher than usual, but as long as we're careful and the wind doesn't pull any surprises, the *Queen* will get us through."

The water was calm tonight, and I tried to follow its cue, smile through my nerves, but Christian's words had sent a new bolt of fear through my heart.

For weeks I'd been convincing myself that I could do it, get back out on the open sea. I'd reached an impressive level of denial, mainly by not thinking about it. It was enough to focus on getting the boat in shape, keeping it clean, preventing piracy, saving the Cove. Sailing? That was a far-off fantasy, nothing to worry my pretty little head about.

But tonight his words made it real.

I twisted the bracelet around my wrist.

"With me, Stowaway?" Christian squeezed my shoulder. The gesture should have been reassuring, comforting. But it only made me feel guilty as I sank deeper into old fears.

I nodded, smiled with extra enthusiasm.

"Hold tight," he said, wrapping a towel around the champagne. He'd swiped it from Mr. Kane's stash, some expensive stuff whose absence his father wouldn't even notice. The cork popped, leaving a trail of cool mist behind.

He filled our cups halfway with golden bubbly, then returned the bottle to its ice bucket.

"To my girls," he said plainly, raising his cup. "Elyse and her *Queen*."

With our eyes locked in a heated gaze, we tipped our cups back. He offered to pour another round, but I shook my head, my heart weighted again with everything that hung in the balance. The houses—Lemon and Kirby's, as well as Mr. Kane's, which directly impacted Christian's chances at coming back next summer. The Black Pearl, the little hole-in-the-wall without a regular menu, the kind of place that might not survive a big tourist boom. Kirby's library, the ocean murals she'd gotten the summer story-time kids to paint. Shipwreck, the magical club beneath the sea. Quiet mornings on the beach, watching the dolphins in the distance with no other observers but the oystercatchers. The orange and lavender sea stars, undisturbed in the tide pools, moving as slow as evolution itself. Sebastian, his big eyes scanning the sea for his beloved mermaids, devoted to them even now, even when he couldn't march in the parade.

Christian sensed my thoughts, pulled me into a gentle hug. He kissed the top of my head, promised me we'd be okay no matter what happened tomorrow.

"I couldn't do this without you," he said. "You know that, right?" I nodded, swallowing the tightness in my throat. He leaned closer then, pressed a soft kiss on my lips, salt and champagne.

With no more words we crawled into the small space at the front of the boat, tasting each other, slow and tantalizing.

He lifted the sweatshirt and shirt from my body, gently unwrapping me. His hands ran along the length of me, lingering on every curve, his warm touch and teasing kisses winding me tight with desire. Though I'd worn my favorite jeans, my sexiest bra and panties, suddenly I hated them. I hated the fabric between us, all that kept me from feeling him completely.

He'd already ditched his sweatshirt, but now I reached for his T-shirt, pulled it over his head, tasted the skin of his neck and shoulder. His chest was broad and strong, warming at my every touch. When my hands fluttered down the firm ridges of his abdomen to the button on his jeans, he let out a growl. In a ragged breath as shallow as the tide pools, he said, "Are you sure?"

I nodded.

He ran his hands over my nipples, tracing agonizingly slow circles with his thumb.

"Is that yes?" His eyes were on my mouth, waiting for confirmation.

Yes, I mouthed. I arched upward, and from my back pocket, fished out a strip of condoms I'd taken from the candy box tonight.

"If you change your mind," Christian whispered, but I cut him off with a kiss, already tearing one of the packets from the strip.

Yes, I said again, slowly forming words against his lips. *I want this. I want you.*

He pulled away, saw it in my eyes and knew that I meant it, that my ache matched his. He couldn't know, though, that I'd been wanting this for weeks, maybe even since our first kiss, maybe even since our first awkward hello. Then it was just attraction, a physical response to the sudden warmth of him, the flicker inside me that had been cold for so long.

But in our time together, through the jokes, through the notes, through the shared glances and smoldering stares, through the lunches, the smiles, the vulnerable moments, through the small touches and deep kisses, through the nights I'd imagined his hands on me, through all of his "sweet dreams" texts, it had changed into something so much more.

We slipped out of our jeans, undergarments, the last threads of all that stood between us.

With our mouths pressed hotly together, he twined his hands into my hair, and I wrapped myself around him, pulled our naked bodies closer.

I drank in the curves of his shoulders, the shadowed line of his jaw, his lips, all of him delicious in the moonlight.

I want you, I said again.

He shifted between my legs, slid inside me. His movements were slow and deliberate, and then fast, fast, faster still. I inhaled the sea-and-mango scent of him, focused on the feel of his body, the muscles of his shoulders and back taut beneath my hands as I arched my hips.

Christian moaned, his lips fluttering down my chin, my neck, landing soft as starlight in the hollow of my throat. This time I didn't flinch, didn't run. I felt his heat, lips tracing the shape of my silver scar, and as my whole body trembled around him, I let out a shuddering breath I'd been holding for five months.

Chapter 29

"Limited-time offer," Christian said. We were lying in the berth later, naked and warm, the moon our only light. I'd been trying to bribe him to reveal his secrets, one kiss at a time, and this was his response. "Ask me anything. But in exchange for answers, I get to do something to you."

What? I didn't bother hiding my grin.

"That's for me to know, and you to experience." He pressed his lips to my mouth, traced the edges with the tip of his tongue.

Before things got too hot and heavy again, I grabbed his hand to stop him, found a Sharpie on the shelf.

On the back of an old nautical chart we mapped out pieces of each other's histories, trading childhood stories for kisses. I told him about being born in the sea, and how we'd gone to Tobago to live with Granna after that. He told me about the day they brought

Sebastian home from the hospital, a bundle of chubby pink limbs with a shock of white-blond curls, and how Christian fell in love with him instantly.

Finally, when all the safe topics had been exhausted, I found the courage to write the question I'd most been pondering.

Once you said you almost weren't his. Why?

The muscles of his jaw ticked. He knew I'd meant his father, and for a moment I regretted bringing it up, weighting the lightness between us. But I was chasing away my own secret admissions, and this was something Christian held deep, almost hidden. Knowing him seemed utterly wrapped up in this mystery.

"God," he said, rolling his eyes in a gesture that failed to be as dismissive as he'd intended. "You don't want to hear *that* weeper. Trust me."

I do, I mouthed. *If you want to tell.*

For a moment he said nothing, his face turned toward the forward hatch, which we'd left open to the night sky. He seemed lost among the stars, and I thought maybe he wouldn't answer after all, that we'd reached the outer boundaries of that limited-time offer.

But then he shook his head, ran a hand through his hair.

"Before I was born," he said, soft and low, "my mother had an affair. He was another long-term renter here, down the north end of the shore, near town."

I tried to keep my face neutral, but shock rippled through me. For all her coldness, her snippiness with Mr. Kane, her awkwardness with me, her long hours hiding away in her office, the tears on tarot night, I never would've suspected Mrs. Kane had been the one to cheat.

Christian's confession was just another reminder that no matter how much you thought you knew about someone, no matter how much you guessed from their movements and actions and words, you never had access to the inside. Never saw the complete, intricate, messy, shades-of-gray picture.

"It went on a few years," he said, "though Dad supposedly had no idea. Fast forward a decade, and it all comes out one night during this huge fight. I'm in the next room, supposed to be sleeping but obviously not."

I tried to imagine Christian as a little boy, ear pressed to the wall, scared and confused. Blood pulsed behind my scar, my throat tightening at the memories as if they were mine.

"After a lot of yelling, Mom admitted that she couldn't say for certain whether Dad was my biological father. Dad said he didn't care, and I felt this . . ." Christian pressed his fist against his heart, spread his fingers. "Like, a wave of relief. But then something shifted, and I got it. He wasn't saying it like, 'He's my son no matter whose DNA he has.' He was saying that he didn't trust anything Mom told him. I was standing in the doorway at that point, and when my father finally noticed me, the look on his face . . ." Christian closed his eyes. "It was like I'd gone from his kid to this disgusting *thing*. He stormed out of the room, didn't even touch me. I felt like a ghost."

I grabbed his hand, squeezed.

"He made us take a paternity test," he said. "I think he was already preparing for the bad news, and a divorce to follow."

Christian turned back toward the stars again, found a bright one to focus on.

Vega, watching over us.

"He loved us, I figured," he said. "He wouldn't have cut ties on his own. But after what Mom did? It's a lot easier to walk away when someone else cuts the ties for you." Christian looked at me again, his eyes sad and lost.

"But as it turns out, I'm his real kid. Lucky me, right?" He sighed. "I waited for weeks for things to get back to normal. Months. Years. But the damage was done. The test results didn't matter, because all I'd ever be was evidence of Mom's affair. Even more fucked up? I think Mom *wanted* to bail. Like she was almost hoping the test would be different, then she could have a legit reason to walk away."

I didn't know what to do, to say. So I just moved closer, pressed my lips to his shoulder.

"It's the thing I'll never understand, never respect about her," Christian said, tightening his grip on my hand. "She could've just divorced him. She stayed, though. Not because she thought they could work it out. She stayed because she didn't know what else to do."

That much I understood.

It was the same reason I'd left Tobago.

I didn't know what else to do.

It was possible Christian couldn't see past his own hurt, the rawness of his own memories, to understand that maybe she had other
reasons for staying.

Webs, sticky and layered.

Who was I to judge?

Maybe I couldn't see through my own hurt and raw memories
either, and I'd pushed my family away because of it. Pushed my sister
away.

Webs, gossamer and strong.

I took Christian's face in my hands, turned him toward me. *I'm so
sorry.*

"Oh, this tale gets better. Sebastian? He was supposed to be the
do-over kid. Mom and Dad wanted to work it out, and I guess they
thought they could get a fresh start. But Sebastian doesn't meet Dad's
criteria for the perfect son either."

Gently I grabbed his arm, turned it over to the pale skin that
stretched over his veins. From wrist to elbow, I wrote:

I think the Kane brothers are perfect.

Christian sighed. "Sometimes I wish I could just take him, you
know? Go start our own thing somewhere before my dad does any
more damage. But he wouldn't want that, not really. Sebastian still
looks up to our parents—poor kid. Yeah, I say that, then I feel like
the world's biggest dick because I'm not married; I don't know what

they went through. Just because they screwed up, does that make them bad people?"

Human, I mouthed.

"Sometimes I think he wants to sell the house because the Cove reminds him of all that bad shit. How could it not? Just because the dude's not here anymore doesn't mean his ghost isn't." Christian shook his head, cleared the cobwebs. "Fuck. You just Oprahed me, didn't you?" He shook his head again. "Forget it. You're not getting anything else out of me tonight. Except, maybe . . ." He flashed me a dangerous look that sent a shock of heat between my thighs.

I pretended to cower away, but he only laughed.

"You're always writing on me," he teased. "Let's see how you like it." He grabbed my foot, stole the Sharpie from my grasp. I squirmed beneath his touch, loving every searing-hot minute of it.

"Hold still," he warned. "You'll mess up my art."

I waited until he'd finished scribbling on the bottoms of both feet before I lifted them to see. Each was inked with a sunshine wearing a pair of sunglasses and a smile.

"Now wherever you go, you'll be walking on sunshine," he said.

I rolled my eyes. *Everyone's a poet.*

He handed over the marker. "Money, mouth. Put them together."

I knelt before him in the small space of the berth, ran my fingers along his jaw, down to his collarbone, then to his chest. I kissed his neck, traced the lines of the tattoo on his shoulder, ship and compass, the black sea.

Beneath my touch, his heart beat strong, steady.

With the marker pressed against his skin, I spun words in the moonlight, tattooed them over his heart.

For all the strength of men
And the divine power of their gods
But for a spell in a pale blue dream
Not even the wisest among them
Can harness the silver moon
Nor cease with thoughts or words
The beating of their own fragile hearts

He read upside down, his fingers lightly touching the words.

"Okay, show-off. That's just . . . epic."

I gave him a casual shrug. *Had enough?*

"Oh, I'm just getting started, Stowaway." Gently he pushed me back onto the bed, took my foot into his hands. He started to write something on the top, but then he ditched the marker. "Wait. I think we're doing this wrong." His lips landed softly on my ankle, trailed a line of kisses up to my knee. "I'm about to make you wish you'd kept your clothes on."

After, our skin bathed again in moonlight, Christian reclaimed the marker, painting letters on my back, slow, soft.

I turned to meet his eyes over my shoulder, raised my brows in question.

"For later," he said, capping the marker. Before I could turn over, he was beside me, close, his hands gathering my hair and lifting it off my neck. His kiss was gentle, drawing a path down the back of my neck, across my shoulder, across the front of my chest, finally landing on my lips.

He watched me endlessly, his eyes tracing the planes of my face, fingers following in gentle strokes that threatened to put me to sleep.

"I want you to do the honors," he whispered, and I knew he meant the boat. My heart swelled at the immensity of the gesture. "We don't have to keep the *Queen* part if you don't like it. Up to you."

It came to me in an instant, a flash. Lemon's tarot cards, the compassionate queen and her golden chalice. The night of the reading, Lemon had said that the Queen of Cups awaited me, that if I could finally let go, find my way back to myself, open my heart to her, she'd be there to embrace me, to help me on this journey. Lemon had meant friendship and compassion, maybe even the chance at love. But it was the boat, too. I was certain now. For me, they were bound—the boat and my heart. Broken and damaged, but maybe—hopefully—not irreparably so.

I thought of all the things that had happened, leading us to this moment, to this opportunity for me to name the vessel upon which I'd spent my first weeks here hiding out. The vessel that might save my home. Chance encounters. Dedication and care. Friendship. Passion. Lots of things had brought us together, and lots of things could make us whole again.

There was no other name for her. I wrote on my hand:

Queen of Cups

I held it up to his eyes, watched the smile stretch across his face.

"*Queen of Cups.*" He kissed me on the mouth, bolted back into the saloon where we'd left the champagne. He grabbed the bottle and nodded for me to follow him above deck.

Nude and free and wholly unconcerned, we christened the boat under her new name, splashing champagne over the hull. Christian poured a final glass, held it to the stars. With a glint in his eyes, he dumped it overboard.

"To Neptune," he proclaimed.

He kissed me passionately, then ducked belowdecks alone, leaving me to whisper my own prayers to the god of the sea.

Moments later, switches and fans flipped on, and the engine purred to life.

"That's our girl," he shouted over the noise. "That's our girl."

Christian eased the *Queen of Cups* out of the slip, and in an instant, a moment, a heartbeat, we were on the open water. Choppy. Foaming at the mouth. Hungry.

Panic flooded my limbs, icing me from head to toe. The boat shimmied against the waves, and everything in me shook. I tried to make my legs move, make them carry me belowdecks to tell him to stop, but they wouldn't budge.

"Elyse," he said gently, reaching for my shoulder.

I turned to face him, shame burning my skin, a painful heat made worse by the compassion in his eyes. I dropped my gaze to his shoulders, the collarbone I'd only moments ago tattooed with my lips, the heart I'd tattooed with my words.

"What the hell happened to you out there?" His eyes were blazing again, belying the gentleness in his voice. I didn't know if he'd meant out there, on the deck of the *Queen of Cups*. Or out there, in the Caribbean. Or maybe some other out there that had scarred me this way, inside and out.

Still, I could only shake my head, lower my eyes in a weak apology.

"We'll figure this out. But you need to trust me," he said.

Understanding. Hope. Encouragement. His voice was thick with all three, and if I'd had the courage to look him in the eyes, I knew I would've seen it there, too.

But it wasn't enough.

Not with my sister, my Granna. Not with my father. Not with all the well-meaning friends and neighbors who'd sent their endless cards and flowers.

And now, it wasn't enough with Christian Kane.

I closed my eyes.

Shook my head.

Slipped his gentle caress.

Reached for my bra and panties and clothes.

"Elyse, look at me. Please."

I finally did.

His eyes seared me. "You can do this."

I've been waiting for you. . . .

Her voice was in my head again, and I shook it to silence her.

"You can," Christian said. Firm. Final. Definite. Uncompromising.

No. I met his eyes again, set my shoulders. Firm. Final. Definite. Uncompromising.

I'm not ready, Christian. I'm just not ready.

Chapter 30

Lemon once told me that a woman's heart was infinite, that there was room for light and dark and everything in between. Now my heart took on a new weight, haunted endlessly by the look in Christian's eyes, the last I'd seen as I'd walked away.

Disappointment.

I knew I'd carry it always, for I was the one who put it there. I let him down, doused the fire in his sea-storm eyes.

I stood in the bathroom at Lemon's, naked before the mirror. Over my shoulder, I turned to read Christian's words.

beautiful soul

He'd written it backward, knowing I'd look in the mirror the moment I could. Wanting me to see it straight. To believe it.

For a moment I almost did.

A curtain of steam parted as I stepped into the shower, and slowly, agonizingly, the searing hot water captured the words he'd written on my bare skin, dragged them down my body to my feet. They swirled for only a second before the tide pulled them under, sucked them back out to the sea where all my stories seemed to end.

Wrapped in a towel, barefoot and dripping on the hardwood floor, I froze in the hallway before my bedroom.

The light was on, spilling out through the doorway.

Vanessa and Kirby were inside.

Kirby was wearing it.

The dress.

My dress.

"That dress is amazing," Vanessa said. "I can't believe she keeps it locked up in here."

"Imagine it in the parade tomorrow? I could so rock this thing." Kirby smoothed her hands over the fabric, her touch delicate. It was all wrong on her; the silky curves sagged against the narrower lines of her hips; her ankles peeked out awkwardly from the bottom.

Maybe if it fit her properly—if I'd walked in and seen her lit up like a runway model, stunning in the gown I could no longer wear—maybe then I would've been able to let it go.

But the dress was custom-made for me. Not just my physical measurements, but everything in me too. My passions, my dreams. All the songs I ever sang, and the dance steps Natalie and I practiced. The dress was cut for the way I moved. The way I breathed.

Fucking breathe, Elyse. . . .

"I should take it off," Kirby said, suddenly deflated. "Before she comes back." She turned to reach for the zipper at the back, saw me standing in the hallway.

"Elyse!" Kirby folded her arms over her chest. "I didn't . . . sorry. I was just looking for a skirt to borrow . . . you know, the red one? Because Noah wanted to go out and I don't have anything cute, and I thought maybe—"

"It's my fault," Vanessa said gently. "I saw the dress hangin' there and told her to try it on. I wanted to see it again. I'm sorry, Elyse."

I nodded quickly, swiping at invisible tears that still wouldn't fall. How long before I could look at a simple blue dress without my heart seizing up?

"Are you okay?" Vanessa asked. "Seriously, I'm really sorry. I didn't think—"

"Stop," Kirby snapped. "Stop apologizing right now." She'd slipped off the dress and was already hanging it back in the closet, burying it once again. She hastily tugged on her shorts and T-shirt and crossed the room to face me. I'd never seen her so enraged.

I took a step back.

"Why are you here, Elyse? What do you want?"

Beneath my bath towel I was naked, and that's exactly how I felt at her words, stripping me down to the bone.

"Sometimes I think you want to be totally alone," she said. "Fine, I try to give you space. Then I think maybe you need a friend, someone to talk to. Or just to hang out with, forget all the bad stuff. I've tried it both ways. *Every* way. Everything I could think of. Invited you out, tried to get to know you, introduced you to my friends. Sometimes you hang out, but it's like you're on the edge, always pulling away again. So I think, okay, I'm coming on too strong, too fast. I do that. But when you're alone, you're just . . . you're sitting here stewing. And what I don't get is if you really want to be alone, why come to the Cove at all? Why come to a place where you have people who are practically family—people who care about you and want to help you? Why spend all that time with Christian and Sebastian? And don't say it's the boat, because we know you told Christian you aren't sailing. He texted us."

"Hey," Vanessa said. "He texted *me*. That wasn't for us to repeat."

"Someone has to say it," Kirby said. "I know I have a big mouth, okay? And sometimes I stick my foot right in it. But not this time. I'm sick of all the tiptoeing. Someone has to speak up around here." She turned her eyes on me again. "Don't just stand here making excuses and pretending everything's okay, when it's so obviously not. You can cry and freak out, you know."

I shrugged, mute and stunted as ever.

"Hey." Kirby grabbed my hand, her voice and eyes suddenly tender. "Elyse, I'm telling you all this because I care. You're like a sister to me."

I shook my head, pulling away from her kindness. *No, thanks. I've got plenty.*

She shrugged. "I don't."

She'd said it plainly, without drama, without heat. It was utterly honest.

My heart throbbed with guilt.

How many more people could I possibly hurt tonight? How many more could I push away?

I glanced from Kirby to Vanessa, expecting downcast eyes, pity. Maybe confusion. But this time, both met me head on. They weren't letting me off the hook.

I loved and resented them for it. The part of me that loved them wanted to grab their hands, to tell them how grateful I was for their friendship, even when I didn't return it in any of the obvious ways. I wanted to tell them that along with Lemon and Christian and Sebastian, they were the first people since the accident who didn't pity me, who didn't have all these expectations for me to move on with my life, make other plans, figure it all out on some arbitrary timetable.

The part that resented them wanted them to know how much it hurt to be with them, how the simplest things like hearing them laugh or sing in the shower shot knives through my heart. How a little thing like watching Vanessa whisper a joke into Christian's ear sent me reeling; not because I was jealous of their relationship, but because it was one more thing I'd never, ever be able to do. How walking in here like this, catching Kirby in the dress had almost stopped my heart. That the gown once held the promise of my entire future but now was nothing but a cruel memory.

I wanted to tell them that I'd fallen in love with the ocean, and now it was my deepest fear. It haunted me, stalked me, filled my nightmares.

I wanted to tell them that I was terrified I'd always feel that way, the warring emotions of love and resentment, trust and fear. That I was so scared I'd never find peace, never move forward. Never live. Never love. That when I lost my voice, I lost everything else, too. And I didn't know how to get it back. Get *me* back. Maybe I never would, and I'd be cursed to remain invisible, inferior because that's how I let others see me.

I wanted them to know it all, the good and the bad. They were, after all, my friends. The best ones, though I never could've predicted it.

But when Kirby finally looked at me with tears in her eyes, and she whispered again, her head shaking, "What do you want, Elyse?" I had nothing for her.

"Fine," she said, wiping away her tears. "If you want to be alone with your dress and your old videos and stuff from the past, go ahead. When you're ready for real friends, right here, right now, you let us know."

"Elyse, I really am sorry," Vanessa whispered. She reached for my hand, but changed her mind, pulled away before touching me.

I closed my eyes, let their words settle on my shoulders like a cold rain.

I don't know how much time passed before I spoke, silent as always.

I'm sorry. I'm not ready. I'm just not ready.

The same insufficient words I'd said to Christian at the marina.

I opened my eyes.

Kirby and Vanessa were gone.

Chapter 31

Even with my eyes closed, my hands found the dress in the back of the closet easily; I knew the weight and feel of it like I knew the smoothness of my skin, the kinks and curls in my hair. Sometimes the dress felt as if it were just as equal a part of me. Just as real.

Kirby hadn't returned to my bedroom since our fight last night, and I hadn't ventured out to look for her. After a restless night I'd spent this morning in a trance, twisting my hair into a cascade of braids secured with jeweled starfish, painting my face to look like a beautiful, dangerous creature from the sea. It was the mask I'd worn on the last best day of my life, and I'd seen so many pictures and videos that I'd memorized it. Recreating it was, like finding the dress, instinctual, a known thing that since that day back in Trinidad had lain dormant within me but not forgotten.

It was an old trick. Sometimes, after a stupid fight with Natalie or Granna, I'd don a different mask, the hair and full makeup and jewels, and pretend I really was a mermaid queen, or an angel, or a butterfly. And when I'd done it for Carnival, it was both relaxing and exciting, watching myself transform before the mirror, waiting to see the costumes Granna had picked out for each performance. She always liked to surprise us, and each one was more beautiful than the last. All the way up to the mermaid dress.

Now, hanging on a hook on the back of the bedroom door and absent its twin, the dress seemed sad in a way that clothing couldn't possibly be. It was as if the fabric carried with it my own shame and fear, prickly guilt about hiding from Natalie, all of it weighing unfairly on its delicate embellishments. Still, time and neglect had stolen none of its elegance. It took my breath away. It was everything I was supposed to be, everything I used to be. Each tiny sequin, every glittering rhinestone, the slip of deep blue silk, all of it held magic.

It was the most beautiful dress in the world.

It was the dress I'd sworn I'd never wear again. The dress that belonged only to the past.

I slipped it from the hook, gathered the fabric in my fists. It would've been so easy to put it back. To stuff it into a plastic bag and bury it in the bottom of the closet under the shoes and Lemon's old books and too many umbrellas. Or better, to shove it into the box with the letter Granna had sent and the chocolates and everything else from my old life, taped up and forgotten.

Kirby was right. I was living in the past. Part of me, anyway. Still locked up with my old videos and music and faults and regrets. I didn't want to live there anymore. I didn't want to live in the dark. Afraid. Alone.

I stepped into the pool of silk, gliding it gently over my thighs. It pulled across my hips a bit more snugly than I remembered, but it still felt familiar, as if it had been waiting for me, for this moment, when we'd be reunited. It hugged me, cool and smooth as water, and though I'd assembled my hair and makeup before the mirror in my bedroom, I couldn't bring myself to look at the reflection of the dress.

I had to go on instinct now, to trust that it looked right, despite its new tightness. I took a deep breath—as much as the dress would allow—and opened the bedroom door, took small steps to the kitchen.

When she saw me standing before the windows that looked out across the sea, Kirby gasped and dropped her lip gloss. "Holy. Fuck."

For the first time since the accident, I really, truly laughed.

Not just a fading smile, a quick breath puffed through my cheeks, but a deep-from-the-belly laugh. It didn't sound like much—a series of wheezes and squawks that reminded me of the gulls fighting over stale bread, and it felt raw and edgy in my throat. But it was mine, a real laugh, a warm laugh, the kind that folded me in half and had me pinching my eyes closed to avoid makeup-ruining tears.

Kirby echoed my hysterics, and when we finally recomposed ourselves, my face turned serious.

You were right, I mouthed.

"I was harsh," she said softly.

Harsh and right. I'm sorry.

I closed the distance between us and grabbed her hands, pulled her into a long hug. A sister kind of hug. When we finally released each other, she gave my dress another once-over, top to bottom.

"Does this mean what I think it means?" she asked. At my nod, her face broke into a triumphant grin. She pulled out her phone. "You're marching with us! Vanessa's going to flip! Mom too! She's already down on Main, setting up the Mermaid Tears booth. The parade goes right past it—she's gonna scream! Elyse, ohmygod, this is so amazing!"

My fingers closed delicately around her wrist, stopping her mid-text. *Wait.*

I rummaged through the junk drawer for the crab stickies, scribbled an explanation.

They still won't let Sebastian march. He's heartbroken.

Kirby tapped her chin. She looked beautiful in her cream-colored gown, a mermaid-style prom dress Vanessa had helped her repurpose with delicate silver sequins, starfish ornaments, and a sheer wrap the color of the sea.

"What do we do?" she asked.

Granna's voice floated through my memory, something she used to tell us whenever we were nervous before a tough competition. *Some days you win the battle just by showing up.*

We weren't going to fight the parade rule makers, to argue in vain to convince them to do the right thing. I wrote:

We're going to show up. And we're going
to make sure Sebastian is the best-looking
mermaid there.

Her eyes sparkled. "Oh, I'm *so* in. What do you need?"

Sebastian had a lot of mermaid gear at home, but pulling this off would require more than a coconut bra and an old bathing suit. He needed something special. Something so amazing it would take the judges' breath away. After everything they'd put him through, it wasn't enough for him to simply march in the parade like a shadow, slipping in behind us.

Fear may have kept me from sailing with Christian today, but there was one Kane brother I could still help.

Sebastian was going to march, loud and proud.

And Sebastian was going to win the crown.

Fifteen minutes later Kirby and I had sufficiently ransacked our closets as well as Lemon's, followed by the gift shop and store room, unearthing every sea-themed accessory and sparkly, sheer, and sea-colored piece of clothing we could find. Individually the items were impossibly ragtag, an explosion of fabric from which we couldn't possibly string together an outfit.

But Vanessa could.

Kirby texted her pictures of everything, along with a rushed explanation of the plan. Vanessa sent back her ideas immediately.

Somehow, with help from the magic of the sea and Vanessa's

devotion to *Project Runway*, we pulled it together. Kirby stood back and surveyed the final assembly laid out on my bed, giddy with pride. "He's going to be amazing."

I nodded, truly impressed. I knew the crowd would fall in love with him as soon as they saw him march, and their applause would likely win over the judges. But I was worried about getting him into the starting lineup in the first place. I wrote:

> I can register on-site, but they won't let him. We have to sneak him in, get him a number.

"We'll figure something out. Just . . . you get Sebastian ready," she said, heading for the front door. "I'll get Vanessa and we'll meet you there in . . ." She checked her phone, eyes widening. "We've got less than an hour. Hurry!"

The Kane house shone through the gray morning mist. The front door was open, and when Mrs. Kane saw me from her perch at the kitchen table, she waved me inside.

It was the first I'd seen her since Christian's confessions last night, and though I knew in my heart his story about her affair was true, it was still so hard to reconcile. I wanted to hate her for what she'd done, for the seeds of doubt she'd planted all those years ago that blossomed into Mr. Kane's anger, his cruelty toward Christian. His dismissiveness of Sebastian.

Instead, my heart ached for her, for all the secrets that must've lived inside, hollowing her out.

"Elyse!" she said as I entered. "Are you marching in the parade? You're stunning!" She grabbed my hands, twirled me around for a complete view. Kirby had had the same shocked reaction, but when I saw it on Mrs. Kane's face—a woman who was a stranger to me, and more cold than hot—my breath caught.

She gestured for me to sit down, and I took the chair across from her at the table, careful not to mess up the stacks of files and devices she'd spread out.

"Sebastian's in his room," she said softly. "I thought he might want to at least *watch* the parade, but he hasn't come out all day. Poor kid."

Mr. Kane? I mouthed.

"Down at the marina. He's still trying to talk Christian out of the race, especially now that he's out a first—Well, you know those two don't exactly see eye to eye."

She looked down at her papers, and an awkward silence settled between us. She finally broke it with a sigh.

"Elyse," she said, "I know it may not seem so from the outside, but Andy and I love our boys."

I wanted to tell her that sometimes it wasn't enough. That love wasn't just a word you used when describing the kids to the neighbors. It wasn't just an obligation.

But instead I only nodded.

"I wanted you and Christian to win," she said. "I knew you could. I would put money on it."

I smiled, not knowing what to say.

"In fact," Mrs. Kane went on, "I *did* put money on it. Fifteen hundred dollars, to be precise."

My eyes snapped to hers across the table.

"We'll keep that between us," she said. "I just thought you should know that I believe in you guys. Just in case you were thinking of changing your mind."

My skin was hot with guilt. She'd been the one to sneak onto the boat, to leave us the money we needed to get the Vega seaworthy when her husband had pulled the plug. I felt the twin shame of disappointing both of them, Christian and his mother.

I took a deep breath, met her eyes again. There was still a chance he could win, could save this property for all of us.

But I couldn't help him. I shook my head sadly, mouthed another apology.

Before she could ask me to reconsider, I grabbed the sticky notes from her pile and told her about our parade plan, asked if I could try to convince Sebastian to come.

"Oh, that would be wonderful," she said warmly. "I think he'd like that."

I rose from the table, turned to head upstairs.

"Elyse," she said, and I stopped, looked at her over my shoulder. "Thank you. For both of them."

I left Mrs. Kane to try my luck with Sebastian, hoping that at least one of the Kane boys would be happy to see me today. I had to knock twice before I heard the doorknob twist. The door creaked

open slowly; Sebastian had already darted back to his bed, lost within the pages of my island fairy tales.

I set my bags on the floor and sat in the chair across from him, waiting patiently for him to glance up. I knew it the instant his eyes caught the sea-blue glint of my dress—the air in the room stilled, the book slid down his chest.

"Atargatis," he whispered.

I stood then, twirled in front of him until the dress fanned out at the bottom, and from the depths of his despair, I fished out a smile.

Now there's *my favorite mermaid*, I mouthed.

"But I'm not a mermaid, remember?" His smile slipped back under. "Boys aren't allowed."

I grabbed his chin, tilted his face toward mine. *That's bull.*

"Yeah, but the mayor and the parade ladies and—"

"Sebastian," I scratched out, a ragged whisper. It shocked him, the hiss passing from my lips to his ears, and his smile returned. I grabbed a marker and paper from his desk.

You are the best mermaid to come to the Cove since Atargatis herself. Now come on, we've got a parade to get to.

"But I don't even have a costume."

I rummaged through my bags and showed him the outfit Vanessa, Kirby, and I had put together: a silver-sequin halter that tied at the neck, a pale blue taffeta skirt cut from Kirby's freshman homecoming dress, a sheer white altar cloth edged with gold and silver beading that we'd use as a cape, and a delicate tiara studded with sea glass. Kirby had texted Lemon about the latter two items, and my aunt gladly donated them to the cause.

Sebastian looked over the shimmering clothes, the seashell hair clips and starfish pins we'd use to make it all fit. He flung himself at me, hugged me so tightly I worried he'd rip my dress.

I untangled his arms and urged him to get ready quickly. *I'll wait outside,* I mouthed. I held up three fingers. *Knock three times when you're ready.*

He dressed himself in record speed, banging excitedly on the door for me to return. The clothes hung off his body, but I'd been expecting as much and immediately set to work wrapping and tucking, folding and fastening in artful, flowing swaths, everything pinned in place with starfish in a way that looked purposeful.

Satisfied, I guided Sebastian to his desk chair and dumped my makeup kit on the desk, expertly separating the silvers, blues, and greens with remembered efficiency. I smiled when I thought of the last time I'd done this: the day of the Bella Garcia show. Natalie rocked at hair, but she could never manage makeup without my intervention. Backstage was a disaster any time she'd tried.

Sebastian sat still as a statue while I painted his face with the sea's blue-green palette, teal swirls outlined in silver and white like waves dancing in the moonlight. His blue eyes were piercing and intense, rimmed in green and gold, and I coated his lips with a simple clear gloss so they wouldn't clash. Makeup complete, I twisted his wild hair into a series of tiny, intricate braids and tendrils, fastening them with seashell clips.

Finally, I removed the tiara from my bag and placed it on his head. The light shimmered through each piece, throwing stars from the bright red gem in the center that dipped into a V against his forehead. It was perfect, a stunning crown of glass.

"How do I look?" he asked, blinking under the weight of the eye makeup and hair ornaments. He reached up and touched the crown with tentative fingers. "Mermaidy?"

Needs one more thing.

The seashell had rested against my throat all summer, gentle and cool, so much a part of me. It was only then, when I'd untied the cord and slid it from my neck, that I felt its absence. I knew my scar lay bare and visible now; the air that kissed it felt like a stiff coastal wind.

Sebastian's eyes never left the shell, and in the wake of his wonder I almost believed it *did* contain my voice, curled into its protective twists and turns, precious and translucent.

I knelt before him and leaned forward, tied the cord behind his neck. The moment was weighty between us; we both felt it. His breath was warm on my cheeks.

"What if you need it?" he whispered.

You need it, I assured him. *I want you to have it now.*

"For keeps?"

I nodded.

His tiny fist closed around it, chest puffed with pride beneath his shimmery halter.

I stretched out my hand, and he grabbed it, held on tight as we marched out to the sea.

Chapter 32

Main Street was swimming with merfolk. Entire families glittered in satin gowns, escorted by eye-patched pirates carrying wooden swords, everyone shadowed by photographers and reporters from the town's only newspaper. P&D sharks were there too, drooling over the future income the gathering could bring them.

Again, my thoughts drifted to home, to Carnival. The scene here, though on a much smaller scale, reminded me of J'ouvert, our festival's official start. By four a.m. on that bleary-eyed Monday morning, the streets of Trinidad would be jammed with people dressed as bats and blue devils and Jab Jabs, covered in mud and oil or paint, marching in time to the beat, all of us anticipating the bands that would come later, the revelry, the bacchanal—complete chaos of the best kind.

The nervous tug of Sebastian's hand reminded me that here in the Cove, today's revelry wasn't a Carnival celebration. We were on a mission.

I stashed Sebastian behind a potted plant in front of Sweet Pacific and wiggled my way to the on-site registration table, one of the only mermaids to sign up this late in the game.

Ten minutes later I had my own number.

One minute after that I was pinning it to the back of Sebastian's cape.

"Forty-two is a good number," he said. "Right?" His voice had lost some of its earlier confidence.

I gave him the thumbs-up. *The best.*

He grabbed my hand, and together we made our way through the crowd, both of us keeping our heads down and our steps quick. Sebastian, as expected, was the only boy in a mermaid gown. But if anyone recognized him, they kept their thoughts to themselves.

Weaving through the throng of mermaids in the parking lot of Cove Community Bank, we took longer than I'd hoped to find the girls. By the time Vanessa and I finished hugging it out about last night's argument, we had but minutes to discuss a plan.

"Wait here," Vanessa said. She slipped into the crowd, came back a moment later with another mermaid—her mother.

"Vanessa, what on earth is going on, sugar?" She looked at me and Kirby, smiled grandly at our dresses. "You girls look stunning! But they're starting the lineup! I need to be back with my age group!"

Vanessa laughed. "I found you with the twenty-somethings."

Mrs. James wiggled her hips. "I can pass."

"I can pass too," Sebastian said, tugging on Mrs. James's bangle-studded arm. "See?"

no matter how hard I'd banged on the table, it didn't change the out-come. Sebastian still walked away with a broken heart.

"It doesn't matter," Christian whispered. I knew he could read my thoughts, see them in the grim set of my mouth. "You showed him that not everyone thinks he's a freak."

He's not.

He nodded toward the doorway, and silently we rose, leaving Sebastian to his dreams.

Out in the hallway Christian pulled Sebastian's door closed quietly, clicked off the hall light.

I was ahead of him just one step, maybe two, when I felt his hand close around mine. He pulled gently, and I turned, following the tide of him until there we stood, chest to chest.

With his free hand he swept the hair from my neck, slipped his fingers underneath. He leaned in close, and our lips brushed.

I shivered.

Inside, the ember flamed back to life, hot as ever.

"You"—his voice was a whisper in the dimness, his breath tickling my lips—"are not what I expected."

Before I could respond, his mouth covered mine.

His hand slid down my back, over the curve of my hip, brought me back to that night at Shipwreck. I pressed against him, slipped my hands beneath his T-shirt, our bodies close and warm.

His whispers turned to moans inside my mouth. I wanted him so badly—to touch him, taste him, feel his breath on my bare skin.

He pulled away for only an instant, took my face in his hands. When our eyes locked, he nodded toward his bedroom and raised an eyebrow, an invitation I accepted without hesitation.

The room was white, bathed in moonlight, with huge windows that overlooked the sea. As the ocean roared beyond, we tumbled onto the bed, peeling sweatshirts and tees off as we fell. From one side of the bed to the other we rolled, our kiss unbroken, devouring. When he was on top again, I wrapped my legs around him, pulled him hard against me as though our jeans didn't exist. His hips dug into my skin, grinding, but his kiss was gentle, sweet and attentive.

When his mouth left mine, I gasped. His lips fluttered down my stomach, against my hip bone, trailing kisses from the left to the right. His tongue circled my belly button, and every inch below it bloomed with desire. Too soon his lips traced a path back upward, between my ribs, through the valley of my breasts, continuing higher, higher, higher. . . .

Everything in me froze.

In an instant his mouth nudged aside the seashell at my throat.

Gentle, his kiss. Lips and tongue against the pale scar, soft as air.

Heavy as the sea.

The heat of him, the tingling pressure on my skin where for so long I'd felt nothing but the cool seashell, was too much. I pulled away sharply, sat up in the moonlight. His eyes were alive, raging like the sea, full of want and something else.

Worry.

He shifted back, giving me space.

"Are you . . . I'm sorry," he whispered, closing his eyes. It took a moment for him to look at me again. "Too fast?"

I shook my head, but it was too late. He thought he'd done something wrong, and when I reached forward, tried to take hold of him again, he slipped away, off the bed in search of our shirts.

"I should've asked you," he said. "Out loud. Waited for a yes, especially since . . ."

His words fell, dropped into the void between us, and my heart followed. It was the first time he'd ever been awkward about my injury, the first he'd ever lost his own words over it. Behind the telltale seashell, my scar burned anew. Instinctively my arms folded over my chest.

"I'm sorry, Elyse." Christian handed me my shirt, holding his own in front of the bulge in his pants. "I got . . . caught up."

He turned away to get dressed, missed the fevered shake of my head. I watched his tattooed shoulder disappear beneath the white T-shirt, then tugged on my own, not sure whether I should reclaim his sweatshirt. I let it be.

I felt like an idiot.

I didn't want it to end here. Every inch of my body didn't want it to end here. But like the ever-shifting tide, the moment had crashed upon us, receded.

"I'll walk you home," he said. "Just . . . give me a minute." And he was gone, down the hall, leaving me alone in his big, cold bed, the moon looking on, embarrassed on my behalf.

Chapter 26

Christian and the regatta may have evicted me from my original hideaway, but all my pensive wandering seemed always to lead back to her, my queen of possibilities, and the following morning I found myself stretched out in a familiar spot.

Lemon had donated some outdoor cushions she'd had in her garden shed, significantly less musty than the ones we'd tossed from the Vega, and I set them up in the saloon and berth. I crawled in on top of them, content to be alone with my endless thoughts.

But when the boat rocked with Christian's steps an hour later, my stomach fizzed.

Hope and desire. Anticipation.

Christian hopped down through the companionway, looked at me across the saloon. "Oh," he said softly, a dim smile sliding across his lips. "There you are."

He handed me his sweatshirt, the one I'd abandoned last night, though it wasn't cold today.

All of last night's awkwardness vanished. Maybe it had never existed. Maybe I'd only imagined it. Feared it.

"I texted you to meet up for breakfast, but when I didn't hear back, I figured you were doing your own thing."

I checked my pockets, realized I'd left my phone at home.

"Scoot over," he said, slipping off his shoes.

I sat up and shifted over in the small bed as he climbed in next to me. We sat with our backs against the shelving, heads bent, and he took my hand, warm and comforting. Solid.

After a long silence, he nodded toward my old poem and said, "I've been thinking about plans. A and B and everything after. You never told me your B."

I shrugged. Singing was everything to me. It was hard, turning a passion into a profession—I'd only gotten a glimpse of that, and already the competition was getting stiffer, the rehearsals more grueling, the disappointments sharper. But I was ready to work for it with Natalie by my side. We'd always given each other strength.

I knew there would be setbacks and letdowns. But I'd never considered the possibility that it wouldn't happen.

I reached for the seashell at my throat, tugged it gently. The doctors had warned me that the physical recovery would be slow, that I'd still feel rawness and discomfort in my throat, maybe for years. They were right; I had felt that. I'd learned to mitigate it with hot tea and honey, with relaxation, with rest.

But there was no mitigating treatment for the deeper wounds.

What happened when the one thing you loved, the song of your soul, was taken from you? What pieces of your old life were you left with, and how could you begin to put them back together? How could you find your way back to the people who'd hurt you the most?

Outside, the ocean churned and hissed, continued its endless dance.

Still, I couldn't answer.

Christian squeezed my hand. "I wish I had the words for this."

I squeezed back. He'd never had a big dream like this—he'd said as much. So he couldn't imagine what it was like to have his dream taken from him, to know that no matter how hard he worked or what sacrifices he made, he'd never get it back.

I tried to tell him as much, in so many silent words and gestures, all the expression I had left.

"You're right," he said softly. "I wouldn't know. Couldn't. I've never had any dream. Never looked for it, never found it, never followed it."

Dreamless, I mouthed, more because that's the word that came to me than because it was right. His story felt like the before to my after, and I thought I'd understood him.

But he shook his head, eyes brightening with some new thought. "No, not like that. More like, limitless."

The ocean shushed before us. I don't know when the tide came in, but it was there, rocking the boat with more urgency. Farther out, were always open. The ocean was a lullaby, an undertone to the constant blare of music, the steel pans from neighboring bands, the chitchatter of hundreds of birds. Someone was always talking, and when my sisters were visiting, there were never fewer than three simultaneous conversations, all of us dipping in and out of them effortlessly.

Here in Oregon, though, the ocean was all of it. The melody and the harmony. The bass and the beat. The simultaneous conversation, an endless symphony of hush and roar. I had to close the windows if I wanted to hear my Granna across the miles.

I messaged: *If I open the windows, all you hear is ocean. All day, all night.*

Granna laughed. "Need to tell Lemon to fix up her music collection. Get some soca, a little spice from the islands."

I almost told her about Bella Garcia. The song that had infiltrated my nights alone on the beach again, got me back to dancing. Since that first time, I'd been out twice more. Never for as long as that first night, never as passionate. But I was moving again, mouthing along with the words. Workin' my way back, as the song went.

The dancing was a small thing though, just for me, and I knew she'd read too much into it.

Lemon has wind chimes, I typed. *And fairy music. Those fairies know how to party, Granna.*

Granna swatted at me with a laugh. She got up to stir the callaloo, humming as she did. "So," she said, sighing when she settled back into her chair. "What about a regatta? You sailing again, gyal?"

I nodded quickly, as if it weren't half the big deal she was making it. I typed her a message about the race, how Christian and I had to patch up the boat first.

Lemon had already told her about the bet, but I wondered if Granna would ask about Christian. *Tell me 'bout dis boy, den,* she'd say, and I'd smile and deny it, no matter that he was quickly becoming the last thing I thought about as I drifted off to sleep, the first when I woke. When it came to boys, my older sisters had always warned Natalie and me to never reveal too much to Granna.

Somehow she figured it out anyway.

But when her words came now, it was as if Christian was the least significant part of the story.

"Sailing again. This mean you coming home soon?" She fixed me with her patented no-bull Granna stare, and all I could do was squirm beneath it. "Not the same here without you."

I tried to smile, to throw her off the trail, but like all the boys that had crossed our paths, sadness was not something I could hide from Granna.

"You can't go on like this," she said, and the lightheartedness that opened our conversation was officially gone.

I sucked my teeth at her, the only sound I could still make. Especially thousands of miles away, where she couldn't smack me for it.

"Don't you give me that steups," she scolded. "It is a tragedy, yes. But it is what fate decide for you, Elyse. Don't throw away your life and your family for this grief. Let it go."

On the stage.

Holding her hands when they'd announced her big win.

It was *our* big win too. The moment that was supposed to launch our entire future together . . .

"Those two," Lemon said, pulling me back to the present. "That's what happens when you see yourself through someone else's mirror, Elyse. You build your dreams for them, ignoring your own heart. One day you wake up and wonder how the fire went out." She squeezed my leg. "Promise me you'll never do that."

Lemon looked out on the sea, gurgling and churning again, and I suddenly realized why she didn't move to Tobago with Dad and Granna when she got pregnant with Kirby—unexpectedly—after a weekend of no-strings-attached Carnival revelry. My sisters told me that Granna had tried to insist, but Lemon was an artist, an old soul. She knew what it was to feel that fire burning inside her, that passion, and for her it was wholly connected to this place, the Pacific Northwest, Atargatis Cove. Staying in Tobago with my family might've made her life easier, more convenient.

But it would've extinguished her fire.

I wanted to ask her if that's why she took me in this summer, if she thought it might help me find my own fire, light it up again. But a fresh wave rose and crashed against the rocks, spraying us with salt water, and in my momentary fear I let the moment pass.

"I don't know what to make of this regatta bet," Lemon said. Her eyes held mine again, serious, and for a minute I thought she might ask me if I'd think about helping Christian. Even just getting the boat patched up. But when she cupped my chin with her palm, a smile softened her face. "But it's not for you to worry. You'll always have a place with me and Kirby, for as long as you want it. Even if we have to move and close the gallery. Even if we end up in a tent on the beach. You're a joy, Elyse, and you're always welcome. Never, ever doubt that this is your home too."

Home.

Each of my older sisters left home after high school, one after the other. Juliette was first, gone to Barcelona, ancient city on the sea. By day she studied at Universitat Autònoma de Barcelona, and when the moon rose, she walked the shores, watched the city glimmering like a jewel. Martine followed the tea leaves through China and India, learning how to plant and harvest, dry and blend, make a "proper cuppa," as she said. Gabrielle was eager to explore the islands, sticking her toes in all the sands of the Caribbean—Jamaica, Barbados, Honduras—but she missed our homeland, and eventually returned to open a dive shop near the cocoa estate. Hazel was the last to leave, following her dreams to Greenland, that vast white fist on the globe, where with her camera she perched on the tips of the tallest icebergs, photographing God's most impossible creations.

Natalie was still home, still waiting for me, but the rest were explorers. Adventurers. Dreamers.

Maybe our island looked different from the shores of Spain, from behind the thick crowds of the Far East, from a ship sailing on the about your own liberations." She tugged on one of Kirby's curls, eyes sparkling with new mischief. "Where *is* Noah tonight?"

Kirby bristled. As she leaned close to Vanessa with a string of denials, I backed up toward our bedrooms. My door was ajar at the very end of the hall, and the light from my desk lamp spilled into the hallway, an invitation to a better place.

Three steps in, my passage was denied.

Anderson Kane.

The father.

"I don't suppose *you've* seen our birthday boy?" Christian's dad pointed at me, his smile forced. Wearing jeans with a button-down and a tie, sleeves rolled deliberately to his elbows, Anderson Kane reminded me of a sandy-blond version of the "corporations are people" guy who ran for U.S. president a while back.

"You must be Elyse. I'm Andy, Andy Kane," he said, not waiting for an answer about Christian. He smelled like mint and expensive cologne and just beneath that, the faint odor of cigarettes.

Behind me, Vanessa and Kirby continued their good-natured teasing, sipping their daiquiris. All around us, party guests drank and laughed, nibbling cheese and those eraser-shrimp from small plates, and this man's eyes were on my scar. I could feel them, behind their glassy politeness, burning through my shell necklace.

"What . . . um . . . what . . ."

What happened. Ask me what happened. Ask me why I can't speak.

"What can I get you to drink?" He pointed at me again. "Coke? Seltzer?"

I held up my glass, still half-full of strawberry-banana daiquiri.

"You're all set, then. Good."

I nodded.

"So. I understand we're going to be neighbors," he said.

I nodded.

"For the whole summer, that right?"

Nodded, nodded.

It was getting pretty awkward, me waiting for Andy Andy Kane to say what he wanted to say, him going on not saying it. I tried to extract myself, edging back toward Kirby and Vanessa. Somehow he kept finding more words.

"Have you met the rest of my family?" he asked, looking around. "I don't know when he'll grace us with his presence, but Christian's my oldest, the birthday boy. Just finished up his freshman stint at Stanford. Sebastian's the little guy, he's running around here somewhere. Meredith, my wife? I know she'd love to say hello."

The way he talked about them felt like a sound bite, a clean arrangement of words he'd mastered but never really meant.

Silence was a fishhook, catching secrets and tugging them from beneath the surface. Since losing the ability to speak, I'd learned to observe, to watch and listen when others had all but forgotten my presence. In ways I'd never noticed before, I'd seen bodies defy words, how a person's eyes and hands revealed truths their mouths were trying so desperately to deny.

"Seriously, Dad? *Seriously?*"

"Companies change the conditions of a deal all the time," Mr. Kane said. "Markets tank. Stock valuations shift. CEOs get booted. You've got to learn to adapt. Otherwise you'll never make it in the real world."

In the real world, I thought, *your parents shouldn't hang you out to dry.*

My heart squeezed. I missed my dad. Granna.

Christian, head in hands, tugged at his hair. I couldn't see his eyes, but his anger was obvious. Still, despite the few barbs he'd launched, I suspected he wouldn't erupt. It was just like the night of the bet; his father was wrong, but no matter how hard the man pushed, no matter how infuriating his words, Christian wouldn't unleash his anger.

A shiver rolled through me.

I wasn't physically afraid of Mr. Kane. He didn't seem like the kind of father who'd smack his kids around, or put his fist through a wall, or even raise his voice above the stern tone he'd always used in my presence. But in him was a deep well of bitterness, the kind that could swirl and tug and yank you under before you even realized you'd gotten your feet wet. I scooted my chair closer to the table, reached across for the syrup.

Next to me, Christian seethed.

"It is, after all, the Pirate Regatta," Mr. Kane said, looking pointedly at us both. "If you're insisting on racing, time to pirate up, kids."

At that Christian tossed his napkin onto the plate and rose

calmly, letting me know he'd be ready to head out to the Vega in a few. He thanked his father for the waffles as though it had been uneventful, just another morning at the Kane house.

Maybe it had been.

I trembled with anger for Christian, but I stayed put, eyes on the coffee that had since chilled in my mug.

Sebastian finished clearing the table, and when he returned, he stood next to his father, tapped his shoulder. "I have an idea. Let's just keep the house forever. When you die, me and Christian will take care of it. And then our kids and their kids and—"

"Why don't you leave that for the grown-ups to take care of?" Mr. Kane said. He offered a belated smile, but even Sebastian could tell it was insincere.

Sebastian sighed. "All the grown-ups do is fight about it."

"Clear Elyse's plate—she's finished eating. Then you can go with them to the boat," he said. "Mom and I have some things to discuss today."

"I know, but—"

"Sebastian," his father said sternly. "It's not a suggestion."

Sebastian's shoulders sank, but he did what he was told, picked up my plate and silverware and disappeared into the kitchen without another protest. Sadness emanated from the space he'd just vacated. My eyes blurred as my gaze drifted back to his father.

"More coffee, Elyse?" Mr. Kane held up the carafe, his fake smile as bright as the sky was gray.

I passed him my mug for a warm-up.

He topped it off.

I gave a tiny smile of thanks, even though I didn't really want more coffee.

Behind its protective seashell, the starfish scar on my throat burned.

There were lots of ways to lose your voice.

Chapter 15

In the stainless-steel kitchen of the main house of d'Abreau Cocoa Estates, Granna sat at the counter, a pot of callaloo simmering on the stove behind her.

I closed my eyes, could just about smell the spicy soup across the miles.

"If you were home, gyal, you wouldn't have to imagine how it taste."

I smiled at the computer. After yesterday's tense breakfast with the Kane family, I was just grateful Granna was home to accept my Skype invite this morning, no matter that she was baiting me.

I'm eating okay here, Granna, I typed. *Hot pepper sauce fixes a lot. :-)*

"Too quiet there, though," she said, narrowing her eyes suspiciously. "I can hear your hair growin'."

She was right; in the house it was quiet. Back home our windows

"Plain latte and a cranberry-orange scone for you," he said. "Afraid I'm not that sophisticated. Black coffee, glazed donut does me fine."

I raised my eyebrows.

"Noah," he explained. His eyes drifted momentarily to the yellow-and-blue boat at the other end of the marina, our nemesis. When he looked at me again, he was grinning. "Apparently you and Kirby are the most regular regulars the Black Pearl has ever had. His words, not mine."

After Christian had left the house last night, Kirby spent an hour lecturing me about him. She said I'd have to stand my ground; he'd either boss me around like a deck hand, try to hook up with me, or both. "That boy can charm the pants off pants," she said.

She didn't mention anything about him getting breakfast. Asking Noah for my order. Waiting for me to arrive before eating his own food.

Balancing the tray on one hand, he stepped over the boat rails and climbed out, barefoot, inviting me to sit down on the dock next to him. I slipped off my shoes and dangled my feet over the edge, same as Christian. We ate in silence, side by side, cold water licking our toes. When I felt his eyes on me again, I turned to face him.

Thank you. I took another sip of the latte. It was hot and creamy, nothing like the bitter, tree bark–flavored brew Lemon had made.

For a moment he didn't speak, just watched, like he was trying to decide what to say.

With a sigh he gathered up our trash and rose from the dock. "Last chance to bail, no judgments. But then we'd have to call this a date. I bought breakfast, after all, and you didn't even spend the night."

I jumped to my feet. *Here to work.*

When we were back on board, he picked up his tools, reassembled them in the box. "I tried to open up some of the instrumentation, get a look at the electrical. Battery's got juice, but it's pretty corroded. Oil needs to be changed. Overall, she's a hot mess. Girl needs a complete scrubdown before I can really get in there. You ready?"

At my nod, he passed me a surgical mask.

"Put it on," he said, donning his own. "Mold. Lead paint. Dust. Who knows what cancer-causing surprises await on the ol' *Queen of.*"

With a janitor's closet worth of cleaning supplies, we each took an end of the boat, Christian in the V-berth and me on the aqua-blue deck.

The filth was as old as the sea; it's possible that my scrub-scrub-scrubbing unearthed more than a few ancient fossils. Judging from the bucket of black water in the saloon, Christian's experience belowdecks was the same.

After what felt like three days, Vanessa stopped by with a picnic basket full of tiny sandwiches, grapes, carbonated waters, and what passed for chocolate bars here in the States.

"Dig in, y'all," she said. "Can't stay—Mom came in early after all, and now she's insisting on a spa day down in Bandon. By insisting, I mean I nagged her until she caved. Elyse, wanna come?" She wriggled her fingers at me. "Matching manis?"

I shook my head, thanked her anyway.

"Poacher." Christian laughed. "Lucky you showed up with food, otherwise I might think you were totally useless."

"I promised to help, and I don't make idle threats," she said. "I also brought intel from Kane HQ."

Christian stilled.

"I stopped by," she said. "Sebastian was outside, said your parents were havin' World War Three up on the deck. I heard them too."

"That's not intel," he said. "That's a snapshot."

"Yeah, well, your mom's really pissed about this whole bet Sebastian told me she was cryin' about it. She doesn't want your daddy to sell."

Christian looked out at the horizon, all the way to Japan, it seemed. "She had her chance to take a stand that night."

"Don't shoot the messenger," Vanessa said.

Christian shivered, hard. It was as if his body had to physically shake off his thoughts. When he looked up again, the ghost smile was back. "Harm a hair on your pretty little head?" he said. "Never. Thanks for lunch."

"Catch y'all at Shipwreck later." She blew us each a kiss, tossed a backward wave over her shoulder as she walked away.

After the too-short lunch break, we hit the decks again for another two hours before Christian finally called it a day. I was relieved; both of us were exhausted, covered in grime and dust and a cold sweat made worse by the encroaching coastal mist.

After securing the cleaning supplies in the saloon, we climbed out to empty the trash and dirty water at the marina dump station, and then headed for Starfish Point. The ocean was getting restless again, frothy in the distance as the waves gathered strength.

I felt Christian's hand on my arm, stopping us.

"Dolphins," he said, pointing to a series of small white peaks in the water. "If we had Sebastian's binoculars, we could see them up close. Watch."

It took me a moment to catch sight of them, but once I did, they were impossible to miss. We couldn't see the animals themselves, but they left a trail of white splashes as they arced through the sea.

I wanted to ask him where they were going, whether they lived here or were just migrating through, but before I could form the words, a wave leaped up from the shore, dousing us to our knees.

I sucked in a sharp breath.

The sea is going to take me. . . .

I saw her then, the mermaid queen, tail shimmering in the distance against the gray water. She laughed, piercing and hollow. Her voice rattled inside my head, scraping the walls of my heart.

I've been waiting for you, Elyse d'Abreau. . . .

I was freezing, shaking, tumbling into the waves, falling into the darkest deep. . . .

"Elyse?"

I opened my eyes. My feet were planted on the shore, legs soaked and shivering. Christian's eyes were full of worry.

He couldn't, of course, and here I stood, cursing again the star at my throat, the gash it had covered.

We went back inside the saloon. I grabbed the nautical chart, found a clean spot where we hadn't written our secrets.

With the Sharpie, I wrote furiously.

I wish I had the words to say this out loud, because I owe you that much.

I've loved our time together this summer, all the work we put into the boat.

I want you to win the regatta. Not just because of the house, or to prove your dad wrong.

But because you love this boat, and the sea, and you deserve it.

I know you'll do it, you'll beat Noah and you'll race through the finish first.

But you won't be doing it with me.

I can't sail.

I can't face the open sea again.

I'm so sorry.

As Christian read the words, I looked out through the hatch at Vega, patron star, and outside, the gray-blue Pacific swirled and sputtered against the boat, as if to taunt me.

I was anchored to the deck, naked and shivering, and all around me the stars blinked into blackness.

I was sinking.

Cold.

Falling.

Dropping like a stone to the bottom of the sea, and Christian wouldn't even know I'd fallen.

I've been waiting for you. . . .

The mermaid's voice was in my head. She reached out through the water, pale fingers stretching to reach me, to ensnare me, to pull me into the depths. . . .

"Elyse!"

I opened my eyes, surprised to find myself on deck, the Vega bobbing innocently in the slip. We'd never even left, I saw then.

Christian was looking up at me through the companionway, his face panicked and confused. "What's wrong? What happened?"

I shook my head. *I can't.*

"Can't what?" He killed the motor and fans, climbed up top to reach me. His hands were warm on my bare arms. "You can't tell me? No way. You can tell me anything."

I shook my head again. *Sail.*

"Sell?"

Sail.

Christian squinted, brow creased with fresh concern.

I looked at him, mute, willing him to fish the words from my heart, to speak them aloud where I could only mutter and hiss. But he didn't.

She beamed at the little mermaid beside us. "Well don't you look adorable, Miss . . . I'm not sure we've met, darlin'.'"

"Mom!" Vanessa gave her mother a playful nudge. "It's Sebastian Kane."

Mrs. James did a double take.

Sebastian giggled. "Fooled you!"

"Sebastian, you look amazing, honey! Look at you!" She twirled him around, checked out the costume. "Well, we'd better get you over with the other kids. Come on."

"I can't," he said. "Boys aren't allowed. But don't worry, because someone has a plan."

Vanessa filled her mother in on the details, all the so-called "rules" that got us here.

Mrs. James looked aghast. "That child has as much right to be here as any of us. We're not about to take this lyin' down, I promise you that."

"What should we do?" Kirby asked, worry pinching her face. "It's starting."

"At this point, girls, there's only one question we need to ask." Mrs. James flashed a clever, confident grin. "WWTTD? What would Tami Taylor do?" She nodded once, her jaw set in some new, determined mission.

"It's from a show," Kirby said to me. "*Friday Night Lights*? Tami's the mom, and there's this whole Texas thing—"

"Texas forever," Vanessa said.

"Texas forever," Mrs. James echoed. "Follow me, mermaids."

We fell in behind her, buffering Sebastian, and onward we marched, our toppling, tiptoed, tight-dressed, gender-bending mermaid brigade.

The parade marshal—the woman who'd originally denied Sebastian at the registration table—shouted into a bullhorn, chasing mermaids onto Main Street in glittering waves of blue and green.

Our group waited patiently behind the throng, and when she saw us, unrecognizable in our costumes, she quickly ushered us along. "You're all mixed up!" she said, shooing us out into the parade. "Try to find your own age groups. Go! Go! Go!"

My insides lit up with nervous butterflies, feeling as we stepped onto Main Street like we'd gotten away with the world's greatest heist. Sebastian's grin stretched from here to the Pacific; I'd never seen him so happy. He waved to everyone we passed, threw candy at the kids lined up on the sidewalks from the satchel he'd brought for just such an opportunity.

With Mrs. James in the lead, Kirby, Vanessa, and I fell in behind Sebastian, ready to confront any assailants, verbal or otherwise.

"He's really into this," Vanessa said. Raising her voice, she called ahead. "You go, Sebastian!"

For all the mayor's huffing and puffing, no one mocked Sebastian. They cheered as we approached, smiles growing brighter when Sebastian's light shone in their direction. It was likely they didn't recognize him with all the braids and makeup, but as he'd been dreaming about all year, the kid just wanted to march; he wasn't concerned with making a case.

We marched down the entire half-mile stretch of Main Street, past Sweet Pacific, past the pet store where Christian had gotten the crickets that still haunted the *Never Flounder*. As we neared the booth where Lemon was selling her small sculptures and handmade soaps, she cheered and whooped, stepping into the street to snap pictures with her phone. We continued on past the Cove's only pizza place, past Big Mike's hardware, past the yarn shop and all the other places I'd come to know this summer. Soon we were nearing the end, approaching the intersection where the parade would turn off, the mermaids lining up with their age groups for judging. On a platform decorated with red-white-and-blue ribbons, on a fake throne the size of a small boat, Mayor Wesley Katzenberg sat, utterly impressed with himself.

The final judge.

My heart sped up, adrenaline coursing through my veins.

Mrs. James turned around, winked at us. "Follow my lead, girls."

From her hip she raised a bullhorn—she must've swiped it from the parade marshal.

"Ladies and gentlemen, my friends and neighbors of Atargatis Cove! Please give a special round of applause for Sebastian Kane!" She tugged him forward gently, giving him space to soak up the spotlight. My eyes were on the mayor, and at Mrs. James's announcement, his face turned red, eyes lasering our little mermaid pack.

Before the mayor was even out of his chair, Mrs. James lifted the bullhorn, boomed across the crowd. "At six years old, Sebastian is the Cove's youngest and first boy to march as a mermaid in the festival parade. That's right, ladies and gentlemen. You're witnessing history today!" She turned toward the mayor, waved with her free hand. "Thank you, Mayor Wesley Katzenberg, for your compassionate open-mindedness in letting this young man embrace and showcase his personal truth!"

All around us, mermaids cheered. Brenda and Gracie, beautiful in their matching gold dresses, blew bubbles into the crowd, screaming Sebastian's name in support. We cheered the hardest, though— Vanessa, Kirby, Mrs. James, and I, with my silent but enthusiastic gestures—all of us clapping for our mermaid, number forty-two.

Mrs. James lifted the bullhorn once more. "Sebastian Kane and Wes Katzenberg, y'all. Let's put our hands together once more to give these pioneers the extra applause they deserve!"

At that the crowd went wild, and all Mayor Katzenberg could do was blubber and smile, sit down in his chair and bask in the gratitude as if he'd earned it.

"That's my momma, y'all," Vanessa said. It was obvious how she'd won so many votes in Texas, gotten so many initiatives passed. That woman knew how to make things happen.

I slipped into the sidewalk crowd to let the judging commence, a two-step process that involved the crowd's vote by noise level and the mayor's final stamp of approval. No longer was I worried about

Sebastian's win, though; he was a shoo-in, thanks to Mrs. Kane's campaign and, first and foremost, the kid's natural enthusiasm.

I was right. At the end of the voting, number forty-two took the title. Mrs. Kane was there with her phone, taking pictures instead of work calls as Sebastian accepted the win. Over his grin, she winked at me.

There were tears in her eyes for him. Our official Mermaid Queen of Atargatis Cove.

Small and glowing under his new golden crown, Sebastian called my name across the crowd, beaming when our eyes met. He made his way through congratulatory hugs and high fives, finally reaching me on the sidewalk.

"Hold on a minute, kids." Mayor Katzenberg was there, suddenly, looming over both of us. His smile was as sharp toothed as ever. "I'm not sure what's going on here, but I thought the rules were clear. Boys cannot be in the mermaid parade."

My heart sped up, heat rising inside me.

Sebastian looked at me.

Looked at the mayor.

Shook his head.

Pointed at his crown.

To Wes Katzenberg, King of the Sea, my little mermaid said plainly, "I think maybe you need glasses, because a boy just won the crown."

The mayor stormed away, mad but finally bested.

My heart swelled with pride. Sebastian was beautiful and rare, a perfect pearl in a sea of gray oysters. I knelt down before him so that our eyes were level. My fingers traced the shell at his neck, our shared voice.

He'd done it. He'd really done it.

"You're my best friend," Sebastian told me, and I knew, the instant he pressed a glossy kiss against my cheek, what I had to do next.

Pirates, wenches, and sea creatures from the depths of the Cove's imagination jammed the docks, and it took more than a few minutes to elbow my way through the fray. In all my lamenting the lost music this summer, I'd nearly forgotten these minor inconveniences, squeezing between walls of costumed bodies without so much as a *pardon me, sorry, coming through.* But pity wasn't part of the plan, so I kept my head down, dove into the mix and swam through arms, legs, and elbows until I finally broke into the light.

The rare sun sharp in my eyes, I gathered the ocean-blue silk of my dress in my fists, and I sprinted to the end of the marina, past the *Never Flounder,* past the other boats bobbing in anticipation, down the last dock, to the very last slip.

Christian, wait! my mind shouted. *Christian! Christian!* I thought his name so many times, so loudly, that when he finally met my eyes, I thought he must've heard me. Really heard me.

But that was impossible.

He stood on the bow, where he'd just been double-checking the mast. Now his eyes held mine, unflinching. *Queen of Cups* bobbed beneath his feet, and he shifted his weight, one foot casually resting on the rails.

"That's enough, Christian." Mr. Kane sprouted up through the companionway, pounding two open-handed smacks against the wood. "You made your point. Let's—Elyse? I thought you weren't seaworthy?"

My heart slammed inside me like a fist.

Mr. Kane was right. I wasn't seaworthy. I wasn't worthy of another chance, of Christian's soulful eyes pinning me in place, making everything inside me hot and hopeful.

But I was asking for it anyway.

Ignoring his father, I looked again at Christian, held his gaze. Matched it in intensity.

Please take me back. Take me to the sea.

Our summer together played behind my eyes, flashed like a slideshow. Weeks and weeks fixing up the old boat. All our pirate missions. Dancing at Shipwreck, bodies pressed together beneath the strobe lights, lost in their own rhythms. Our mermaid wedding by the sea. The hike. The kisses. The caresses. The passion. The secrets and stories we'd shared, all the things I'd written on his heart, on the walls of his boat.

And that first night, where it all began.

There's a girl writing on my boat.

I kept my eyes on his, though they'd started watering from the glare, and finally he shook his head and stepped down from the hatch.

"Thanks for the pep talk, Dad. We got it from here."

Mr. Kane closed his eyes. "I thought we agreed—"

"This is my gig," Christian said. "And I said, we got it from here."

Without further argument Mr. Kane stepped off the boat, a bit wobbly as he steadied himself on the dock. He looked at me, scanned the dress, shook his head. To his son, he said only, "Screw this up, Christian, and that's on you."

We watched in silence as he marched down the dock, back into the marina's throbbing masses.

"You're late, mate." Christian thrust his hand toward me portside, unfurled his fingers and a smile to go with. It was like he'd been waiting all along, like he always knew and trusted I'd be there.

You sure? I wondered it, even as I grasped his hand and climbed aboard.

Christian smiled. The real one. It broke over my lips in a single kiss, deep and certain. With his forehead pressed to mine, he said, "Get your sparkly hot mermaid ass on that tiller. We've got a boat to race, Stowaway."

Chapter 33

Seas the Moment, Daring Delilah, Chasing Sunsets, The Other Woman, Black Star. Like photographs, the name of every boat told a story.

But of the two dozen vessels lined up for the regatta, there were only two stories I cared about: *Queen of Cups*, and our number one competitor, *Never Flounder*.

This was it.

Race day.

I looked up to the sky, and though I couldn't see the constellations in the daylight, I stared into the brightness until white sparks appeared before my eyes.

Please, Lyra. Vega, I thought. *Keep us steady. Look out for us today.*

"Ten minutes," Christian said, and I nodded, headed belowdecks to get ready.

As Christian made his final checks, I changed out of my dress, putting on a sweatshirt and a pair of drawstring pants Christian had left on the boat. There was no time to wash off the makeup or twist the ornaments from my hair, so for now, part mermaid I remained.

Steadying myself for the race, I scanned the cabin one last time before the start, taking in the final items Christian had brought on board this morning: First aid kit. Extra food and clothing. Two fire extinguishers. Flare gun. Foghorn. Life buoy.

I took a deep, salty breath, counted the waves lapping against the boat until the fear finally left my limbs.

We wouldn't need any of those things, I told myself. They were just precautions. This wasn't even a real regatta—not like the hardcore competitions you'd sometimes catch on television. This was the Pirate Regatta of Atargatis Cove. Loose rules. Shorter course. Untrained weekend sailors. Cheating encouraged.

"This is it," Christian said, peeking at me through the companionway, and his enthusiasm was sudden and contagious. Captured by the warmth in his smile, I forgot about the houses, the stakes of this race, what it meant if we lost. I forgot about my fears. Instead, I imagined us together on the open seas, here and in Tobago. Maybe, I thought, I'd take him there. From the deck of the *Atlantica* we'd float on the warm Caribbean, and I'd show him my places, all the old haunts that still haunted me.

"You ready?" he asked. His eyes sparkled like the sea, and I answered him with two steps forward and a kiss as vast and deep as our dreams.

❖ ❖ ❖

A shot rang out across the great Pacific, and the line of boats wavered and broke, all of us jockeying for the best position.

I manned the tiller while Christian worked the sails. Per my captain's orders, we'd started behind the line, building up speed and crossing the line the instant the race began. The strategy paid off; we'd gotten a clean lead, breaking away from the knot of inexperienced boaters and successfully avoiding their bad air.

From his position at the boom Christian said, "Noah's main weakness is *Never Flounder* herself. He's so protective of her that he gets skittish when other boats get too close. He'll round the marks too wide or too tight to avoid a hit, and he'll back off if we're coming at him too hard. That'll be our best chance to gain on him."

I nodded, reviewing the course again in my mind, just as Christian had mapped it out for me. There were three marks we'd have to round, plus other obstacles, and that tricky spot by Seal Rock.

"Elyse," he said, and when I looked up at his face, he was alight with joy. "We got this."

As the mainsail captured the sea air, fluttering and then smoothing quickly, Christian's smile was unchecked. The breeze was moderate as we headed upwind, and after a moment he flattened the sail to pick up some speed. While the cockier sailors put more draft in their sails, banking on more power, we maintained our lead, moving at a steady clip through the first leg of the course.

Christian was so at ease on the water, such a natural sailor. It was the first I'd seen him really let loose, and though he was focused and serious, he was also at peace. Completely in his element. No matter the outcome of the race, in this moment I was as proud of him as I'd been of his little brother at the parade. I hadn't even told Christian about the big parade win; I had a feeling Sebastian wanted to share that news himself.

As Christian predicted, we easily left most of the boats several lengths behind, and if any caught up, it wasn't long before we outmaneuvered them again.

Only *Never Flounder* pulled ahead, soon taking and holding the lead. Despite the inexperienced first mate, Noah seemed more than capable of handling the boat.

"Let's jerk the sheet," Christian said as Noah gained another length on us. "She's luffing." He followed through on his own order, gaining a little on Noah when the sail filled smoothly again, carrying us out.

So far we were doing everything by the book, and our calm tactics were keeping us steady. The Pirate Regatta wasn't about entertaining the crowd with fancy tricks and daring moves—things that could mess with your head during a race and lead to sloppy mistakes and showboating. It was about speed and strategy, about getting to the finish line first.

Still, the *Queen of Cups* drew a graceful, elegant wake through the water, gliding across the waves as though she barely touched the surface. She was stunning, and I was at ease in a way I hadn't thought possible.

"First mark," Christian said as we neared it. I shifted the tiller as he worked the boom, guiding us through. The boat heeled into the first turn, picking up speed as Christian trimmed the sails.

Against the other boats, *Queen of Cups* and *Never Flounder* were unmatched. The course seemed too easy, the wind and water too cooperative, it almost felt as if we were just out with Noah for a friendly sail. I could just about taste the picnic lunch we'd drop anchor for, just about feel the cold water on my skin as we jumped in the ocean for a quick, refreshing dip.

"This is where it gets tricky," Christian said, bringing me out of the reverie. He nodded at the choppy water ahead, the area around Seal Rock whipping into white peaks. "Something's really churning it up today. Hold on."

Up until now the tiller had barely given me any trouble. But I grabbed it with both hands, preparing for the jagged waves ahead.

Christian let some wind into the mainsail. Over his shoulder, he turned to check on me, my position. "You good?" he shouted.

I nodded and stood up straight to get a better look at him and the rock ahead, still gripping the tiller, holding steady.

The look in his eyes changed in an instant.

Caution to fear. Impossible, bone-chilling fear.

"Elyse!" he shouted, unable to let go of the boom. "Hang on! Hang the fuck on!"

The desperation in his eyes told me exactly what would happen next. I didn't have time to react—I couldn't even sit down. I could do nothing but close my eyes and try to keep my heart from leaping out of my chest.

The wave slammed into us portside, and *Queen of Cups* hiccupped.

The tiller jerked away, stinging my palms, and the boat leaped up again, then crashed down. My teeth smashed together. Christian was shouting and there was blood in my mouth and then the sky turned dark and I was floating among the stars.

Look, Natalie, I said, but it wasn't my voice. It was Granna's, and then it changed to my father's. I reached out, touched the air before me. *So many stars, baby. I think you can hold them.*

"Elyse!" Christian made it across the deck in a blur, grabbing me and pinning us both against the coaming just as another wave hit. The unmanned sails flapped wildly in a gust of rabid wind, jerking us about.

Instinctively my arms wrapped around him, held on with a death grip.

Christian shouted in my ear, so loud and fierce it hurt. "Don't let go!"

We'd lost control of the boat, and the sea tossed us like a toy. Water shot up before us, crashing down on me in an icy plume.

My body was bathed in salt water. The shock of it yanked me back to my senses.

Queen of Cups.

Atargatis Cove.

Pirate Regatta.

Christian Kane.

Just as quickly as it had hit us, the wind died. The waves passed. The boat leveled out beneath our feet. Bobbing gently, innocently, the rigging squeaking softly as though nothing had happened.

Christian held me to his chest, his breathing ragged. I couldn't feel his heartbeat through our life jackets, but I suspected it was as wild as mine. Overhead, grommets and ropes clanked against the mast.

He pulled away slowly, searching my face for signs of distress.

"Talk to me," he said gently. His fingers probed my head, my neck. "Are you hurt?"

I couldn't move. Not even to shake my head.

"Elyse!" he said. "Say something!"

His urgency chased away the fog. I snapped to attention, checked the inside of my mouth with my tongue. I'd bitten it, but it wasn't bad, just a little blood. My teeth seemed intact, despite the jarring impact.

I shook my head. *Not hurt.*

Christian let out a gust of breath. "Okay," he said. "Can you get back to the tiller?"

No. I couldn't get my legs to work, and no way was I letting go of Christian.

It was happening again, playing out in my memory, flashes of water and pain. The stars and the moon. Choking, no air. The blade on my throat. The end of it all.

I wouldn't risk it, wouldn't budge. I knew if I moved, if I let him go, the sea would rise up again. Sweep me away, suck me down to the underneath.

"It's okay," Christian said, soothing. He ran his hands over my arms. "You're safe. The boat is fine. We've just got to steer her around Seal Rock, then it's a smooth ride to the finish. We can easily overtake *Delilah*. And after that, Noah's not that far up. Look."

He pointed ahead, and I caught sight of *Daring Delilah*, *Never Flounder*'s yellow-and-blue sails just beyond. Behind us, *Seas the Moment* was closing in, a trail of slower vessels bringing up the rear. We still had time to make this up, if we hurried.

There was excitement in Christian's eyes; he'd done the same calculations.

But I couldn't move.

Just go, I told him. *I'll be okay*. It was a lie; I was paralyzed with fear, but I was holding us up, wasting time.

"Come on, Stowaway," he said through a smile. "Don't fall apart on me now."

He'd said it playfully, but still, I snapped. I shot him a desperate glare. *Just go, Christian! Hurry. Go! Catch up!*

"Elyse," he said, calm and gentle as ever. "I'm not pushing you because I'm worried about the time. I'm pushing you because I believe in you. You can do this. Just let it go."

His hands grabbed mine, warm and reassuring. "Let. It. Go."

Gently he slid his fingers beneath mine, prying them from his life jacket.

"I'll be with you every step," he said.

I closed my eyes, took a deep and salty breath. Another. And another.

And I let it go.

Took a step away from him.

Felt the sun on my face.

Never Flounder's bright sails were once again in my sights.

Okay, I said. *Ready.*

"You sure you're up for this?" Christian asked. His voice was soft, but he couldn't hide the hope there, and it felt raw, this glimpse. Like last night in the boat, passionate and fragile, together. Fire and spun glass.

I leaned forward and pressed my mouth against his ear. "All in," I croaked. It was scratchy and low, but he'd heard me, and my breath spurred him into action.

"Get on the tiller!" he shouted. I scurried back to my position and grabbed the tiller as he shouted again. "Hold on. We need to pick up some serious speed. Might get bumpy again until we get around this rock. Okay?"

I gave him our salute, suddenly fierce and determined.

With speed and deftness Christian gathered up the lines, pulled and fastened, yanked and released. Despite our losing temporary control, he managed to readjust the sail and flatten her out again, sensing the wind and the water more than watching them. He sailed on instinct, on feel, as though the boat were an extension of his body. His soul.

It worked.

We caught up easily to *Daring Delilah*—the only boat other than Noah's we'd seen beating us around Seal Rock. After we passed her, the captain overcompensated in his eagerness for speed, losing his wind and stalling out.

"There's *Never Flounder*," Christian said. Like *Delilah*'s crew, Noah and his mate were too hasty in their reaction to us. Their mainsail billowed and pouched, the jib tightened, and though the boat glided away from us, it was sloppy and uneven. As we passed them, moving ahead and away from *Never Flounder*, Noah shouted something to his first mate.

Suddenly they changed course.

With renewed determination Noah was approaching our starboard side from behind, closing in fast.

My heart sped up again as I awaited Christian's next orders. But above me at the boom, Christian only laughed.

"I was hoping he'd fall for this. We're going to lee-bow him. Hold her steady, and trust me." Christian adjusted the sails. "Okay, time to get closer. Go." He pointed at Noah's boat.

I steered us as he directed, sending the *Queen of Cups* careening toward *Never Flounder*, so close it seemed we were on an unavoidable collision course.

At what felt like the last possible second, Christian shifted the boom, I pushed the tiller, and we swerved away, almost as if we'd bounced right off *Never Flounder*.

Noah's boat slowed considerably, rocking unevenly in the water.

We'd trapped him in a pocket of bad air, all but killing his chances at a win.

"Go, go, go!" Christian jerked the sails again. We picked up speed as the wind carried us forward, and within minutes *Never Flounder* became a yellow-blue blur behind us.

Hope rose in my chest like a wave, even as the sun hid behind a wall of thick, gray clouds. The temperature dropped, wind picking up again. But not even those icy gusts could dampen our mood.

"We're doing this, Elyse. We're doing this!" Christian secured the sails and leaped down from the boom, capturing me in another embrace. Ahead, the marina docks shone like a beacon, calling us back to the harbor. To the win that was just within our grasp.

The sea was calm, the wind strong enough to push us forward unaided.

Christian grabbed my hand, squeezed.

Standing on the aqua-blue coamings, smiles bright enough to keep the gathering clouds at bay, we sailed past the final buoys and cruised into the harbor.

Never Flounder came in behind us.

Cheers floated on the wind, welcomed us ashore.

We did it.

We beat the *Never Flounder*.

Chapter 34

"What a race it's been!" the announcer boomed. "That's the *Queen of Cups*, captained by Christian Kane and first mate Elyse d'Abreau, trailed by our own Mayor Wesley Katzenberg's son Noah and first mate Wayne Prentice in the *Never Flounder*. It's official, ladies and gentlemen of the Cove. The three-year Pirate Regatta champion, *Never Flounder*, has finally been dethroned."

The crowd whooped and roared, cheers crashing over us in waves.

"Congratulations, *Queen of Cups*. You've earned second place with a time of two hours seven minutes, putting *Never Flounder* in third with two hours nine minutes."

Christian lifted me off my feet, pressing his lips to mine. It wasn't until our kiss ended that I processed the words.

Second place.

His confusion set in at the same time, a mirror. We separated and looked out across the harbor, and sure enough, she was there. The *Black Star*. The dark horse must've overtaken us after I'd frozen on the deck, totally paralyzed. In the short time that Christian's attention was focused on me, talking me through it. Trying to save me when I didn't need saving after all.

Shocked and wordless, we docked the *Queen of Cups*, tied her up. Shed our life jackets and disembarked, footsteps as heavy as our hearts as we marched along the dock toward the marina lot.

"You guys rocked out there," Vanessa said. She'd been waiting in the crowd with Gracie and Brenda, all of them hugging us. "Kirby's with her mom at the booth, but I texted them the news. They'll meet us at the Black Pearl later."

We nodded mutely, trying to smile through the crushing disappointment. Up ahead Noah was elbowing his way through the crowd. When he finally reached us, he had only one word.

"Dude."

Christian pulled him into a hug, the two of them clinging to each other like they were trying to make up for lost time.

"Get a room, y'all," Vanessa said, and finally they broke it off.

The regatta award ceremony was a blur, the crowd cheering and chanting, trophies passed along, pirates and mermaids showering us with congratulatory wishes, saving the biggest and the best for the *Black Star*. Christian and Noah didn't recognize the guy—just another summer renter, passing through. No idea how his win had changed the fate of the entire town.

Christian, Noah, and I seemed to be the only ones who'd realized what our loss meant. None of the cheers around us would save
Lemon's house, would keep Mr. Kane from holding up his end of the
bargain. Noah hadn't won either, but those weren't the terms. I'd been
there when the men shook on it. I remembered, too late.

Christian wins, he walks away with the *Never Flounder*.

Christian loses, his father sells the property.

No matter that he'd beaten Noah, he lost the race.

The loophole was only obvious now.

Christian and I still hadn't spoken a word to each other when,
soon after the ceremony, our friends wandered into the Black Pearl
and Christian's father called out from the other side of the mob. We
followed the sound of his command, the tight wave of his arm. In the
midst of the celebration, Mr. Kane stood grim faced and cold, his hand
tight on Sebastian's.

My little mermaid offered a weak smile. "Congratulations," he said.
"You guys beat *Never Flounder*!"

Christian high-fived him, lacking the heart to tell him it hadn't
been good enough.

"And guess what?" Sebastian beamed. "I won too!" He pointed at
his crown, and for a moment Christian seemed to forget about our loss.

Before Christian could officially congratulate his little brother, his
father sighed loudly, shaking his head. He didn't have a smile for me
this time. He looked at me, almost sneered, raising Sebastian's hand
near my face. "I understand this is your doing."

I hated him for that tone, how he'd made the word "this" sound like a piece of rubbish, some great inconvenience he'd have to deal with.

This.

His youngest son.

My mermaid.

Sebastian's head sagged under the weight of his father's endless disappointment.

Christian stepped in front of me, grabbed my hand. "Dad, not now."

I looked at Sebastian, the sadness in him, only hours after his triumphant parade win, after he'd stood up to the mayor. I saw Christian, the tick in his jaw, the tense set of his shoulders, and I knew that it would always be this way for them, for my Kane boys. That their father would always have the last word, the final say. And that nothing either of them did would ever be good enough to make up for their parents' mistakes.

It was a losing game.

With a surge of adrenaline I stepped in front of Christian, grabbed Sebastian's hand. I was holding the Kane brothers at my sides, staring down their father, my heartbeat ragged.

I met Mr. Kane's eyes, let the fire blaze in mine.

He looked at me like he'd never seen me before.

But he didn't speak.

Call it off, I mouthed.

"All of what?" he said.

I tried again, slowly. *Call off the bet.*

The man bristled, taking a step back. "You don't call off a bet the moment you lose it, Elyse d'Abreau. That's not how things work."

But—

He silenced my lips with a wave of his hand, turning to his eldest as if I wasn't even there. A smudge, a wisp, a nothing.

I shrank.

Again.

~~Failed.~~

"Christian," he said firmly, "it was a decent effort, but you didn't follow through. I understand you're all disappointed, but the bet is over, and the houses are going to P and D. That's final." He looked at me again, his tone leaving no room for argument. "Elyse, I'm sorry that you and your family might be inconvenienced by the development plans, but it is what it is. Boys, let's go."

It is what it is?

When Andy Kane talked, people listened. His voice preceded him, and when he walked into a room, people stood up and took notice. I imagined it had always been like that for him. All of his business dealings. His first job interviews out of graduate school. Defending his thesis. Debate team in college. Even when he was a kid, I bet he always got his way, always got his say.

No wonder the mayor was so bent on burying him.

The funny thing was, for someone with so much power, so much conviction in his words, he sure did waste them.

If I had a voice like that, I wouldn't waste it.

My lips formed the words, but Mr. Kane wasn't listening. He'd already turned away, dragging Sebastian by the hand.

My body shivered beneath damp clothes and a fresh splattering of rain, and instinctively I moved closer to Christian, tucked myself under the familiar comfort of his shoulder. I'd learned the skies of Atargatis Cove well enough to know that this was just a warning, that we had about thirty seconds to seek shelter before the downpour.

The excitement of the day quickly fizzled. Parents grabbed up sticky child hands and herded everyone to their cars, to the Black Pearl for the last party, to Kat and Ava's Sweet Pacific for their famous mermaid cookies. Mr. Kane was already partway down the shore with Sebastian in tow, and the Mermaid Queen of Atargatis Cove looked back at me with a blank expression, blue-green swirls of makeup running down his cheeks.

I turned my face to the sky.

Drench me, I willed it.

Pour your heart out; soak me through.

Wash away the makeup, the tears, the blood,

the day, the week, the month.

Wash away the entire last year and bring us all back to where

we began.

As if to answer, the rain sluiced from the gray mist, pelted my eyelids and lips. Salt-tinged water ran in rivulets down my chin, my neck, my pale silver scar.

But it didn't change anything.

The marina was nearly empty, but Christian was still next to me, his arm around me like a life preserver, and when I turned toward him, I saw his face tipped toward the sky too. Eyes closed, mouth open to catch the rain on his tongue.

Sebastian and his father were two dots in the distance now, one gray and tall, the other tiny and silver-blue, and in that moment I knew without a doubt that for the rest of forever, I'd look back on this moment as my one regret, the one thing—unlike so many other events in my life—I could've done something about if only I'd been brave.

If only I'd found my voice.

Wordlessly I laced my fingers through Christian's and caught his sigh on my shoulders, slumping beside him. *Black Star* couldn't have been more than five minutes ahead, ten at most. It was less than the amount of time I'd spent frozen on the deck, paralyzed by fear. It was less than the time it had taken Christian to talk me down, to convince me to trust him, to trust the *Queen of Cups*, trust my sailing skills, my own deep, lost love for the sea.

It was less time than it had taken for him to kiss me, to tell me that he knew I had the strength to do it. That he believed in me.

I tightened my grip on his hand.

Christian turned, pressed his mouth to mine, his kiss cool and wet from the rain. "I can't think about this right now," he said. "I just want to spend as much time with you as possible. Okay?"

My eyes drifted back to the *Queen of Cups*. I mouthed, *Go back out?*

"Back out? In this weather?"

I nodded. *Anchor. Sleep. Watch the sunrise. Do-over?*

Christian looked exhausted and half-wrecked, but he tightened his arm around me anyway, leading us back to the *Queen* to shelter from the gathering storm.

Chapter 35

The ocean was placid and sleepy, as if it had been worn ragged by today's regatta and the rain, which had thankfully passed quickly, and it needed time to regain its strength. Christian and I sailed back out and watched the Mermaid Festival fireworks from a distance, but we agreed not to talk about the regatta, about what the loss meant, about what tomorrow or the next day would bring. So after the smoke faded from the sky, after we shared a sailor's meal of canned stew and oyster crackers, Christian and I floated wordlessly above deck, shoulder to shoulder, fingers intertwined as we watched the stars blink to life in the deep blue sky.

When the moon was high over the marina, we retreated to the saloon, sitting again in comfortable silence. I thought of the first night I'd met Christian, how I'd watched him at the Solstice party, jealous that he and Vanessa seemed to have so much history together. I'd been wrong about them, of course. I saw it now, felt it, knew it by heart. The sign of a deep connection wasn't necessarily outward affection, but silence. The ability to sit still with another, wholly aware of him, neither needing nor desiring anything but his presence, the shape of him, his breath in the air between you.

A wave jostled our little vessel, and I finally stirred, looking up to meet Christian's eyes. He'd been watching me, I realized, and when I rose from the cushion, his smile turned wolfish. I grabbed his hand, leading us both to the berth.

Despite the exhaustion of the day, my body was wild with wanting, my own breath ragged and rough as I slid my hands inside his sweatshirt. My touch lingered only a moment before I pushed his sweatshirt up, slipped it over his head, and tossed it on the floor. The rest of our clothing quickly followed, and then he was, blissfully, inside me.

His kisses were more hungry, more desperate, more devouring than ever.

Our time together, we both knew, was finite.

I closed my eyes, searing this moment into my mind, committing his touch to eternal memory.

Hours later something tugged me from a deep sleep, and when I opened my eyes, I saw that it was the moon, shining down on me in a silver beam. I rose from the bed, careful not to disturb Christian as I slipped out from our warm cocoon.

In the saloon my mermaid dress hung from the hook where I'd put it before the race, blue silk spilling down the wall like water, just as shimmery. For a moment I thought I could put my hand through it, feel the cool wetness run through my fingers. But it was only my old familiar dress after all, and I lifted it carefully from the hook and pulled it up over my nakedness. If the night air was chilly, I no longer noticed.

I crept out through the companionway, silent as the stars on the sea. Out on the deck, alone, I heard nothing but the gentle lapping of water against the hull, and beneath the vast diamond sky I felt both all important and utterly insignificant, the goddess and the damned in equal measure.

I thought about Lemon's tarot cards, the deceiving moon, the call of something deep within, and wondered for a long moment whether looking at a reflection of the moon in the water made it the opposite of deceiving. I wanted to trust this pale and lovely moon, the flicker of starlight that seemed to glow from the bottom of the ocean. The sea was so impossibly still, so dark, that the longer I stared, the more uncertain I became. Was the night sky reflected in the Pacific, or was the Pacific reflected in the heavens? Had they switched places as I slept?

How had everything I'd ever known been turned upside down?

When I'd volunteered as Christian's first mate—despite my res-ervations about sailing—I truly believed I could help. That we might actually win this thing, prove Christian's father and the mayor wrong.

Show them all by saving Lemon's house, Christian's house, the fate of the entire mystical town.

But again, the ocean had other plans.

Again, I'd failed. The people I loved. Myself.

And again, everything would change.

The night was so calm, the ocean so inviting, offering none of its usual warnings and threats. Entranced, I reached my fingers out and trailed them through the black soup, through the moonlight, as though I could capture the stars beneath the sea.

Soon I was in up to my wrist. My elbow. The tender skin of my underarm didn't register the cold, though I thought it should.

I am a mermaid, goddess of the sea.

Midnight is upon me.

Her lover is near.

Death, come to take me home.

And then I was slipping into the void, a tipping forth that seemed both uneventful and inevitable, not even a splash to mark my descent.

Silent, as ever.

Chapter 36

"World tour! World tour, Elyse!" My twin sister, Natalie, throws her head back, howls up at the Tobago stars.

It's March. Carnival season. And we're celebrating. We've got every reason to, after all. Dreams like this don't come true very often.

"You crazy, gyal," I tell her, but I'm giddy too. Rum and adrenaline, the electric buzz of wishes granted. All around us the night shines with promise.

"Tell me it's real," Natalie says, and I roll my eyes. "It doesn't feel real."

I grab her arm, pinch it until she shrieks. "It's real, see?"

We're laughing again. Last night we opened in Port of Spain on the main stage for Bella Garcia. She loved us so, the crowd loved us so, and her manager, too.

Everyone loved us so much that when Bella took the crown later, Queen of the Bands, she called us out, introduced us to everyone watching.

Cameras. Videos. Reporters. International tourists.

"Elyse and Natalie d'Abreau," she said. "Rising stars, mark my words."

Later in our dressing room, as we slipped out of our matching mermaid gowns, we got the invitation from Bella's assistant. The note was handwritten, black ink on fine, cream-colored stationery, words swimming before our eyes.

So talented.

Potential.

World tour, expenses paid.

Singing with Bella.

Recording at Trinidad's top studio.

Dreams, dreams, dreams, rushing at us at once. We'll finish school in a few months, continue singing, rehearsing, and then, come summer, get on that plane.

Now we laugh again, rehearsing the words we memorized from Bella's note. Alcohol and joy have loosened our tongues, all formality and properness gone.

Natalie howls again, tells me she's a werewolf inside.

"Shut up, gyal," I say. "You'll call Mami Wata from the deep with that crazy noise."

"Let her come, then." She sucks her teeth, leans over the rails. "She got nothin' on us. Hear, Mami Wata?"

I shake my head, but soon I'm howling too.

"First thing I'm gonna do after we drop our album," she says, like it's a list, something we should write down, and I reach for our note-book, because I think maybe she's right, we should make a list.

"I'll buy Granna a house in the country," she says.

I laugh. "Granna already live in the country, what's wrong with you?"

"Another country. She always wanted to visit Grenada, all their spices and chocolate growing. I'll buy her a big house. We can stay with her when we tour."

"Let's get through school first, okay?" I say, as if I'm the boss. "Before you start with your spices."

But her spirit is contagious.

Natalie, the quiet one, the gentle soul brought to life by music.

"Allya talk so much nonsense," Julien, my boyfriend, says. He came with us tonight, out on the boat to celebrate the start of the rest of our lives. He dives into the cooler for another round, comes back out with more punch for each of us. "Don't forget your friends when you get all famous."

"Nah," I tell him. "We ain't forgetting. You coming too. You could carry the suitcases."

Natalie laughs. "For real. You can bodyguard us."

"To friends," I say, tipping my cup in toast.

Julien slaps me on the boomsie, and my sister howls again. The three of us clank our cups loud enough to make a shark's teeth rattle.

"Julien," Natalie says, and my boyfriend smiles at us both. "This party needs some Bella Garcia. Our patron saint."

I laugh. "Don't let Granna hear you talk like that."

"Granna be laughing," she says. To Julien, she says, "You heard us. Hook it up, boy."

"Already giving me orders," he says, but he's laughing too.

And then Bella's voice is on the speakers, floating out across the Caribbean Sea.

Instinct, heartbeat, soul flow, Natalie and I stand together. Break into melody and harmony, verse and chorus. In sync we wine our waists, dip our hips.

We know every word, every step, and we sing it like this:

We dance up on it, dance up on it
The floor rise up when it see we comin'
We dance up on it, dance up on it
Beats bom-bom when they see we comin'
We dance up on it, dance up on it
Boys in the house when they see we comin'
We dance up on it, dance up on it
Drop to they knees when they see we comin'
We dance up on it, dance up—

"No! Elyse! Wave!" Julien shouts. A warning, his face suddenly slack and afraid. "Hold on!"

My heart sinks.

Impact.

Natalie slips, screams as the boat shudders beneath us, and though I try to grab the rails, the lines, anything to keep from tumbling out, it's no use. I feel myself tipping backward, and I brace for the warm, wet dip, try to remember to breathe out my nose so I don't get salt water burn.

But I don't hit the water.

There's only the hollow crack of bone against fiberglass, and for a second I wonder if my sister fell again.

Fear seizes me as I recall the old legends, wonder in a panic about Mami Wata.

All of this happens in a heartbeat. The moment I realize the noise came from my own head, I go numb.

I slip from the deck, into the deep blue sea.

Which is black at the bottom, where the impossible things live.

Been waitin' on you, gyal, the voice says. Maybe it's Mami Wata, come to claim my soul for the sea. Maybe it's Death, come to claim my soul for himself.

I don't open my eyes, just hold my breath as the warm water presses in, tries to choke me. To break me.

I can't fight. I open my eyes, fall to the bottom where I stare in wonder at all the stars beneath the sea.

Claws are around my neck, sharp and tight. Pulling my hair, tugging, yanking.

Inside, I go black, black, black.

Dim.

And then a bright, sharp pain like nothing I've ever felt.

Knives and blood, blood and knives.

My throat is bathed in warm liquid, and as the light rises around me, I tremble. I'm on the deck again, calm waters, the stars overhead where they belong.

Shivering, I am, body wrecked and ragged.

Something is pulling at me, threatening to take me under again.

I try to speak, try to reach out, but hands tighten on my shoulders, hold me down.

I think I see it—my soul.

Shimmery and pale as it drifts out through the searing hot gash in my throat, floats over the water.

It vanishes.

My sister's face hovers suddenly before me, a dark moon streaked with panic and tears. "Elyse! Fucking breathe, you hear me! You fucking breathe!"

I gasp, choke, my breath a blade that rips through flesh and bone to find me.

"You got her," a boy says. Julien, his name returns, lands on my tongue. Julien who plays the steel pan. Julien who loves me.

But he can't hear me when I call.

"You got her," Julien says, again and again and again. "You got her. She all right. She all right. She gonna be all right." He's shouting into the shortwave radio, something about an ambulance on shore.

I can't be sure, but I think his cheeks are streaked with moonlight.

"Shh, shh, shhhh," Natalie says, her breath tickling my sticky throat. My sister holds my hands at my sides, though I struggle to pull away. Her hands are coated in blood. There's something trying to choke me, I'm certain, to carve out my throat. But she tells me I'm okay, that I'm okay, that I must lie still.

This is what my sister says.

But then I don't know if it's really my sister or the sea, or maybe the last sound I'll ever make, and everything goes dark anew.

And then bright. Impossibly, silver-white bright. Sterile-light bright.

A hospital, a doctor with a downturned mouth, pity in his eyes.

"You're lucky to be alive, gyal," he says. "Lucky to breathe."

I think I must be having one of those out-of-body experiences. Like I'm in a coma, and my family is all watching over me, waiting for me to wake up.

Julien Natalie Juliette Martine Gabrielle Hazel Dad Granna.

Granna Dad Hazel Gabrielle Martine Juliette Natalie Julien.

I have to be dead, or near dead, because why else would everyone be here? Why else would everyone look so sad?

In and out of my body, hours turn to days to centuries and eons, back to days. On one of them the doctor says this:

"Your sister saved your life."

He lets that sink in, then continues in the tight, uncomfortable tone reserved for bad news. "You hit your head, slipped underwater. Natalie eventually pulled you out, but she says you weren't breathing."

Natalie is there, her moon face grim. She takes my hand in hers and it's warm, and I think that it's a good sign, because if I were dead, I wouldn't feel warmth.

Would I?

I try to smile to show my relief, but there's tape across my mouth, holding the tubes in place, and it pulls and pinches my skin.

"You were blue, gyal," Natalie says. "Not even alive. We tried everything—bang on your chest, breathe into your mouth, pray, everything." She's shaking with upset, words choppy and raw as the sea. "On the radio Julien called for help, and they ask him, is there a first aid kit on the boat? Yes. Then they tell me what to do and I do it, anything to bring you back." She smears her nose with the back of her hand. "You were . . . you were dead, Elyse."

She's sobbing, sobbing. I can't understand her. There was blood on her hands that night, I remember. So why isn't she the one in the hospital bed? I want to tell her to slow down, to breathe, to say what she means, but I can't.

The doctor puts a steady hand on my sister's shoulder, quieting her. To me, he says, "Natalie had to perform an emergency tracheotomy. When you went under, your larynx contracted. You were drowning." He wraps a hand around his throat, closes his eyes. "You could not breathe on your own. Natalie had to make a new way for the air."

With his finger he slices delicately across his neck, makes an invisible gash.

My sister cannot stop trembling.

"I'm so sorry, Elyse," the doctor says again. "Natalie . . . the procedure . . . it saved your life. But it nicked your vocal cords. Damaged the nerves. Badly."

There is more jargon, medical terms that I don't understand. In and out of my body, hours turn to days to centuries and eons, back to days. On one of them I ask for paper, for pen.

Granna hands me my notebook, where Natalie and I write all of our songs and dreams and secrets. It's wrinkly and warped, like someone got it wet.

I scrawl quickly, my writing barely legible for the shake in my hand.

Are we postponing the tour? When I'm better, we'll go, right?

Natalie sits on the other side of the bed, her face streaked with tears. "I did this to you," she says. "Your vocal cords are permanently damaged. There is no cure, baby. No getting better. Not better enough, anyway."

The rest of her words fall on me one by one, like drops of rain.

"You

  can't

sing

  anymore.

Gyal,

 you

  can't

even

  speak."

Chapter 37

I suppose I thought it was a dream at first, whatever called me out of Christian's embrace, luring me to the sea. The kind where you know it's a dream, and you just settle in for the ride and see what your wild subconscious might invent. Flying, perhaps. Or breathing underwater. Or time traveling, back to the past.

But by the time I realized what had happened—that I'd slipped beneath the *Queen of Cups* in the middle of the night, left Christian sleeping soundly in the berth—I was wide awake.

The sea had finally come to make good on its promise.

To claim me.

Not to ruin the story, but if you've come this far, you should know how it happens.

The end begins, as all things must, in the water. Now.

Ropes of black hair twist before my eyes, swaying like reeds.

One by one, red clips loosen from the braids, tiny jeweled starfish that
  drip-drip-drop
  into the deep.

Midnight stands before me, her body ebony and deep blue, half
woman, half moon. Long black hair tipped with moonlight spills down
over her breasts and hips, and with one eye open she watches me,
imploring.

I nod, and she turns to lead the way, enticing me to follow.

Every step sends knives through my limbs, so tight is my dress,
so restrictive. My mouth tastes of blood, my lungs burn with red-
hot pain.

But still, I follow.

Finally Midnight turns, one finger pressed to her lips.

Before her a pale soldier appears, dressed in a red coat with
golden buttons, loose but well-appointed over bone-white breeches.
Tattered bandages hang from his head and limbs; in the water they
sway and shift, wrapping around Midnight's ankles.

He wears no skin, only bones. Death.

Death bows his head, hiding from me the sunken black caves of his
eyes. Midnight's legs run red with blood.

Behind them a new figure emerges from the darkness.

The mermaid queen. She's been expecting me.

I am Atargatis. I am the First. Her scarlet lips don't move; I hear
her voice inside me. Her eyes shine with yellow flame, the same light
emanating—impossibly—from double-ended wands she holds in

each hand. Her breasts are pale and bare, save for a tiny golden crab in the center of each, and at her throat a starfish clings to her skin. *Witch queen of the watery realm.*

At my nod, her beauty turns to rot and ruin. I dare not look away, dare not flinch.

"But *I* am Atargatis," I say. The sound of my own voice is shocking to my ears.

Her laughter drifts like soap bubbles, each landing and bursting against my lips. *Do you not see? For I am you,* she says. From the blackness behind her a serpent slithers forth, coiling around her waist. The snake consumes its tail, vanishing when it reaches the end. *And you are me.*

The serpent reappears, encircles her, consumes itself again.

Again. Again.

The yellow flames extinguish.

A flash of silver, and her knife is in my mouth, her fingers cold and slippery between my lips. Blade against my tongue.

I don't fear her. There's peace in knowing it will finally end, that I will exit as I arrived, last breath as my first. Salt water. The sea.

I'm ready.

But as my heartbeat stalls, as my limbs give their final tremble, as all around me turns to darkness, I can't help but wonder. . . .

If the sea had offered me one last chance—if I could've bargained with Death to make this broken wing mine, a soul with all its beautiful imperfections—would I have taken it?

Even after everything I'd lost?

Blackness envelops. . . .

No, child. Her voice is a painful hiss inside, fingers digging into my jaw. *I've not yet released you from the realm.*

At the crush of her hand, ice rushes through my veins, and I open my eyes again.

This is not the first time our paths have crossed, Atargatis says. *But you had much to learn then.*

She regards me for another long moment, then releases my jaw. The knife is still in my mouth, though, sharp and bloody.

Oddly, my final thoughts are not of Christian, but of his brother, Sebastian. Of his words that day on the Vega, just after I'd signed on as first mate.

I read a story about a mermaid who couldn't talk because the sea witch cut out her tongue. . . .

I'd stuck out my tongue then, shown him it was still intact. But I was wrong. I *did* let the witch cut out my tongue. Not now, with the blade of Atargatis pressed against me. But then.

In March.

In a hospital in Port of Spain.

The accident took my voice—my physical voice—the ability to make sounds emanate from my mouth.

I'd given up the rest all on my own. My *voice.* The inner power that comes from neither sound nor form, but from soul, from truth, from one's deepest self. That's what I'd let the witch cut out.

And ever since, she's been stalking me, haunting my steps and shadows. My dreams. My future.

Now Atargatis's voice is in my head again. *Do not trouble yourself with such things, Elyse. I want only your tongue. In exchange, you will be free to love whom you wish, live as you wish.*

She slips the blade out from my mouth so that I might answer.

Lips closed tight, I hesitate.

Love requires great sacrifice, she presses, a warning slithering beneath her cool tone. *You must give something up to get something in return. It is the way of all things, Elyse. Life, death, life again.*

I consider her words. My words. My voice.

I think of Christian, our first meeting and our last, our naked bodies entwined above.

Love has its own costs, its own sacrifices, yes. But in its true form, love is borne of neither spell nor bargain.

I won't take it through trickery.

"I will give you what you ask," I tell the sea witch, and my voice is strong and clear, vibrating across my tongue. "But only *because* you ask, and I have come to your domain. It is a gift, as it must be. I'll take nothing in return."

As you wish, she says.

I open my mouth against her silver blade. Her cool fingers again hold my chin as the knife does its work, cold and quick. Copper and salt fill my mouth. The pain I'd been expecting, though . . . it doesn't come.

In its place instead I feel a lightness, a freedom.

Atargatis cut out my tongue, with my permission, yet a veil falls from my eyes, my heart suddenly unburdened.

Death, who'd been silent thus far, bows to the queen.

And then he is gone.

At once the ocean warms.

You've asked for neither love nor life in return, Atargatis says, *but I will freely grant you one thing. An answer, child. If you've a question. Consider it my gift to you.*

I nod in thanks. There's so much I wish to know—how long she's lived here, whether she's still looking for her lost shepherd, what other great mysteries dwell in the deepest places of the world. But as the words form on my lips, I sense danger, the trouble that comes from being too greedy for sacred knowledge.

Instead, I ask only, "How is it that you've taken my tongue, yet I can still speak?"

Atargatis raises her arms. Twin serpents—eels, sleek and black—slither from her wrists. I'm not afraid. They circle me, twine around my ankles, and still I don't move.

Before my eyes, the serpents turn to words.

My words.

My scribbled-on-the-wall words, scrawled-in-my-journal words, whispered-into-the-wind words. My summer words. They wrap around me gently, limb to limb, toes to curls. All the poems, the fairy tales I'd told Sebastian, the boat lists I'd made for Christian, all the raw

THE SUMMER OF CHASING MERMAIDS

and heartfelt things I'd written on his body without a single utterance passing my lips.

My dreams. My stories.

My voice.

A warmth pulses behind my scar, a golden-blue glow I can feel more than see, and in an instant the haze lifts. The word-serpents release me, slithering back into Atargatis's sleeves.

From her pocket Atargatis pulls forth a net of stars, scattering them before us. Hundreds, thousands, millions twinkle, lighting a path from the sea to the moon.

You are ready.

With no further wisdom or warning, Atargatis vanishes.

My body convulses with the desire to breath, but I fight it, focusing on the path of stars and the bright white moon overhead. With all the strength left in me, I scissor kick my way to the surface.

Rising.

Rising.

Rising.

Chapter 38

When I finally broke through, everything was calm. Everything was clear. I'd journeyed to the witch's watery realm beneath Thor's Well, but here above the water it seemed that only a moment had passed. The moon cut the same silver-white path across the Pacific, the *Queen of Cups* floating gently beside it. Just as it was when I'd gone under.

My mouth was whole, unbloodied.

Deeply I drank in the cool night air, but though I'd risen out of the water, I still couldn't fully breathe. Something was pressing against my lungs, squeezing. Restricting.

I felt my body, pressed my hands against my chest.

The dress.

The dress that once held the memories of the best day of my life, the promise of an entire future. Now it was only the past.

I slipped the straps from my shoulders, slid my arms out.

I hesitated only a moment, heard Atargatis's words again.

You are ready.

Sometimes life's most important moments are quiet, a decision made quick and calm. Still bathed in the sea, I slipped the dress from my torso. There was no struggle, no herculean, adrenaline-fueled tearing of fabric and lace. Just a simple shiver, a loosening, one last shimmy.

I slipped the dress.

Set myself free.

Naked, I pulled myself up the safety ladder with exhausted but triumphant limbs, floating in a state of suspended wonder. The instant my feet touched the deck, Christian emerged from the companionway, wrapped in a blanket, his eyes glossy in their half sleep. When he noticed me, they narrowed, then widened.

"Elyse?" It was a whisper first, laced with grogginess. I waited for the fog to lift, for it was still clouding my memories too, and when it finally passed he burst through the companionway, launching himself at me, at my wet nakedness. "What are you doing? What happened? What—"

I pressed a finger to his lips, smiled to let him know I was okay.

"Okay, okay . . . you're okay." He was stammering, shaking his head as if it really might've been a dream. His arms closed around me, pressing our bodies together beneath the blanket "You're freezing. God, Elyse. I woke up and you weren't here, and . . . Come inside."

I turned my head then, glanced at a point in the water just beyond the stern where a slip of blue silk twisted and floated in the gentle waves. Beneath the glitter moon, it lingered only a moment longer before the sea, finally claiming the life it'd been promised all those months ago, dissolved it into foam.

The most beautiful dress in the world—all that I was and all that I could've been—was gone, the old life shed to make way for the new.

I followed Christian into the saloon, where he wrapped me up alone in the blanket, clicked on the lantern, and quickly tugged on a pair of sweatpants. He sat me on one of the benches, frantically rubbing heat into my arms and legs. Once I stopped shivering, he leaned me over the small sink to wring out my hair, then gently wrapped my head in a towel.

"Were you sleepwalking?" he whispered. I shook my head. "Did you fall in? What happened?"

I shrugged. *Don't remember.*

He narrowed his eyes, waiting for me to explain, but that was the truth. One minute I'd been counting stars, my heart heavy with the weight of our loss, of all we still had to lose.

And then I was underwater.

Weightless.

I shivered again, the whole thing fading before my eyes like a dream not quite remembered. If not for the water pooled at my feet and the chill in my bones, I might have been able to convince us both it really *had* been a dream.

It didn't matter.

Despite the worry in Christian's eyes and the tremble in my limbs, I was practically giddy, light with life. Christian didn't return my smile, though; he was still frantic, concern giving him speed and purpose. He was on his knees before I could stop him, rubbing my feet between his strong, determined hands.

"I need to get you warm," he said. "Fast."

I watched in silence as he boiled water on the hot plate, poured most of it into the bilge bucket with some fresh water from the tap. With the rest of the hot stuff, he made a mug of tea, then placed the steaming bucket on the floor and instructed me to put my feet inside. The feeling was utter heaven.

"So this was your Lieutenant Dan moment, Stowaway?" He lifted an eyebrow in question, and I realized then that I'd waited a beat too long, expecting to hear Kirby's whisper at my neck. *It's from a show,* she'd say. Or maybe a movie or a song, some bit of American pop culture I'd clearly missed. I smiled now, thinking of her.

"Ah. You never saw *Forrest Gump,*" Christian said. "Remind me to show you next time you come over."

Anticipation rose in my limbs, grateful that there would even be a next time.

"Come to terms with the sea?" he asked. His voice was lower now, but insistent. Concerned.

My fingers trailed up my sternum, found the familiar star on my throat—that pale marker that had, up to now, divided my life into its befores and afters. With Christian's eyes full of worry, watching my every move, I mouthed the words I'd never before been able to find.

I'm never going to speak or sing again.

It hurt, saying it like that, but not as much as I'd expected. Feared.

I wanted to tell Natalie. To say it, as best I could, across the distance.

But there would be time for that later.

Christian's smile softened. He handed me the tea, now steeped.
"Drink this. Small sips, okay?"

I wrapped my hands around the offered mug, closing my eyes as
the steam enveloped me. Unbidden, unexpected tears slipped from
behind my lids, warm and salty, streaming into my mouth. I'd nearly
forgotten the taste of them, the feel of their soft tracks on my cheeks.

The ocean.

Tears.

Illumination.

With my eyes still shut, I found Christian's face with my free hand,
pulled him close. With the strongest breath I could call forth, I said it.

"I love you."

The words flowed in a whisper without expectation, and for the
first time in my life they didn't make me feel as though I was giving
something up, giving away some irretrievable piece of me. Instead, my
heart expanded, embers burning, and when Christian lifted the top
edge of the blanket and pressed his lips to my bare shoulder, my heart
expanded farther still, and I knew, this time, it *was* real.

Christian was the first boy to know me after the accident, the first
person I allowed to get close. His feelings weren't connected with old
memories of the girl I used to be, and the pity that inevitably followed

whenever someone realized I couldn't be that girl anymore. When Christian looked at me, I didn't see sadness reflected in his eyes, sympathy and sorrow.

I saw a boy who wanted to know my soul.

A boy who believed I still had one.

Beautiful soul . . .

I set my mug on the table, rose from the bench, and walked to the berth. I let the blanket slip from my shoulders, and I turned, standing before him, naked in the moonlight.

Christian's eyes never left mine. In a ragged, barely restrained voice, he said, "You're beautiful."

I'd lost track of time and space the moment our bare bodies touched, but after, I opened my eyes, desperate to see Christian, to know he was real. His eyes were on me, too, smoldering.

"Elyse . . ." It was a soft moan, half whispered into my mouth, and in it were all the promises and hopes of a boy who wanted to believe we could still save each other. Save the houses. Save the Cove.

I breathed heavily in return, the haze of ecstasy tricking me into copying his motion; my lips formed his name, but the sound didn't reach his ears. His stillness shattered the illusion, and I knew in that moment he'd never know the pleasure of hearing his name on my breath, of feeling the melodic rhythm of my accent. When I opened my mouth against his ear, the only sound he captured was a wet emptiness, a faint heartbeat that echoed through the canyon where once my voice rang true.

I whispered his name anyway; this time, I knew it would be enough.

"Sure you're all right?" he whispered, and when I nodded, he covered my mouth with his, kissing me with fresh hunger. I returned it, desperately alive.

Repaired, renewed, recovered.

Rejuvenated.

Restored.

All the *RE*s complete, and I was whole.

Because I'd always, always been whole.

Hours later, when dawn's soft glow awakened me, Christian and I were still entwined. I lingered in his arms, overwarm but glad for it, until his eyes finally fluttered open.

I held my hand before him, opened my fingers to reveal the message I'd written on my palm as he slept.

We're not giving up, Captain.

Chapter 39

The Pacific was frothing mad with rain and wind. After the placid night, it had recovered, channeling with urgency all its vast power to delay our return, to keep us at sea.

But Christian had seen the determination in my eyes this morning, and he'd made it his, shaking off his exhaustion and piloting us through the storm. When we finally reached the marina, it was near afternoon and the docks were deserted, every boat battened down and tied up. Gone was the evidence of yesterday's race, the portable barbecue pits, the balloons, the pirates and mermaids.

It was as though none of it had ever happened.

But I knew better. The race had happened. Our *Queen of Cups* had taken second. Admirable, but not enough to save the houses.

By the strength of Atargatis, I had to make my last stand.

As soon as Christian had safely navigated the boat into the slip, he waved me on. "Go," he shouted over the storm. A fierce wind howled, clawing at my hair, at the too-big sweatshirt and pants Christian had given me. "I'm right behind you, soon as I tie her down. Be careful!"

I kissed him, and then I disembarked.

My feet hit the dock.

Rain needled my face, my neck.

I ran.

Bare feet slapped the wet cement, gritty with sand. I ran faster, harder, ignoring the sting on my feet and the burn in my calves. I ran all the way through the marina, into the sand and up the beach, past the small cottages and then the larger homes, and still I didn't pause. By the time I hit the last of the dunes and saw the rise of the houses of Starfish Point, I was winded, but I didn't feel the cold. Adrenaline and purpose kept me warm until I finally reached the Kanes' door.

"Elyse?" Mr. Kane stood in the doorway, a glass of scotch in hand. His face said a lot of things, all at once: *What the hell happened to you? I'm tired of your meddling. I'm just plain tired. Is this summer ever going to end?* But all he said out loud was, "Where's Christian?"

He's fine, I mouthed. I pointed inside the warm house. *May I?*

"Oh, of course. Come on in." He finally stepped aside. "Sorry. Let me get you a towel." He led me into the kitchen, gestured for me to sit at the counter.

He returned with a fluffy bath towel, fresh out of the dryer, then put on the kettle. With a smile that wasn't altogether unfriendly, he said, "Looks like you could use something hot to drink."

I nodded, grateful, and asked him for a pen and paper.

Christian's fine. Tying up the boat. We had it out all night, just got back. He'll be here soon.

I showed him the note to alleviate his concern about Christian, then held my finger up, asking for some time.

This, I thought, *might take a while.*

As Christian had drifted off to dreamland after my return from the ocean last night, I lay awake, thinking about this moment, this plan taking vague shape from the mist in my mind. It was a long shot, but we'd lost the bet—a long shot was all we had left. Andy Kane had no reason to listen to me, but after everything, I couldn't just *not* try.

Somewhere deep inside I felt the flames of Atargatis, twin lights with just enough warmth to keep me going.

I set my pen to the paper and wrote, straight from the heart.

Mr. Kane,

I know you made a bet, and Christian and I lost. I get it—you don't go back on your word.

But despite the name on the deeds, the houses were never yours to bet. If you go through with this deal, Ursula and Kirby will be forced to move, and I'll probably go back to Tobago. Inconvenient, yes, as you've said, but that's not why I'm not asking you to reconsider.

When I say the property wasn't yours to bet, I mean this: Whatever it once meant to you, to your father and grandfather, it's clearly just a house to you now. A burden, perhaps, one you can easily turn into a profit. If it meant any more to you, you never would've taken the mayor's wager.

But to Christian and Sebastian, it's a home. It's old memories and new ones. Summers that you've spent together as a family.

In the time I've been with your family, I've seen enough to know things aren't perfect (whose family is?). I don't pretend to know the ins and outs of that, but I do know this: Those boys love each other, and they love being here. Together, where Sebastian can look for mermaids and Christian can sail, where they can hike and spend time together as brothers and friends, and where they can be accepted and loved by the friends they've made here.

Mr. Kane set a steaming mug on the counter before me. "I understand you're not a fan of American chocolate, so I skipped the hot cocoa and went for tea. Okay?"

I nodded and set down my pen.

He read what I'd written so far. At the end he let loose a heavy sigh, taking the seat next to me.

"Elyse," he said, choosing his words carefully, "I realize that I've been unfair to you. Particularly yesterday, after the race. With Sebastian. I'm sorry for that. As a father, it's not easy for me to . . . I just want what's best for my boys. That's the truth. It's a harsh world, and people don't like what they can't label and stick in a box." He let his eyes drift to my scar, purposely lingered to make the point. When I nodded, he continued. "I appreciate that you've gotten close with my sons this summer. Christian and I don't have many conversations these days, but it's obvious how he feels about you. And Sebastian can't stop talking about you either." He laughed. "Frankly, if you go back to Tobago, we may have to send him with you."

I smiled, thinking immediately of all the things I'd show him. The cocoa pods, how they grew, how they transformed from puffs of red and yellow into fine chocolate. The birds, hundreds of species all over the island, with colors as varied and bright as a rainbow. And the massive leatherbacks, giant turtles who swam thousands of miles every year to lay their eggs on the moonlit beaches of Tobago.

He'd go bananas for it.

"I know you care a great deal about the boys," he said, bringing me back across the seas. "But I'm not sure what you're asking me here." He slid the paper toward me again, his gaze weighted and serious, tired but not impatient. Whatever he was about to say, he meant for me to answer honestly. "Elyse, what do you want?"

The question, simple and obvious as it was, shocked me.

Not because it was unusual, or even unexpected. I had, after all, shown up soaked and shivering on this man's doorstep, asking for his time and some paper. I'd obviously wanted *something*.

But in his asking of it, I remembered a similar conversation with Christian on the Vega, Fourth of July. I'd asked Christian the same question, and he'd told me that he didn't know. That no one had ever asked him.

Now, with Mr. Kane draining the last of his scotch, waiting for my response, I realized that before I came to the Cove, no one had ever asked me, either.

For so long there was never a need. I was a singer, a dancer, a performer. I'd been singing almost as long as I'd been speaking, and the moment Natalie and I joined our voices in song, our entire future spiraled out before us, solidified years later at our last Carnival performance. With Bella Garcia, and the promises of greatness she'd offered us.

Last March.

But all of that had changed. One night. One moment.

Last March.

And I'd gone from someone with a future to someone who needed to be asked what she wanted. Someone who needed to consider options, to make a decision.

And Mr. Kane, for all his faults and flaws, for all he'd intimidated me this summer, for all he'd made me burn with quiet rage at the things he'd said to his sons, was giving me a chance to think about it. To make a choice.

To speak up, just like Kirby had done the night I'd found her in the dress. *What do you want, Elyse?*

I grabbed the pen, dashed off the last of all I'd come here to say. The most important part.

Mr. Kane, I want you to call it off. Back out. Cancel the proposed offer, turn it down. Yes, I realize I'm asking you to put your winning reputation on the line, and to disappoint the corporate buyers, and to walk away from a profitable deal.

But sometimes life asks us to make those kinds of choices.

The hard ones, the inconvenient ones, the ones that feel like anything but our first choice, the best choice, the plan A.

That's why I'm sitting here now, asking this of you, even though I'd rather be anywhere else.

For Christian. For Sebastian. For the brothers I fell in love with this summer.

I know that I'm no one to you. And maybe

you feel the same way about Ursula, despite having known her your entire life. But please, consider my words. My request. For your boys.

I want you to keep the houses.

That's what I want.

I signed the letter and slid it across the counter, closed my eyes. Waited for him to read it.

Moments passed in silence. He rose, finally, and his heavy steps thudded across the kitchen. The freezer creaked open, three ice cubes clinked into the highball. A bottle cap twisted off, liquid sloshed into the glass, ice cubes shifted and settled. The bottle was re-capped, put back on the shelf.

A sigh, another one, the sound of the glass lifting from the counter and tipping back, landing once again on the counter, and still Mr. Kane didn't say a word.

I opened my eyes, met his across the kitchen.

My hope was small, fragile.

"I'm sorry, Elyse," he said softly. "Truly. But there's nothing I can do."

Dashed.

"Nothing you can do about what?" It was Christian, panting and soaked in the doorway.

Mr. Kane sipped the scotch, set the glass firmly on the counter. When Christian reached us in the kitchen, his father looked at the floor. "Parrish and Dey already bought the place. Done deal, guys."

I tossed Christian the towel.

"But . . . already?" he said, scrubbing his head dry. "We just lost the bet last night."

For a tense moment no one spoke but the rain outside, lashing the house. Mr. Kane had the decency to look apologetic, but I knew things were about to get worse. The air inside was electric, as though lightning would strike any moment.

"Christian, this house was becoming a liability for us," Mr. Kane said. "Your mother and I don't have the time or inclination to keep up with it. P and D offered a more than fair price—well above market value. I'd have been a fool to turn it down."

"A fool? Or maybe just a father." Christian threw the towel into the kitchen sink, leaned back against it with his arms crossed. "So you were planning to sell all along. You thought this'd be our last summer at the Cove?"

Mr. Kane shook his head. "I had no idea P and D would be interested. But when I heard about it? Come on, son. Do the math."

Christian pinched the bridge of his nose, spoke into his hand. "So the regatta was just, what? Your way of proving what a screwup you have for a son?"

"I tried to talk you out of it," Mr. Kane said, but it was a weak attempt, and he knew it. "Christian, I didn't . . . it just . . ." He let the words die. There was no explaining this bitter game, the way he'd so casually yanked his son into the middle of his own childhood rivalry, the way he couldn't just back down from the mayor's taunts. No apology would excuse the invisible, nameless faults he'd found with Christian and Sebastian again and again. No words would erase the pain he'd caused in all his years of doubting, of judging, of resenting, of projecting his own failures onto his sons—one, a mermaid queen; the other, a boy who almost wasn't his.

My heart broke for them. Despite everything laid bare before him, Mr. Kane still couldn't see how much he'd hurt his family.

Christian's eyes left his father, landed on the counter, the letter I'd written. My last-ditch plea. He picked up the paper and read, eyes scanning faster and faster, just as I'd written it. Frantic to the end. Desperate. Hopeful.

"You wrote this?" he asked me.

I nodded. I hadn't told him the details of my plan this morning, only that I thought I could talk to his father, get the houses back, stop the inevitable.

Christian dropped the paper, took my hand instead.

"I want you to know something, Dad," he said, pulling me close. There was no rage left in his voice, only honesty. "I'm not you. I don't want to be you, a man with no heart, all ambition. My whole life, that was your favorite word. Ambition. The key to your love and respect. But the thing you taught me about your kind of ambition is that it means selling people out. Always."

"Christian, I—"

"No, you're going to listen to me. Elyse was right in her letter—I love it at the Cove. Sebastian loves it here. But you wouldn't know that, because you never asked. You sold us out."

Mr. Kane took a step back, folded his arms over his chest. "Last time I checked, it's my name on the deeds to this property. I regret that I've hurt you guys, but I stand by my decision. I don't need your permission to sell homes that I own and pay for."

Christian sighed. "No. But you could've told us you wanted to list it. Could've warned us that we wouldn't have a place at the Cove next summer. Never mind what the Cove's going to become, thanks to Wes and those douches from P and D."

"What's a douche?" Sebastian asked. He'd been lingering in the hallway at the bottom of the stairs, and now he joined us, climbed up on one of the counter stools. "And why are you guys all wet?"

"Out chasing mermaids, kiddo," Christian said, ruffling Sebastian's hair. "Slippery as ever."

Christian clearly had more to say to his father—he'd held it in for years, and now that he'd cracked the seal, there was no going back. But he stowed it for now, turning his attention to his brother. The kid was hungry, asking about grilled-cheese-and-hot-dog sandwiches, and Christian got to work, glad to have a job, some concrete goal he could actually accomplish.

"Anyone else for the Christian Kane special?" Christian asked.

My growling stomach answered for me.

"Dad?" Christian said. "Lunch?"

"No, no, you guys go ahead." Mr. Kane rinsed out his glass, set it in the dish drainer. He was slipping away, every muscle in his body telling me he'd soon have an excuse, some urgent work situation to extract him from the uncomfortableness of right now, right here.

But I caught his eye, held him in place.

He'd asked me what I'd wanted, and when I finally told him, he turned me down.

But the forces of Atargatis Cove worked in magical, mysterious ways, and in all the time I'd spent here running from my own mistakes, hiding from the wreckage of the dreams I'd lost in Tobago, I'd managed to figure out one thing.

When one dream burns to ash, you don't crumble beneath it. You get on your hands and knees, and you sift through those ashes until you find the very last ember, the very last spark.

Then you breathe.

You breathe.

You fucking *breathe*.

And you make a new fire.

On my left hand I inked my last request, held it steady before Andy Kane's eyes.

I want the e-mail for the P&D guys.

Chapter 40

It was a sunny day in Atargatis Cove, diamonds glinting off the Pacific as I stood watch on Lemon's deck. Barely a mile from shore a school of dolphins dove through the waves, their gray fins whipping the water into meringue peaks.

It had been my vista all summer. The deck, the dunes below, the vast ocean beyond, all its beautiful creatures.

And now, two weeks after we'd lost the regatta and the chance to save it, I was looking to the sea for strength.

Lemon was right when she'd said that Mr. Kane hadn't shown up at the Cove with an agenda to sell, but a seed was planted the night of the Solstice, blooming into a plan and a handshake during those long days Christian and I had worked on the *Queen of Cups*. The houses had been sold. If all went according to plan, Parrish and Dey would close in the fall, determine fair market value for

Lemon's rent until Prop 27 came to a vote in November.

Mr. Kane expressed regret at hurting his sons, at hurting Lemon. But once the opportunity presented itself, he'd wanted to sell. To break free of the place that in so many ways reminded him of his own failures, the way he'd lived his life for so long to impress Wes Katzenberg. The way he'd neglected his wife in that fruitless pursuit. The affair, the arguments, the pain.

Despite the added strain it was putting on their marriage, Mrs. Kane was doing what she could to contest the sale, to throw a wrench into the inspection, to hold it up just long enough for us to figure something else out. But she wasn't the owner, and legally there wasn't too much she could do.

Not everyone gets a happy ending, however deserved it may be. Life had been doing its damnedest to teach me that, starting with my first saltwater breath, the day my mother died at sea.

But that didn't mean we were giving up.

"Almost time, Elyse." Lemon found me on the deck, her auburn hair wild with the day's potential energy. "The food's all arranged, laptop and projector are good to go, goodie bags are out, the Be Amazing candles are lit, the coffee is on.... Are we missing anything?"

I took her hand, gave it a reassuring squeeze.

"Your calm demeanor is an inspiration to us all," she said.

Yours, I corrected her. I held up my wrist for a whiff of her Calm Down Balm, a blend of chamomile and lavender she'd cooked up last week. *Thank you. For everything.*

She shook her head, that wise smile rising on her lips. "Elyse, these people aren't coming today for my candles and coffee. They're coming because you've shown them that you're a woman with something to say. They're coming because they want to hear it."

It hardly seemed real, but I knew she was right. I felt it inside, way down where new things grew from ashes and dark.

"So you're all set with your slides?" she asked. "Your notes? Visual aids?"

I nodded.

Though they were surprised and a bit uncertain, three representatives from Parrish and Dey, along with Mayor Katzenberg and a couple of other town officials, had accepted my invitation. An informational luncheon, I'd suggested, at the very gallery they'd just purchased. Noah had convinced the Black Pearl to provide the lunch, and I'd be providing the information.

A proposal, actually.

Everyone kept saying that P&D, with the mayor's blessing, wanted to turn the Cove into a tourist trap. But what all of these developers really wanted, multinational and local alike, was to bring in money.

In Tobago, our little organic cocoa farm became an exclusive hot spot, a place that still produced the same sustainable crop, but now attracted some of the world's wealthiest celebrities and clientele. Our friends and neighbors had also helped grow the ecotourism industry through guided cultural and wildlife tours, dive and surf shops, and organic restaurants.

Here, as much as some of its residents wanted Atargatis Cove to stay off the map, the reality was that this town needed a boost—the mayor had been right about that. But there were ways a town could bring in tourist money without falling into the traps that so often rendered places homogenous and overrun. It wasn't about attracting lots of small money with the same old splash, but attracting smaller bursts of big money by protecting and showcasing the unique details that made a place different, that made a place worth visiting over any other, worth cherishing.

With help from my Cove friends and inspiration from my family in Tobago, I'd spent these last two weeks researching and putting together my presentation. My pitch. The mermaid lore alone was a gold mine of marketable ideas, not to mention the rugged coastal beauty and wildlife viewing the Cove offered. If P&D was willing to keep the new development in check, while at the same time better capitalizing on the unique products and experiences the existing local businesses already offered, the eco-friendly possibilities in a place like the Cove were endless.

I had the data to back up my claims; Lemon had asked Dad and Granna to send over statistics from the resort as a case study, and Granna would be Skyping in for the meeting in case they wanted more details.

To balance out the money-making ideas, Kirby and Vanessa—with assistance from Brenda and Gracie—had gathered video interviews from the locals, from people who wanted the town to retain its

charms, but who were open to creative ideas for bringing in more business. People like Noah, who was already making plans to buy the Black
Pearl. People like Kat and Ava, who were more than happy to provide
custom-decorated cookies for today's meeting. People like Lemon, who
not only offered her gallery space, but who made miniature sea glass
trees for each guest from the jar I'd been filling, the hourglass by which
I'd long ago stopped measuring my days.

Even Sebastian pitched in, crafting handmade mermaid cards for
everyone.

It was the ember in our ashes, our hope for a new fire.

"I'll be inside," Lemon said, giving my hand a final, confident pat.
"Let me know if you need anything."

Lemon went in to recheck the food display, the coffee, the gleam
on the big sea glass tree. Everything had to be perfect.

They'd be here in fifteen minutes.

"Have I told you how amazing you are?" Christian crossed the
deck, wrapped me in his arms from behind. I felt his lips, warm and
comforting on my neck.

He'd stayed up with me the last two nights, running on fumes,
helping me rehearse.

No matter the outcome of today's meeting, I couldn't have done
this without him.

Without any of them.

Had I really only been at the Cove three months? A quarter of a
year, and so much had changed. So many impossible things became

possible. And so many other things, once bright stars in my imagination, winked out.

Growing up, I couldn't wait until I was old enough to embark on my own adventures, just like my sisters had before me. For so many years I thought that my adventure meant singing, touring with Natalie, seeing the world from its stages and concert halls. I thought my life would bloom in the spotlight, and that's what I worked for.

But my real adventure wasn't even close.

And now another journey was about to begin.

Changing tides, as always.

"Because you are," Christian said, his lips warm near my ear. "Amazing. Among other things. I'll run through the list again later." He rested his chin on my shoulder, strong arms around my waist, and together we looked out at the sea, at the dolphins that still frolicked in the distance, and I thought about all the people who'd brought me here. From afraid to amazing. From lost in the sea to wholly found in it.

I thought of Atargatis, the First, frightening and beautiful. The mermaid goddess who lived on in the soul of every woman who'd ever fallen in love with the ocean.

I thought of Sebastian, my little mermaid queen, how happy he was the day of the parade, just getting the chance to express himself, to *be* himself.

I thought of Vanessa, the story about how she and her girlfriends became feminist killjoys to get a women's literature core in their school, the way she'd accepted me this summer without question, gently pushed me out of my self-imposed shell. Of her mother, Mrs. James, how she'd grabbed that bullhorn at the parade and paved the way for Sebastian's joy.

I thought of Lemon, so wise, so comfortable in her own skin, full of enough love to raise a daughter as a single mom and still have room for me, for her friends, for everyone whose lives she touched with her art.

I thought of Kirby, her fierce loyalty, her patience and grace, her energy, what a good friend and sister she'd become, even when I'd tried to shut her out. I thought of all the new things I wanted to share with her now, all the things I hoped she'd share with me.

I thought of my mother, a woman I'd never known, but one whose ultimate sacrifice gave me life.

I thought of Granna, stepping in to raise her six granddaughters when my mom died, never once making us feel like a burden or a curse. She'd managed the cocoa estate with her son, personally saw to the comforts of every resort guest, and still had time to tell us bedtime stories, always reminding us how much she treasured us.

I thought of my sisters. Juliette, Martine, and Hazel, their adventures to faraway lands, new experiences. Gabrielle with her island-hopping, her ultimate choice to follow her heart home.

And Natalie, my twin. My mirror image, my dream sharer. I knew I hadn't been fair to her this summer—she'd saved my life, done the best she could. And I wanted to thank her for that, because as long as it had taken me to realize it, I *was* thankful. Thankful for her. Thankful to be alive. To breathe.

It still hurt to picture her on tour with Bella Garcia, as much as I wanted the world for her. It was messy, it was complicated, my heart still torn in two. But I loved and missed her, there beneath the resentment and jealousy, the loss of my singing voice from which I was still reeling.

Last week Kirby had helped me put together a video message for Natalie. I wrote out everything I wanted to say, everything in my heart. Then, as I mouthed the words into the camera, Kirby read them aloud, offstage, lending me her voice so I could better express mine.

It wasn't perfect. I'd started, stopped, started, and stopped a half dozen times before I could get through it. But it was a start.

I had no guarantee she'd listen, no promise that she'd hear me after all her unreturned efforts. But Natalie had always been the one to pick me up after a hard rehearsal, to lift my heart after a disappointing performance, just as I'd done for her. I called up that love again now, held on to the hope that maybe, someday, we'd find our way back to it.

The sea whispered beyond, and I smiled, grateful all over again.

All of the people who'd brought me here, past and present, ancient and young, legend and life and lore, I channeled. I welcomed them into my infinite heart, alongside the ghosts, the shadows, the ache I'd always carry. I made their strength mine, a part of me. My inspiration. My voice.

And still, amazing heart, limitless, there was room for more.

I turned around in Christian's arms, pressed my lips to his until I knew he could feel the words in my heart. How happy I was to be with him. How proud I was. He'd finally told his father that he didn't want to follow the well-beaten Kane family path—that he was eager to continue studying at school, but not in the way that Mr. Kane had planned. From here on out, he'd be remapping his own route, his own dreams. And always, he'd return to the Cove, again and again, even without a permanent home here.

After all, we had a boat to finish restoring. To care for. To sail.

And we had each other.

It was me, Christian confessed, who'd given him the courage. Who'd inspired him, through my own quiet strength, to find his.

My sisters used to tell me stories about falling in love, about girls finding their princes. In all the old tales, love saved the girl from her wretched life, from the depths of grief, from some undefined spiritual poverty.

I'd arrived at Atargatis Cove alone and afraid, feeling like the most unloved, unlovable woman on two legs.

Since then I'd fallen in love many times over. With the Cove itself, its magic. With the people I'd come to cherish as friends and family.

And I'd fallen in love with Christian Kane, official summer scoundrel and champion heart stealer of Atargatis Cove, standing but a breath away, his eyes on mine, amazed and dazed and full of fire.

I was in love, just like in the stories.

But unlike those fairy-tale girls, love didn't save me; it changed me.

Changed me into someone who could save myself.

Christian pulled out of our embrace, grabbed my hand. On my palm, with the Sharpie we'd so often shared, he wrote a secret missive, folded my fingers gently around it.

"They're here," he whispered, nodding toward the gallery. "Ready?"

I took a deep, cool breath.

Ready. Such a big question for such a little word.

The answer idled on my lips, suspended suddenly with a million what-ifs. What if they hated it? What if I froze up? What if they whispered and scowled?

What if I let them make me completely invisible again?

Christian's eyes didn't leave mine. He read the doubts as though they'd scrolled across my face in a neon blaze.

He squeezed my hand, held it between us.

I took another deep breath.

Unfurled my fingers.

I believe in you.

When I looked at him again, Christian's eyes were their brightest green-gray-blue, like the sea that glittered and danced behind him.

I smiled at them both, my life's great loves, and I had my answer.

Yes. I'm ready.

Christian held open the door, kissed me once more for luck.

Hopeful, strong, unafraid, loved.

I crossed the threshold.

Passed through the shadow of the sea glass tree.

Stepped into the light of the gallery.

And there,

in the place where possibility lived,

I shone.

Acknowledgments

When I set out to write from the perspective of a young woman born and raised in a culture I'd never experienced, from a place I'd never visited, I knew that my first responsibility was to ask questions. Lots of them.

Lynn Joseph and Andre Daly answered. Thank you doesn't seem to cover it, but I'll say it anyway: Thank you! Lynn, I couldn't have done this without your encouragement, your help, your willingness to push me to challenge my assumptions, and of course, your friendship. I'm so grateful our paths crossed. Andre, I sincerely appreciate your insider's perspective on life in Tobago, and the fact that you didn't laugh too hard at my many Americanisms. Because of you I now smile when I buy "locally sourced" produce!

Readers, Lynn and Andre kindly shared their knowledge and experience, bringing me to Trinidad and Tobago in a way that none of my other research could. Any mistakes or misrepresentations are my own.

I would also like to acknowledge the following people who've supported and inspired me in countless ways:

My amazing agent, Ted Malawer, who keeps on believing in me, cheering me on, and helping me shape and share my voice with the world. Ted, having both meaningful work and such a passionate advocate for it is a privilege for which I'm eternally grateful. Thanks also to Michael Stearns and everyone at Upstart Crow Literary who helps my books cross oceans and continents.

My publishing team, including Patrick Price, who followed me and the crew of the *Queen of Cups* to the depths of the sea in search of the pearls; Sara Sargent, who sailed this book through the finish line, which was no small feat; Regina Flath, First Mate of Design, because OMG that cover; Kelsey Dickson, Publicist of Awesome; and everyone who brought all hands on deck to support this book, including Mara Anastas, Craig Adams, Brian Luster, Nicole Ellul, Michael Strother, Kayley Hoffman, Carolyn Swerdloff, Liesa Abrams, Teresa Ronquillo, Christina Solazzo, and the entire Simon Pulse crew.

Jessi Kirby, the most dedicated literary soul mate ever. Jessi, every time I feared the worst, you were there with the good chocolate, saying, "You got this, Ockler!" I'm pretty sure our ability to "Be Amazing" together is matched only by our ability to fill up the recycle bin together, but I look forward to re-testing that theory for many years to come (by the sea, of course).

Zoe Strickland. Thanks for being in my corner, HT! Your texts and letters are always like a much-needed hug.

Leo Quinn, who gave the *Black Pearl* its name.

Anna Hutchinson, the original feminist killjoy. I'm honored to make the list.

My parents, my parents-in-law, and the family and friends who continue to read my stories no matter how many I write.

Librarians, booksellers, bloggers, and teachers, whose passion for reading keeps me coming back to the page with new ideas.

And most of all, my husband, Alex, my pet monster and bestie. Thank you for bringing me to the sea, and for giving me the most amazing adventures every day. As long as you're with me, I'm home, and I'm okay.

Finally, dear readers, there's one more thing I'd like to say, specifically to the teens and young adults reading this book.

As Elyse discovers, there are so many ways to lose one's voice. Elyse's initial loss is literal, but she comes to know and care for people who've experienced all kinds of silencing, both subtle and forceful, both accidental and purposeful.

The intentions and methods by which people silence one another may be wildly different, but the outcome is always the same: Someone's voice goes unheard.

So, for anyone who has ever been hushed, shushed, shut down, shut up, shut out, shut off, cut off, flamed, shamed, silenced, suppressed, oppressed, dismissed, disempowered, discouraged, disrespected, rejected, ignored, intimidated, talked over, talked at, denied, cast aside, outshouted, outvoted, overlooked, unnoticed, unheard, or unacknowledged in any way: this is your acknowledgement, whenever you need it. I wrote this story for and because of you. Know that you're not invisible. Know that you matter. Know that your voice matters. And know that there are people out there who want and need to hear that beautiful voice of yours, whenever you're ready, however you're able to express it.

Believe in you. I do.

With respect and admiration,

Sarah

#NOTEVENCLOSE

If a picture is worth a thousand words, a picture tagged on Miss Demeanor's Scandal of the Month page is worth about a million. Especially when the story all those words tell is an absolute lie.

Well, mostly a lie.

The part about falling asleep in his arms is sort of true. I don't remember the details about the horse, or how it got into the living room exactly, but judging from the smell that morning, that part's true too. And yes, the Harvard-bound debate team captain definitely cannonballed into the pond wearing only tuxedo socks and silver fairy wings. *Everyone* got shots of that.

But there's no way the other stuff happened.

Not like the pictures are saying it did.

A SPECIAL MESSAGE TO LAVENDER OAKS SWORDFISH ON THE OCCASION OF PROM

MISS DEMEANOR

2,002 likes 👍

~~92 talking about this~~

Friday, April 25

It's prom weekend, fishes, and you know what that means: Sex! Scandal! And . . . glitter?

Yes, glitter, as you'd expect from Lavender Oaks's first-ever Mythical Creatures Promenade. I'm not sure what that even means, but everything's better with sparkle, so let's raise a glass to the planning committee for spreading a dash of pixie dust on an otherwise pedestrian tradition. Cheers!

For those of you who haven't planned the ruination of your innocence at one of the many after-parties, may I suggest popping by the east field for the school-sponsored medieval joust and mutton roast? Principal Zeff assures me that while the lances are made of foam, the horses and meat (mutually exclusive, despite recent legislation) are the real deal.

Chain mail not your thing? Rumor has it the (e)lectronic Vanities Intervention League is hosting a postprom reenactment of the fake moon landing on the grassy knoll, but they don't believe in Facebook; we can neither confirm nor deny reports. Still, if anyone spots any (e)VIL club members at the dance, snap a few pics. I'd love to see those girls rock an updo with their tinfoil hats.

Team Tinfoil Hat pics aside, don't forget to upload and share your juiciest weekend shots here on the Miss Demeanor page, tagged #scandal to enter my Scandal of the Month contest. This is it, kids—the very last #scandal before graduation. Make it count! Winners will be immortalized with a blinking gold star and, of course, eternal humiliation. Can't put a price on that!

Speaking of fame and glory, today we crossed the magic number: 2,000 fans! But it's no time to rest on our überpopular laurels. Millions of Americans have yet to profess their loyalty. I'm saying! So do your part and tell a friend, tell an ex, tell a nana to hit that thumbs-up button!

On a serious note, a message from Students Against Substance Abuse: Driving dry is hella fly. The SASA president will personally monitor the punch bowl for suspicious activity, and the VP has the smoking lounge on lockdown in case you have any nontobacco smoking plans. With all that glitter and gossamer, something tells me you won't need hallucinogenics to have a funky trip, anyway.

While you're out bustin' a move in your satin and sequins tomorrow, I'll be home reclining in my zebra-print Snuggie, knuckles-deep in a box of Fiddle Faddle. Not very mythical, perhaps, but I've got a date with *Danger's Little Darling*, and after last week's killer episode, I can't wait to see what Angelica Darling has in store. God, I love me some Jayla Heart. That saucy starlet's the hottest thing to ever come out of Lav-Oaks. Don't believe me? Check out her fan page, the Jayla Heartthrobs. 200K fans? There's a girl who knows how to bust a move.

In closing, a Facebook message even Team Tinfoil Hat can't protest: Have fun this weekend, fishies. Be safe. And don't forget to smile for the spy satellites!

xo ~ *Ciao!* ~ xo

Miss Demeanor